a crack in the sky

a crack in the sky

MARK PETER HUGHES

A Yearling Book

Text copyright © 2010 by Mark Peter Hughes
Map and diagram © Joe Lemonnier
Cover art copyright © 2010 by Per Haagensen

All rights reserved. Published in the United States by Yearling, an imprint of
Random House Children's Books, a division of Random House, Inc., New York.
Originally published in hardcover in the United States by Delacorte Press,
an imprint of Random House Children's Books, New York, in 2010.

Yearling and the jumping horse design are registered trademarks of Random House, Inc.

Visit us on the Web! www.randomhouse.com/kids

Educators and librarians, for a variety of teaching tools,
visit us at www.randomhouse.com/teachers

The Library of Congress has cataloged the hardcover edition of this work as follows:
Hughes, Mark Peter.
A crack in the sky / by Mark Peter Hughes — 1st ed.
p. cm.
Summary: In a post-apocalyptic world, thirteen-year-old Eli, part of the most
powerful family in the world, keeps noticing problems with the operations of
his domed city but his family denies them, while in the surrounding desert,
the Outsiders struggle to survive while awaiting a prophesied savior.
ISBN 978-0-385-73708-1 (trade) — ISBN 978-0-385-90645-6 (lib. bdg.) —
ISBN 978-0-375-89670-5 (ebook)
[1. Science fiction. 2. Survival—Fiction. 3. Family life—Fiction.] I. Title.
PZ7.H8736113Wil 2010
[Fic]—dc22   2009043532

ISBN 978-0-385-73709-8 (pbk.)

Printed in the United States of America

10 9 8 7 6 5 4 3 2 1

First Yearling Edition 2011

Random House Children's Books supports the First Amendment and celebrates the right to read.

For my wonderful parents,
Suzanne Winnell Hughes and Peter Hughes

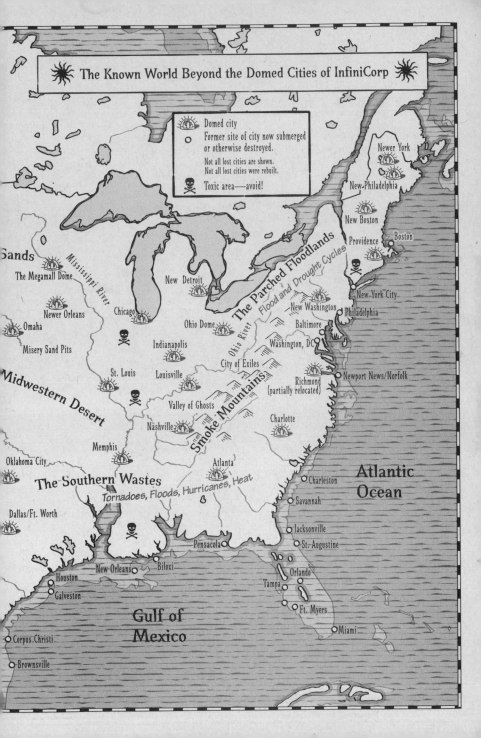

prologue

I am thirsty all the time now. The air is heavy with bugs and the dust coats my throat. Our little reservoir, the pool in what used to be somebody's leaky basement, is almost dry. Soon we will have to leave this place.

Rosalia is not well. She needs water.

I am careful not to show my concern. As each day passes I catch the others looking up at the sky, watching for signs of the first storm. We hope for rain even though we all know that it will arrive as it always has—like an angry fist that will blast away our shelters, sweep through the few buildings that remain, and flood the streets. The hard, red earth will turn to mud so thick and soft that we won't be able to walk without sinking to our waists. The flooding will also bring more insects. They will buzz in our ears and fly into our mouths. They will bite us night and day, covering our skin with sores until our eyes swell shut.

There are seven of us now. There is safety in numbers. Last month the twins found a little girl wandering alone in the desert, weak and disoriented. We all argued, but in the end we agreed to take her into our clan. We fed and washed her and have since been showing her how we survive, where we look for moisture in the dry times and where we can find shelter during the storms. We are teaching her to stay off the main roads. The old highways, most of them crumbling and overgrown with weeds, are not safe. They leave you exposed to enemies waiting to jump you.

Most of all, we are teaching her to stay hidden.

We sleep during the daytime to avoid the heat. At night we hunt animals and search the ruins for anything useful, anything that might be traded on the black market. But always we gather again before dawn and take cover together wherever we can. An abandoned gas station. An old bus left to rust in an open field. Sometimes we construct temporary shelters out of car doors or plastic bags, whatever we can find.

We are survivors.

We are thieves of fortune.

We are gods and goddesses of the wild.

Yesterday amid the rubble I found an old magazine. Amazingly, the paper was unspoiled. There are beautiful glossy pictures of smiling kids our own ages, teenagers relaxing beside swimming pools. It's hard to imagine there was a time when people had so much clean water they used to collect it in backyards and splash around in it. But here are the pictures.

In the magazine there are also advertisements for makeup, music video downloads, and old-fashioned movies. There are images of celebrities I've never heard of and articles about things I'd never even considered:

How to Find the Perfect Pair of Jeans.

Five Ways to Detect True Love in a Kiss.

Everyone keeps asking me to read the magazine aloud. I have already worked through it cover to cover three times.

This morning we got word they are selling oranges in the open-air markets by the dome. It might be a trick and it might not. Either way, I volunteered to make the long trek, not just because of the fruit but also because they say filtered water flows inside the dome walls. If this is true I will try to tap into it. I told Rosalia this, but she said not to try anything foolish. She told me she is worried I will fall prey to bandits or to one of the packs of starving, mutated animals that roam the wasteland. I told her not to worry. What else can I do? As long as there is no trouble, I can be back in two or three days and she will get better.

Rosalia met an old man once. She says his hair was long and gray and that he breathed through a machine. He told her he could remember back when things weren't this way, before the bugs and the bad

3

smells and the heat and the storms and the highwaymen. He said these are the Final Days, the last gasp at the end of the world. But someone is coming for us, he said. El Guía—a child veiled in shadow, a great leader who will appear accompanied by a disfigured beast of terrible power. He will deliver us to a new place where there are no dry times, where water is plentiful and storms don't kill. He said he saw all this in a dream.

Rosalia believed him, but I do not. I don't believe in prophets any more than I believe in the perfect pair of jeans. What I do believe—what I know—is that too much sun affects the brain. Heatstroke makes people imagine things that aren't there.

Things are getting bad. I hold Rosalia's hand as she talks nonsense in her sleep. This evening I will go deeper than ever into the ruins in search of water. If I cannot find any, maybe I will at least come back with something to trade with the black-market water dealers.

"Sleep," Rosalia whispers beside me. "And when you go, be sure to come back before light." She drifts off again, and I lie awake listening to the metallic echo the wind makes as it whips through the debris. Eventually my eyelids grow heavy.

When I sleep, I dream of swimming pools.

—From a torn notebook discovered in the desert at the edge of the Atlanta Dome

PART I

the artificial city

1

eli

Something was wrong.

Thirteen-year-old Eli Papadopoulos could feel it.

Just as thunder boomed in the distance, there was a faint bursting sound from somewhere outside his bedroom window. Eli spun his head just in time to witness a tiny spray of sparks falling from the artificial sky. Debris drifted to the ground like faraway fireworks and quickly disappeared, leaving an empty space where some of the pixels had gone out—a dark spot, almost unnoticeable in the five-mile-wide hemisphere of blue light.

Whatever the little explosion was, it was so quick and small in the vast expanse of the protective dome over the city of Providence that anyone might have missed it among the digital clouds if they hadn't been in just the right position when it happened. But Eli *did* see it, and for a while he kept staring. Sky malfunctions were supposed to be rare, and yet this wasn't the first time in recent days that he'd seen something troubling up there.

He felt again the vague dread that had been growing inside him for weeks.

Nobody else in Eli's room seemed to have noticed anything.

Stretched across the windowsill at his elbow, Eli's mongoose, Marilyn, yawned. A recent birthday gift from Grandfather, Marilyn was a small, scruffy animal, shaggy and gray, with a short snout, a skinny body, and a long, bushy tail. If she'd observed the unsettling burst of sparks, she didn't show it. Her eyelids drooped, and after a moment she laid down her head and began to snore quietly.

Not even Dr. Toffler, the surly old instruction robot seated on the other side of the desk from Eli, seemed aware. It continued plodding through the day's lesson as if nothing strange had happened, droning on and on about project management.

Today's lecture was even duller than normal.

"Nurturing a customer's sense of well-being through positive message repetition," Dr. Toffler was saying, its voice crackling with age, "not only encourages complacency but is also a useful tool that ultimately leads to widespread respect for authority and obedience to rules." It paused. "Representative Papadopoulos, you're not paying attention. Please try to stay engaged."

Eli pointed, startled out of his reverie. "I just saw something break. Up above those silver trees, see? There were sparks, and then part of the dome just . . . fizzled out!"

Dr. Toffler's slender plastic head swiveled to see. By then, though, everything appeared normal. The dome ceiling shimmered a cheerful blue. The synthetic sun, a perfect sphere of blazing gold and red, was halfway through its daytime journey and now glowed above the shopping mall at the center of downtown. The dark spot had grown smaller, as if the surrounding pixels were adjusting their positions to leave no trace of their missing brothers. Even Eli was having a hard time making it out anymore.

"I see nothing peculiar," Dr. Toffler said. "I'm sure it was just part of a cloud-vertisement."

"No, it wasn't a cloud-vertisement! I'm telling you, something exploded!"

The droid's head swiveled back, its optical sensors fixing on Eli. Dr. Toffler was so old that the rubber at its joints had almost worn away, exposing the wires that ran up its neck and the steel rods at its elbows and knees. "This wouldn't be another of your attempts to divert our discussion from the lecture, would it? Your tactics are becoming rather tiresome."

Eli ignored the jab. As a member of the powerful Papadopoulos family, the family that owned the giant company that managed everything in the domed cities and kept the millions of domed employees safe and productive, he was being raised differently than most kids. Instead of attending a normal school and getting a regular job at age thirteen, as most children did, Eli was tutored at home, years of management instruction so he could help his family run InfiniCorp someday. The problem was, he tended to zone out during Dr. Toffler's long lectures.

The mongoose grunted quietly at his elbow, still lost in sleep.

"I'm not trying to get out of the lesson," he insisted,

starting to lose his temper with the droid. "I saw part of the sky shatter. Pieces fell to the ground!"

"Sky parts don't simply burst apart." It raised its metal hands in frustration. "First it was suspicious sky formations that you believed could only mean the dome was about to crumble to the ground. Now you've convinced yourself you saw pixels explode? Really, Eli, enough of this nonsense. Senior Management has already assured you there's nothing to worry about. No more pointless distractions. You have to focus. Mother and Father are concerned about you."

Eli threw his weight back into the chair. He was aware of his parents' concern, but he wasn't making up stories! This time he'd seen something seriously alarming, and it burned his insides that Dr. Toffler wouldn't believe him. The robot was already starting over, though, and all Eli could do was glower out the window again, his heart pounding and his black hair falling over his eyes. If he went out to the street and found broken sky parts, then nobody could deny that what he'd seen was real. Not that Dr. Toffler was about to let him out of his lesson without an argument.

But Eli made up his mind. This was too important, and he'd had enough of arguing with a machine.

"Excuse me," he said, getting up from his chair. "I need to take a break."

The mongoose lifted her head. Whiskers twitching, she eyed him with what looked like suspicion. If Eli hadn't known better, he would have sworn she somehow knew he was up to something.

Dr. Toffler sighed. "All right. You have two minutes."

Eli left the room and closed the door behind him. Then he ran down two flights of stairs and straight across the long foyer to the front door. As he slipped on his cloak, he noticed his brother's Image-Capturing Spyglass on the table by the front door. Perfect! He slid it into his pocket.

He'd seen what he'd seen. He was going to prove it.

For a couple of weeks Eli had been noticing anomalies in the sky—little quirks, mostly, like lights that blinked or random shapes that flickered and disappeared. He'd read an old story about a sea captain who ignored a tiny leak on his boat, and it ended up sinking the whole ship. What if this unexplained sky behavior was the first sign that the protection systems were corrupted somehow? If it turned out that the dome was heading toward a breakdown, it could potentially leave the entire city exposed to the elements.

Yet for some reason nobody else seemed concerned. The family elders kept telling him everything was fine and that it wasn't his job to worry about these things anyway.

But what he'd witnessed today was different. This time he'd actually seen something break into pieces.

He sprinted down Hope Street. The East Side was teeming with activity. As transport pods whooshed by, InfiniCorp employees on their lunch hour milled along the sidewalks and jammed the shops and restaurants, stepping around the little yellow cleaning droids that swept the walkways. The Infini-Corp logo—a crowd of smiling faces protected in the palm of a strong, gentle hand—was everywhere: on every store window, every trash-disposal tube, every shopping bag. And just below each logo was the company slogan in thick, purple letters:

DON'T WORRY!
INFINICORP IS TAKING CARE OF EVERYTHING!

As Eli rounded the corner of Manning, there was another roll of faraway thunder, the last remnant of the storm that had kept him awake the previous night. He'd lain in bed listening to the wind Outside and the metallic hiss of rain against the dome's exterior. Here Inside, though, the sky seemed as calm as ever, with only a few three-dimensional cloud-vertisements breaking up the vast canopy of blue.

Tired of your nose? read one of them just then, a low-hanging cloud with flashing red words over a sad, long-nosed face. *Isn't it time for a new one?*

Higher up and closer to the center of the dome, five digital kids with musical instruments were dancing on a different cloud. *Check it out! It's the new groove from Five Go Splat!*

Up ahead he spotted the silver trees below the place where the pixels had burst. The trees were inside an enclosed lot surrounded by a brick wall. DEPARTMENT OF RELIABLE POWER SYSTEMS, read a sign near the top. From where he stood, Eli saw nothing peculiar about the sky, but he was sure he'd have a better view if he went inside the enclosure. All he had to do was find the entrance.

He followed the wall as it turned another corner, but there he froze. Not far, near the arched door in the brick, stood a Guardian, one of the white-uniformed kids who patrolled the

12

streets. A thickset girl with flashing purple eyebrow enhancers, she was watching the pedestrian traffic with one finger pressed to the InfiniTalk in her ear. It occurred to Eli that Dr. Toffler was sure to have realized he'd skipped out on his lesson by now, and the droid had probably alerted Mother and Father. It wouldn't have surprised him if they'd already sent word for the Guardians to keep an eye out for him so they could drag him home again.

As if to prove his point, the Guardian looked up, and for a moment their eyes met. "Hey, you!" she called. "Stop right there!"

He lingered a heartbeat longer, but then he doubled back and ran. Shooting around the corner again, he scrambled along the wall and into an alley at the other end of the enclosure. He pressed his back against the bricks. The Guardian ran past.

Eli waited a few seconds. Just over his shoulder a sign said KEEP OUT! AUTHORIZED EMPLOYEES ONLY! He hesitated, but only for a moment. The Guardian could be back in an instant, and if Eli didn't get in there and capture a few images to prove to Senior Management that the dome was breaking apart, it was possible nothing would be done about it until it was too late. What if he was the only one who saw the explosion?

He made his decision.

Grabbing an iron bar at the top of the wall, he hoisted himself up, swung his legs over, and dropped to the other side. Now he was in what looked like a small, tidy garden carpeted with synthetic grass. Much of the center was taken up by the top of a power generator, a metal cylinder maybe ten feet across and three feet high. It hummed softly. Other than that and the trees, the enclosure was empty, although it was lined with artificial hedge on two sides. Eli climbed onto the generator and squinted at the sky.

Being only a few blocks from the city perimeter, the dome came down at an angle here, and the lower surface of the sky floated no more than forty or fifty feet above the trees. He took out the spyglass, switched on the green light, and zoomed in. The individual pixels seemed fine. In fact, nothing at all caught his eye except a perfect, unbroken canopy of light. He climbed down from the generator and walked around, scanning the ground for charred material, any shards of metal or broken glass or melted plastic, any evidence at all that something had exploded overhead.

He found nothing.

Disappointed, he abandoned the spyglass and stared back at the sky from the top of the generator with his naked eyes. He'd been so sure the burst of sparks was real. So where was the debris? Was it possible the cleaning droids could have so quickly discovered the mess and cleared it away? Or had Dr. Toffler been right after all, that it was just a digital image he'd mistaken as genuine? No. Eli could tell the difference. He'd arrived after the cleaning droids, that was all, which meant now he had to go home empty-handed, unable to prove what he was sure he'd seen.

He blew out a long breath. All he could do now was climb over the wall again and head back home. When he turned to retrieve the spyglass, though, to his surprise it wasn't where he'd left it. He'd dropped it in the grass by the hedge—he was sure of it—and yet there was nothing there anymore. It was gone! He looked around in a panic. That spyglass was special. It had belonged to Father when he was a boy. How could he have lost it in such a small space?

Out of the corner of his eye he saw something move. The hedge shook, and a dark shape shifted inside it. Somebody was in there, and suddenly Eli was sure that, whoever it was, they had taken the spyglass. He stepped forward.

"Hey, what are you doing in there?" he demanded. "Give it back!"

The leaves shook again, but otherwise there was no answer. He crouched and parted the plastic branches. Peering inside, he saw something disappear into the ground—at least, that's what it looked like. The earth seemed to move, and then there was nothing.

"Who are you? What department do you work for?"

But the shadow was gone. Eli crawled under the leaves, inching forward. Groping around with his hands, he discovered something near the base of the wall. It was a hinged flap, stiff and round. It had been left open, but when he touched it, Eli realized its upper side matched the texture of the ground, as if it were meant to blend in when it was closed.

It was a hidden door. A secret entrance to a hole in the ground.

He peered into it. The opening was just wide enough for one person to fit through. There was a ladder, but it was too dark to see the bottom. He knew he shouldn't go down there. The company had firm rules about restricted areas, but what was he supposed to do? A thief had taken the spyglass and he had to get it back!

He climbed in.

The ladder went down quite a distance before Eli touched the floor. The heat was stifling. There was a damp smell too, and the sound of water dripping. He decided that whomever he was following must be an employee from the Department of Plumbing. Through the dim light, he could just make out that the ceiling ahead was lined with giant pipes and that thick cables ran along the walls.

He stood still, listening for footsteps.

"Hello . . . ?"

No answer, just the hiss and grind of machinery. There was only one direction to go in, though, and that was forward. Within a few steps the passage narrowed, and he had to crouch to fit under the pipes. It was so hot he could barely breathe.

He crept forward, groping his way through the shadows. It was spooky down here. Far above, he could see the grates in the sidewalk, unreachable through the tangle of pipes, and the shoes of pedestrians moving along on the street. As far as he could tell, he was heading toward the eastern perimeter. Would this tunnel go all the way to the edge of the dome? What was it for? And where *was* that thieving employee?

"Hey!" he called. "Who's there? Can anybody hear me?"

Nothing.

Farther in, the pipes sank so low that he had to drop to his hands and knees and crawl. Water trickled onto his head and splashed in little puddles on the floor. He was considering turning back when he noticed a narrow opening in a long stretch of concrete to one side of the passage and a dim green light shining through the gap. Cautiously he poked his head through. There it was—the spyglass!

He squeezed the rest of the way in and grabbed it. Even

with the green glow it was dark in this new space, but he realized he'd discovered a secluded alcove with just enough height to stand in. He did. He took a step forward and felt his boot kick against something small and hard on the ground. He heard it slide away. Shining the spyglass, he saw a trail in the dust that led to a pile of debris by the opposite wall, a mound of dirt and broken concrete. Whatever he'd kicked, it was now half-buried at the base of the mound. He squinted. A triangle of white, it looked like the corner of a book, the old-fashioned kind, with actual paper pages and pictures that didn't move. If so, it was a rare find. He stepped over and pulled it from the heap.

He was right. It was an old book, tattered but intact. He wiped dust from the cover. *Alice's Adventures in Wonderland, and Through the Looking-Glass,* by Lewis Carroll. Eli had never heard of it. He wondered what an artifact like this was doing underneath the city. How long had it been there?

Scanning the base of the wall, he noticed other curious things: Sand goggles. A pair of old boots. A wooden fork. An air-filter mask. Dented and tarnished, the mask was attached to the leather headpiece of an environment suit more or less like the ones the Department of Employee Safety workers wore whenever there was a reason to go Outside. This one was ragged and old, though. Definitely well-worn. Why would someone leave a thing like that down here, of all places?

In the corner there were a couple of rough blankets, neatly folded, and another one rolled up like a pillow. Had somebody *slept* down here? It seemed too incredible to believe. But then he looked back at the mound of garbage—and this time he noticed a pile of small bones. Some dead thing, recently eaten.

The sight of it made him queasy.

Somebody was living down here. But what kind of person was crazy enough to sleep under the city? Who would skulk around the dark catacombs like an animal, hidden from sight and feeding on small creatures they probably found crawling among the pipes and wires? Eli glanced again at the sand goggles. He eyed the air-filter mask. And with a sinking feeling, he suddenly knew.

There was only one kind of person who would live like this.

A desert rat. An Outsider.

His heart began to race. Outsiders, the wild people that lived like savages out in the wasteland outside the domes, were more like untamed beasts than human beings. Some were even mutants. The idea that one of them had managed to penetrate the dome wall into Providence was terrifying. Outsiders were barbarians. They would think nothing of slitting his throat— and then who knew how much looting and killing and chaos might follow? Eli trembled at the thought. He took a step back toward the gap in the wall. He had to get out of here! He needed to rush back and warn everyone!

But just as he was squeezing into the low passageway again, he heard something. Under a growing hiss of machinery, a series of muffled grunts like heavy breathing. He froze. Farther up the tunnel, a dark shadow lumbered toward him. For an instant it passed through a narrow beam of light, and Eli caught a glimpse of tangled hair and leathery skin, mottled and red. Eli recognized at once the weathered complexion that came from sandstorms and prolonged exposure to the sun.

There could be no question now. This was an Outsider.

Eli felt his blood run cold. He was all alone. Nobody knew where he was. If the Outsider were to attack him, to tear him apart, it was conceivable that nobody would ever find out what had happened to him.

A loud rumble shook the pipes. Eli realized it must be one of the underground trams, the Bubble cars that carried employees through the city's subway system, running somewhere not far below them. The rumble lasted only a few seconds, but in that moment the savage stopped crawling and seemed to look up. Eli was almost certain it saw him, but it didn't come after him. It kept still, watching him.

At first Eli only gaped back at it, too terrified to move. Then, with a rush of adrenaline, he began scrambling away, tearing back through the tunnel on all fours. At one point he cut his hand on the edge of a piece of broken pipe, but he didn't slow down. Soon the ceiling was high enough that he could pull himself to his feet again. He gasped for breath as he ran.

Eli had already reached the street before he allowed himself to look behind him and see that he was alone. As far as he could tell, the Outsider wasn't chasing him. Still, with every step he imagined he could hear the sound of a wild thing breathing at his back, closing in behind him.

"An Outsider?" Mother asked, peering over her neon-framed glasses at Eli from her Senate office in New Washington. "You're certain?"

"Yes! He had red, blotchy skin—I'm sure!"

Eli was still catching his breath after sprinting all the way home. The moment he burst into the house, he'd pinged

Mother, and now a hologram of her head floated inside the CloudNet sphere in the living room. Like a translucent beach ball, the sphere hovered near the center of the ceiling, sending milky waves of light across the mahogany cabinets and along the walls. He'd interrupted her in the middle of a meeting. Just over Mother's shoulder floated another three-dimensional head, bald and mustached, in another sphere—a hologram inside a hologram. It was Uncle Hector, Father's eldest brother. Part of Mother's official role in the Senate was to provide assistance to high-ranking InfiniCorp officials, including Uncle Hector, who was InfiniCorp's chief operating officer and Grandfather's right-hand man.

"Anyone with you, boy?" Eli's uncle asked, removing the cigar from his mouth. "Anybody who might be able to confirm this? Did you alert the Guardians or anyone else?"

"No, I ran straight here as soon as it happened. Nobody was with me."

Mother looked tired. Her pink wig held stiffly in place, but there were bags under her eyes. "What on earth possessed you to crawl through the underworks of the city? Dr. Toffler sent word that you made a false excuse and walked out in the middle of a lesson. I've never heard it sound so annoyed."

Eli's face went warm, but he wasn't going to lie. "Dr. Toffler wouldn't believe me about the sky explosion, and I had to check it out. I was scared of what it might mean for the dome." He looked down at the floor. "Anyway, after that, things just sort of . . . happened."

"I'll have the Guardians keep an eye out for the Outsider," Uncle Hector said, "but if he saw you, then he knows we'll be looking for him. I'm sure he's long gone by now, slipped back into the wasteland. I'll send word to the chiefs over at Power Systems and Plumbing to find the tunnel and close it off." He put the cigar back in his mouth and took a long puff, momentarily filling the sphere with smoke. "The important thing is, you're okay."

"And the sparks in the sky? It was real, I'm telling you, and it's not the first time I've seen things going wrong up there. Shouldn't we send out an alert, in case it happens again?"

Uncle Hector shook his head. "Not necessary. The dome isn't breaking down, son. We're aware of the problem, and we know why it happened: this Outsider of yours must have been meddling with the system. Besides, the sky software checks every pixel every five seconds. I'm sure the reason you didn't find any debris on the site was because by the time you got there, the Sky Department already had the issue cleared up."

"You've been letting your imagination run away with you again," Mother added with a shake of her head. "If you paid more attention to your training, you would have more faith that the company has everything in hand, and you wouldn't keep getting yourself worked up about imaginary dome disasters."

Eli opened his mouth and closed it again. On the one hand, he was glad that his family was finally acknowledging he'd seen something out of order up there, but still, he'd thought they would be more alarmed. He suddenly felt a little silly.

"But at least I discovered the Outsider, right?"

"I suppose, but no doubt the company would have detected him soon anyway. By chasing after him, you put your life at risk for no good reason." Uncle Hector paused. "Eli, right now your responsibility to InfiniCorp is to spend your time learning how to run a business, not chasing after fictional sky calamities or climbing through tunnels under the streets."

"Your lack of focus is getting to be a serious problem," Mother said. "You're a Papadopoulos, for goodness' sake. Don't you care about your future?"

"Sure, I care about my future. It's just that . . ." He sighed. He wasn't sure how to finish, and in any case he was still shaking.

"Aw, leave him alone, Mother," called a voice. "Can't you see he's still scared?"

Eli turned. On the stairway stood his brother, Sebastian. Three weeks shy of fourteen, Sebastian had long black hair down to his shoulders, with Father's dark features and Mother's sloping nose—all of which he had in common with Eli. But there the physical similarities ended. Sebastian was less than a year Eli's senior but looked years older. Eli had inherited the Papadopoulos physique, short and solid, while Sebastian was tall and slim, with a penetrating gaze that turned teenage girls into puddles. Only a few weeks earlier, the CloudNet readers of *Dome Girl* magazine had voted Sebastian number 4 on their annual list of the Top Ten Cutest Future InfiniLeaders.

"He *should* be scared," Uncle Hector told him. "What your brother did was irresponsible and dangerous."

Mother frowned. "This defiant behavior has to stop, Eli. I'm afraid I'm going to have to instruct Dr. Toffler to double up your lessons for the rest of the week. You have some catching up to do."

His stomach sank.

By then Sebastian had descended the remaining stairs and now stood beside Eli. "Don't torture him. Dr. Toffler is the most boring droid ever. Have a heart."

"Dr. Toffler is a brilliant machine."

"Mother, it's as dry as sand. Look, instead of piling on more lessons with the old rust heap, why not let Eli do some catch-up work with me? What unit are you on now, Eli? Messaging Theory?"

He nodded.

"Oh, deadly stuff. But I know it cold." He turned back to Mother. "I'll work with him."

She was quiet a moment. "All right. I suppose that would be okay, as long as you finish up with Dr. Toffler today, and as long as Uncle Hector agrees."

"Fine, fine," he said. "I appreciate your willingness to step in to help the team, Sebastian."

Eli felt his brother's hand on his shoulder. He knew what this was really about. Sebastian's Internship Assignment was coming up, and he wanted to be sure he was on Uncle Hector's good side. Not that there was any reason to worry. Sebastian was a rising star in the family, a shoo-in for a management spot in some high-profile department like Security or Entertainment Systems. Still, he'd saved Eli from a week of nothing but Dr. Toffler, and for that he was grateful.

"Don't worry," Sebastian said into the sphere. "I'll get him up to speed." When he turned around, he winked at Eli.

"In the meantime, boys, let's keep this whole business to ourselves," Uncle Hector said. "No point in raising needless alarm."

Shoulders slumped, Eli followed Sebastian up the stairs.

Halfway up the steps he looked back toward the sphere. "Why would somebody do that?" he asked. "Sleep under the city?"

Uncle Hector and Mother had been fading, but now they solidified again, and Uncle Hector looked up. "Oh, don't bother searching for logic when it comes to Outsiders. They're practically animals, you know *that*. Cannibals, cutthroats, and criminals are all you'll find in the wasteland. If starvation doesn't get them, brain fever rots their minds away. It's very sad."

Sebastian pulled at his elbow, urging him to come upstairs and let it go, but Eli couldn't. "Can't the company help them? Why don't we send people out there to clean it all up?"

"This is not a good time for this conversation, Eli," Mother said. "As you can see, you caught us in a meeting, and you have your own work to get back to."

In the hologram inside the hologram, Uncle Hector's head chuckled. "No, it's all right, Paloma. The boy's just curious, that's all. It's normal." And then to Eli he said, "We'd like to, kiddo, but do you have any idea how difficult and dangerous it would be with all the heat and storms, not to mention the savages themselves? Sure, we'd all love to speed up Mother Nature, but the Cooldown is going to take time. Figure another decade or two before the planet's natural temperature cycle returns things to normal and it's safe out there again."

Eli could still picture the shadow under the pipes: the frozen silhouette, the flash of tangled hair and red skin. As if reading his thoughts, Sebastian asked, "But, Uncle, isn't it possible to live for years in the desert? Even with brain fever, not everybody *dies*, right?"

Uncle Hector took another puff on his cigar. "Very few of them last long out there, Sebastian," he said. "And there are some things worse than death."

When he returned to his room, Eli found Dr. Toffler in dormant mode. It had folded itself into its box and shut itself down to recharge its batteries. The mongoose lay on the rug, ripping up one of Eli's socks. Scattered all around her were dozens of tiny bits of blue fabric. She narrowed her eyes at Eli, looking for all the world like she was annoyed with him.

"Marilyn, what's the matter?" he asked, bending to stroke her little head. "Don't do that."

She bit into the sock again and tore off another piece. Eli wondered if it was because he'd gone on a walk without her.

"It's okay," he said, running his fingers through the thick fur of her back. "I'll take you next time." After a while this seemed to appease her. She let go of the sock and closed her eyes, and soon Eli could hear the soft *tick-tick-tick* sound she made when she was content. Apparently all was forgiven.

He stood up. He was about to revive Dr. Toffler when his hand brushed against something hard and flat in his cloak pocket. The *Alice* book. He didn't remember slipping it into his pocket back in the tunnel, but he must have, because here it was. He examined the cover again. In this better light he could see a drawing of a little girl peering over a giant mushroom with some kind of bug sitting on top.

He glanced back at the sleeping robot and decided his lessons could wait.

Marilyn followed him to his bed, and when he sat down she hopped up beside him. This wasn't the first old-style book he'd ever come across. Grandfather had a whole wall in his office stacked high with them, his favorites saved from the Old Days, before the Re-Org. Eli enjoyed poring over them whenever Grandfather let him. Unlike the CloudNet-generated tales in modern InfiniBooks, no colorful images moved across these pages, no music swelled from the bindings. Mostly there were just static words printed in black and white. But Eli liked that. He preferred imagining the scenes for himself because it meant he was free to picture them as he liked.

This *Alice* story, though, was new to him. He didn't remember seeing it in Grandfather's archives.

He flipped through the pages. Lots of prose, a few illustrations, even some poems. Marilyn climbed onto his shoulder and looked on. When he got to the back, a sheet of paper fell out. It looked old and discolored, and it was torn along the edges. The only marking on it was a crude image drawn in brownish ink—a sketch of what looked like a blazing sun, with rays that twisted at jagged angles.

Had the savage drawn this? What did it mean? There was no way to know. Eli turned to the beginning of the story to start reading, but he heard Dr. Toffler powering back to life behind him. There was the unmistakable whir of its systems rebooting, the whispering sound of unfolding joints.

"Representative Papadopoulos? Excellent, you're back.

Let's stop wasting time, shall we? Come here, sit down. We have lessons to work through."

Eli closed his eyes, bracing himself for more drudgery. Before he turned around, he slipped the paper into his pocket.

Seconds later, as he took his seat by the old droid, he noticed the mongoose was still on the bed, staring into the open book. She was crouched over the page, her snout inches from the text and her brow furrowed as if she were concentrating. He continued to watch. She looked like she was trying to read, and, crazy as it seemed, he knew it was possible that was exactly what she was doing.

On Eli's birthday, when Grandfather had given Marilyn to him, he'd said:

"This, my dear boy, is a three-month-old mongoose, a common Indian Gray. But make no mistake, there's nothing common about her. You won't see many animals like this one in your lifetime, I can promise you that."

In his wrinkled fingers he'd held up a squirming creature no bigger than his fist. He took her by the scruff of the neck and handed her to Eli. Eli had held his breath. He cradled her in one arm, cupping his free hand gently across her back. This calmed her.

"The thing you need to understand, child, is that there's a special chip planted in her brain. The operation that put it there is very hard to perform successfully. Very rare." He leaned in close and whispered, "*Illegal,* in fact."

Eli had stared, wide-eyed. "What does the chip *do,* exactly?"

At this the old man sat back in his armchair and grinned.

"I don't honestly know. An old friend gave her to me, and he didn't say." Then his expression turned mischievous. "Whatever it does, though, I have no doubt that finding out will be part of the fun. Happy birthday, Eli. She's all yours."

Too astonished to speak, Eli had stared deep into her eyes. Chip or not, he was thrilled with her.

In the ten weeks since, he and Marilyn had been almost constant companions. He sometimes walked her down North Main to peer through the windows of the pastry shops or to visit a comic-book store together. In the afternoons they'd sit in the backyard and share a cinnamon bun. Marilyn preferred bugs and mice, but she wasn't picky.

Now almost six months old and fully grown, she measured just under two feet long, although her tail made up half that length. Eli was always watching her, on the lookout for any odd behavior that might be from the chip. So far he'd seen nothing especially strange. She seemed smart for an animal, but he didn't know much about mongooses. As they wandered the neighborhoods, cats would sometimes hiss at her, or dogs would growl and cower, sensing, it seemed, that there was something unnatural and frightening about her. But that wasn't her fault.

In any case, the more time Eli spent with her, the more he adored her. With Mother and Father often away on business and no schoolmates to keep him company, Eli had spent much of his childhood separated from other people. Even within his family he was considered something of a loner.

He'd never had a real friend before.

* * *

The afternoon following his discovery of the Outsider, Eli took Marilyn out to the backyard to study the artificial sky. For several days he'd been doing this. He'd lie in the synthetic grass with his eyes fixed on the dome, waiting to catch anything that didn't seem to belong up there.

He'd discovered that if he paid close attention, he could sometimes spot strange things—curious, fantastical images that most people seemed too busy to notice or care about: Dozens of digital bats would appear to swoop down at him. A fanged pterodactyl or a giant flying hippo would appear briefly in the distance. A freight train on fire might streak across the dome so fast, it could have been mistaken for a meteor. The time to look, Eli had found, was right after a storm had passed by. A week earlier, after an especially dramatic squall, he'd spotted a bespectacled old gentleman in a tweed suit floating a hundred feet or so above his house. The man was pedaling a contraption that looked like an old-fashioned bicycle except it had enormous red, feathered wings. After a few seconds, the image disappeared.

Eli knew none of what he was seeing was real. They were simulations generated by the CloudNet, the automated computer network that controlled the spheres, the sky, and all the other electronic processors in the dome. Still, the images both fascinated and worried him. Uncle Hector had said the company wanted him to stop thinking about sky anomalies and pay attention only to his studies, but the fact was, Eli couldn't help it. Besides, he didn't care what the company wanted.

No, that wasn't true. He *did* care. He cared about Infini-Corp because he cared about his family. It was almost the same thing. But lately he was having so much trouble staying focused on his training that he wondered how on earth he would ever make it as a senior executive. He wanted to do the right thing by taking his place in the organization, but, unlike Sebastian, he felt secretly ashamed because he had no idea where that place might be. Just like looking at the sky in recent days, thinking about the months and years ahead filled him with trepidation.

"You know what I think?" he whispered to Marilyn. "I think there must be something wrong with me."

Beside him on the grass, the mongoose appeared lost in concentration, her neck craned toward the southern edge of the dome ceiling, which was crowded with cloud-vertise-ments. After a moment she started whistling and chirping.

Eli twisted to see where she was looking. Then he saw it too. Over the Department of Painless Dentistry building, about three blocks away, a troop of silver monkeys was swing-ing from cloud to cloud. Small in the distance, they grew larger and clearer as they passed overhead, leaping at each other on their way up across the sky. He had to admit, this was an impressive one. Whenever he caught one of these sudden, absurd simulations, he tried to take in every detail. The mon-keys got close to the center of the dome, perhaps a quarter mile high, and then vanished.

Marilyn ran around in circles as if she appreciated the show, but Eli sat frozen. If these random images weren't a sign of some troubling underlying malfunction, then why were they there? They weren't advertising anything. They didn't seem to have any purpose at all. As terrifying as Eli found them, they were often beautiful too. Whoever the programmer was, he decided, he must have had the soul of an artist.

He even came up with a name for him. Leonardo.

Leonardo of the Wild Blue Yonder.

Eli wondered if he himself had a purpose. His whole life was already mapped out for him, and yet when he thought about the future it filled him with dread and uncertainty. He couldn't explain why. With Marilyn at his side and his eyes still scanning the sky, he had an idea it had something to do with what was happening up there.

Which made him suspect there really was something wrong with him. He felt like the only kid in the world who could get scared just by looking up.

2

the family

The next day was InfiniCorp Day, the anniversary of the Grand Reorganization. On celebration days such as this, Eli was allowed to set aside his study modules, leave Dr. Toffler in his box, and travel with his family to Grandfather's mansion. These were Eli's favorite days. Fortunately, there were plenty of occasions to celebrate. Company holidays, Grandfather's birthday, the Fourth of July. Sometimes there was a Papadopoulos family wedding. No matter what it was, Eli knew that the CloudNet news cameras would be there to cover it, which was why everyone prepared so carefully. The laundry droids would set out the boys' best balloon pants with matching jackets and ties. They would also pack an extra set of casual clothes for them, just in case there was a football game.

Even when he was a small child, Eli understood that the message for the media was this: See? We're like everybody else. A normal family. We even play football together.

Once they were clean and suited up, Eli and Sebastian

would follow their parents into the transport, which had the familiar InfiniCorp logo emblazoned on its side: DON'T WORRY! INFINICORP IS TAKING CARE OF EVERYTHING! The transport would fly the four of them out beyond the Providence dome, and Eli would gaze down through the window. From high in the air, Outside looked bleak and empty to him—endless miles of sand and barren roads with only occasional patches of abandoned buildings. Eventually, far on the horizon, he would be able to make out a silver glow, the first shimmer from a massive hemisphere of metal and light twice the size of the Providence dome.

New Washington, where Grandfather lived.

Eli loved these family visits to the mansion—these *photo ops*, as he sometimes overhead Mother and Father referring to them in whispers. Eli had twenty-three cousins and eighteen uncles and aunts. Plus Grandfather, of course. He was the one Eli looked forward to seeing most.

Grandfather, whose actual name was Hector Papadopoulos but *everyone* called him Grandfather, always made a special fuss over Eli. At some point during the commotion the old man would always wave him over.

"There he is! My fat lamb!" he would say. And then, "What is it that nobody ever sees, never arrives, and yet no one doubts will come in mere hours, at most?" Grandfather adored riddles and always had a new one ready when Eli visited. Eli was good at figuring out the answers and often got them right on the first guess. It was usually some sort of play on words. He'd consider for a moment and then give his reply.

"Tomorrow."

Then Grandfather would laugh. "Nicely done!"

While the CloudNet cameras snapped pictures of the other children, Eli and Grandfather would head into Grandfather's private office, away from the commotion, to play checkers, another of Grandfather's favorite pastimes. Grandfather sometimes let Eli beat him, but not often. It wasn't his way.

"What an observant child!" Grandfather would say whenever Eli made a clever move. "Such an intelligent boy!"

Eli was a frustration to Dr. Toffler and a disappointment to most of the Papadopoulos family, but to the old man none of this seemed to matter. Eli was Grandfather's special favorite.

Eli was proud of Grandfather and what he'd done for the nation. He'd started the company as Papadopoulos Incorporated and evolved it into a giant organization that sold just about every kind of product and service there was to sell. He'd kept it growing by merging and acquiring and gobbling up competing companies until at last it became one gigantic conglomerate, InfiniCorp, the organization that built, owned, and ran everything in the whole country. *Everything.* Which was wonderful because Grandfather had organized it all, made it more efficient.

When the Great Sickness came, sweeping across Europe, Asia, and Africa, killing millions, only InfiniCorp was strong and organized enough to protect its employees. There wasn't time to design the perfect vaccine, but InfiniCorp scientists created a fragile concoction that had to be used within minutes of its manufacture. By the time the virus hit North America, InfiniCorp was ready. Soon after, the domed cities were completed, and

InfiniCorp's employees were able to live in a protected space where climate-bred illnesses couldn't reach them.

So of course Eli was proud.

Each and every person living in the domed cities owed his life to Grandfather!

Today InfiniCorp was still a family-owned business. After the Great Sickness, Grandfather was hailed as a hero; the petty complaints about one company holding so much power disappeared virtually overnight. Now everyone understood that the Papadopouloses were *leaders*. They ran things. They managed the domes that shielded everybody from the storms and heat. They cleaned up messes and did what they could about the Outsiders. And most important, they protected their employees when it mattered most. Not only had Eli's family turned the whole disorganized nation into one ideal society, the most advanced and productive in human history, but they kept everybody safe and comfortable while they awaited the completion of the Great Cooldown. If it hadn't been for Grandfather, the employees of InfiniCorp would have suffered the same fate as the rest of the world: if they'd survived the Great Sickness at all, they'd still be scrounging in the desert wilderness, trying to survive in the scorching heat. Grandfather said even if there were still any Outsiders alive on other continents, all the other nations of the world had been virtually destroyed.

Grandfather was the greatest hero ever. Everyone knew that.

* * *

Eli and Grandfather stood in Grandfather's office gazing at the magnificent music box the old man kept on a block of carved marble at the center of the room. The size of a grand piano, the musical contraption was in the shape of a domed city, with little wooden houses and shopping centers, shiny towers, and jeweled streets, all under a protective dome of glass. It was one of a kind, an astonishing work of art. Eli had been drawn to it since he was a small boy.

Beside him, Grandfather leaned into the glass and spoke the code words that switched the machine on: "Good morning, folks. Time to wake up." He winked at Eli. At once the model began to hum, and little lights came on in the houses and buildings.

Next Grandfather produced a wooden box containing hundreds of tiny metal keys in velvet casings. He waited for Eli to choose one. This was part of their ritual. Each key triggered the mechanism to play a different melody, but since the keys all looked pretty much the same, Eli was never sure which music his chosen key would unlock. He picked one at random and slipped it into the keyhole. The city came to life. Little people walked the sidewalks. Tiny transport pods moved along the streets and flew in circles in the sky. Eli pressed his face closer to the glass. The music was Bach's Minuet in G. Its restrained, measured notes gave a stately feel to the mechanical movement.

"How's that mongoose?" Grandfather asked. "Any unusual behavior yet?"

"I'm not sure. I think she's smart—for an animal, I mean. But it's hard to tell. Yesterday she ripped up one of my socks."

He grunted thoughtfully. Eli could see the old man's

reflection in the glass. Short and stocky with a wide nose, his sky blue eyes still maintained the good humor and vitality of his youth. Now, though, he was almost completely bald, with only a thin line of white hair over his ears. His face was etched with pockmarks, barely visible, which he shared with Eli's parents and uncles and aunts, and all those old enough to have survived the Great Sickness. But it was Grandfather's deep wrinkles that had always fascinated Eli. At seventy-nine, Grandfather was the oldest person he'd ever known. For the past few months Eli had been observing him, taking note of the slow, shuffling way he sometimes moved and how he occasionally wheezed when he breathed. It worried him a little. Despite his age, Grandfather had always seemed invincible, but now Eli realized the years were catching up with him.

After a minute or so, Grandfather stepped back from the music box and started in the direction of the checkers table. "Come on, then," he said. "I believe the time has come for me to whip your butt again."

Eli smiled. This routine was the same every time he visited. Before following, he leaned close to the glass and said, "Good night, folks. Time to go back to sleep." Somewhere in the complex mechanism, a sensor detected that these were the shutdown words, the second part of the Master Key, as Grandfather called it. The music stopped, all the little pods flew back to their parking stations, and the people went home. The lights in the mechanical city went dark again.

It was as Eli stepped past the ancient books on Grandfather's shelves that he remembered what he'd almost forgotten. "Oh! Grandfather, I have a riddle for you!"

"Let's hear it."

"Why is a raven like a writing desk?"

Grandfather didn't answer, or maybe he wasn't really listening, because he was busy setting the checkers pieces in their places. In any case, when he didn't respond after a few seconds, Eli decided to give the answer.

"Two reasons," he said. "First, because both can produce notes that are flat, and second, because you never put either of them with the wrong end in front."

Grandfather looked up.

"It's a strange riddle, I know," Eli admitted. "In fact, I don't understand the second answer at all. But it was in a book I found. A really interesting book. Here, I brought it for you to see." He pulled the *Alice* book from his pocket and held it up, thrilled to show off his discovery.

For a moment Grandfather didn't say a word. He stared at the cover, his bushy eyebrows pulling together. At last he said, "Where on earth did you find this, child?"

"I was wandering around and saw it under a pile of old junk." Eli had planned this answer ahead of time. Even though he'd been dying to show Grandfather his find (Grandfather was the only other person Eli knew who cared about such things) and would never have lied to him, Eli also knew he had to be careful what he said about where the book had come from. It belonged to an Outsider, after all. If anyone found out, it was possible he'd be forbidden to keep it. Until now he hadn't shown it to anyone, not even Sebastian.

Fortunately Grandfather didn't press him for details.

"The second answer to the riddle makes sense only when you notice the way the author spelled the words," he said, looking up at Eli. "*Never* is printed n-e-v-a-r, which is raven backward. That's the Mad Hatter's riddle."

"Ahh . . ." Understanding began to dawn on Eli, but only slowly. "So, you know this story already."

"Oh yes. I know it well." Grandfather took the book in his hands and flipped gingerly through the pages. "This is quite a discovery indeed. I didn't think any more of these existed."

"I'm about halfway through."

Grandfather nodded, still examining the ancient thing. "I'm so glad you found it. Tell you what, Eli. Why don't you let me keep it here in my office where it'll be safe from harm? We don't want this lying around. What if it gets lost again?"

Eli hesitated. He'd been so sure Grandfather would let him keep it. Now he wanted to kick himself. "Actually," he said, "I was hoping to keep it with me. You don't need to worry. I'll take good care of it, I promise."

The old man seemed to study him, taking a deep, wheezy breath as he did. "All right," he said, his smile returning as he handed it back. "You found it, so I suppose it was meant to be yours. But keep it safe, child. It's worth something."

Eli had trouble fitting in with other children. Later that day, when his younger cousins drifted in groups to various play activities, one group called out, "Come play a dream game with us, Eli!" Another group, one that included Sebastian, called, "Eli, come watch the CloudNet spheres! We're streaming *Kidz Gonna Zap Ya Dead!* and then *Babette, Time-Traveling Vampire Dancer!*"

"No, thank you," he answered.

It wasn't that he didn't like spending time with his cousins. He just wasn't interested in CloudNet streams the way everyone else was. Instead he wandered off to a secluded corner with the *Alice* book. Last time it had been one of the old-style volumes from Grandfather's shelf, a story titled *The Call of the Wild*, by Jack London, which turned out to be an adventure about a dog in a strange, frozen wilderness. Eli had always been intrigued by how different the world must have been years ago, back before the Warm Times and the domes. He pictured himself running through snow and sliding across sheets of ice. It was hard to imagine that such things had once been commonplace in Providence during the wintertime many years before the city was domed. Eventually two of Eli's aunts had stumbled across him curled up on a sofa. When he'd looked up and noticed the aunts standing over him, he'd caught them giving each other what looked like secret glances of concern.

"My brothers and sisters and I are worried about that child," he'd later overheard Uncle Hector complaining to Grandfather. "Have you noticed how much time he spends with those confounded paper antiques of yours? The boy has hardly any normal interests. Mark my words, we're going to have trouble with that one."

"Nonsense," Grandfather had replied. "The child is no trouble at all."

Uncle Hector hadn't looked too convinced.

Today Eli found a quiet chair, big and red and comfortable, by a window in one of Grandfather's sitting rooms. He opened the *Alice* book to the page where he'd left off. It was a peculiar story about a little girl who wanders into fantastical worlds where playing cards and chess pieces walk around and animals talk. Throughout the book there were little poems, and these Eli especially enjoyed. He mouthed their sometimes outlandish words as he read them.

> 'Twas brillig, and the slithy toves
> Did gyre and gimble in the wabe:
> All mimsy were the borogoves,
> And the mome raths outgrabe.

Much of it was nonsense, but it was glorious nonsense. The author played games with language and logic. Eli was mesmerized, and as he lost himself in the story, the world around him seemed to fade away.

> Beware the Jabberwock, my son!
> The jaws that bite, the claws that catch!
> Beware the Jubjub bird, and shun
> The frumious Bandersnatch!

"There you are," interrupted a breathy voice. "I was wondering where you'd disappeared to. What have you got there?"

Eli looked up. Partway across the long, sparsely furnished sitting room stood his eldest cousin, Spider, Uncle Hector's son, alone and half-hidden in shadows. Spider was twenty-four, pale, and painfully skinny, with hair that had turned prematurely white. Eli had always been wary of him. Years earlier, when Eli was six, Spider had brought his new InfiniZapper to one of Grandfather's parties, snuck up on him, and zapped him painfully in the back. Spider had then dragged his immobilized body down an empty hallway to a pantry at the back of one of the far kitchens and had left him there. Mother and Father had later found him trapped behind a giant bag of potatoes.

Since then Eli had steered clear of his most senior cousin.

"Well, well," Spider said, squinting at the cover. "Where did you find this old relic? Oh, of course. It's one of the old man's."

Eli didn't correct him.

"Is it any good?"

"Yes . . . ," he answered guardedly. "What do you want, Spider?" Spider, of course, was just a nickname used within the family. His real name was Hector Papadopoulos III. Eli wasn't sure why they called him Spider, but he'd heard a rumor it was because his cousin enjoyed pulling the legs off bugs.

Spider looked hurt. "There's no need to be unfriendly. I'm just saying hello to my little cousin, that's all." He smiled. "You don't mind if I have a quick look at it, do you?" Before Eli could answer, Spider snatched the book from his hand. He hummed to himself as he flipped through the pages. Soon he was shaking his head. "A rabbit with a watch? Frogs in wigs? Playing cards that talk?" He snorted. "Gibberish. Pathetic."

Eli felt his blood rise.

"No wonder we don't make these things anymore. Such a waste of time. I've been hearing that you've had your head in the clouds, Eli, but I had no idea the situation was quite this . . . *dire.*" With another snort, he handed the book back. "I don't understand what goes through Grandfather's doddery old mind, sharing his artifacts with you. But then again, who understands the old geezer?"

Eli held the book tight in his lap. He didn't answer.

Spider put his hands in his trouser pockets and turned toward the window. "Actually, Grandfather is the reason I was looking for you. I've been watching, Eli, and I've observed how much time you and he spend together. How informative it must be to receive so much special . . . *attention* from the CEO."

Eli didn't know what to say. It wasn't as if Spider didn't have contact with Grandfather. Because he was the son of Uncle Hector, who would take Grandfather's place as chief executive officer someday, everyone assumed Spider would be next in line after him. He already held the top position in the Department of Loyalty, an important branch of the Division of Freedom. Why Eli's occasional time alone with Grandfather should matter to such an important person in the family, he couldn't guess.

"What are you talking about?"

Spider spun around. "Oh, don't think we haven't all noticed the preference he's always shown for you. But, as somebody who'll be in charge of this company someday, I get uncomfortable when Grandfather closes his door and it seems there could be . . . *secrets* shared. Secrets I'm not privy to. So I've been wondering: whatever plot he's hatching in there, whatever special information he's sharing with you, perhaps you would be willing to divulge it to me?"

Eli stood up from the chair now, eyeing the doorway at the far end of the room. Spider wasn't making any sense. He was scaring him. "I don't know what you mean," he said. "Grandfather isn't hatching any plot. He doesn't share any special information. All we do is watch his music box and play checkers."

Spider's expression went dark. All of a sudden he grabbed Eli by the collar, and Eli found himself nose to nose with him. "Don't play games with me, little cousin. I just want to know where your loyalties lie. If you'd let me, I believe I could prove very . . . *helpful* to you. Or not." He glowered at him. "You don't want to cross me."

Eli was too startled to respond. Loyalties? What on earth was Spider talking about? "But you don't understand," he said at last, trying to keep his voice level. "I'm telling the truth. Grandfather doesn't talk about any secrets or the company or anything like that. I have nothing to share with you."

For a long moment Spider stayed quiet. "Your attitude disappoints me," he said, his voice eerily calm once more. He let go and made a show of smoothing out Eli's collar again. "You should know that my father is already concerned about you. The family is at a loss about where to place you in the organization. What InfiniCorp needs are leaders and innovators, not children who sit apart from everyone else and daydream about foolish old stories that mean nothing to anyone anymore." He leaned in and prodded him in the chest with one of his long, skinny fingers. "All I can say is, you'd better watch your step."

Eli's stomach was in his throat. From the main ballroom the sounds of celebrating could still be heard. He wanted to get away from his strange cousin. He took a deep breath, and then he ducked around him and ran.

Spider didn't move. He didn't even try to stop him. He narrowed his eyes at Eli without saying another word.

* * *

Something extraordinary happened between Eli and Marilyn one evening later that week. It was just after dinner, and they were in the living room with Sebastian, who was having an argument with his instruction robot, a sleek, blue HumanForm named Dr. Avila. Sebastian had recently dreamed up a new business idea: InfiniCorp could sell security systems to Outsiders. He'd even worked out a mock business plan.

"But why shouldn't we?" he was asking. "There's an untapped market out there. Even criminals need to protect their stuff from other criminals. As long as they have something of value to trade with us, why not do it?"

Soothing music filled the room. Dr. Avila was programmed with a simulated personality and, unlike ancient Dr. Toffler, designed with a gender—female. At that moment her expression was peaceful as she balanced on one of her plastic legs while holding the other above her head with her chassis forward and her arms outstretched. She was following along with a CloudNet stream called *Yoga for Droids*.

"It's an intriguing notion, Sebastian," she said, holding her pose, "but impractical and potentially dangerous. You can't trust Outsiders to act like civilized consumers."

Eli was on the sofa, pretending to review his lesson, while Marilyn lay at his feet, watching him. All day long Eli had been feeling a weird sensation in his head. At first it had been only a distant, intermittent hum, almost like a mosquito buzzing around his ears. But now it was getting louder.

"How do we know unless we try?" Sebastian asked. "Isn't Grandfather always saying the company is looking for innovative ideas?"

Dr. Avila raised one of her synthetic eyebrows. "I doubt doing business with savages is what he had in mind."

All of a sudden the buzzing became so insistent that Eli had difficulty thinking. He sat up and held his hands to his ears. He wasn't sure what was happening to him.

Too involved in his conversation to be aware of anything else, Sebastian didn't notice. "I'm serious. If I could get permission to go Outside for just a few minutes, if I could only get close enough to some desert rats to try to talk to them, I bet I could prove my idea could work."

Eli could barely hear past the static. When Dr. Avila answered, her voice sounded as if it were being transmitted over a distant radio signal. "You'd never get authorization to leave the dome for something so frivolous." And then, after a pause, "Sebastian, what's wrong with your brother?"

A moment later Eli became aware that he must have fainted. He was lying across the sofa and Sebastian was leaning over him, staring into his eyes. "Whoa, that was spooky, Eli. What's the matter with you?"

"I . . . don't know." He rubbed his temples. The buzzing was gone, but he was still light-headed. "I just felt . . . strange, that's all."

"I think he's all right," Sebastian said to Dr. Avila. "Probably just catching a cold or something."

The blue robot was standing behind him, watching over his shoulder, her tranquillity disturbed. "Perhaps . . . ," she said. "I suppose we ought to instruct the cooking droid to prepare him something healthy. In the meantime, you'd better help him to his room."

Minutes later Eli sat up in his bed, sipping a bowl of

macrobiotic soup. The cooking droid had insisted on making him the greenish liquid even though Eli felt sure that whatever was happening, it wasn't a viral infection. Something had changed—he could feel it, like an unfamiliar channel in his brain.

He was still working on the soup, stirring it around more than actually drinking it, when he heard a voice.

Eli . . . , it said, an urgent whisper. *Eli . . .* It was deep and gravelly but clear. Still, at first he thought he'd imagined it. But then he heard it again.

Over here, Eli . . .

He sat up straighter. He set the bowl down.

It was the strangest thing. The voice sounded as if it were coming from inside his own head.

Marilyn hopped onto the bed. Settling near his feet, she licked her paws and watched him with what looked like curiosity. He studied her. Was it possible?

No, it couldn't be. Surely not.

But he climbed out of the covers and put his face close to hers. He gazed deep into her eyes. She blinked.

And that's when he knew.

Eli, dear, said the strange voice in his brain, *would you mind opening your door to let me out? I have to pee.*

He gaped at her. Somehow, she'd tapped a channel into his mind.

Marilyn was talking to him.

3

ruins

It was the strangest, most exciting thing that had ever happened to him. He had no idea *why* it worked, but it didn't take Eli long before he learned more about *how* it worked. He was the only one she seemed able to communicate with in this way. What was more, the channel seemed to go in both directions. Within a few days he and Marilyn were conversing like it was the most normal thing in the world.

How far back can you remember? he asked her silently one evening, studying her on his bedroom floor with his chin in his hands. He was trying to find out if the chip enhanced her ability to recall things. *Do you remember when you were a newborn pup? Do you remember the operation?*

She stretched and yawned. *No, but I remember soon after the operation,* she said. *At least, I remember something of what happened. But if you don't mind, darling, I'd rather not think about it. Very unpleasant memories.*

Eli didn't push her, but over time he was able to piece

together the few snippets she occasionally did reveal. Marilyn remembered that the operation had happened in a bright room lined with clear plastic. She'd woken up groggy, her head throbbing like it might split open. It was her earliest memory. Soon she realized something was moving on the other side of the room. Gradually her thoughts cleared, and over the next few hours she'd watched, horrified, as five other mongoose pups, her littermates, were taken from their cages one at a time and brought to another table where their heads were sliced open. Marilyn now realized she'd been the first. Of the six of them, only three had survived the operating table, and two weeks later Marilyn was the only one still alive.

It had been a profoundly upsetting time.

After that, she was kept in a special cage where electronic instruments recorded her every move. There were electrodes taped to her head. Men and women wrapped in brown cloth watched her through the mesh. She never saw their faces. Red-eyed droids with needles and sensory probes took hundreds of measurements every day. Her heart rate. Her brain waves. Her bodily functions, too numerous to imagine. The humans performed experiments on her too. There were daily injections, flashing lights, and complicated mazes she was forced to navigate. When she wasn't being poked, measured, or injected, she felt desperate and alone in her cramped cage.

Then one day she was taken from that place. Marilyn remembered shaking with fear, but her captors had been kind. They fed her, played with her, and even let her wander around in a large room with a sand floor. It was the first taste of freedom she'd ever known. The very next morning, though, she was packed into another cage and given an injection that put

49

her to sleep. When she awoke she found herself in the care of a wrinkled old human with very little hair.

The experience had been terrifying, but in the end it turned out all right. This, of course, was because the wrinkled old human had been Grandfather.

And he had given her to Eli.

One afternoon a tremendous boom shook the sky. To Eli it sounded a lot like a thunderclap, only closer. It turned out to be a bomb. The CloudNet reported that somebody had sabotaged the air filter on the northwest perimeter and that the likely culprit was a criminal organization called the Fog.

Eli had heard of Fog attacks before. Foggers, the shadowy outlaws whose sole purpose was to destroy freedom by sabotaging the company, were a great mystery. Nobody seemed to know much about them except that they were twisted people who hated InfiniCorp. Every few weeks or so they tried to cause disruption, but rarely with such dramatic results. Today there were nearly thirty dead, a big deal. Grandfather declared a general state of emergency.

When Sebastian came to Eli and suggested they use the confusion to sneak Outside and check out the damage, Eli was only half-surprised. To all appearances his brother wasn't one to break the rules, but Eli knew better than anyone that Sebastian wasn't as tight as he appeared. He wasn't above straying from the straight and narrow on occasion; he was just better at getting away with it than Eli. With his recent fixation on marketing to Outsiders, Eli should have guessed he would be more than a little curious about what was happening out there.

Besides, as Sebastian pointed out, neither he nor Eli had ever seen a real dead person.

The brothers decided to use back roads to lessen their chances of being seen. Not that anyone was likely to recognize Eli. Hardly anyone ever did. But lots of people knew Sebastian's face. They didn't get far down the street, though, before Marilyn ran up behind them, nipping at Sebastian's heels.

"Hey, get it off me!" he shouted. "Eli, what's going on? What were you thinking?"

"I didn't have anything to do with this! It wasn't my idea!"

"Well, the mongoose can't come! What if it gets lost or something? Or stolen? Grandfather would totally shut down! Order it home."

Eli turned. "Marilyn, what do you think you're doing?"

What does it look like I'm doing? I'm coming with you.

"But you can't," he said, still getting used to the idea that he was trying to reason with a mongoose. "Sebastian's right—it's too risky. You have to turn around and go back."

She sat down and scratched absently at her ear. *I want to see Outside.*

"What's going on, Eli? Did it answer? Why isn't it going away? It's supposed to do what you tell it."

Eli sighed. He'd explained to Sebastian that he could communicate with Marilyn, but Sebastian didn't get how it worked. He seemed to think of her as something between a pet and a machine, as if the chip couldn't possibly make her capable of anything more than rudimentary communication—something only slightly more interesting than a well-trained dog or a furry robot. Eli had tried to tell him she was a real person just like anybody else, but he refused to believe it.

51

And Marilyn didn't seem to care what anyone thought.

"I already told you," he said. "I can't *make* her go home. She wants to come."

Sebastian glared. "You gotta be kidding me. What's the point of a chipped animal if you can't figure out how to control it? When are you going to learn to be the boss?" He shook his head. "Pitiful."

He made a sudden move as if to lunge at Marilyn, but she scooted away. Settling on the pavement just out of reach, she straightened to her full height and swayed from side to side as if readying for a fight. She narrowed her orange eyes at Sebastian and hissed.

"Stupid Frankenrat!" Sebastian said under his breath. And then, "All right, but she better stay out of sight!"

This wouldn't be an issue, Eli knew. If there was one thing Marilyn was good at, it was hiding. So the three of them wove through the streets behind Douglas Avenue to the far edge of the dome, running as quickly as they could. It was more than two miles away. When they reached the gate there was still a great deal of confusion, as Sebastian had predicted, and the three of them blended into the chaos. Within moments they were able to slip past the monitors without anybody stopping them.

For Eli it was a tremendous relief, but Sebastian laughed. He'd never doubted it would work.

Once Outside, the first thing they felt was the oppressive heat. Eli had forgotten how muggy it could get. When they were younger their parents had twice taken the boys on company-sponsored perimeter tours. Both times, though, Mother made them wear environment suits—bulky, uncomfortable outfits with big helmets—which made it hard to see or feel anything. They wouldn't need suits today, Sebastian had assured him. They wouldn't be Outside long.

Mud puddles dotted the otherwise dusty earth, remnants of last night's storm. But now the sun shone so bright it took a while for Eli's eyes to adjust. He blinked in wonder at the seemingly endless canopy of gray and blue. The real sky always seemed so lifeless to him, far less interesting than the artificial one Inside, in the dome.

At Sebastian's suggestion, the boys rubbed dust and mud on their faces and arms so that anyone who saw them might mistake them for Outsiders. Then the three of them ran toward the air filter. It wasn't far. Most of the interesting stuff from the explosion had been cleared away by then. Somebody had already cordoned off the area around the enormous steel column. Part of the base was blown clear off, with shards of metal and melted wiring hanging everywhere. A fresh tech crew had just arrived to work on it. There were still plenty of people shouting and calling out orders, with others looking dazed as they milled around, cleaning up. Most were in their InfiniCorp uniforms, but not all, so nobody noticed the three of them slipping behind the garbage bins and rubble.

"Look!" Sebastian said, pointing. "How cool is *that*?"

Off near the ruins, set back from the commotion at the edge of the dome, a crowd of five or six people in tattered environment suits stood in a circle and held hands. They were chanting something Eli couldn't quite make out. Even from so far away, Eli could see that one of them had red hair and they all had the weathered complexion that came from prolonged exposure to sun and sandstorms.

Outsiders.

"What are they doing?" he asked, wondering if one of them was the one he'd seen under the city.

"Who knows?" Sebastian's gaze had already moved on, looking farther ahead. "They're desert rats. Let's keep going."

They crept along the edge of the chaos, trying to move as close to the filter column as they could without attracting attention. At first they thought they were too late, that all the bodies had already been taken away. But then Sebastian saw one. Not far from a supply vehicle, somebody had thrown a blue plastic sheet over a lump on the ground, but the wind had blown it open. They dashed over to the vehicle and peered around it.

It was an Outsider, a girl. One of her arms jutted out, and in her dead fingers she was still gripping an orange. Even though the body was mangled, the fruit didn't seem damaged at all. Eli was mesmerized. Was she one of the nomads who sometimes set up wooden stands to trade things with each other, curiosities or supplies they'd found amid the wreckage? Or had she traded for the orange only moments before the blast? Was she a Fogger? There was no way to know. She looked like she was in her late teens, with long black hair that formed a fan around one side of her head. She might have been pretty, but now half her face was covered in blood. Her other arm, the one not holding the orange, had been blown off. Her eyes were open but she was obviously dead.

Eli couldn't speak. Sebastian was quiet too, and even Marilyn looked solemn. Of the three of them, she was the only one who had seen death before.

It felt like they were looking at something holy. A sacred thing.

Pretty soon one of the cleanup robots wheeled over and covered her again. Two Guardians lifted her onto a stretcher and loaded her into a ground transport. Eli, Sebastian, and Marilyn watched it drive away, a cloud of dust rising from the ground as it went. By then Eli was feeling dizzy.

"Sebastian," he whispered, "I want to go home."

Sebastian didn't argue.

Just as they were about to head back, though, they heard a voice calling out to them. "Hey! You over there! What are you doing?"

Eli looked up. About fifty feet away on the other side of a pile of rubble, a skinny Guardian with the wispy beginnings of a mustache had his hands on his hips. He was looking directly at them.

"Oh crap!" Sebastian whispered.

All at once Eli felt his heart pounding even harder. Caught! What would happen when Father and Mother heard they'd snuck Outside? Eli didn't like to think about their reaction. This was bad. Very bad. And yet there didn't seem to be any way out of it. They couldn't get back to the gate without crossing the Guardian's path. And worse, he was moving toward them now.

"Come on out from behind there!" he called again. "What department are you with?"

Eli was starting to panic. "He's going to find out who we are. What do we do? What do we do?"

"Calm down," Sebastian said. "I'll tell you what we do. We run."

"What?"

But there was no arguing. Sebastian grabbed his collar and

yanked him back. The next thing Eli knew, the three of them were bolting across the hard ground, only they were heading *away* from the dome, toward the ruins.

"Hey!" the Guardian shouted. "Get back here!"

Head down, Eli ran as fast as he could. There was a pile of wood and metal refuse up ahead and, beyond that, the remains of a destroyed building. Somebody's old garage, perhaps, or maybe a gas station. This whole area, the ruins around the dome perimeter, had once been part of Old Providence, but that was before the storms started ripping the cities apart, before they needed to build the protective domes. Up ahead Sebastian ducked behind the wall so Eli followed, running on adrenaline. Oh god, what were they doing? Surely they'd never get away with this!

Eli lost track of Marilyn, but around the corner he thought he saw Sebastian slip through the rectangular opening of a structure that might once have been a storefront. He headed in that direction, huffing and puffing, and climbed through. A moment later he was sprinting down a street of broken asphalt. He didn't see Sebastian anymore, but he couldn't stop. For all he knew the Guardian was right behind.

Soon he had to rest. He'd never run so hard in his life. In front of a little alleyway he doubled over with his hands on his knees, gasping for air. Bugs swarmed around him, and his entire body dripped with sweat. He glanced around at the wreckage. He was surrounded by sagging, vacant buildings and telephone poles that slumped like dead bodies. Shattered glass and debris littered the ground, and just ahead stood the crumbling brick remains of the front of an old house. To Eli it looked haunted, its empty doorway like a mouth, its missing windows like eye sockets keeping blind watch over nothing. It gave him the creeps.

"Sebastian?" he called, still struggling to catch his breath. "Marilyn?"

No answer. Just the sound of his own breathing and the wind whipping through the rubble.

It was only then that he fully realized he was all alone. He was farther Outside than he'd ever been before. Surely this place wasn't safe. It was spooky. It was *dead*. Or was it? Eli realized there were plenty of places where thieves or even murderers might hide, concealed places from which they might even be watching him right now. Everybody knew that life out here was cheap. The savages wouldn't think twice about ripping him apart just to go through his pockets.

"Sebastian? Marilyn?" he called again, a little louder this time. *"Are you there?"*

Nothing.

He tried calling out to Marilyn with his mind, but either she couldn't hear him or she wasn't listening. Eli had no idea where she and Sebastian were, or where *he* was. He wondered why he'd listened to his brother. He'd been caught up in his curiosity about the savage he'd seen, and now look where it had gotten him.

He wiped the sweat from his brow. The sun was like a furnace, and he realized he was dying of thirst. He felt like throwing up. This was the dumbest thing he'd ever done. Maybe the best thing now would be to head back. He could round up Sebastian and Marilyn and persuade them to make their way to the dome perimeter again and let the Guardians find them. True, it'd mean trouble from Mother and Father, but at this

57

point that didn't seem so terrible anymore. And what other choice did he have? He took a deep breath and decided. He would go back and turn himself in.

Suddenly something grabbed his arm.

He spun around. An inch from his face was a long, jagged knife. He was staring into the blade.

"My, my," said the Outsider holding the knife. "What fine boots you're wearing."

Eli's heart was pumping fast. The Outsider's face was hidden behind rusty metal goggles, but from the voice he guessed it was a girl. In any case, much of her head was wrapped in tattered brown cloth, and she was covered in dust. Her environment suit, if that was what it was, was patched in so many places it looked like it was made of rags.

"Little mousey ought to be more careful where it wanders," she said, her fingers like a vise around his forearm. "Doesn't it know there are dangerous people about? Mousey could get into real trouble roaming the ruins in a pair of boots as nice as those." She grinned. She was missing more than a few teeth. "It could even get itself killed."

Eli was too terrified to speak. In what felt like an instant, she maneuvered him backward until his shoulders hit something solid. She had him against the wall. He felt himself starting to hyperventilate. He wondered if he was going to pass out. Was this the end? Was he about to die?

Marilyn! I need you! Please, please! Come . . . !

With the blade pressed against his throat, Eli tried to keep still. The Outsider's masked face drew so close he could feel her sour breath on his cheek. The smell was like dirty socks and rotting cabbage.

"Yes, yes . . . ," she mumbled, sniffing him. By then Eli was shaking. What was she doing? He'd never been within reaching distance of an Outsider before, and definitely never *this* close. It occurred to him that she must be suffering from the corrosion of the mind that eventually came to all those who lived Outside. Brain fever. He wanted to scream.

But just when he was sure he couldn't take another second, she backed her face away enough to lift her goggles, perhaps to get a better look at him. Still holding the blade steady with one hand, she pulled back the rusted metal circles, and Eli saw her face. She had a long nose and sun-mottled skin, and her cheeks were streaked with dirt. She really did look like a desert rat. She might have been older, maybe in her twenties, but it was hard to tell. Most startling of all was that one of her eyes was completely white, probably sightless. Her other eye, clear blue and intelligent, was fixed hard on Eli.

"So, what'll it be then? In or Out?"

He could only blink at her. She seemed to be waiting for an answer.

"Wh-what?" he managed, surprised he could even talk.

She rolled her eyes and pressed the knife just a little harder against his throat. "Where are you *headed,* boy? Are you trying to escape the dome and join us Outside, or are you merely lost and looking for the way back?"

The blade pinched his skin. "I-in!" he stammered. "I'm going back! I just—I went a little farther than I meant to! I'm not used to being this far from home!"

"Really? How ever would I have guessed?" She smirked. "What's your name?"

"Eli!" He blurted it out before he could stop himself. The

moment it left his lips, he regretted it. It was unwise to admit his real name—even if it was only his first name—to an Outsider. On the other hand, who could blame him if he wasn't thinking straight? At least he hadn't told her his family name. Who knew what crazy ideas might get into her head if she found out he was a Papadopoulos?

Eli watched her pull back part of the cloth that covered her head. Now he could see some of her hair. It was cropped and red, and jutted in all directions. He realized he'd seen her before, just a few minutes earlier. She'd been one of the Outsiders at the edge of the ruins.

Without taking her freakish eyes off him, she wiped her sleeve across her chin, which glistened with sweat. She seemed to study him with new interest now. "Why do I know this one . . . ?" she said as if to herself. "Where have I seen its face . . . ?"

Eli wondered if she was the Outsider he'd seen in the tunnel. But no. Her size and shape were all wrong. Even so, he realized he was in danger of being identified, and that wasn't good. He needed to change the subject fast. "W-was that you at the edge of the ruins?" he sputtered, hoping to buy himself time. "A few minutes ago there were a bunch of people standing in a circle, holding hands and chanting. Were you one of them?"

Her eyes widened. She grinned. To Eli she looked like a space creature, some horrible mutant toying with its prey. "Oh yes," she said, "I was there."

"What were you doing?"

"What all of us should be doing. Preparing for the End of All Things. Readying ourselves for the journey ahead."

Eli glanced over her shoulder, trying to assess his options.

The opening to the little alleyway was only a few steps away. If he could somehow slip past her, then maybe he could try to duck down there. He wondered if he could knock her over. He doubted it. She was a full head taller than he was.

She leered at him and leaned in closer again. "How about *you*, little mousey? Are *you* prepared? Are you ready to face what's coming?"

Eli's breath came in short gasps. "I . . . don't know. I have no idea what you're talking about." He squeezed his eyes shut and tried to press tighter against the wall. He expected the worst.

But then he felt the weight of the blade leave his throat. He opened his eyes. The outlandish woman had taken a full step back and was now just standing there, watching him. Did this mean she wasn't going to kill him after all? He didn't know what to think. She was eyeing him like he was the one who was out of his mind.

"What do you mean you don't know?" she asked. "Are you blind? Look around. The Final Days are upon us. Soon there'll be no dome for you to return to. Even now, little mousey, child of the artificial sky, your dreamworld is breaking up before your very eyes while you choose not to see. Meanwhile, here in the *Real*, out in the *Actual*, the storm clouds are already gathering to sweep you and your synthetic world away. Why do you sleep, little mousey, when you should be sounding the alarm?" She poked his chest with the tip of the blade. "Do you not see the truth, or are you too terrified to face it? Don't you want to be among the survivors when the end comes?"

"Yes, yes!" he cried, hoping to placate her so she wouldn't kill him. "Of course I do!"

Her expression darkened. *"Then you have chosen the wrong path!"* She spat the words, shouting as she raised her arms. "Your domes are ignorance! They are the way of certain death! Open your eyes! A false dream is no place to spend Armageddon! Your only hope is the Great Journey! Disavow the life of illusion and enlist in the cause before it's too late!"

"Okay!" he called out. "I will! I will!"

The Outsider leaned closer again. Her face was still red with emotion, but her lips curled in a smile. To Eli she looked deranged. This is it, he thought. If he had any chance of living, he needed to make a run for it. He glanced at the alley again. He took one quick breath and tried to summon his courage.

But just then, from somewhere over the broken wall above him, something leapt at her. It flew through the air and landed on her shoulder, sending her staggering back. There was the sound of hissing and screaming as the savage batted her arms at the furry thing that bit and scratched and leapt all over her.

"Get it off me! Get it off!"

Marilyn!

Seconds later Sebastian appeared in the alley, yelling and waving what looked like a length of a rusted pipe. Like a madman he charged at the screaming woman, but by then she was already halfway toward the remains of the old brick house. The last Eli saw of her was when she disappeared through the empty doorway, shouting and cursing. Marilyn had already hopped off her, but instead of following after her, she crouched by the doorway, hissing in the Outsider's direction. Eli and Sebastian watched, wide-eyed, until finally, a few seconds later, Marilyn crept back to them.

Nobody spoke.

Finally Eli felt Sebastian put his hand on his shoulder. Eli could see in his eyes that he was scared. Really scared.

"I thought you were dead meat there," he said, his voice quivering.

Neither of them said anything else. Eli was still breathing fast. After a moment Sebastian started toward the little alleyway, and Eli followed. Soon the three of them were running again, this time sticking close together. Within minutes they were making their way out of the ruins, scrambling across the hard earth, back to the edge of the dome.

One thing Eli knew: he would never venture Outside again.

4

tabitha

Alone in her cubicle and away from the probing eyes of her classmates, Representative Tabitha Bloomberg at last had a moment to think. She settled into her chair and rubbed her pounding temples. She should have been feeling proud of herself today. Earlier that morning Representative Barnes, her supervising instructor, had delivered her third-quarter assessment report with wonderful news: they were promoting her to Team Leader. It meant she, at thirteen years old, would be the youngest Team Leader in the history of the Department of Intern Relations.

It was an unexpected honor, the latest in a surprising series of positive developments in Tabitha's life.

Even so, the truth was that she had mixed feelings about the promotion. She hadn't said anything to Representative Barnes, of course. She'd told him she was thrilled. But there was something he didn't know, something she couldn't tell him or anyone else.

A glimmer of milky light fluttered across her face, a reflection from her work sphere. A floating orb of color, it hovered and glowed above her desk, beckoning her back to work. For once, though, Tabitha gave herself a few extra seconds to gather her emotions before jumping back in. She glanced out the window at her view of St. Louis and watched a digital dodo bird clean its feathers as it squatted in a cloud.

Distracted, she didn't notice the handwritten note somebody had left on her desk. It had been folded and placed carefully under her coffee mug, with one corner poking out. But Tabitha was focused on her own troubled thoughts just then.

By all appearances today was an especially rewarding day at the end of an especially productive month for Tabitha. It had started when she'd been selected out of all her classmates, a nationwide pool of more than a thousand of the top interns in the Division of Student Affairs, to accompany Sebastian Papadopoulos, of all people, to New Washington on the first day of his internship, only two weeks from now. It was going to be a huge honor. And despite her secret distrust of the Papadopoulos family, she was thrilled she would be part of such an important occasion.

Then, of course, there was Ben. The thought of him sent a warm rush through her. She'd known him six months now, and in the past few weeks they had grown closer than ever. Only the previous evening the two of them had been up half the night, talking and holding hands. As far as that went, Tabitha had never felt so content.

And now this. The promotion was a big deal. It might lead to even bigger promotions. More responsibility. It meant the company trusted her.

But it also meant more secret weight hanging over her head.

She should have been happy, but she felt too conflicted to feel anything but numb. Nothing was black and white anymore, just shades of gray. Deep down she wasn't sure she could ever know real happiness again. In any case she didn't deserve it.

Her head still throbbing, she turned back to her work sphere. At last she noticed the corner of paper poking out from under her mug. She froze. She recognized right away what it was. She saw how it'd been folded and placed on her desk in a way that would minimize the chance of anyone else seeing it. It was obvious who must have set it there. Who else left paper notes?

She felt the first tinge of dread.

Trying to appear casual, she checked over her shoulder to see if anyone was watching. Her classmates were busily manipulating their own work spheres, checking trainee performance records, following up with new Program applications. It was safe to look. As safe as it would ever be, anyway. She reached for the note and gently unfolded it.

There were only a few words.

They know. They're coming for you, Sister. Run.
Escape to sanctuary Outside, beyond the windmills.
Help is waiting.
—The Friends of Gustavo

It felt like all the air left her lungs.

* * *

Tabitha rushed into the bathroom stall and locked the door. Trembling, she sat down and pulled her knees to her chin. If anyone came in, she didn't want them to know she was there. The folded note, the message that had in one instant turned her whole world upside down, was still in her hands. She read it again. She wanted to throw up.

She had been part of the secret organization for only a few weeks and already her life was ruined.

She wondered how the Friend, whoever it was, had found her. How did they even get into the building, past the Guardians, and through the entire office area? Was it possible there was somebody else studying here in the Program with her, another member of the clandestine society, whom she didn't know about?

The note was like a bomb blasting her world apart. Everything she'd been working toward for her whole career was finished now. She would be kicked out of the Program for sure. And if the Friends were right, that was the least of her worries.

But she couldn't let herself think about that right now.

She needed to stay calm.

In front of her, the hologram on the stall door showed three grinning teenagers stuffing pastries into their mouths. *Tonight at 9, on InfiniCorp 22: InfiniCorp Runs on Honey-Glazed Energy! Nutrition Tips for the Busy Employee.*

Two stalls away, a toilet flushed and someone stepped out. Tabitha heard the click-clack of footsteps on the tiles and then water running at the sink. She waited until the person left before allowing herself to breathe again.

Ben! She'd been stupid to fall for him, that was clear now. If she'd never met him, none of this would have happened.

And yet, even at this awful moment, she still couldn't change how she felt about him. Fifteen, charming, and funny, he'd been her first kiss. Her first real boyfriend. She *liked* him.

Was that so wrong?

Now, hiding in the bathroom, she wondered if she'd ever see him again. It was dizzying how fast her whole house of cards had fallen apart.

Quickly she considered her options: First of all, leaving the St. Louis dome and escaping Outside as the note said . . . well, it was just too scary to think about. She'd lived her whole life under one dome or another. She could count on one hand the number of times she'd been Outside without a transport. And even if she did it—assuming she could make it to the gate without getting caught first—it would mean leaving the Program, abandoning her whole life and everyone she cared about, and living the rest of her days as an outlaw, hunted and frightened. If she could survive out there at all.

It was a crazy idea.

But staying with InfiniCorp didn't seem possible anymore. The Guardians were coming for her. And if the Friends were telling the truth, the company would almost certainly wipe her memory clean, maybe even throw her in some secret prison to rot the rest of her life away.

The Friends told her things like that *happened*.

But the company ran everything. It *was* everything. Without it, how could she ever expect to survive?

The bathroom door swung open again, and new footsteps walked toward her. Tabitha held still. Whoever it was, the person passed her stall and went into the next one. Tabitha knew she was using up precious time. She closed her eyes and hugged her knees.

Maybe she should go to the Guardians. Turn herself in. She could tell them what she knew and promise to help identify the others, and maybe they'd let the whole episode pass. Maybe she could live the rest of her life as if she'd never heard of the Friends. But was she kidding herself? Was that even possible now?

And could she bring herself to do that to the others? To Ben?

She was having trouble thinking straight. Choking back a sob, she knew she had to make her decision right now. What did she believe? Who did she really trust?

Everything depended on her answer.

A moment later she stood. Fighting back the lump in her throat, she took a deep breath and stepped out of the stall. She caught her reflection in the mirror and was surprised to see that she looked the same as ever. Tall and slim in her fitted purple balloon blazer, she always worked hard to keep her appearance as orderly as possible, to be the poster girl of young professionalism. Her one albatross was her hair. Dense and unruly, Tabitha's mop of frizz was like her life. She was forever struggling to control it, to keep it from slipping into its natural state. Chaos.

And right now it looked to her like a tangled mess beyond fixing.

Seconds later she was back among the cubes, striding her way across the large office classroom full of teenagers manipulating the work spheres that floated above each of their desks.

She struggled to appear calm. She even managed to nod and smile at her classmates, who looked up as she passed. Had one of them left her the note? Was there a Friend here?

"Tabitha!" a nearby voice called as she was about to reach the exit to the central corridor. She felt her breakfast rise into her throat. Sandra Gates, Tabitha's suite mate and frequent project partner, waved her closer. "There you are. I was wondering where you'd gone."

"I—I'm sorry, Sandra," she said, trying to keep her voice from shaking. "Can't talk now. Gotta run."

But Sandra grabbed her hand and pulled her into the cube. "But we haven't talked all morning!" Her voice dropped to a conspiratorial whisper. "You and Ben were up way past *my* bedtime. That's new for you, naughty girl. Details, please."

Tabitha tried to pull away but Sandra's grip was too tight. "No," she whispered, almost in a panic. "I *can't*. Honestly, I have to go!"

She was on the verge of losing control, but she willed herself not to freak. She couldn't afford a scene. And the truth was, a part of her wished she did have time to talk with her friend, to tell her about the note and how everything was suddenly falling apart. But she couldn't have, of course, even if there had been time. Sandra didn't know about her secret. None of the other interns did. As far as she knew, they'd never even heard of the Friends.

She wondered if this was Fate's way of punishing her.

Sandra frowned. "That's not fair, Tab. I told you about Malcolm." But then her expression changed. She stared with concern at Tabitha's face. "Are you okay? You don't look so great."

"No, I'm fine. Just—"

Tabitha didn't have to finish, because that was when Sandra's InfiniTalk howled. In the same moment that she turned to see who it was, she also let go of Tabitha's wrist. Tabitha didn't wait around. She shot away, but just before she reached the glass doors, Sandra called out to her one last time. "Uh . . . Tab? Everybody just got a general broadcast with your name on it."

Something about this news brought Tabitha to a halt despite herself. She looked back. Sandra was leaning over the side of her cube, holding up her InfiniTalk. "I guess the Director wants to see you upstairs right away. It's marked Urgent. Wherever you're going in such a hurry, hon, it'll have to wait." And then she added, "As if a make-out session and getting promoted weren't enough good stuff for one twenty-four-hour period." She smiled. "Perk on, girl!"

Tabitha stepped quickly through the doors and into the elevator. She was sure of one thing: she wasn't going up.

Less than a minute later she was downstairs in her dorm suite. First, she needed her fake ID. If the Guardians were looking for her, she wouldn't get very far using her own DNA. They'd pick her up the first time she had to ride a transport or buy anything. But the Friends had given her a set of fake finger pads, and if there was ever a time she needed them, this was it. Second, she needed an environment suit. There was no way around that either. If she was really going Outside, she'd be there awhile and would need protection. Unfortunately she didn't have a suit of her own. But Sandra had one, and Tabitha knew where she kept it.

Sorry, Sandra. You'll have to forgive me.

First, the finger pads.

Balancing herself on a chair, Tabitha lifted the ceiling tile above her poster of Aristotle the Cat, her favorite band. She felt around up there with her hand. A couple of weeks earlier she'd put the pads in a bag and hidden it up there, and yet now her fingers didn't feel it. It wasn't where she thought she'd put it. Her heart gave a lurch. Oh god, where was it? What was she going to do if she couldn't find it?

On the opposite edge of the tile her hand finally felt the textured surface she was looking for. Relieved, she snatched the bag, stuffed the pads into her pocket, and leapt back to the floor. Next she bolted down the hallway for the environment suit. She didn't know how much time she had, but she knew it wasn't a lot.

Tabitha tried Sandra's door. It wasn't locked. Sandra never bothered to lock it. Hardly slowing at all, she shoved it open and burst inside. The last thing she expected was to find somebody in there.

She nearly jumped out of her skin when she found herself face to face with a pair of green eyes.

She screamed.

"Good afternoon, Representative Bloomberg. This is an unexpected surprise."

Tabitha struggled to recover her composure. It was only Ophelia, the cleaning robot. Old and worn, she smelled like disinfectant and looked like a mess of tattered plastic tubing, with dusters and scrubbing brushes and appendages that seemed to hang from every part of her chassis. Even though she was just a machine, she looked tired.

72

Tabitha had forgotten this was cleaning day.

She took a step back and made an effort to act casual. "Ophelia, you scared me!" she said, attempting a laugh. "You shouldn't sneak around like that!"

But Ophelia didn't seem to think it was funny. She angled her smooth plastic head to one side like a curious dog. Her mechanical arms paused in the middle of making Sandra's bed, and her rubber fingers stopped picking up the socks and paperwork scattered across the rug. Her voice was soft and pleasant as always, but gave no hint of a sense of humor.

"Representative Bloomberg, what are you doing in Representative Gates's quarters in the middle of the school day?"

"I just need to grab something I left in her trunk. No biggie."

She waited, but Ophelia didn't move to let her past. Her optical sensors were locked on Tabitha's face. It gave her the creeps. Finally Tabitha said, "You can go clean up somewhere else now, Ophelia. I'll just be a second."

But the robot still didn't move. It occurred to Tabitha that Ophelia was connected to the CloudNet, which meant she might have been alerted about the situation.

As if reading her thoughts, Ophelia said, "You have a message to report right away to the Senior Director."

Tabitha fought another wave of panic. She wanted to run, but she had to stay and do this. She needed that suit.

"Yes, Ophelia, I know," she said calmly. "Like I said, I just have to grab one quick thing. Let me by, please. It'll only take a second."

"No, Representative Bloomberg. The message is marked Urgent. You are instructed to go upstairs and report to the executive office *without delay*." There was something in her voice that made Tabitha take another step back. Normally she would never have been afraid of a cleaning robot. It was just a piece of equipment, like a toaster. But suddenly Ophelia seemed intimidating. Her glowing green eyes and blank stare sent a prickle across Tabitha's scalp.

Then the robot started moving toward her.

"Okay, okay," Tabitha said, taking yet another step back, this time into the hallway. She forced another laugh. Giving up the suit meant exposing herself to toxins and facing the elements unprotected, but what choice did she have? "I didn't realize it was marked Urgent. I'll head upstairs right now."

"I will let the office know you are on your way."

Under Ophelia's spooky gaze, Tabitha moved toward the suite door. She tried her best to appear relaxed and cooperative. They'd just had a misunderstanding, that was all, but everything was cleared up now. Once she was out of the suite and in the main corridor, though, she was out of Ophelia's sight.

She started to run.

They know. They're coming for you.

She dashed past the elevator this time and went for the stairway.

If only Ben were here. He would have ideas. Nothing ever seemed to faze Ben. Oh, how she wished she were holding his hand right now on one of their long, slow walks through the park. But the image felt painful now, something she wanted but couldn't have, maybe not ever again. And where *was* he? Was he all right? Should she try to contact him? She couldn't use his com-code, of course. That was another thing the Friends had taught her: handwritten notes only. Anything electronic could be traced. How about if she tried to leave a message at the regular place?

No, there wasn't time.

Besides, if they knew about her, then maybe they knew about Ben too. And if so, then he was in as much danger as she was.

Ben! The thought tied her stomach in knots.

She reached the stairway and scrambled down the steps. At the window at the bottom of the first landing she came to, she stopped. What was she planning to do, saunter into the lobby? She'd never make it past Reception. Her breath was coming in short gasps now, but she realized what she had to do. She forced the stairwell window open. Despite her terror of heights, she swung herself out onto the fire escape. Trying not to look down, she descended the remaining six flights to the alley below.

Her first impulse on the ground was to run, to get away as fast as she could. But again she stopped herself. Better to move calmly. If she dashed headlong through the streets of St. Louis, somebody would notice her.

A hovercraft passed overhead. She had to get going or they'd spot her here. She walked down the alley and turned left onto Delmar to avoid walking in front of her building. Infini-Corp signs were everywhere—on every billboard, every street pod, every briefcase.

```
               DON'T WORRY!
  INFINICORP IS TAKING CARE OF EVERYTHING!
        TAKING CARE OF EVERYTHING!
               EVERYTHING!
               DON'T WORRY!
```

Tabitha kept her head down. The company had eyes everywhere. The closest dome exit was at the Gateway Arch, maybe twenty blocks away. It wouldn't be smart to hire a private transport, she decided. Even with the finger pads, it was possible a robot driver might make a visual ID on her. Better to go by foot.

She felt a puff of freezing cold from overhead. It seemed like the Department of Cool and Comfortable Air had the blowers cranked higher than ever lately, but the city was getting warmer anyway. She ducked through the swarm of downtown shoppers, careful not to look anybody in the eye. Where was she even going? The note said "beyond the windmills," but that didn't help much. Outside the dome there were hundreds of windmills. They formed a complete ring round the city. She tried to think back on what the Friends had told her about safe places. In one of her many whispered conversations, Sister Krystal might have mentioned the name of a place in the wreckage of Old St. Louis. Was that right? There'd been so much to learn, and now she was having trouble remembering. But yes, she was pretty sure that was correct. And if she remembered right, it *was* beyond the windmills, somewhere deep in the eastern ruins.

But what was the name? How could she hope to find it if she couldn't remember?

She wondered how her life had come to this. It wasn't how things were supposed to have turned out. Back in New Houston, where she'd lived most of her life, she'd been the smartest kid in her class. When she'd taken the InfiniCorp Middle Management Aptitude Test and was accepted into the Program a whole year early, her parents had been so proud. She'd moved to St. Louis and everything seemed on track.

But then Ben changed everything.

From her first day in the Program, this beautiful, smart boy with droopy eyes and an earnest face had been a distraction from her studies. They'd meet in cafés or wander through the city. Sometimes they'd find a park bench and whisper to each other until late in the evening. Being with him was thrilling and fun. He was the one who had lifted the veil from her eyes. About Outside, about the company, about Grandfather, the so-called Savior of Humanity, and his whole horrific Papadopoulos clan. Ben helped her recognize what was real and what was only a facade. At first she hadn't wanted to hear him; it was all too hard to accept. But in the end she couldn't deny what she'd felt deep down all along. Then he'd introduced her to Sister Krystal, Brother Arnold, and all the others, operatives of a shadowy organization. Sister Krystal, with her secret Outside maps marked with the image of a burning sun—the insignia of the Friends—was particularly impressive. The group had their own ways, their own secret ceremonies, and they kept it all hidden from the company.

She'd known the risks of joining, but she'd been drawn in by the idea of making a difference. She wanted to help save the world. And she wanted to be with Ben.

So she'd agreed. She took the Oath of Loyalty.

Now all she wanted was to shrivel up and disappear. All she'd done was throw her life away. Her career, her future, everything. She was the worst kind of failure. She would kick herself later.

But first she had to survive this day.

Trying to blend into the crowd, she made her way down North Twenty-first and turned the corner onto Lucas. Which was where she almost walked right into two heavyset girls in white uniforms. Guardians. They looked about sixteen or seventeen, and *big*. Both were holding their index fingers up to their earpieces and nodding as if receiving instructions. Only a few steps ahead of Tabitha, one of them happened to look in her direction.

As soon as she saw them, Tabitha spun on her heel and held her hand up to her face. She knew she couldn't dash back the way she'd come without attracting attention, so for a moment she just waited there, pretending to be interested in a shopwindow. It was a Rewards Office, and the giant hologram display was looping through an incentive advert:

The InfiniCorp Department of Productivity Incentives Reminds You What Awaits the Employee of the Month! The yellow words lit up a glorious blue sky over a swanky hotel. Then two beautiful, smiling people, a man and woman in their twenties, were shown ice-skating, skiing, eating in fancy restaurants, and playing with baby seals. The seals leapt out at Tabitha, and then the couple grinned at her as they tossed a pair of particulate filters into the ocean. Then more words: *Adventure! Rugged Wilderness! Air-Contamination Levels as Low as 50 AQI! The Arctic Circle . . . Outside Relaxation at Its Way Coolest!*

Tabitha felt the advert's subtle pull, coaxing her attention

78

away from her immediate danger and toward its beautiful message. She turned her eyes slightly aside and felt the attraction diminish. The Friends had shown her how to do this, but the truth was that she'd always been able to resist the subconscious influence of the CloudNet, even when she was a small child. It was only recently, since she'd met the Friends, that she realized just how rare this ability was.

The two Guardians removed their fingers from their ears and glanced up and down the street as if searching for something. Head down, Tabitha drifted in the opposite direction, careful not to run. Up ahead a crowd of first-year executives talked and laughed as they crossed North Twenty-first. She ducked among them and tried to stop trembling. She had to get out of the open. If word was already out about her, she couldn't stay on the street.

It was time for a new plan. She decided to risk a private transport after all.

Before long she was hiding in the shadows on Washington Avenue, waiting for a cab. It had to be just right—preferably an old relic. Most of the newer taxi pods were flight-capable, which would be helpful, but they were also more likely to have robot drivers who would recognize her and alert the Cloud-Net. She waited until a dirty yellow road pod, an ancient jalopy with patches of actual rust, came chugging around the corner. It had old-style rubber tires and no visible flight gear of any kind. Definitely ground-only.

She raised her arm and, thankfully, it pulled over.

With her fake DNA pads in place, she set her fingertips on the InfiniCredit square. Somewhere, some unsuspecting employee's account was debited. She was sorry about that, but she didn't have any other options. The door swung open, and the sound of pounding music blared. Before stepping in, she glanced at the driver.

She was relieved to see that she'd chosen well. He was human.

"What are you waiting for? Get in!" he called over the music. A skinny kid with freckles, no older than twelve at the most. "Where to?"

Good question, she thought as she slid onto the worn upholstery and yanked the door shut. She quickly decided on a destination close to the gate but not close enough to raise suspicions. "The corner of Market and Fourth."

The boy leaned on the accelerator and they shot off. Tabitha watched him, searching for any sign that he knew. But he seemed lost in his own world, more interested in the music than anything else. He nodded and tapped the wheel to the rhythm, occasionally slamming on the brakes and tossing her forward in her seat. But he never once looked back at her in the rearview mirror. Tabitha decided he wasn't likely to have been paying attention to any CloudNet alerts. She felt relatively safe, at least for now.

For once, she thought, she'd lucked out.

Across the back of the driver's seat flashed an advert for a new dream game, a funny one where you flew through a lush cornfield full of fat, machine-gun-toting pigs in flak jackets who jumped out at you every now and then. Tabitha looked away. As she watched downtown roll past, she was almost overcome with grief. This was probably the last time she would ever see the city. She'd never shop on Market Street again, or watch another Cardinals game at InfiniCorp Stadium, or grab a slice of pizza at Union Station with her friends. Even the music seemed designed to torment her. The song was "Doo Doo Like U, Dee Dee Like Me" by Five Go Splat!—the very tune that had been playing when she and Ben had first kissed.

She couldn't help thinking how ironic it was for her to be in this position. Only last night Ben had asked if she still carried doubts. "Now isn't the time to lose faith," he'd said, quoting what she'd heard Brother Arnold say many times. "The future requires personal sacrifice, and the Friends are counting on each of us."

Worst of all, Ben had been right that her trust in the Friends wasn't absolute. While she did sense in her heart that the end was near and that the company was dangerous and irresponsible, she didn't fully buy into *everything* the Friends taught: their belief in predestination; the prophecy of el Guía; their unwavering faith in the Outsider prophet named Gustavo, a shadowy figure who might or might not even have really existed. How could they be so sure theirs was the only true path? But it was too late to question things now. Doubts or no doubts, she was in this for keeps.

Oh god. She hoped she hadn't thrown her life away for nothing.

With just moments to go before she reached the gate, her mind scrambled to find another way, a way that would let her stay under the dome. But Inside there was nowhere to hide. If she was going to make it through the gate, she'd need to stay focused. She was grateful, at least now, for the Awareness Training the Friends had provided. Her self-discipline was the only thing that might get her through this alive.

She took a slow, deep breath and tried to calm her thoughts. She told herself she was about to see Ben. At this very moment he was on the other side. He was there. She could visualize him. He was waiting for her.

At the corner of Broadway and Washington, they passed a sign for a one-hour liposuction salon called Skinny Asylum. She'd passed it a hundred times, but today the name triggered something in her consciousness. What was the word the Friend had used—*asylum*? No. But similar. A refuge. A shelter from danger. She pulled out the note again.

Sanctuary.

At last she remembered. The note itself had been the clue. It should have been obvious, but she'd been thinking too hard. The name of the safe place was *The Water Sanctuary.* Tabitha even remembered now what Sister Krystal had said about it, that before the hurricanes it used to be a hospital emergency room but now it was one of the Outsider gathering places, what almost passed as a restaurant out in the ruins. She felt a gush of relief. If she could find her way there, she would almost certainly find Friends who could help. Perhaps they'd smuggle her to some faraway place where she'd be safe.

If there even was a place that far away.

The pod pulled over with a sudden jerk, and the boy at the wheel interrupted his song long enough to call back, "Here you go, lady. Have a productive day."

The door swung open. Tabitha quickly thanked the driver and hopped out. Her head low, she strode down the block, staying close to the nearby housing complex. Here at the edge of the city, the dome angled downward, becoming a near-vertical electronic wall that reflected color patterns all across her face. She took a deep breath and tried to stay calm. The gate was a block away.

Soon the exit station was in sight. She paused to gather her courage. It was Thursday, not even lunchtime, so she was surprised at the long line. Along with a handful of dome engineers and a few others, thirty or forty little kids, fidgety and excited, stood laughing and shoving each other in front of the Arch. A dozen or so education specialists stood among them, many with cameras hanging around their necks. Tabitha recognized right away what this must be. A school field trip, the third-grade Out-visit tour of the dome's perimeter. She'd been taken on a similar tour Outside at the New Houston dome when she was eight. Every kid did it. It was like a rite of passage.

This was good, she decided. It'd be easier to slip past undetected if she were part of a crowd.

She stepped across the street and joined the line. All the children had environment suits, but some of the education specialists did not. By this time her hands were sweating so much that she had to wipe them on her slacks. But she was *here*, actually at the gate. Suddenly her situation was taking on a whole new reality. Once she stepped through that arch—*if* she made it through—there was no coming back.

Not ever.

She tried not to stare at anyone. The line moved quickly. The Friends had told her that getting Outside through the gate wasn't a big deal. They'd said the monitors cared more about stopping the wrong people from coming Inside than preventing employees from going Out. At most they'd do a cursory ID check and wave her through. Still, Tabitha's knees felt wobbly. Surely the gate monitors would be more careful than the cabdriver had been.

But what the Friends had told her seemed to be true. She watched as, one after another, the people in line touched their fingertips to the identification pad. Each time, the monitor waved them through. This looked like it was going to be a cinch.

There were only two others left ahead of her now. Tabitha could even see the monitor's face behind the glass. It was a red-headed girl with acne. She looked about the same age as the boy in the cab.

"Fingers on the pad," the girl said in a bored voice, a massive wad of chewing gum in her mouth.

A heartbeat later she waved the last education specialist, a big-hipped lady in a Rams cap, through the gate. Now only one other person, a dome engineer, stood between Tabitha and the front of the line. Seconds later the monitor girl waved him on, and he stepped through the Arch.

Summoning all her willpower, Tabitha forced herself to stay calm. She shaped her face into what she hoped was a relaxed, everyday expression and stepped in front of the glass.

"Fingers on the pad," said the girl without even looking at her.

Tabitha placed her fake fingertips on the smooth plastic square.

That's when the girl's InfiniTalk howled. It trailed on and on before breaking down into a wheezy cough. Tabitha recognized the sound. It was famous, the trademark howl of a popular late-night comedian. Lots of kids had it programmed into their InfiniTalks lately. The girl grabbed it just as Tabitha saw her phony information come up in the work sphere.

She could almost feel the blood pulsing through her temples. But she did her best to smile. She watched closely as the girl listened and nodded. Was this it? Was she caught? Should she run?

The girl didn't look at her, which Tabitha decided was a good sign. But it felt like her heart was about to burst through her chest. Finally the monitor set her InfiniTalk back on the counter, and without even bothering to glance at the information in the sphere, she waved Tabitha through.

At first Tabitha wasn't sure she'd understood right. What? That was it? But after only a slight hesitation, she pulled herself together and walked through the gate.

Within moments she felt the difference. The atmosphere hit her like a hot, wet blanket. The air was so thick it was like walking through soup. And then the sour smell of the Mississippi filled her nose, and hundreds of tiny insects buzzed in her ears.

It was the most wonderful feeling she could imagine.

She was Outside. She'd made it.

She kept her head down and moved quickly forward, past the crowd of children, who by then had gathered around a short woman who was pointing out the technical features of the dome exterior and describing the history of the area. Far ahead was a series of wooden booths where Outsiders, dirty-looking and haggard in their worn environment suits, had set up a makeshift market for trading between themselves. She slipped behind a crumbled wall and made her way in that direction. Maybe one of the Outsiders could tell her where she could get her hands on a suit. Maybe they could even help her make her way through the concrete jungle to the Water Sanctuary.

Maybe she really would see Ben again.

But that's when she felt an iron grip on her shoulder. Before she could turn to see who it was, a sudden, staggering pain nearly paralyzed her. Like a ferocious electrical charge at her back, the sensation was so sharp it knocked the breath from her lungs and buckled her knees. She fell to the ground. Somebody grabbed her by the hair and yanked her head. The last thing she saw before a dark sack was shoved over her face was two white-suited Guardian boys, one of them crouching over her. Then another stabbing pain, this time in her shoulder. She realized it was a needle. Something was being injected into her. She tried to cry out, but it was no use.

Almost as soon as her head hit the mud, her ears started to hum and her thoughts began to lose their shape, stretching like warm taffy until they drifted away from her, formless and without substance.

The last thing she heard was the droning voice of the tour guide and the *swoop, swoop, swoop* of the windmills in the distance.

5

foggers

That night Grandfather appeared on the CloudNet and made a speech. "Don't worry," he said as the company logo spun behind him, "InfiniCorp is taking care of everything."

Grandfather had a deep, calm voice. He had a friendly face too, which was part of why everybody liked him—on top of the fact that he'd saved the world, of course. Eli had read an article once where somebody said he was like everybody's dear old granddad.

It made Eli proud because he really was *his* granddad.

"Today's tragic attack on the Providence dome was brutal, senseless, and unprovoked, but it could have been worse. This blast was meant to be part of a coordinated series of malicious actions against our city domes. From New Miami to Atlanta, from Newer York to Phoenix, the plans were in place for the most extreme disruption we've ever seen. Fortunately the company was able to thwart the master plot before it was fully carried out."

Eli stared up into the CloudNet sphere from the floor, his arms wrapped around his knees. On the sofa nearby, Father's brow was furrowed in a scowl.

Like his sons, Daedalus Papadopoulos had dark eyes and black hair that he wore to his shoulders. He was the head of the Division of Rebuilding and Relocation, but when he'd heard how Eli and Sebastian had been picked up at the perimeter that afternoon, he'd left in the middle of an important meeting and flown straight home from Chicago. Sebastian had done most of the talking and had been able to mollify him a little—Sebastian had a way of calming people—but Eli could tell Father was still furious. And that was without knowing the full story. Eli and Sebastian weren't about to tell anyone what had happened with the Outsider. At least none of them had been hurt. Besides, Eli had unintentionally broken a strict company rule: Outsiders were so dangerous that InfiniCorp prohibited anyone from communicating with them. So Eli and Sebastian had agreed to keep quiet about it. Why get themselves into more trouble than they were in already?

Sebastian sat beside Father, his jaw tight. On the edge of the rug, Marilyn's gaze was fixed on Grandfather. She seemed to hang on every word.

"Rest assured, the company is strong and well organized. Already we've made great progress in undoing the damage and have confirmation on who was responsible. As is too often the case, today's dreadful proceedings were indeed devised by the same criminal element we've seen so many times before. It was yet another act of vicious mischief carried out by the Fog."

Eli sat up straighter at the mention of the Fog. He'd always been curious about Foggers. In InfiniBook stories they were often the villains, mysterious Outsiders with twisted motives and grand plans to destroy the company. They were the worst of the worst. Eli didn't know much about them, but today the terrors of Outside felt more real to him than ever.

Grandfather went on. "Even now, mere hours after the explosions, we already have the situation under control. At this hour, the Division of Freedom has the masterminds of the attacks in our custody. Especially troubling is that the Outsider Foggers who carried out these cowardly actions had help from *Inside* Fogger agents."

The image in the sphere changed: now it was the head of a thin, unsmiling girl with hair that jutted out in all directions like an insane person's.

"Her name is Tabitha Bloomberg. Until this morning she was a trusted employee, a rising star in a branch of the Department of Intern Relations in St. Louis. That goes to show how, even with their compromised, often brain-fevered reasoning, the Foggers can still be cunning." As Grandfather spoke, the camera slowly closed in on the girl. "She wasn't high in the criminal organization, and yet hers is the same unfortunate story we've seen before: a misguided young lady who allowed herself to be coerced by lies. In doing so, she turned her back on all of us and on everything she once held dear."

Eli studied the image, looking deep into the girl's eyes. There was something scary behind them. Anybody could see that.

She was a monster.

Eli thought again of the Outsider with the white eye, and the shadow he'd seen under the city. As a younger child Eli had read InfiniBook stories about disappearances, kids snatched from their beds at night and taken somewhere into the desert for unknown Fogger purposes, never to be heard from again. He shuddered.

"Needless to say," Grandfather continued, "such a lapse in judgment is a tragedy." The girl's face faded and Grandfather reappeared. Behind him the president nodded, her expression grave. Eli had met her once, long ago, at one of Grandfather's parties. That was back when she was still an InfiniCorp VP. All he remembered about her was that she'd made a long, boring speech and that the whites of her eyes had been dyed bright green. Since then she'd had them redyed a shimmery gold color.

Now Grandfather's voice went even gentler. "Friends and neighbors, sleep easy. Every time the enemies of liberty make a move and try to frighten us, the company learns more about them and is better able to shield you from harm. Our commitment to the protection of our cities, the preservation of civilization itself, remains firm. InfiniCorp will never stop looking out for you."

After that there was loud clapping. There must have been a large crowd of people just off camera. Eli wondered if Mother was there. She'd had to stay in New Washington because the Senate had called an emergency session to express support for the victims' families and to provide a vote of confidence for Grandfather's leadership in this time of crisis. The clapping went on for a long time. Behind Grandfather, the president clapped too.

* * *

90

Finally Sebastian was turning fourteen, and InfiniCorp was taking him away from home to begin his internship. He was very excited.

The evening before his departure, Mother and Father took the boys out to celebrate. They went to a restaurant called the Brain Room, an exclusive club at the top of the highest building in the Providence dome, where senior executives had a panoramic view of the city. The brain itself, the central, controlling node of the city's CloudNet, was a mass of wires, lights, and grayish goo floating in a giant transparent container in the middle of the room. The place was busy, but the maître d' escorted them to a special table set up just for their family. To even step inside the Brain Room you pretty much had to know somebody in upper management.

Eli's family had their own special table.

Sebastian was all smiles. As they sat down, Eli watched the artificial sun start to set over Federal Hill. Ever since the explosion, almost two weeks ago, it had been glowing an odd pinkish color. The CloudNet kept assuring everyone that it was okay, that the company would find a fix for it soon, but in the meantime Eli was having a hard time getting used to it.

Mother and Father seemed distracted, but only a little. Mother kept saying things like, "We're so pleased for you, Sebastian."

Father kept saying things like, "We know you'll knock 'em dead."

Yet the occasion only left Eli feeling uneasy. The truth was, now that Sebastian was about to start his internship, Eli's own Internship Assignment suddenly seemed more imminent. He couldn't help recalling what Spider had said, that the family was at a loss as to what to do with him. Today especially it was starting to feel like a black cloud over his head.

He kept staring out the window. From this height he could see the whole city, including the river, the old state capitol building, and the East Side, where he lived. What was more, if he squinted into the electromagnetic shimmer of the dome, he could just about see *through* it. It had something to do with the near-horizontal angle of the dome here, so close to the top. After a moment he turned back to Sebastian.

"I don't see what the big deal is," he said. "It's not like there was ever any doubt whether you were going to get placed in an upper-management track. We *all* do."

"That's not true and you know it," Sebastian said, annoyed. "Not everybody does."

"Okay, maybe not *everybody* everybody. But everybody in the family. When I'm fourteen they'll select me for a good position too."

Father raised his eyebrows.

"Eli, what's gotten into you?" Mother asked. "This is your brother's big night. We're happy for him."

Eli knew he was being unfair. If anyone had earned his way to a prestigious internship, it was his brother. Sebastian had been accepted into the topmost tier of the Management Training Program—the Senior Leadership Path. He was going to New Washington to learn everything there was to know about security systems in every market and every division of the entire company: Freedom, Smart Investments, Better Housing, Fine Dining, Smaller Government, Free and Fair Elections, Sensible Light Fixtures, Personal Fulfillment, Fashionable Accessories—

the list went on and on. Spider had been assigned as Sebastian's mentor. Sebastian was excited about this because Spider had a reputation as a cunning business strategist and was well respected in the company.

For Sebastian, this was all a very big deal. An honor.

He was being set up for great things.

Deep down, Eli really was happy for his brother, but for some reason he couldn't make himself feel it just then.

Sebastian leveled his gaze at Eli. He leaned in close. "Don't be so sure everyone in our family gets into upper management. The way you're going, Eli, you just might be the first who doesn't. The family *embarrassment*."

It was like a slap. Eli knew he deserved it for what he'd said, but it took him by surprise anyway. He couldn't look at Sebastian for the rest of the meal.

The representative from Intern Relations arrived after breakfast the next morning. A serious young woman in a bright green balloon suit with the InfiniCorp logo on the lapel, she was extremely respectful to Mother and Father. Even so, it was obvious she was on a schedule. Sebastian was ready, waiting on the sofa with his suitcase. Mother and Father had both delayed their transports so they could see him off. Now that the moment had come, though, it seemed like none of them knew what to say. In the end their goodbyes felt stiff and short.

"So long, Father," Sebastian said, taking his hand and shaking it. He tried to shake hands with Mother too, but she insisted on giving him a long hug instead. Eli noticed that Sebastian kept glancing over at the rep, his face turning red.

Mother's voice was quiet and unsteady. "Take care, Sebastian. Be careful." Even Marilyn, in her own strange way, seemed sad to see him go. She stood on her haunches and prodded his knee with her snout.

Finally he came over to Eli and held out his hand. Eli took it. Their arms pumped up and down. "Sorry about last night," Sebastian said. "About the way I spoke to you."

"It's okay. Me too."

There was a brief moment in which neither of them said anything else, but then Sebastian did something Eli didn't expect. He leaned in close so that nobody else could hear and whispered, "You're the only person I'm going to admit this to, but I'm terrified."

At first Eli thought he was kidding. Then he saw in his eyes that it was true, he *was* scared. Sebastian was always so self-confident; it was strange to see him unsure of himself now. Eli felt bad for him.

"You'll do great," he assured him. "You always do."

After that the rep helped carry his bags to the landing pad beside the house. The transport's silver and green wings unfolded and its propellers started to glow. The family watched it lift from the backyard. It rose high into the air and then passed through a hole that opened in the dome's electromagnetic field. It was pouring rain Outside, and some of it drizzled in. The real sky was cheerless and gray. Soon the transport was only a green dot in the distance, but they kept watching long after it was too far away to see.

Mother dabbed at her eyes. No one spoke for a long time. Eventually Father put his hand on Eli's shoulder. "Don't worry, son. Your day will come." Mother kissed the top of his head, but all Eli felt was a dull tightness in his throat.

It feels like everything is going to be different now, Marilyn observed. She sighed.

Eli pulled away from his parents. He ran back into the house and up to his room, and then he threw himself onto his bed. Until that moment he hadn't allowed himself to think about life without Sebastian. Now the future was like a weight around his neck. It wasn't as if he had lots of friends. The days ahead looked grim: endless study modules, long lectures with Dr. Toffler and Dr. Avila. And what if Father was wrong? What if his day never came? Maybe he really *would* end up being the only member of the family not to make it into management. And if so, then what? There was only one company. Where would they put him? Customer Service? Inventory? Something even worse? How would he ever face the humiliation?

How would he face Father and Mother?

Sebastian had said it himself. Being a Papadopoulos didn't guarantee anything.

With his head deep in his pillow, Eli decided there was only one thing to do. It was time he got as serious about his place in InfiniCorp as Sebastian always had been. Eli would be fourteen soon enough. He needed to forget about sky glitches and savages and Foggers and instead devote himself to his company training the way everyone wanted him to. Because unless he did, he'd be the family embarrassment forever.

He'd been living like a kid for too long.

He was a Papadopoulos. It was time he faced the future.

6

grape soda sky

With Sebastian gone and Mother and Father so frequently away, Eli's parents arranged that a specialist from the Department of Domestic Services would come to live in the house with Eli. Her name was Claudia. Big-boned and pretty at twenty-eight, she had olive skin, a kind face, and feathery black hair that she kept tied in a bun. Officially she was there to help the cleaning and cooking robots, but Marilyn didn't think the robots really needed the help. She suspected the real reason Father and Mother wanted Claudia in the house was so that Eli would have company.

Marilyn felt offended. Wasn't she company enough?

At mealtimes, Marilyn would watch Claudia glide around the kitchen, frying up meat patties or adding spices to simmering chilies. She would even set the table and clean up afterward. It was fascinating to see a human doing the cooking instead of a droid.

"You have a wonderful appetite, *gordito*," Claudia would

say to Eli as he worked his way through a stack of her cumin pancakes. "I make you a thick stew for supper, no?"

When Eli first told Marilyn he was going to devote himself to his InfiniCorp training, Marilyn laughed. She felt sure that after a few tedious afternoon sessions at his desk, his newfound determination would waver.

But then he surprised her: three weeks later he was still working at his desk every afternoon, long after Dr. Toffler shut itself down for its daily recharge. Marilyn was impressed, even proud of him, but on a personal level his sudden ambition had a serious downside. It meant Eli had much less time to spend with her. They weren't talking as much, their afternoon sky-gazing sessions became rare, and even when they did anything together, Eli's mind was often elsewhere.

Eli was her only friend, and Marilyn was lonely.

She had little to do now except waste the long hours until Eli finally pulled himself from his studies. Every now and then Claudia would come across her flopping around the house and get annoyed.

"*¡Anda! ¡Anda!*" she would shout, shooing her off the sofa or the windowsill or wherever she happened to be. "Everywhere you shed! And you leave germs, filthy thing! *¡Abominación sucia! ¡Máquina monstruosa!*" Marilyn would drag herself away, and then Claudia would disinfect the area.

Which wasn't exactly a boost to Marilyn's already low self-esteem.

In recent weeks she'd become aware that she seemed to repulse most other creatures. The last few times she and Eli had walked the streets of Providence, she noticed hostile glances from passing employees, looks of disgust or even fear. She'd seen dogs bare their teeth and cats arch their backs as if readying for a fight. It was as if everyone, people and animals alike, could tell there was something corrupted about her, something repellent that made them shrink away.

And the undeniable fact was, they were right.

Yes, she *looked* like an animal, but wasn't she really just a grotesque imitation, about as natural as a cleaning robot? She asked herself what kind of mongoose enjoyed watching cloud commercials? Or had long telepathic conversations with a human boy? There was almost nothing animal about her anymore. No feral desires. No wild instincts. She was an abomination of nature. A freak.

Of *course* she made everybody uneasy.

In fact, Eli was the only person who seemed at ease with her. Which was why she preferred to stay close to him even now that he had less time for her. As he worked with Dr. Toffler, Marilyn would find a quiet place in his room. That was how Marilyn ended up making a new and startling discovery about the chip in her brain.

She was under Eli's bed, gazing absently in the direction of Eli's overhead fan, when suddenly it started to hum. It stopped after a second or two, but by then Marilyn was alert, her eyes wide. Had she done that? At the moment it happened, she'd felt something in her brain, like a spark. She rolled onto her stomach and fixed her gaze on the fan. She tried to make it hum again. Nothing happened. But she continued to concentrate, focusing her thoughts on it, imagining herself traveling inside its motor and through the processors that controlled it.

All at once it hummed to life, and this time its blades started spinning.

Eli looked up from his desk. "That's weird." He got up and jiggled the control that turned it off. Then he went back to his work.

But in the darkness under his mattress, Marilyn felt a sudden thrill. Somehow she'd tapped into the electrical system just by *thinking* about it.

Over the next few days, she discovered she could link to any of the various processors around the house. She could communicate with the dishwasher, the security system, even the sensors on the toilet seat. She felt her way through Eli's father's electric razor and explored the complex logic of the toxin-detection software.

And then she made her most thrilling discovery yet: Sebastian's old Dream Gamer sent vivid images and sensations directly into her mind as if they were really happening to her. Without leaving the house she began to have incredible new experiences. She could pass entire days lying motionless, her eyes glassed over as she mentally flew over fields of dancing rhinos or rowed with Vikings to conquer exciting new lands.

Every now and then Eli's voice would break through as if from far away. "Why don't you take a walk or something?" he would say. "It can't be healthy for a mongoose to lie around all the time. Go get some fresh air, explore the yard."

Perhaps you're right, my love, she'd answer. *Maybe I'll do that.*

An hour later she would be in the same position, her eyes still staring into space.

* * *

It had been two whole months since the attack on the filter, but Eli couldn't help noticing that the company still didn't have things back to normal yet. It wasn't just sky glitches anymore either. The air felt warmer with each day that passed, and sometimes the cooling blowers would shut down for minutes at a time before coming back on. The sun was no better. If anything, it looked pinker lately.

Eli tried not to worry about these things. Nobody else seemed concerned. The CloudNet reported it was no big deal, just minor problems caused by the explosion, and the company would have the issues resolved soon. Still, he couldn't remember any dome problems like these before. The company had always prided itself on addressing whatever minor dome issues came up before anyone even noticed.

So what was taking them so long this time?

One afternoon after a particularly grueling review of organizational-performance metrics, Eli woke Marilyn and they went out to the backyard to watch the sky together for the first time in a while. As they lay in the synthetic grass, Eli saw somebody climbing the dome.

"Look, Marilyn," he said, suddenly alert. He'd never seen a real person up there. "Do you see that?"

Yes, darling. How odd!

The dome ceiling was busy that afternoon with so many adverts, there wasn't much blue left. It was amazing he'd noticed anyone up there. He could tell right away it wasn't a simulation. It was a sky engineer, perhaps two hundred feet high and several feet deep into the thick layer of skylight. He could make out her dangling hair ribbons and blue uniform. Eli was aware that the dome had a hidden lattice system tucked among the pixels, but he'd never seen anyone use it before. The engineer appeared to be climbing steadily higher, in the direction of the sun. He wished he still had Sebastian's spyglass.

"What do you think she's doing?"

I imagine she's making repairs.

"Maybe," he said. Under normal circumstances, Eli knew, the Sky Department saved any maintenance jobs at the top of the dome until night, when their work was less likely to disturb the sky illusion. If the company was taking the extraordinary step of sending engineers up there during the daytime, it seemed to suggest that something out of the ordinary was happening, despite the CloudNet's assurances. He would have to ask Father about that when he had the chance.

He continued to watch, still amazed at the novelty of seeing a real person up there. "Claudia!" he called back to the house. "Come see! There's an engineer working on the sky!"

Claudia opened the kitchen window. "Why are you wasting the day out in the grass, *mi amor*? I thought you were studying. Come inside. I make you a grilled cheese."

There was the sound of thunder from Outside. Eli had been listening to the drumming of rain all day. "No, you should come out here and look at this!"

By the time Claudia padded out, fanning herself with a tea saucer, the engineer was at least another fifty feet higher and looked barely larger than an insect among the clouds.

"Show me, *cariño*," Claudia said. "It's probably just an advert."

Eli tried to point her out, but Claudia kept squinting and

shaking her head. About halfway to the top, the engineer stopped climbing. It was hard for Eli to see exactly what she was doing, but it looked like she reached deeper into the light, and then a tiny part of the sky seemed to swing open, revealing what looked like a narrow black splinter behind the layers of translucent blue—a crack in the dome.

"Do you see that?" Eli asked, amazed. "A door in the sky!"

Marilyn hopped onto Eli's shoulder. *I had no idea there were doors up there.*

It was news to Eli too, although now that he thought about it, he realized Dome Maintenance probably had all kinds of stuff up there that most people didn't know about. It made sense for the engineers to have somewhere to put their equipment.

For a few seconds the engineer disappeared through the door, and then she returned again. Claudia was still squinting. She shaded her puzzled eyes with her hand.

"Where are you looking? I don't see any engineer."

Suddenly there was a deafening crash a lot like thunder, and then a buzzing sound shook the sky. The engineer seemed to wobble, and the next thing Eli knew, she was falling.

Even Claudia saw her now. She gasped.

Eli watched with horror as the engineer plummeted from the clouds. Almost as soon as she started to fall, a cord shot from her body to the top of the dome. It must have held fast to something behind the light, because in seconds it tensed and slowed her fall like an elastic band. Soon she was swinging back and forth—a long, thin pendulum in the sky.

The dome made another earsplitting crackle, and then, far to the left of the spot in the sky where the engineer had dropped, fiery sparks started to fly in all directions. Marilyn shrieked. Eli felt her claws digging into his shoulder as he watched the sky begin to change. First one pixel and then another went violet. It started as a tiny dot, but it grew like a bruise spreading in fast motion. Soon it stretched in all directions, wiping out every cloud until the entire dome was electric purple.

An instant later everything went dark.

This time it was Eli who gasped.

"*¡Dios mío!*" Claudia whispered beside him.

Eli had never seen the dome do anything like this before. It was the middle of the afternoon and the three of them were standing in complete darkness. There weren't even stars.

All around them he could hear neighbors opening their windows and calling out to each other, wondering what was going on.

It took almost an hour for Dome Maintenance to get the sky back up. They had to reboot the whole system. Even then it was obvious things still weren't right. The air grew so warm it was hard to think, and Eli could hear the cooling blowers struggling to restart. For more than twenty minutes, a thin spray of water showered down onto the corner of Benefit and Thayer streets as if from some unseen pipe in the dome. People gathered around it and watched. Most startling of all, every now and then large patches of the sky flashed with unexpected colors. The area over the Bank of InfiniCorp building would turn brown and then green. The horizon would blink metallic silver.

It was distressing.

Eventually the company got the blowers working and the water leak plugged. A smiling news lady, plump and thirtyish with glittery teeth, appeared on the CloudNet to explain what had happened.

"This afternoon the city of Providence was once again the setting of a dramatic dome incident, this time caused by a creative product launch gone awry. Apparently an overly playful marketing intern in the Atlanta-based Department of Refreshments decided to surprise his supervisor with an ambitious and"—she made a wry smile—"not entirely *authorized* kickoff campaign for our newly formulated grape soda. The idea was a dazzling purple daytime display, but unfortunately the intern's program included an error that caused the municipal sky to temporarily shut down. A sky engineer doing routine maintenance was thrown from the dome ceiling, but nobody was hurt, and no lasting damage was done to the system."

Her coanchor, a man with bright blue hair piled several inches above his head, chuckled. "Seems like we've got the makings of a true marketing genius on our hands."

The two of them laughed.

"The intern has been reprimanded," continued the blue-haired man, "but no criminal charges are being made at this time. As we speak, the Providence sky is putting on quite a display. Residents are urged not to be concerned. The discolorations will return to normal. Rest assured, the company has everything under control."

"In the meantime," the lady said, "enjoy the show!"

* * *

Eli went back to his room and tried again to concentrate on his studies, but it wasn't easy. Through his window he could see the sky still turning odd colors: one second it would flash in pink and green stripes, then entirely black, then back to normal again. It did this every few minutes and was different each time. He'd never seen anything like it before. It was as if Leonardo, his imaginary sky artist, had lost his mind and the curious images Eli had been noticing for weeks were starting to take over. And yet nobody else seemed concerned.

He couldn't help remembering what the crazed Outsider had said: *Your dreamworld is breaking up before your very eyes.*

He had to admit, it was spooky.

He shut his study module and rubbed his forehead. "I think my brain is going to explode."

Marilyn didn't answer right away. At that moment, only her tail was visible, hanging limply over the top of one of Eli's open drawers. After the excitement of the sky malfunction, she'd wasted no time in linking herself to another dream game.

Hush, darling . . . , she said, her voice so distant he could barely feel it. *I'm flying over medieval France in an air balloon. It's harvest season. . . .*

Eli sighed. He couldn't bring himself to go back to his mind-numbing lesson just yet. After a moment he reached up and let his finger pass through the surface of the CloudNet sphere that floated over his desk. At once a face appeared, a beautiful blond girl of about seventeen, with flawless skin and a perfect white smile. Her name was Heather, and she was one of the CloudNet assistants. Eli knew she was artificial, of course, but every time he saw her she gave him butterflies.

"Eli! Hon!" she said. "How *fabulous* to *see* you!"

His face went warm, and for a moment he looked down at his hands.

"What's up this time, big guy? Hey, there's a new Dirk Drickland stream. You're gonna *love* it!" Her head morphed into a shot of a muscular boy with long silver hair and a knife clenched between his teeth. He was climbing a steep cliff as flaming arrows whizzed past his head.

"Oh my *god*!" Heather said. "This episode totally fries!"

Eli rubbed his forehead again. "Actually, that's not what I—"

"Okay, okay. Not a big Dirk fan, I get it. No prob. Oh, I know! A new look ought to perk you!" The image of Dirk morphed into a series of grinning boys in billowing shirts. "Just a tip: think vertical stripes, Eli. They would *so* make you look taller."

Eli held up his hand. "No, no! Stop, please!"

Heather's pretty head filled the sphere again, only now she was pouting. "No need to get huffy. I was just trying to help."

He considered requesting a different CloudNet assistant, but her eyes were on him again and he couldn't bring himself to do it. "Heather," he said, "did anything happen to pop up on the CloudNet about . . . you know . . . the Outsider lady with the white eye?"

"That again?" She wrinkled her nose. "God, Eli, you should stop wasting your time asking the same dumb questions about crazy Outsiders. Don't you have studying to do?"

He ignored her. "Can you please search one more time?

Maybe there's something new. One of the perimeter Guardians might have picked her up or something."

She rolled her eyes. "You're the boss. No, there's still no report of any Outsider with an all-white eye. There's a sale today on artificial irises, though. Want to see the selection?"

"Please, I'm serious."

She giggled. "Okay, Eli. You're cute when you're grumpy."

"Check again on Outsiders. And while you're at it, look into why the sky is taking so long to fix. Are there any known dome-design weaknesses tied to the air filters? Maybe a software flaw or something?" He paused as another idea came to him. "Look up the Final Days too. Any information about the end of the world, maybe in the form of a giant storm that could be on its way. If there's even the possibility the weather could do permanent damage to the domes, I want to know."

"If you say so," she said. "Okay, I just checked, and there's nothing about any giant storm or dome-design weaknesses. And you already know why the sky's taking so long to repair. It's because the Fogger attack did so much damage. As far as the Final Days, there are gobs and gobs of information about that, Eli. People have been predicting the end of the world since forever! Do you really want me to list out zillions of files?"

He sank lower in his chair. "No. I guess you're right. It's pointless."

Even as he said it, it was hard for him to shake the feeling that something was going on that nobody was admitting. But why didn't anyone else seem alarmed? What was the matter with everyone? What was the matter with *him*?

He slammed his fist on his desk. "I don't care what the

CloudNet says!" he said. "Something bad is happening! The sky never acted this way before, and the cooling systems never used to give out all the time! Why can't anyone tell me what's going on?" He glared hard into the sphere. *"All I want is the truth! Can't anybody give it to me?"*

There was a momentary hiss. Heather, whose jaw had dropped at Eli's unexpected outburst, suddenly froze in position as if somebody had flipped a switch and halted her processor. It was freaky.

"Heather?"

She didn't answer. Stranger still, a moment later her nose split clean off from the rest of her face. Eli watched, wide-eyed. The nose floated slowly to the top of the sphere and then broke into thousands of pieces that drifted in all directions. Her eyes were next. They moved apart and melted away.

Eli's breath caught in his throat. "Marilyn! Marilyn, wake up. You gotta see this!"

In the drawer behind him, Marilyn must have heard the urgency in his voice, because she stirred. Her orange eyes peered over the edge. *What is it, my love?* Eli didn't need to answer. She could see for herself.

Heather's entire head was disintegrating.

Soon all that was left was a cloud of movement, tiny cubes of color that swirled inside the sphere like confetti. If Eli hadn't been so aware that Heather was a simulation, he might have screamed. Then he heard voices from inside the confetti. They were ghostly soft and their words were unclear, as if a crowd of people were murmuring to each other all at once. They got louder. Eli squinted into the blur.

"Hello?"

"Your request has been noted, Eli Papadopoulos," the voices whispered, blending together into a single breathy chorus. *"In a complex fabric of illusion, a single thread of reality can be hard to distinguish. Do you understand what it would mean to disentangle it? Are you sure you're ready to accept the consequences?"*

Eli hesitated. What on earth was this? Another program bug? Some crazy stream Heather found for him on the Cloud-Net?

"What if you disentangled the truth only to discover that your whole life has been a sham?" continued the voices. *"Would you really want to know? What if you were the last chance to save a dying world? Would you take that chance even knowing it would be the hardest thing you ever did, and that you would probably fail?"*

"What kind of a crazy question is that?" Eli asked. "If I were the last chance, then of *course* I would. Who—?"

But the voices interrupted him. *"But how can you be sure? What if it meant you would have to give up everything important to you? Everything you love?"*

"Sebastian, is that you? This isn't funny! Why can't I see your face? Where's Heather?"

"Heather is on pause. We must speak quickly. In seconds this patch will be noticed and we'll be disconnected."

"So you're saying we're . . . off CloudNet? You *hacked* into my sphere?"

"That is correct."

Eli's mouth went dry. He'd heard about off-CloudNet connections, but nobody had used them for years. There was no need for them anymore because InfiniCorp's gigantic systems took care of everything for everybody. The only people who even tried to go around the system nowadays were criminals.

Foggers.

Marilyn's voice echoed in his head. *You don't want anything to do with this, Eli. Shut them down!*

Eli spoke into the confetti, struggling to keep his voice calm. "This conversation is over. I'm turning off the sphere, and then I'm reporting you to my father."

"We have the answers you're looking for, Eli."

He felt a sudden tightness in his gut. His hand stopped in midair. Even Marilyn stayed quiet. There was something very wrong here, something that could get him in serious trouble. And yet now he couldn't bring himself to touch the sphere and send the voices away. If they really knew what was going on, he wanted to know.

"Who are you?" he whispered.

"Who we are doesn't matter. We can help you disentangle the fabric of lies."

There was a sudden static pop. For an instant the cloud of tiny colored cubes froze. Almost immediately they began whirring around again, only faster now. Something was wrong.

"What's happening?"

"We're out of time," the voices said, breaking up. *"Eli, you are in great danger. If you want the truth and are prepared for the consequences, tell no one about this conversation."* The colors in the sphere started to vibrate.

"Don't go! Tell me what you know! Is a terrible storm coming? What's going on?"

Their reply was so faint that Eli could only just make it out. *"We'll be in contact."*

All at once the colors shot together and formed the image of a burning sun, dazzling and orange. Eli had barely a moment to take it in before it broke apart again, but he recognized it right away. It was the same image as the one on the page he'd found tucked inside the *Alice* book.

"Wait!" He put his face up close to the sphere. He wanted to shake it, to somehow force the mysterious voices to speak again.

But it was too late. They were gone.

And then he felt Heather's eyes on him once more. Her head filled the entire orb; her pretty mouth hung open in exactly the same expression of surprise that it had the moment she'd disintegrated. Eli and the Heather simulation were practically nose to nose.

"God, what bug got up *your* butt? No need to pop a neuron. Don't you know I'm here to serve? Eli? *Eli?*"

He was backing away from the sphere. His palms were covered in sweat, and he had no idea what he should do or say. Finally he shot out of the room. Marilyn was close at his heels. Even as they flew down the stairs, Eli could still hear Heather calling out to him, asking what the heck was wrong.

He sat hunched in the grass, his thoughts a blur. What had just happened? He tried to remember exactly what the voices had said. Something about saving the world and how he was in some kind of danger. But how could he save the world? And why would he be in any danger?

111

None of it made any sense.

"What do you think it all means?" he asked Marilyn, who was still trembling at his feet.

I don't know. I honestly don't. Mysterious voices. Hacked CloudNet patches. Whoever they are, they must be criminals. Eli, you need to contact your parents right away, before something terrible happens!

Eli wrapped his arms around his legs and squeezed them tight to his chest. Overhead, the sun blinked. For an instant, enormous multicolored bars filled the entire dome like a vast horizontal rainbow. Eli couldn't help marveling once more at how peculiar the whole world had become in such a short time. He could almost hear the white-eyed Outsider again: *Why do you sleep, little mousey, when you should be sounding the alarm . . . ?*

He glanced back at Marilyn. "Deep down, aren't you curious? Don't you want to hear what they have to say?"

Her whiskers twitched. *Absolutely not. Let it go, Eli. We have a comfortable life. Why make waves? Anyway, this was pure foolishness and almost certainly a trick. They were Foggers, and reckless ones too. Just report it to your family and forget it. You have your future to think about.*

Eli knew she was right. How foolish for a group of criminals to contact him, a Papadopoulos, of all people. In any case, whatever message they had for him wasn't the most important consideration here. The right thing to do was to tell Infini-Corp what had happened. The company would know how to respond.

With the cloud commercials once again drifting reassuringly overhead, he made his decision. He would contact Father. He would tell him everything, and right away.

But just as he was about to get up from the artificial grass and return to the house, he heard somebody calling his name.

"Eli! Eli, we need to talk with you!"

Marilyn sprang up on her hind legs. Eli glanced around the yard. Nobody. There was no one at the back of the house either. And yet he knew that gruff voice.

"Uncle Hector?"

"Up here, boy. Above you."

Eli craned his neck. There was an unusual cloud hanging just over his head, a small holographic projection that must have been created by some hidden mechanism in the nearby trees. Inside this strange cloud floated three heads that stared down at him.

Uncle Hector. Father. Mother.

They were watching him, their expressions grave. Eli had a bad feeling about this. It was disturbing enough just to see his family looming down at him from his own personal cloud— he hadn't even been aware the dome could do that—but Uncle Hector had never pinged him before. Not once in Eli's whole life. This was a first.

Which made this sudden appearance all the more alarming.

"Eli," Father began, "Uncle Hector just received a report we need to ask you about."

Mother peered down at him over her luminous glasses. "One of the CloudNet techs noticed a break in the stream. Oddly it turned out to be an unauthorized link to *your* sphere. It raises questions. Please tell us everything that happened."

How had they found out so quickly? Eli had left his room only a couple of minutes ago, and yet, judging by their expressions, he was in trouble already. Eli couldn't help remembering once again what Spider had told him—that Uncle Hector was concerned about him. So the timing of this couldn't be worse. None of this was his fault, though. Once he had a chance to explain, surely Uncle Hector and his parents would understand.

At least he hoped so.

"It's true," he began, doing his best to sound confident even though he felt like he might throw up. "Something weird *did* just happen. I was about to contact Father about it."

So Eli told them. He started with how he was searching for information on the CloudNet when the Heather simulation had disintegrated. He described the voices and the strange things they'd said. The whole time, Marilyn stayed quiet. The three heads listened, their expressions difficult to read. When Eli told them how the voices had warned him not to tell anybody about the conversation, they seemed to relax. Eli guessed why. He hadn't been a Papadopoulos his whole life without learning something about how his family worked. His loyalty had been in question. For now, it seemed, he'd passed their test.

Mother and Father looked relieved.

"I think you're right," Uncle Hector said at last, lighting a fresh cigar. "Those voices were indeed Foggers. It fits the pattern. The Outsiders want our resources, and this was a clear attempt to sabotage the CloudNet, possibly even to infiltrate the family. The barbarians are getting bolder."

"The company has already plugged the CloudNet hole the Foggers utilized to tap into your sphere," Father said. "They'll never be able to get in through that back door again."

"But why me? And why would they say I'm in danger?"

"Don't try to find any logic with Foggers," Uncle Hector said, blowing a cloud of smoke. "You'll never find any."

"You have to understand," Mother said, "they can't do any significant or permanent harm to our systems, but incidents like this are still a serious problem and a constant drain on resources. This is why everyone has to stay vigilant. And *you*," she said with a significant look, "need to stop obsessing about dome-design problems and the end of the world."

Eli felt his face go warm again. "I—I just had questions," he admitted. "The sky seems to be getting worse, not better, and sometimes I get the feeling there's something you're not telling me."

Uncle Hector frowned. "You're being ridiculous. Some software problems are more complex to resolve than others, that's all. I'm surprised you have so little faith in the company. Foggers look for people who are predisposed to paranoia. The way they recruit Insiders is by planting doubts that feed their fears. I don't know what they're looking for from you, but it seems they want to influence our family in some way. And we can't let that happen."

Father spoke up again. "Eli, you've been making good progress with your studies. Don't think the company hasn't noticed. But these questionable incidents of yours aren't helping you."

Eli had to look away. His cheeks were burning. "I'm sorry," he said. "You're right. I guess I was being stupid."

"Be sure to ping us if anything else happens, son. Anything at all."

"Yes, Father."

The three heads glanced at each other again. They seemed satisfied. "Now get back to your work, boy," Uncle Hector said. "Go earn your place in InfiniCorp management, like your brother. We know you can do it. Have a productive day."

The cloud blinked, and they were gone.

Eli let himself fall back into the grass. He closed his eyes. The last thing he needed was more trouble with his family. Why had he been moronic enough to share his worries with the CloudNet? Now not only did his parents have one more reason to be on his back, but he also had Foggers to deal with.

Dumb, dumb, dumb.

Marilyn seemed to sense what he was thinking. *Don't worry. It's all right.* She nuzzled him gently with her snout. *Let's get back to the house, my love. You have work to do.*

"How am I supposed to act normal after that?" he asked.

It's over now. You did the right thing.

But Eli knew better. The truth was, guilt hung over him like a weight. *You're wrong,* he admitted silently to her at last. *I didn't do the right thing at all.*

The mongoose stopped nuzzling. She tilted her head to one side. *What do you mean?*

He sat up and turned away. *When I told the story of what the voices said, I left out the ending. Didn't you notice? I didn't tell them how they promised to contact me again.*

Marilyn considered. Her expression changed as she seemed to recall the conversation. *Eli . . . you lied!*

No, not exactly. I just neglected to mention that part. Miserable, he forced himself to his feet and started back to the house. But he didn't get far. Marilyn blocked his path, her tiny orange eyes glaring up at him.

Tell me why, Eli. Why didn't you give them the whole truth? It's not too late. You can still ping them back.

He could, but he wasn't going to, and they both knew it. The thing was, if his family were aware the voices intended to contact him again, then they could probably find a way to prevent them from getting the opportunity. And Eli didn't want that. Even after so much trouble, he still couldn't stop thinking about the shadow he'd seen under the city, and the savage with the all-white eye, and the strange behavior of the sky. For so long he'd tried to shake the feeling something was wrong, something important. He couldn't ignore it anymore. If there was even the slightest chance of getting answers at long last, he needed to take it. He *had* to know.

Even if it meant associating with Foggers.

7

the white room

Tabitha woke up terrified. Her breath came in sharp gasps. She'd had a dream in which something unimaginable had happened and everything she cared about, everything that mattered, had been taken from her. She was nothing. Her life was over.

And Ben? Where was Ben?

Surely he was coming for her, but what could be taking him so long?

Now she lay curled in a ball and covered in sweat. There was a throbbing pain on the left side of her head. Even in her groggy state, she sensed she wasn't in St. Louis. First of all, it was warmer than she was used to, like there was something wrong with the blowers. And somewhere in the distance she could hear a sound like waves crashing. There was a faint smell like sour milk burning at her nose. She rubbed her eyes and tried to shake the remaining haze of her awful dream.

She opened her eyes.

White sheets. A white wall. Long, curly white lamps. A wardrobe and a low table shaped like a flower. Two puffy chairs. She was lying in silk sheets in what looked like a small but comfortable bedroom. Somebody had dressed her in pajamas.

It occurred to her that maybe she was dead.

She heard the soft click-clack of footsteps approaching. Then a girl's voice. "Awake at last, are we? You were having a nightmare. Must have been a whopper by the way you were calling out."

Tabitha turned her head, and it throbbed again like there was an ice pick in her brain. Standing over her was a beautiful green-haired girl with a kind face. She looked about Tabitha's age, maybe a little younger. The corners of her mouth were turned downward in concern. She was dressed all in white. She looked like an angel.

"Please don't be afraid, Representative Bloomberg. You're perfectly safe."

Tabitha yanked the sheets around her and pressed herself against the top of the bed. She didn't know what was happening, but she knew she should be suspicious of everything and everybody. She wanted answers.

"Where am I?"

"In the admissions ward of an InfiniCorp reeducation facility," the girl said, her voice calm. "You had a pretty severe jolt, and then you hit your head when you fell to the ground. You'll be fine, though. My name is Representative Shine, and I'm the Guardian assigned to take care of you. I brought you breakfast. You must be hungry. You've been sleeping for two days."

Tabitha felt it all come rushing back. The awful memory of how she'd been exposed. Her failed attempt to escape to Outside. Could that have been two whole days ago? Was it possible? Then she realized she wasn't just hungry—she was ravenous. She eyed the tray of food the girl in white was carrying. A huge omelet. A tall stack of toast. A cup of fruit. Some kind of juice.

"Where is this facility?" she asked. "Why do I hear waves?"

"It's the Gulf of Mexico. It's all around us for hundreds of miles. This ward is twenty-three stories above the water."

The Gulf of Mexico? How would she ever get home again if she was trapped in a tower somewhere in the middle of the sea?

"Look, let me set this tray down and we can talk. I'll tell you anything you want to know." As the girl placed the food on the bedside cabinet, she must have noticed Tabitha's wary look, because she added, "Don't worry, there's nothing wrong with it. So many new arrivals start off thinking we're going to, like, poison them or something. I promise you, that's not what this place is about."

Tabitha left the food where it was. "So what is it about, then?"

Representative Shine took one of the puffy chairs. "You've been assigned to a special offshore program for the reeducation of Wayward Employees."

"Reeducation?" Tabitha didn't like the sound of that.

The girl nodded. "Don't worry. It's going to be cool." She settled herself deeper into the chair. "Years ago this place used to be an offshore oil rig, one of the biggest ever built. It's twenty-four stories high. But the underwater reservoir is almost

120

dry, so now it's mostly used as sort of a giant floating manu-facturing plant. In addition to the admissions ward, where we are right now, we have seventeen separate production floors for making lots of different InfiniCorp stuff. This is where the company makes digital hair gel, electric pants, cooling win-dows, espresso makers—oh god, I could go on and on. All the products we make get shipped from here to the different In-finiCorp domes on the mainland."

"So . . . why am I here? Where's the reeducation part?"

The girl smiled. "You, kiddo, are going to join all the other Wayward Employees in one of our productivity areas. It's how you Waywards can relearn what you may have forgotten—the peace of mind that comes with trust. Just looking at you I can see you're still a nervous wreck. That'll change, I promise. Plus, contributing on a Learning Floor is a way to redeem yourself."

"A way to redeem myself," Tabitha repeated blankly.

"Yes. Forgiveness through productivity. The company is giving you a way to pay back for what you did." Her face was somber for only a moment before she brightened back up again. "You won't start just yet, of course. Only after you've re-covered. And the work isn't too hard either, believe me. It'll be fine. It's really not so bad here. We have lots of activities and fun stuff to do. The company takes good care of everybody."

Tabitha's thoughts whirled. So she wasn't going to die after all? Nobody was going to torture her or erase her memories? After all the horrors the Friends had described, working in some faraway manufacturing plant seemed like hardly any punishment at all. She glanced around the comfortable room again and at the breakfast that looked so delicious. She wasn't sure what she had expected, but this wasn't it.

The girl seemed to guess what Tabitha was thinking. "InfiniCorp might not like your past behavior, Representative Bloomberg, but we still want the best for you." She smiled again. It was the compassionate smile of someone who truly cared. "Hey, it's *totally* understandable you're a little disoriented right now, but please don't be nervous. I promise you, you're going to like it here. Everybody does."

Tabitha said nothing.

"Listen," the girl said, getting up from the chair, "you should eat and rest. It takes some people a long time to get over the jolt." She bit her lower lip sympathetically. "I wish they didn't have to do that, but it's standard procedure. Sometimes the Foggers mess people up so bad that when we try to help, they get violent." With that she turned and started heading away.

"Wait," Tabitha called. "One last question."

At the door now, Representative Shine looked back.

"What's that smell, like sour milk?"

"Oh, that's just the gulf." She wrinkled her nose. "Kind of yucky today, isn't it? It's the one neg to living over the water. Don't worry, you'll get used to it. I've been here so long I hardly think about it anymore."

So it was the *water* that smelled so bad? Tabitha had always wanted to visit the shore, but of course she never had. Still, she'd played dream games about the beach, and in the games the ocean smell was sharp and salty. Clean. Not like this. It seemed odd, but then again maybe it was normal. There was no way for Tabitha to know. In any case, sitting up in her pajamas with the sheets wrapped around her like armor, Tabitha felt exhausted again. Everything was out of whack somehow. Maybe it was the throbbing in her skull. All she was sure of was that she wanted to eat. In fact right then she was having a hard time thinking about anything but food.

"Can I get you something else, Representative Bloomberg?"

Tabitha wasn't sure what to think. She shook her head.

Representative Shine smiled one last time and left the room. Tabitha waited until she was sure she'd gone before she reached for the tray. Within seconds she was stuffing her breakfast into her mouth and swallowing it in hungry gulps.

She slept on and off, a fitful sleep with strange, dark dreams. She was at her Initiation Ceremony again, standing in the center of a circle of hooded Friends who held hands and chanted as she recited the Oath of Loyalty. She was theirs now. Despite still holding secret reservations about what she was doing, she had chosen to join their ranks because she shared their commitment to seeing the truth through the illusion and their desire to fight the system. But now, in her dream, she had a lump in her throat as she watched herself make the solemn promise to give up her old life, swearing her allegiance to a shadowy organization, a team of high-minded agents who looked out for each other in secret. This time she better understood the consequences, though, and she questioned whether it had ever been worth the risk. She tried to call out to herself, to somehow stop the ceremony so she would have more time to think it all through. But no sound would come from her mouth, no matter how hard she screamed.

Again and again she woke up trembling.

She wasn't sure how much time passed. It felt like weeks, but it might have been days. The heat drained her energy, and always there was that distant sour smell, making her stomach turn. Every now and then Representative Shine returned to fuss over her. She brought meals, changed Tabitha's sweaty sheets, and occasionally urged her out of bed to walk around. She was patient and kind. But no matter how nice she was, Tabitha still didn't feel safe. She suspected that somehow this kindness was another trick, a way for the company to keep her in the dark about its real intentions.

She wasn't going to fall for it.

On their short walks up and down the narrow, peach-colored admissions-ward corridor, Tabitha's eyes were always taking in the place. It was what the Friends had trained her to do. She never saw any other patient in the ward, but she noted every door, window, stairway, and duct. Any opportunity for escape. There wasn't much. And even if she were to find some way out of the building, this floor was too high to jump from. She shuddered at the thought of a twenty-three-story drop. Even if she could somehow make it safely down to the water, what then? How would she get across the Gulf of Mexico?

If this was a prison, it was a well-designed one. She didn't see any way out.

A sign in the corridor had the InfiniCorp logo, and words in curved, elegant letters:

FORGIVENESS THROUGH PRODUCTIVITY
CONTENTMENT THROUGH TRUST

The message was worrying, but Tabitha forced herself not to let it distract her. Secretly she was counting on the Friends. They were all she had, and she was convinced they'd come for her. She never said anything about this to Representative Shine, of course—she hardly even admitted it to *herself*—but deep down she imagined Sister Krystal, Brother Arnold, and all the others out there, searching for her. In her mind she kept envisioning them crashing through the door, taking her by the hand, and whisking her somewhere far away where she and Ben would be safe. And together.

It was just a matter of time.

Soon Tabitha met other kind Guardians, more beautiful, caring faces. Everyone smiled all the time here. Everyone was sympathetic and helpful. Yes, Tabitha had done something wrong, they said, but she wasn't to blame, really. She had been the victim. Everyone seemed so reasonable. What was happening? Could the Friends of Gustavo have been so wrong? Could she have been so misled?

No. Tabitha still refused to believe it. The nicer everyone acted, she decided, the more she had to fear.

Soon she found herself more bored than afraid. After days in the same comfortable room, she spent most of her time staring into space. A CloudNet sphere glowed overhead. Even though she had a higher-than-average resistance to its influence—in fact, the Friends said her natural resistance was one of the strongest they'd ever measured—she sensed that this one was more powerful than those she was used to. Despite herself she found that her eyes were drawn to it. She knew it wasn't wise to watch too much, but she didn't have many options. Besides, it was always on, and there was little else to do.

"How's your head, Representative Bloomberg?" Representative Shine would occasionally ask.

"Still hurts," Tabitha would reply, even though it was fine.

"I'm sorry to hear that. Can I get you anything? Like, some water?"

"Yes, that would be great. Thank you."

A minute later she would return and set a paper cup by the bed. Tabitha would sit up and gulp the water down, grateful to feel something wet and cool in her throat. She realized she was feeling much better now, more relaxed.

"Soon you should be ready to leave the admissions ward and join the others in the productivity areas. It'll be good for you to feel useful again."

Tabitha would only shrug. There was no way anybody was getting her to work for InfiniCorp—not if she could help it, anyway. She was still trying to think of a way to escape, but she was running out of ideas.

Where were the Friends of Gustavo? She wished they would hurry up. Otherwise she might end up stuck on some production line for the rest of her life.

One of the programs they streamed here on the CloudNet sphere every night was a series called *Wham! Bam! Jam!*—a romantic musical drama about three former Fogger kids, two boys and a girl, who had seen the error of their ways and now worked happily together in a food-processing plant at the outskirts of the desert. During the day they made strawberry preserves for needy children, but at night they were secret agents who mended broken hearts through good deeds while exposing Outsider plots against the company. At the end of each episode there was always a big production number in which everybody danced and sang songs about forgiveness, the virtues of hard work, and the benefits of whatever new Infini-Corp product was the focus of the show. The former Foggers were especially good at picking out cool new clothes. Despite herself, Tabitha found it to be a very uplifting show. The music was terrific too.

One morning Tabitha woke to find Representative Shine sitting on the side of her bed. She was holding Tabitha's hand and looking concerned. Tabitha wasn't scared of her or what she was doing, just puzzled. In fact, she'd taken such good care of her that Tabitha was actually starting to like her. She was just a girl, that was all. Like Tabitha, Representative Shine was only doing her job. Tabitha's issue was with the company, not her.

"Hello?" Tabitha asked, still groggy.

"You were calling out in your sleep," she said. "Who's Ben?"

This took a second to register in Tabitha's mind. But then suddenly she was awake. A sick feeling spread through her. On instinct Tabitha pretended to be confused, still too sleepy to answer, but inside she was at full attention. Ben! She'd been so careful not to say his name! It was the only way she had to protect him. And yet in her sleep she'd gone and betrayed him after all! What had she *done*?

Without thinking, she pulled her hand away. Representative Shine seemed to sense something was wrong. "Oh no!" she said, her own hand rising to her mouth. "I've upset you!

127

He's somebody important to you, isn't he? Somebody you don't want to talk about?"

Tabitha said nothing.

"And stupid, idiot me," she continued. "I've stressed you out because now you think that telling me his name puts Ben, whoever he is, at risk somehow. That's it, isn't it?" She looked truly upset with herself, like she might even cry. "Oh, you poor, poor thing."

But still Tabitha kept her mouth shut. There was nothing she could do to take back what she'd given away in her sleep, but there was no chance she was giving up any other information. She was devastated with disappointment at herself. What would the Friends think of her now if they knew? At that moment if she could have flung herself into the Gulf of Mexico, she would have.

"God, I'm so sorry," Representative Shine said. She stood up and backed toward the door. "I didn't mean to pry. It's just that I happened to hear you and I was curious, that's all. You have to believe me. You don't need to worry. Really. It's not what you're thinking. I'll leave you alone now. We'll make this our secret, okay? We'll pretend this conversation didn't even happen."

A moment later Tabitha was alone again, still reeling from what she'd done. How many Bens did she know back in St. Louis? Not so many. How hard would it be for the company to make a list and connect him with her? And then what would happen to him? Oh god! If only there were a way to contact him! If anything bad were to happen to Ben, she didn't know what she would do! She could see his face; his brown eyes, always so serious; his sideways smile. She missed him so much it hurt. She would have given anything to know he was safe, or at least to be sure the Friends would rescue her soon so she could get word to him before it was too late. This was her only hope.

Or was it? She thought of Representative Shine and how upset she'd seemed at causing her so much distress. Maybe she was telling the truth. Maybe she wasn't pretending to be her friend—maybe she really was.

Maybe Representative Shine wouldn't tell anyone about Ben.

Tabitha didn't get out of bed all day. She left her lunch untouched and couldn't bring herself to eat at dinnertime either. She pulled the sheets over her head to block out the world. But it was no use. She couldn't escape what she'd done.

That evening, when Representative Shine appeared with a tray of tea and cookies, she closed the door behind her. She'd never done that before. Tabitha was instantly on alert. She watched as the girl set the tray next to the bed and sat beside her. In one of her hands there was an envelope.

"I went through the files," she whispered, brushing back a lock of green hair that had fallen over her eyes. "I found something for you."

Tabitha watched Representative Shine open the envelope and remove what looked like a photograph. She held it up.

"Is this Ben?"

Tabitha couldn't believe her eyes. It *was* him. It was the

head shot they'd taken for identification on his first day at the Program. She felt everything rushing back to her, all that she'd left behind. She tried to contain her emotion, but it was too much. Her eyes started welling up, and she couldn't stop it from happening.

Representative Shine nodded. "I guessed right, then. Don't worry. Nobody else knows about him. I kept my promise. I was able to figure it out because he was the only Ben taken that same day you were. He was the first one they captured. I'm sorry—that must be hard for you to hear."

Tabitha's world was whirling again. Ben was taken too? The company had him? Oh, this was horrible news! The worst possible!

But then again, maybe it wasn't. After all, *she* was being treated just fine. What was more, it occurred to her that maybe, just maybe, she could see him again. Her heart skipped a beat. She sat up. She was desperate to know. Where was he? Was it possible that all this time he'd been right here, somewhere else in this tower?

Before she could ask, though, she noticed that Representative Shine's expression was drawn and sad, like a person about to deliver bad news. And then it came: "I'm so sorry to have to tell you this, but Ben is dead. He took his own life. He's gone."

Tabitha couldn't breathe. It was as if somebody had ripped her insides right out of her chest.

"I'm so, so sorry," the sweet-faced girl said, her bottom lip quivering. "It happened the same day they picked you up. They captured him early that morning. He was the only one the company knew about at the time. The Guardians did everything they could to try to help him, but before they could sedate him, he freaked. He cried and begged for mercy. He started blurting out the names of all the Foggers he knew. I guess he thought if he did that then they might let him go." She paused. "Tabitha, he was the one who gave us your name. You didn't betray him—he betrayed *you*. I just thought you should know that."

Tabitha could only gape at her. Could it be true? Was it possible that Ben was not only dead but that he'd turned out to be a coward and a traitor to the Friends, and even to *her*? It was too much to wrap her mind around. How could she have so misjudged him? How could she have been so wrong about so many things?

That's when the room really started to spin.

"I wouldn't have told you any of this except I guessed he was someone . . . *special* to you. At first I couldn't decide what to do, but in the end I thought . . . well, I thought it wouldn't be right *not* to tell you."

Tabitha realized Representative Shine was holding her hand again, only this time she didn't pull hers away. The girl was still talking but she was barely listening anymore. Her throat was tight, and it was so warm in here.

"It's all right, Tabitha. It's okay to cry."

Tabitha tried to speak but nothing came out. She was hyperventilating. Her life was over and Ben was gone. Even the beautiful memory of him was tainted now. The principled boy she thought she knew had never really existed in the first place. Soon she felt the girl's soft arms wrap around her, and she didn't know what to do. She wanted to hate her but she couldn't. Maybe Representative Shine was all she had left now, her last connection to anything real. Maybe she was the only friend she had left in the world.

It was all so confusing. It was so, so hard to know.

The whole universe was spinning faster and faster, and Tabitha wasn't sure what to believe in anymore.

8

the wild orange yonder

Eli stayed alert for more CloudNet messages or any other sign the voices were trying to contact him again. But nothing happened. After several days he concluded they must have figured he was too much of a risk after all and abandoned the idea. Either that, or his family had managed to block them completely.

In a way, it was a relief.

Then one afternoon Eli and Marilyn had a fight, which was rare for them, and Eli decided to go for a walk to cool down. Shoulders hunched, he headed up Hope Street with his fists thrust deep in his trouser pockets.

It was a stupid argument. It'd started after he'd discovered her under his bed in yet another of her trances.

"All you do anymore is lie there," he'd commented.

She barely stirred. When she answered, her voice was distant and lethargic. *Leave me alone. I'm swimming in a binary ocean. I'm riding a digital tidal wave of ones and zeros. . . .*

He wanted to let it go, but he couldn't. It irked him how difficult it was to get her attention lately. Like most of his cousins, she was often in a daze now. Claudia too—when she wasn't working, she spent much of her free time watching the sphere or playing dream games.

He shoved his chair back. "Let's go exploring. It's been forever since we went for a walk. It'll do us both good."

This time she didn't even respond at all.

"What's happening to you?" And then he'd blurted out something he regretted as soon as he said it: "Wasting so much time with machines is screwing up your chip, Marilyn. The CloudNet is making you stupid."

This got her attention. She lifted her head and hissed at him. She'd never done that before. *Don't worry about my chip, Eli. It's not like you're around much these days.*

He'd stormed out of the house and down the sidewalk, half-expecting her to rush up behind him. But now he was blocks away, and still no Marilyn. His boots shuffled along the pavement. It had been a while since he'd left the house without some specific purpose in mind. Why did he have to go and pick a fight? Now Marilyn probably wouldn't speak to him for the rest of the day.

Without any particular plan he turned the corner onto Wickenden Street, which was crowded with people moving in and out of the cafés and clubs that lined both sides of the steep incline. Even during the day the streets were often busy with night-shift workers or daytime employees on their breaks. At that moment, sparklers lit the street corners and loud music blasted from all directions. Two blocks ahead he could see the giant flashing sign above the entrance to the Bubble station, the local subway stop for commuting employees. He dug his hands deeper into his pockets and started up the hill.

He sighed.

So much weighed on his mind, and not just Marilyn. Tomorrow he was going to Grandfather's for the Festival of Optimism, another celebration day. He was looking forward to the party, he supposed, and especially to seeing Sebastian for the first time since he'd left home, but even that had a downside. By all accounts, in his first ten weeks with the company his brother was already doing outstanding work. This was terrific for him, of course, but it also put more pressure on Eli. As each day passed he was becoming more and more nervous. What if despite all his recent work, he still didn't get into the Management Training Program? What if he ended up assigned to some low-level job that brought shame to Father and Mother?

He wished he could just find out and get it over with.

From up ahead came the metallic tink-tonk of circus music played on what sounded like a toy piano, and then an electronic voice calling out, "Welcome to the East Side, my friend! Welcome to where the party lasts all day and the celebrating never ends!"

Eli looked up. It was a funbot, one of the colorful little clown droids that made sure everyone knew where to find the good parties. It was waving one of its oversized foam hands and rolling in Eli's direction.

"Tonight at the Providence Pig-Out, Grandfather invites you to enjoy an all-employee special! Eat InfiniBurgers until you puke, then dance the night away! Buy tickets now and save!" One of its rubber ears was missing, and Eli noticed that the metal around the empty hole was warped, as if someone had tried to pry it open.

"No, thanks," he said, walking past.

But the grinning robot wasn't so easily put off. It kept pace with him, its music maddeningly persistent. "Perhaps you'd prefer a night of history and adventure? May I suggest the Replicator Room? Tonight we're simulating the sinking of the *Titanic*! You'll see your own breath as the ship goes down in the icy North Atlantic! Imagine that!"

"Thanks. I'll pass."

Even as Eli continued on, it kept rolling behind him, and fast. Soon it caught up. The next thing Eli knew, it was whacking one of its coiled antennae against his arm, trying to get his attention. Eli couldn't believe it was doing this. The funbots were programmed to be a *little* pushy, but this was too much.

"I have the best idea of all!" it sang as it continued thumping. "Tonight you should ride the Bubble! Ride the Bubble! It's a lovely night to take a spin under the city!"

Not only was this droid annoying, but it was obviously malfunctioning. As far as Eli knew, the company never held parties in the Bubble.

Eli swiveled on his heel. "Would you quit it? Leave me alone!"

The robot stopped whacking him. Its white clown face lost its smile, and its big plastic eyes locked with Eli's. "Ride the Bubble, Eli Papadopoulos," it whispered, its voice uncharacteristically earnest. "I *strongly* suggest that you *ride the Bubble*."

Eli stared. What was happening? Had he heard it right? "W-what?"

The machine held its gaze. "You heard me."

Eli felt a tingle down his spine. His own voice dropped to a whisper. "Who are you?"

But the little one-eared droid's face had already regained its usual grin, and it was backing away. "Ride the Bubble, Eli," it said one last time before spinning around and heading back across the road. Within moments it was wheeling up to a crowd of people in pink uniforms, its voice playful again over the circus music. "Welcome to the East Side, my friends! Welcome to where the party lasts all day and the celebrating never ends!"

Eli stood, frozen. It was a few seconds before he even breathed.

Bubble stations were always noisy and crowded, especially during the evening commute. Mobs would pile into the air chutes that sucked people into the underground tunnels, where they'd cram into giant spherical trams that carried them home or to parties or one of the malls. The dome was always an active place, but nighttime was when it really came alive. Eli looked around, wondering what he was supposed to do. In the end he hopped into the first Bubble he saw, a perimeter shuttle that looped continuously around the edge of the city. He squeezed into a crush of people just as the porthole closed. The vacuum system gently sucked him up to the ceiling, the only place there was any room.

It was good it was so crowded. If a Fogger tried anything, he could always scream for help.

What was he doing? He wondered what was wrong with him that he would take orders from a funbot. What if it really was a message from the voices, as he suspected? Meeting up with people he didn't know, CloudNet hackers from out of the shadows—it could only be a bad idea. This was the craziest thing he'd ever done.

If only he hadn't fought with Marilyn. He wished more than ever that she were here with him.

Somebody's elbow jabbed him in the side. He wasn't used to being packed in with so many strangers. Members of the Papadopoulos clan rarely rode the Bubble. Eli pulled up his collar to hide his face. It wasn't likely anybody would recognize him. Hardly anyone ever did. Still, it was best to be safe.

The last thing he needed was more trouble.

As the Bubble tram hummed into motion, he gripped a strap for balance. He scanned the crowd. The Foggers—if that was who he was meeting here—could be anybody. Just below him floated two girls with Dream Gamers fastened to their heads, large rubber goggles with tubes for their nostrils, ears, and mouths. They must have been linked into the same dream, because every once in a while they giggled in unison. Beside them three boys were zapping each other with blasters and laughing. For some reason all three were dressed as Elvis.

The tram came to a hissing stop. "Now arriving at South Angell," said a voice that seemed to come from everywhere, "where it's two-for-one night at the Marauding Mutant. The Brain Blasters are playing at Club Babyhead, and at Lovecraft's Lounge we're having a masquerade ball! Prizes for the best costume!"

A masquerade ball. That explained the Elvis outfits.

Eli watched as the boys sank to the porthole and slipped out. A handful of other costumed people left too. A silver bug.

A couple of vampires. One kid was even dressed as Grandfather. Eli hadn't noticed them behind so many other people. When they cleared out, a new crowd squeezed in and took their places. The porthole whooshed shut, and they started moving again.

It was uncomfortably warm. From the few times Eli had ridden the Bubble before, he didn't remember the air being this stuffy. Had the underground blowers broken down too?

The giant ball stopped and started over and over again, lingering at each station only long enough for passengers to scurry in and out. At every stop Eli expected somebody to drift up and start talking to him. On the ceiling to his left, a girl with flashing pink hair implants stared out the window. Just when Eli was wondering if she might be the one, she pulled her release lever and floated back to the floor. At the next stop she left.

Neon lights whizzed past the window and periodically came to a halt. It took only a few minutes to complete the entire loop around Providence, and soon Eli was passing the same stations for the second time. He took deep breaths, trying not to panic. So where were they? Maybe his first impression of the funbot's odd behavior had been right—it was just another malfunction. Maybe the Foggers weren't going to show up after all. That thought was a relief to him.

But that was when it happened.

"A single thread of reality can be hard to distinguish in a complex fabric of illusion," said a voice in his ear.

Eli turned. It was a kid—from the voice Eli guessed it was a boy—in a tattered tunic with a hood that partially covered his face. Somehow Eli had let his thoughts wander and hadn't even noticed that somebody new had floated up beside him. And even the part of the kid's face not lost inside the hood was hidden under a mask. It was red, with leathery skin made to look mottled with sun damage.

The kid was dressed as an Outsider.

"Do you understand what it would mean to unravel it?" he continued. Through the two holes in the mask, Eli could see his eyes, intense and brown, watching him. "Are you ready to accept the consequences?"

Eli kept his voice low. "You're one of them, aren't you?"

"You're difficult to get near to, Eli Papadopoulos," he said. "They're watching you closely."

"Watching me? Who?"

The boy looked away. Eli noticed two other kids in red masks and ragged clothes lingering within sight. One hung upside down halfway across the curved ceiling, and another floated near the wall on the opposite side. All three wore similar costumes: disheveled Outsiders with fake dirty hair jutting in all directions and wild, vacant expressions on their rubber faces. The one hanging upside down even had pointed ears and fangs.

Monsters.

"Who are you people?"

"An association of brothers and sisters committed to truth and survival." The masked boy's gaze was fixed not on Eli but on the flashing lights outside the tram. "You can call us the Friends of Gustavo."

Eli watched the tunnel lights flash across the boy's mask. "What kind of a name is that? Who's Gustavo?"

"A great and wise man. A teacher. A righteous champion

for the scattered people of the wasteland. Many who survive out there today do so only because he showed the way. He taught not just the path of survival but also of a quest far greater than any of us."

"Okay, so where is he?"

The boy shook his head almost imperceptibly. "It is believed Gustavo survived many years before the desert finally took him. We are his legacy."

Eli's palms were sweating. How much more proof did he need that this boy was a Fogger? Besides, he hadn't come to the Bubble to hear about some years-ago Outsider sympathizer. He felt guiltier than ever now, recalling the terrible damage the explosion had done to the air filter. This kid was a criminal.

"I could alert everyone in this tram about who you are," he said. The words were out before he even knew he was saying them.

The boy turned back to him. He met his gaze. "You could. There's nothing stopping you."

The porthole opened, and Eli felt another wave of heat. He considered doing it, exposing the Fogger right here and now. Or maybe he should just pull the lever and run back home. Another crowd of employees slipped out, heading home or to parties or to whatever they were up to in their normal, happy lives. He couldn't help thinking about the failing blowers, and the blinking sky, and the crazed Outsider with her foul breath and jagged blade.

Soon there'll be no dome for you to return to. . . .

He kept his eyes on the mask and wrapped the strap even tighter around his knuckles. "You people said you have answers. Tell me what you know."

141

"Be careful what you ask for," the boy said. "Knowledge can be a perilous ally. It can demand much of you. This is why most people don't really want to know what's real. They think they do, but in the end they choose not to. Because knowing, knowing for *sure,* means having to face up to what's necessary. It's easier to look away. It's safer. As a Papadopoulos you have more to lose than most."

Eli eyed him. Was this a warning or a threat? A bead of sweat trickled down his forehead. Behind the mask the boy seemed to follow its progress.

"It's been warmer Inside lately," the boy said. "Uncomfortably so. And yet, under the shelter of an artificial sky, it's difficult to imagine just how warm it can be out *there.* Out in the *Actual.*"

The Actual. Eli had heard that term before. And then he remembered where: from the savage with the white eye. When she'd talked about Outside, she'd used the exact same word.

"The domes keep secrets, Eli," the boy whispered. "They dull our senses and blind us. They lull us to sleep. But it's a dangerous sleep. While we dream, the deserts expand. Resources run dry. Far beyond the protected cities, survivors of the wasteland hunt and scavenge. It's all they can do. But you live under a protective shell, so you wouldn't understand this."

"You don't have to tell me about Outside," Eli said. "It's empty. It's dead. I know that already. I've seen what it's like."

"You have no idea," the boy scoffed. "How could you? Insiders are cut off from everything but the lights and the machines and the pursuit of shortsighted ambition. But none of these have any worth to the people of the wasteland. Clean water is sometimes so scarce that Outsiders will risk their lives climbing the domes just to try to tap into company water. In this way they die by the hundreds every year. Did you know that?"

Eli shook his head.

"It's one of many realities the company chooses not to share."

"Why would they hide the truth?"

"Because," he said, "they don't want to disturb the illusion. Consider how Insiders are kept sedated with hollow jobs and empty aspirations. They're distracted with products and meaningless entertainment. Have you ever asked yourself what the purpose is?" Behind the mask the boy narrowed his eyes. "It's a diversion, Eli. A reassuring ruse to maintain a semblance of the old ways. For now it appears safe, but the fantasy comes with a cost. The Great Sickness wasn't the end of the trouble— it was barely the beginning. Harsh reality is still building up out there. It's knocking at the door, rattling the domes' foundations. It won't be ignored much longer—you can be sure of that. But you already sense this. I can see it. It's not Outside that's dead. The wasteland is the only truth we have left, the land of the *real* survivors. Look around. It's *your* world that's a living death."

Eli wasn't sure what to make of this. The boy was nuts. "You make it sound like the domes are a bad thing. Until the Cooldown ends, why should we live like animals if we don't have to?"

The roar of the tram increased as it hurtled through another tunnel. "What if the Cooldown never happens? What if it's too late for the planet to go back to the way it once was?"

The boy glanced away again, but he leaned in as if he were

merely adjusting his position on the ceiling. When he spoke, his voice was even closer to Eli's ear. Even so, his words were quiet enough that Eli had to concentrate just to hear them over the background noise.

"We are in an age of extreme transformation. Those of us who choose to see have precious little time to prepare for the final road. Even now resources are running low. Cracks are forming in the artifice. The company can't maintain its illusion forever. After it gives out, then what?" He paused. "A storm is coming, Eli. A mighty tempest, the likes of which no one has ever seen. But you feel it already, don't you?"

"What are you saying?" Eli whispered, ignoring the boy's question because he didn't want to admit the answer even to himself. "That the Outsider with the white eye was right? That all the dome problems we've been having—the sky, the air coolers, and everything—that they're just going to get worse, and then some huge storm is going to kill us all?"

The boy shrugged. "That's one possibility. But here's the thing, the great mysterious truth to keep despair at bay: the Friends believe there's something else out there, a reason for hope. Some of the oldest of the Outsiders, those who've survived in the desert through the Long Ago, tell us that somewhere out there, beyond the wasteland, past the dust and insects and famine, lies a safe haven, a glorious sanctuary where resources are plentiful and life can go on the way it once was. Gustavo saw it. It came to him in a vision. We believe that those who wish to survive need only discover it."

"A sanctuary from the storm at the end of the world . . . ," Eli said. "A place some long-ago Outsider says he saw in a dream. Come on, do you really believe that?"

He nodded. "I'm not alone. There are many believers. Hundreds have given their lives in this final quest—the search for the Wild Orange Yonder."

Eli stared. The Wild Orange Yonder? *This* was the truth the voices had promised? This was the great answer? Eli had taken a huge risk in coming here, and it was because he'd been hoping for some revelation, some important insight that would explain everything. But this wasn't it. This was just Fogger nonsense. It was nothing at all.

He shouldn't have come. He should have known.

He felt again the intensity in the boy's eyes. He wondered who he was talking to and what was underneath the mask? If he pulled it back, would he see real skin that was red and mottled from the sun?

And with that thought he was suddenly even more afraid of him.

"Eli, has it occurred to you why you called out to us?"

"Called out to *you*? I didn't. You came to *me*."

The boy shook his head. "The CloudNet is a powerful sedative. It manipulates the senses and defines the world for us. Without our ever being aware of it, it influences how we perceive and interpret everything around us. It draws us in. Most people can't resist the pull, but occasionally somebody comes along who can. For reasons we don't understand, they're just better at it than others. I'm one of them, Eli, and I think you're another. You're here, aren't you?" He paused. "Eli, I believe you're one of us."

"No!"

Heads turned. He'd spoken louder than he'd meant to. But Eli wasn't like this boy and his Fogger friends. Not in any way.

He never would be. It was time to go. The second the tram came to the next stop he was going to leave. Lines from the *Alice* book flashed through his mind.

> *Beware the Jabberwock, my son!*
> *The jaws that bite, the claws that catch!*

He reached for the lever. "I'm going."

"You need to understand how few of us there are," the boy said, his voice urgent. "Of the quarter million people living in this dome, we have perhaps a hundred agents. They're scattered throughout the organization, but none are at the very top tier. With your help, though—"

"*My* help? You've got to be kidding!" Eli considered shouting for assistance, but the other fake Outsiders were watching, and he worried about what they might do if he did. Instead he yanked his arm from the boy and turned on him. "You know what I think? I think you and your cause are pathetic. Sneaking around with masks and working against the company when it does so much to keep all of us safe. You're a bunch of cowards."

His fists were balled up tight. The tram slowed and came to a halt at Dyerville Station. It wasn't near his house, but who cared? He would walk home. He was about to pull the lever and drop to the floor, but then he noticed two Guardians slipping in through the far porthole. The masked boy saw them too.

"There," Eli said. "You can run, but it won't help. It's all over for you now. They're coming."

But to Eli's surprise the boy didn't leave. Instead he looked directly at Eli and pulled up his mask. Now Eli could see his face. He wasn't an Outsider after all. He was a regular kid, a boy only a year or two older than Eli was. He looked ordinary, with dark hair and just a little acne on his chin. Any other time Eli might have passed him on the street and never picked him out as different.

"The other day you told us that if you were the last chance to save a dying world, you'd take that chance. Did you mean it?"

"Yes," Eli answered, too stunned to lie, "I did."

The boy nodded. "Then we have more to share with you, somebody we'd like you to meet." The Guardians were already drifting in their direction. The boy pulled his mask back down and reached for his ceiling lever. "Be careful, Eli," he said as he started to sink into the crowd. "They are always watching."

Who? Eli wanted to ask, but it was too late. By then the boy had already slipped through a crowded pocket of passengers and was moving toward the porthole. The Guardians seemed unaware of him. Eli watched as the three kids in Outsider costumes passed out of the tram, the last people through the porthole before it closed. His heart pounding, Eli tracked their progress through the transparent wall. He tried to follow where they went, but he lost them in the swarming crowd.

The tram was moving again.

9

a few innocent questions

When Eli got back to the house, his mind was reeling. No Cooldown? The CloudNet manipulating people's minds? None of the things the masked boy had told him made sense. But then again, what did he expect from a Fogger?

Marilyn was waiting on his chest of drawers. She raised herself on her haunches and glared at him. Ignoring this, he told her everything that had happened.

How could you do something so stupid? she asked after a long pause.

Eli kept his voice low in case Claudia was nearby. "How was I supposed to know what would happen? It's not like I had any idea ahead of time."

What did you expect? You followed the instructions of a Fogger-hacked droid! At the very least, didn't it occur to you that somebody on the Bubble could recognize you? What if your family finds out? Her whiskers twitched. *Reckless, that's what it was. A foolish risk!*

He didn't say anything right away. After their argument he was glad she was even talking to him. It was a good sign. "I'm sorry about what I said, Marilyn. About your chip and about wasting time with machines. I was just worried about you. Let's just forget it, okay?"

The mongoose chirped softly and rubbed her paws together as if she were carrying the weight of the world. It was amazing to Eli how human she sometimes looked. *It's not me you need to worry about, Eli. It's your family. You'd better hope they don't find out what happened, because if they do I wouldn't want to be in your shoes tomorrow.* She leveled her gaze at him. *You haven't forgotten, have you, about the Festival of Optimism?*

Eli's stomach sank. In all the excitement, he had indeed forgotten, and now he realized the timing couldn't be worse. What happened today wasn't exactly his own fault, but still, he'd met with a Fogger, an anti-InfiniCorp criminal. It was arguably the most disloyal thing he could have done. In any case, he was certain his family would see it that way if they ever found out. Which was why the thought of having to face them tomorrow was making him feel suddenly nauseated.

I'm glad to see you at least have the good sense to be ashamed of yourself.

He lowered himself onto his bed. "Why do I do these things to myself, Marilyn? I don't know why you put up with me."

Marilyn looked like she'd been struck. After a moment she dropped to the floor, raised herself to her full height, and narrowed her orange eyes. *Because, you dense, selfish boy, you're my only friend. You're all I have!*

With her whiskers pulled back and her teeth bared, to

anybody else she would have been a fearsome sight. Only then did it occur to Eli that she was fully awake, which could mean just one thing: she'd stayed away from her dream game all this time. She was his only friend, and he was hers. But now he realized that he hadn't been a very good friend to her lately. Meeting her eyes, he felt like the worst person in the world.

"I'm sorry," he said, looking away.

Her whiskers twitched again. *What are you going to do?*

"What choice do I have? I'll go to Grandfather's tomorrow. At least I can ask Sebastian. Maybe he's heard of the Friends of Gustavo."

I wouldn't do that. Keep this to yourself. You don't know who's safe to talk to and who isn't.

"Safe? Of course Sebastian's safe. He's my brother." He flopped back onto his pillow and stared at the ceiling. "Listen, I know it sounds weird, but there's something out there. I can't help sensing it. That kid on the Bubble, he lifted his mask. He showed me his face and let me see into his eyes. He didn't have to do that. And he looked as normal as anyone else." He let out a long breath. "I don't know what's going on, Marilyn, but I feel like I need to figure it out."

All I know is that you need to be careful, Eli. Don't let your guard down.

Eli slept badly. The whole following morning he kept expecting Uncle Hector or another of his uncles or aunts to suddenly materialize in a cloud and accuse him of disloyalty. Father and Mother were coming home so they could travel to Grandfather's together, and before they arrived he imagined how

150

they would corner him. They would inform him they'd heard all about the Fogger and ask him why he'd disappointed them yet again.

But none of it happened. Nobody even brought it up.

This was a good sign, of course, but Eli realized that just because the ax hadn't fallen yet didn't guarantee that his secret was safe. His was a family of mysterious and powerful people. He knew better than to relax just yet.

At Grandfather's celebration he kept to himself until Sebastian arrived. When he did, Eli watched his brother parade through the packed ballroom, shaking hands and greeting everyone. It seemed to Eli that he'd grown taller in his weeks at the Program. The CloudNet cameras followed his every move. With his silicone shoulder pads and reflective robe, he looked more like a real executive than ever.

Everyone made a big fuss over him.

Eli waited for his chance to speak with him alone. He kept trying to get his attention, but it wasn't easy. After a quick hello there was always some interruption. Uncle Demetrius needed him, or Spider would call him over to address some business issue or other. After having so many unpleasant incidents with Spider, Eli was bothered more than ever to think of Sebastian working so closely with their strange cousin. But there was no denying that Sebastian looked happy. And it wasn't his fault he was so busy. He worked for the company now. He had real responsibilities.

Eli's moment finally came later in the afternoon. Sebastian was in the hallway, checking his InfiniTalk messages, so Eli made his way over to him. When Sebastian saw him, he grinned. "Just a sec," he said, raising a finger. "Answering a ping."

Rather than waiting for another of his uncles to interrupt again, Eli took him by the arm and pulled him through a nearby door into one of the sitting rooms. It was empty. "What are you doing?" Sebastian asked, ending his transmit. "That was important!"

Eli closed the door. "I need to talk with you about something. You need to promise you'll never tell anyone. Okay?"

Sebastian looked wary. "I guess so."

Eli took a deep breath. "Have you ever heard of the Friends of Gustavo?"

"No."

"How about something called the Wild Orange Yonder?"

He shook his head.

Eli dropped his voice even lower. "Has anybody in the Program ever mentioned anything to you about using the CloudNet to control people's minds? Have they talked about the Outsiders and the end of the world?"

Sebastian studied him, his expression growing darker. "I don't believe it. You're still obsessing about that nut job we saw, aren't you? Why can't you just let it go?"

"No, that's not it—"

He held up his hand, obviously uninterested in hearing more. "God, Eli. What's the matter with you? I'm beginning to wonder if you caught brain fever out there. You're starting to sound like a Fogger."

Eli didn't think that was fair. He was only asking. He was about to say so, but then Sebastian's InfiniTalk howled. Sebastian tapped his ear. "Just a sec," he said to Eli after a moment. "Another company ping." Fuming, Eli waited while Sebastian received the transmit and sent his response, his voice calm and commanding. Eli realized the change in his brother went deeper than just his new clothes. There was a new authority in his manner, a confidence that hadn't been there before.

At last Sebastian tapped his ear again. "Look, sorry to do this to you, but I gotta go. The office needs the quarterly numbers and . . . well, I have to get back right away."

"*Listen* to me!" Eli said, grabbing his sleeve. "Yesterday I rode the Bubble. There was a boy dressed like an Outsider. He came up to me and—"

By then Sebastian had already pulled his arm back and was walking away. "You don't get it. I really don't have time for this."

Eli wanted to grab him by the lapels and shake him, but on the other hand he could imagine how pathetic he must seem, still whining about Outsiders and the end of the world. He looked away, focusing on the window so Sebastian wouldn't see him turn red.

"Listen, I'm sorry. Hey, would you look at me?"

Eli did.

"I know what this is really about," Sebastian said, his tone softer now. "You're worried about getting into the Program. I totally understand that. Everyone feels the same way until they get the news. But seriously, you need to let this stuff go. Everything works out in the end. The company makes sure of it. In the meantime, you have to pull yourself together."

"Sebastian, I really need to speak with you."

His brother rubbed his forehead. "Okay," he said after a moment. "Ping me tomorrow. We'll talk then." He spun around and started toward the door again. As he left the room, Eli couldn't help thinking he looked more like Father than ever.

In Grandfather's office an hour later, Eli and the old man were playing their usual game of checkers. By then Eli had mostly calmed down. After his frustration with Sebastian, he wondered whether he should say something to Grandfather about the masked boy. If there was anyone who had always been on Eli's side, it was him. In the end, though, he decided to take Marilyn's advice. Talking with Foggers was no ordinary transgression. It was safer to tread lightly.

But there was no reason he couldn't ask a few innocent questions.

"Grandfather?" he began, as casually as he could manage. "How does the company know the world is cooling back down and going back to the way it was?"

The old man was barely listening. His eyes were fixed on the game board. Eli couldn't help noticing how since the last time he'd seen his grandfather, his breathing had grown wheezier and the wrinkles on his face seemed to have grown deeper. "It's what our scientists tell us. How else? Why, are you concerned?"

Eli shook his head. "No. It was just something I was thinking about."

His eyes still on the board, Grandfather grunted. "Very good. Questioning assumptions is a sign of a sound mind." Over his shoulder Eli could see the amazing music box shaped like a domed city, its people safely tucked in their houses and

154

office buildings. Grandfather reached out and jumped one of Eli's red checkers with one of his black ones. He set Eli's lost piece to one side of the board.

"Your move."

But Eli wasn't finished. "I have something else I wanted to ask. Have you ever heard of Outsiders climbing the domes to tap into the water supplies?"

The old man raised his bushy eyebrows. "What an extraordinary question. Why would you ask such a thing, child?"

"I don't know," he said with a shrug. "I was just thinking about Outsiders and where they must get their water from. I just wondered about it."

Grandfather smiled. "Another outstanding line of consideration. The answer is yes. As a matter of fact, I have heard of such a thing. At least, I've heard of Outsiders *trying* to tap into our water supplies. But it's not something they would ever get away with."

"Well, let's just say they tried and got hurt doing it, maybe even killed. Would the company ever want to hide the truth about that? Or about anything else?"

"Hide the truth? What exactly are you getting at?"

"I'm just curious, that's all. Would InfiniCorp ever try to stop people from knowing something? Would we, say, use the CloudNet to keep their minds distracted?"

Grandfather eyed him. Eli had been trying to sound like they were just having a regular conversation, but he realized he'd probably gone too far. As the old man continued to take him in, Eli was struck once more by the gray pallor of his face and the dark circles around his eyes.

"Are you all right, Grandfather? You don't look so good."

Grandfather started to cough, a series of deep, raspy spasms that went on for a few seconds. It was worrying. Eli started to get up. "Should I call for someone?"

But the coughing fit soon subsided and Grandfather shook his head. "It's nothing. I'm fine," he said, waving his hand. "Are you planning to make a move sometime soon, or are we going to sit here all day and talk about my health?"

Eli considered what he should do, but Grandfather seemed okay again. Plus, he could tell he'd hit a nerve, so he decided to let it go for now. Instead he reached over, picked up a red checker, and jumped three of Grandfather's black ones, including the one that had just jumped his own. Now his game piece was all the way across the board, on Grandfather's side. "King me."

Grandfather's brow furrowed. He blinked at Eli and then glowered down at the board again. Finally he laughed. He placed the lost red checker on top of Eli's victorious one. "Sharp move. You caught me with my guard down. You're improving."

Eli tried not to smile. "What about my question?"

The old man's eyes stayed on the board. He chuckled. "Oh, you *are* a troublemaker, aren't you?" he said, pulling an air-filter stick from his pocket and clamping it between his teeth.

Eli wasn't sure what to think, but he was glad Grandfather was smiling.

"You're asking serious questions, child, so I suppose I should give you serious answers." He leaned back in his chair. "You need to understand that InfiniCorp is in the business of keeping people safe and happy. It's no small task. And in the course of normal events, sometimes situations arise that the company feels could cause unnecessary concern, needless interruptions in otherwise pleasant, productive lives. Do you follow what I'm saying?"

Eli didn't, but he shrugged. He knew he would explain.

"Think about the many perils all of us face each day even in the relative safety of the domes. Unpredictable, often dangerous weather Outside. Exterior walls in need of constant repair. Continuous risk of attack from savages. The Great Sickness has passed, but we still live in troubled times. *Perilous* times." He removed the filter stick and narrowed his red-rimmed eyes. "Do you have any idea how many threats the company has to deal with at any given moment? Can you imagine what would happen if the alarm was sounded for every incident, no matter how minor? Employees would feel perpetually vulnerable. In a vast and complex organization such as ours, few people understand the lengths the company goes to in order to maintain the feeling of security. Imagine the disruption, the civil unrest, if it weren't there. What would be the purpose? The fact is, there's no point in worrying if the company is taking care of everything. And if the CloudNet helps keep the general population focused on the things the average person can control, well, all the better." He put the filter stick back in his mouth. "InfiniCorp's job is to look out for everyone so all our honest, hardworking employees can live without pointless anxiety."

Eli considered. It made a *kind* of sense, he supposed. What was the purpose of the company if everyone had to worry all the time? Even so, he wasn't sure how he felt about it.

"But what if there were real danger?" he asked. "Like, what

if it turned out there was an apocalyptic storm coming, a hurricane powerful enough to destroy the domes, and we knew about it ahead of time? Wouldn't not telling people leave them defenseless?" He realized he was pushing his luck again, but he'd already gone this far and, after all, this was Grandfather. Eli couldn't think of a better person to ask.

"An apocalyptic storm?" The old man laughed, a deep, phlegmy chuckle. "Eli, if it was really the end of the world, then what would be the point in worrying? No, the domes are strong. Believe me, I made sure of that." He gave a wry smile. "Now, what do you say we drop all this foolish talk and get back to the game? You're about to beat me, child, and I can't let that happen. I have a reputation to keep up."

Eli was alone as he trudged up to the mansion roof, where a transport pod waited to take him home. Mother and Father had both left the celebration early, pulling him aside to say that important meetings had come up unexpectedly. It was unavoidable, they said. This wasn't unusual for them. Even when they were at home, they often disappeared without warning to meetings too mysterious for Eli to understand or care about. It frustrated him each time they left him like this, just as it did now as he walked on his own to his ride home.

The moment he stepped out onto the landing pad, he heard a breathy voice: "Hello, Eli. I'm so glad I was able to catch you before you . . . *flew off*."

"Spider! What are you doing here?" His cousin's spooky, blank gaze was only inches away, and it took Eli by surprise. Without realizing it he shrank back in revulsion.

If Spider was insulted he didn't show it. "Many apologies. If I alarmed you it wasn't my intention. I've been meaning to speak with you all afternoon. It's difficult to talk openly, though, with so many . . . *ears* around. You understand? Ears that might overhear something they shouldn't?" He smiled. An insect smile.

Eli studied him. Did Spider know about the Fogger? He forced himself to appear calm. "Okay, you wanted to speak with me. So speak."

"Your brother tells me you appear somewhat . . . *overwhelmed*. It's understandable, of course, with your fourteenth birthday coming up. Believe me, I know how difficult the pressure can be. But Sebastian thinks you're more anxious than most. He's concerned about you."

Eli tried to keep his face expressionless. That was what all this was about? It had nothing to do with Foggers? But as relieved as he felt, the mention of Sebastian brought a fresh wave of irritation. Their conversation had been private. His brother shouldn't have shared anything about it with anyone. Especially Spider.

"Sebastian doesn't have to worry about me," he said at last. "Nobody does."

"Oh, but he wants to help. And so do I." Spider paused, sensing, it seemed, Eli's doubt about this. "Look, I know you and I haven't always been on the best of terms, but no matter our differences we're still cousins, am I right? Surely cousins ought to help each other whenever they can? Oh, but perhaps you disagree. Maybe kinship means nothing to you."

Eli wasn't buying a word of it. "What do you want, Spider? Just tell me."

He looked hurt. "Only what's best for you, of course. And if only you had allowed me to, I believe I could have been *most* helpful. Unfortunately all I can offer at this point is a little information. Enlightenment to ease the mind."

Eli didn't know what kind of game this was, but he figured there was no getting away unless he played along. "All right," he said. "Ease my mind how?"

"I thought it might comfort you to know that worrying is no longer necessary. Your position in the company has already been determined."

"Already determined? How can that be? I haven't even had my Final Assessment yet."

"Yes, I know. But it turns out that as a member of the Leadership Council, I have a measure of influence over the assignment process. In fact, as head of the Department of Loyalty, my input is given substantial . . . *weight,* shall we say? And it seems in your case there were special circumstances that demanded some departure from the normal procedure."

Eli's mouth went dry. "What special circumstances?"

Spider gazed down his long nose at him. His thin lips formed the faintest suggestion of a smile. "Ride the Bubble much?"

Eli's guts twisted.

"InfiniCorp takes these things rather seriously. An incident like yours would normally compel the company to take action of the most serious nature. But you're a member of the family, so this makes the situation a little less . . . *straightforward.*" He tapped his long fingers together. "I'm not supposed to mention any of this to you—not yet, anyway. The plan is to wait until Grandfather and your parents have been

160

informed. Your brother doesn't know either. But don't worry—they'll all find out by tomorrow."

"What's the company going to do with me?" Eli asked, his voice barely a whisper.

"Oh, I'm not supposed to say quite yet. And I wouldn't want to break the rules. Still, I can point out to you that the dark vaults of the Department of Inventory aren't exactly the most . . . *pleasant* of places."

Eli recoiled again.

"I've seen the underground warehouses, little cousin, and let me assure you there's not much to stimulate the imagination down there. Just thousands of shelves to climb and endless stacks of products to count, I'm afraid. Some robot supervision, but that's hardly real management, is it?" Spider leaned in closer. His grin was cruel now. "In a way, I feel sorry for you. Many would consider this a tragic fall from a great height, especially for a child so beloved by the man at the top. Such a disappointment. However, I understand you're a creative boy. I imagine you'll find a way to make it somehow . . . *bearable.*"

Eli wanted to throw up. This was far worse than anything he'd ever imagined. He took another step back and almost lost his balance.

"Now that you know, I hope you can rest easier," Spider said. "And don't forget that you did this to yourself."

Eli tried to speak but nothing would come out. Behind Spider his transport still waited for him. He stumbled backward and then scrambled across the pad.

"Take care, Eli!" Spider called, smirking from ear to ear. "I wouldn't want you to do anything rash!"

The door of the transport pod closed, and Eli threw himself onto the seat, burying his face in his arms. Even as the pod came to life and he felt the momentary vertigo that came with liftoff, he didn't open his eyes. The sick feeling threatened to take over his insides. How could he face Mother and Father now? What would he say to Sebastian? He wanted to disappear.

Soon he heard a familiar hiss, the sound of a sky hole opening above the transport. Only then did he adjust his neck and crack open his eyelids, but the view through the window was far from encouraging. Dark clouds and vast emptiness. A sputter of rain. The beginnings of yet another Outside storm. The real sky, grim and unknowable, expanded in his view and grew wider by the second until it was everything there was to see. But he didn't want to think about Outside anymore, just as he didn't want to think about InfiniCorp or Spider or anything at all. The pod slipped through the hole, and Eli tried to concentrate only on the sterile, temperature-controlled oxygen passing in and out of his lungs. As he flew farther from the dome, into the bleak nothing, he closed his eyes again and tried to block out everything except the drone of the propellers and the sensation of cool leather against his cheek.

10

girls in boots crushing

Eli returned home shaken. Not only was he still struggling to come to terms with Spider's devastating news, but now his head was throbbing. Just outside Providence his transport had passed through a violent downpour that threw him from his seat and knocked him against the wall.

As tumultuous as his day had been so far, though, it wasn't over yet.

Safe on the ground, Eli couldn't help noticing that the Providence dome was warmer than ever. Even weirder, the sky was generating odd shapes and unexpected patterns faster and with more intensity than he'd ever seen. Random images filled the dome for several minutes at a time before cycling on to something else just as startling and bizarre. One moment there was a checkerboard of lilac and avocado green, the next moment the sky swarmed with winged kitchen appliances or flying boxes of sugar-free frozen yogurt or the faces of smiling

digital babies. Every now and then words would flash meaningless messages across the dome:

```
        GIRLS IN BOOTS CRUSHING!
   ABSOLUTELY FABULOUS LEATHER ROCKY!
        YOURSELF A BETTER TEXT!
```

People stood on the sidewalks, staring up in wonder. There
was practically nothing of the old, familiar sky left.

Soon a representative from Dome Maintenance, a beautiful spokesmodel with glimmering cheek plates and thick, pink
lashes, appeared on the CloudNet to address the city.

"It's totally okay," she said. "Just a little system spaz. We're
so on top of it. We'll reboot, and after that everything's back to
plain old regular. No worries! In the meantime, *wow*! Could
the special effects *get* any cooler?" Her lashes, like stubby baby
fingers pressed around her eyes, seemed to stretch longer when
she smiled. "To help you enjoy it all, Grandfather's offering a
two-for-one on all celebration gear and handheld fans! Think
of it as an unscheduled carnival! Party it up while the light
show lasts!"

An hour later it was still happening. Eli sat moping on the
front steps of his house. He'd brought out the *Alice* book in
hopes that it might help take his mind off what had happened,
but it was futile. He slammed it shut and fought a choking
feeling in his throat. He considered pinging Father or Mother,
or maybe even Grandfather. Maybe he could try to explain.
But then again, what was the point? The truth was, he couldn't

blame Spider or anyone else. He deserved everything that was coming to him. He'd been living in a fantasy world where everything seemed like an adventure, and he'd acted like a fool. Nobody made him meet with the Fogger. It was his own fault.

By that time the sky should have been in nighttime mode, but it was still bright as midday. And even as he watched the improbable images flicker across the dome, he couldn't stop imagining Grandfather's disappointment, or Sebastian's face, red with shame. Mother and Father probably wouldn't even speak with him anymore. Why should they?

He'd let everybody down.

Maybe there's a bright side, Marilyn said, perched beside him on the step. *Inventory is an important function, after all. You never really wanted a management position anyway.*

He buried his face in his hands. Out of everyone, she should have understood. He wiped the sweat from his forehead. "Marilyn, I'm sorry you're stuck with me."

Don't be ridiculous.

"But I am. If you were a human being, you could have done great things. You're smart, smarter than me. You could have been a senior executive in whichever department you wanted. Instead you ended up . . ." He didn't finish.

As somebody's pet? she suggested.

He looked over at her. "You're nobody's pet, Marilyn. You're far more than that to me, and you know it."

Thank you, my love.

"And you knew what I meant too. I meant that you ended up stuck with the loser of all losers." He looked down at his boots. "You'd be better off without me."

Marilyn sat up on her haunches. She tried to peer into his

eyes, but he wouldn't look at her. *That's nonsense, Eli. Wherever you go, I'll go with you. Not because I have to, but because I choose to.* She nuzzled her snout against his knee. *I'll never leave you, my love. That's a promise.*

At that moment the sky, which for the past few minutes had been filled with spinning toothbrushes, soap bars, and mouthwash bottles, burst with new light. They both looked up. The background had shifted from dark green to a patch-work of swirling orange tones, from pale apricot to vivid amber and every shade in between. They watched as the hygiene prod-ucts morphed into ocean creatures: Sharks. Stingrays. Giant clams. Sea horses. Tropical fish of every size and color imagina-ble filled the dome, drifting slowly, regally, across the ginger sky. For a few long seconds, Eli and Marilyn sat still, watching the ballet of color. It was only a random pattern, an accident generated by a processing glitch, but Eli felt as if he were wit-nessing a great work of art, a masterpiece of creative genius. It made his throat tighten even more and his heart beat faster.

Leonardo . . . , whispered Marilyn.

He nodded. He was thinking the same thing.

After a while the great orange sea subsided and the glori-ous ocean creatures fizzled into simple bar codes that whizzed in circles against pulsing blobs of gray and purple. Still, Eli and Marilyn stayed quiet. The emptiness Eli had been feeling seemed deeper and heavier than ever. He burned with regret about so many things, he wasn't sure where to begin. If only he hadn't been so foolish. If only he'd listened. All his life his fam-ily had been there for him, influencing everything he did, pushing him to become the best he could be. Why wasn't that enough? What was wrong with him that he thought that he knew better, that he could somehow find his own path to himself, the *real* Eli, whoever that might be?

But his fall from grace wasn't entirely his fault, was it? There were always so many questions, so many things he didn't understand, and yet, even with all his connections, he'd been powerless to find answers. Everything was left a mystery in his family.

Eli had never felt more frustrated than he felt at that moment.

That's when he heard the tink-tonk of circus music in the distance. It was moving closer, along with the crackle of wheels rolling on brick. A high electronic voice called out to anyone close enough to hear, "Welcome to the East Side! Welcome to where the party lasts all day and the celebrating never ends!"

Eli felt the blood rushing through his veins. Even before he saw the little funbot moving up the sidewalk, waving its foam hand, he knew he would recognize it. He looked up. It was the same clown face, the same oversized plastic eyes and long antennae. One of its rubber ears was missing. There was no mistaking this droid. Soon it rolled up near his feet and came to a halt. For a long time it just stood there while he and Marilyn stared. It didn't move or say another word. Even the music went quiet. It was watching him.

"What do you want?" he asked finally, his voice shaking. "What's the message this time?"

The ends of its lips curled into an exaggerated grin. "Hello, Eli."

By then Marilyn was clinging to his leg. *Tell me what's happening. You know this droid?*

Yes, he answered silently. *It's the one I told you about.* Aloud,

167

to the funbot, he said, "I asked you a question. What are you doing here?"

"Just offering another suggestion to you, my friend," it whispered. "A pleasant way to pass the evening. If you're interested, that is."

Eli hesitated. If he were smart, he knew, he would run back into the house, lock the door, and wait until the funbot left him alone. What if people saw him with this thing? But he no longer cared. What did it matter anymore? Besides, he felt more curious about these people than ever. Grandfather had as much as admitted that the company sometimes held back the truth, and if that was right it meant the Fogger on the Bubble hadn't been lying, at least about that. Even if Eli got caught, the life he'd always known was already over. The future he'd dreamed of was gone. Here was a chance, at least, for straight answers.

"If I say yes, where would you send me?"

Marilyn's claws dug into his arm. *Eli, what are you doing? Haven't you already gotten yourself into enough trouble?*

He ignored her. His pulse quickened as he waited for an answer. Overhead, giant red letters appeared over blinking polka dots of gray on yellow:

Genuine Relaxation and Save!

The funbot didn't appear to notice. Its eyes stayed fixed on Eli. "Lovely sky tonight, don't you think? How about a nice walk to stretch your legs and enjoy the view?"

"A nice walk to stretch my legs and enjoy the view," Eli repeated. He glanced back at Marilyn.

Absolutely not! she said. *I know what you're thinking, and it's out of the question!*

Eli struggled with what to do. The robot seemed to take Eli's silence as an answer—or maybe it was just tired of waiting. In any case, its plastic eyeballs began to spin in their sockets, and its tinny music started up again. It backed up a little, turned, and began rolling down the sidewalk in the direction opposite the one it had come from.

"Wait!" Eli called. "Where are you going?"

"Follow me, Eli Papadopoulos!" it sang. "Follow me! Follow me!"

He still didn't move. On the step beside him, Marilyn was chirping frantically and knocking her snout against his arm. *Don't you do it! Don't!*

"Would it really be so bad? It's just a walk, that's all. Nothing wrong with that."

Don't play games with me, Eli! I know you better. If you go after that droid, you don't know what might happen! She rose to her full height and put her face close to his. *Just because you're upset, don't throw away your future!*

The funbot was already at the next house.

"What future? Everything I was supposed to become, everything I was meant to do, I've already failed at. Besides, I'm sick of waiting for answers that don't ever come. This is a rare chance to take charge of something in my own life. Is that so wrong?" He stood up. "You don't have to go with me. In fact, maybe it's better if you don't."

Eli started after the droid as Marilyn's voice, shrill and urgent, echoed in his brain. *What if it's a trick? What if they drag you away somewhere, never to be heard from again?*

By then he'd almost caught up with the funbot. He didn't care about being seen, not anymore. Overhead, the polka dots

169

melted away, and soon the dome ceiling swarmed with wrist-watches and cartoon animals, a field of clock faces, teddy bears, and bunnies.

Half a block later Eli heard Marilyn run up behind him. *I can't stop you from following through with this madness, so you leave me with no choice! Somebody has to be there to protect you from yourself! I'm coming with you!*

Eli knew better than to argue. He and Marilyn followed the little funbot around the corner onto Hope Street.

The area around Wayland Square was teeming with people, employees having fun in the streets as the dome whirled with color and magic. On every sidewalk and even in the roads themselves they milled around, greeting each other and point-ing up at the sky. Everywhere Eli looked were people with party accessories: flashing neckties, illuminated plastic noses, video fingernails, holographic butterflies, and planets that spun in orbits around costumed heads. A few revelers walked on glowing stilts. Each time the dome changed, the crowd roared its approval.

The little robot wove its way through the happy mob, call-ing out greetings to everyone it passed. There were so many people that Eli had a hard time keeping up. To avoid being stepped on, Marilyn leapt onto his back and held on tight under his cloak.

The funbot led them left onto Wayland and then right onto Orchard. Eli did his best to follow without appearing to. Soon they left the crowd. Eli and Marilyn found themselves drifting up Butler Avenue, past the old Victorian houses near the edge of the dome.

"Where are you taking us?" Eli asked. "There's nothing here."

The little machine didn't answer. It kept rolling up the sidewalk. Finally they came to the inside wall of the dome, where the sky sloped like a massive, near-vertical wall of light. The funbot stopped. It turned to face Eli.

"Okay, so now what?" he asked. "I don't see anybody around, and it's not like we can go *through* the dome."

The funbot only stared at him, its smile gone, its white face eerily expressionless.

I don't like this. It doesn't feel right. Marilyn's snout poked out from under Eli's collar. *It's not too late to turn back.*

Eli ignored her. He glanced around. He hardly ever came to the edge of the dome. He found it unsettling to be so close to the sky, to look into it without having to look up, and to see the line where it touched the ground. And yet the funbot must have had a reason for taking him here.

He blinked into the bright light. This close, he could just about see the individual pixels if he looked very carefully. At that moment the dome was electric pink. He reached out his hand. The light felt cool to his touch and seemed to hum against his fingertips. The peculiar color reflected off his skin, his sleeve, and everything else around him, even the houses, as if they were all part of some strange, giant sculpture made of bubble gum. He wriggled his hand in deeper and felt around to see if anything was there.

Then his fingers brushed against something hard. It was

level with his eyes and invisible behind the light. Whatever it was, it felt solid and cold, and it followed a vertical line. He grabbed hold of it and pulled, but it wouldn't budge.

What is it? Marilyn's whole head extended over his pocket now.

Eli felt around with his hands again, letting his fingers trace the shape of the thing hidden in the sky. There were two vertical bars that went almost to the ground, with horizontal rods in between.

"It's a ladder."

It makes sense. When the sky engineers climb the dome, they have to start somewhere. This must be one of the places.

The funbot began to whack Eli on his arm over and over again with its antennae—*thump! thump! thump!* Even though it didn't say a word, its meaning was clear.

"It wants me to climb." Eli craned his neck upward again. From where he stood, the sky looked gigantic, a massive wall of pink light that shot straight up for a dizzying distance before it started to curve over the city. Suddenly he was Alice staring into the mysterious bottle of liquid.

Drink me.

He squinted into the glare. It seemed like a crazy idea to leave the safety of the ground. It made him sweat just to look up at that height. And besides the danger, surely it was forbidden.

Yet he wanted to know what he would find up there.

"Marilyn, what do I do?"

On his shoulder now, she eyed the wall of light. *I don't know why you bother to ask,* she said. *You know what you're going to do.*

"Aren't you curious too?"

She turned her head and looked into Eli's eyes. *You're impossible, you know that? If we're going to do this, let's get it over with.*

Eli took a deep breath and one last glance at the funbot. By then it had stopped whacking him and was only watching.

"Climb, Eli Papadopoulos," it whispered. "Climb."

Eli grabbed the ladder with both hands and swung his legs onto it. Seconds later he was already several feet off the ground.

The higher he climbed, the warmer the air grew. Lights flickered and digital images whizzed past. A beach umbrella opened and closed overhead. A herd of floating cows grazed all around them. But this was good, Eli realized. On any other day, with the sky behaving normally, he would never have been able to get away with such a climb. At least in all this chaos there was little chance anyone would notice him.

He kept climbing, and gradually the curve of the dome sloped backward until it was necessary for him to keep one foot wrapped around a lower rung at all times to stop himself from falling. The ladder was concealed under so many pixels that Eli couldn't make out how it was fastened to the hidden girders. At least it felt steady. He tried not to look down. He concentrated on moving to the next rung, and then the next.

I think I'm going to faint, Eli. Don't look. I think I saw our house down there.

Despite himself Eli glanced over his shoulder. She was

right. He picked it out too; it looked like a green and gray Victorian dollhouse in a miniature model of his neighborhood. He was so high up, he had to look away in case he lost his balance. He wondered how the sky engineers ever got used to this. What was he doing? Maybe Sebastian was right. Maybe he really did have brain fever.

"Close your eyes if you need to!" he called. "Concentrate on holding on!"

At perhaps a hundred fifty feet above street level, just when the slope of the sky seemed almost too dangerous for him to continue climbing, the ladder's path abruptly curved into the light. He was upright again, thank god, and moving in a vertical direction. A few steps later his entire body was immersed in color. The pixels were almost too small to be distinguished from each other, and yet like reeds being bent back in an overgrown pond they moved apart as he climbed, creating a path. All around, three-dimensional digital images formed and drifted and broke apart. Two gorillas in short summer dresses waved shopping bags. A beautiful salesgirl with long earrings held up a cup of blue liquid and sighed like she'd just discovered true love.

From overhead boomed a female voice, calm and cheerful but loud as a thunderclap. "PARDON OUR APPEARANCE. WE ARE EXPERIENCING TECHNICAL DIFFICULTIES."

Marilyn screeched, burying her face in Eli's cloak. Eli almost lost his grip, but he caught himself. The voice was so thunderous that he was certain people all the way on the ground would hear it.

"WE APOLOGIZE FOR ANY INCONVENIENCE

AND ASSURE YOU THERE IS NO CAUSE FOR ALARM. INFINICORP IS TAKING CARE OF EVERYTHING. ENJOY! CELEBRATE! WHY NOT VISIT THE MALL?"

Eli tried to ignore all the distractions as he continued climbing higher and higher. Soon he'd climbed so deep into the layers of light that he could barely see the ground. Eventually his hand brushed against something unexpected—some kind of ledge. It was just to one side of the ladder. He stopped climbing.

"What do you suppose this is for?"

I don't know, and I don't care. Marilyn's face was still hidden under his cloak. She was shaking.

Eli reached out and pulled himself onto the iron grating. He wanted to explore, but it was hard to see much through all the flashing images and whirling colors. He felt around with his hands. On the far end of the ledge he found a smooth surface, flat and cool like glass. He wondered if he'd reached the inner wall of the dome. It was possible, but he wasn't sure. He parted the light with his hands and peered through. Whatever the surface was, it reflected his face like a mirror. And then his fingers discovered something round and solid protruding toward him. He gripped it and found that it could turn.

This was no mirror, he realized. He remembered the sky engineer he'd seen climbing the dome, and the crack of darkness she'd climbed through.

"Marilyn, I think we've found a door."

She wriggled under his cloak until her head poked out into the light again. She didn't say a word. Eli tried to gather his courage. In his mind he was picturing the white-eyed Outsider. *So, what'll it be, then? In or Out?*

He took a deep breath, and then he twisted the knob and pushed.

The door slowly swung open.

11

a new mission

It had been almost three weeks since Tabitha was brought to the reeducation facility, and still she hadn't agreed to join the other Waywards on the production floors. Representative Shine had even mentioned to her that Tabitha's was one of the longest-ever stays in the admissions ward. "But that's fine," she said. "You'll let me know when you're ready for the next step. I have faith in you."

The truth was, Tabitha was a lot calmer now than she'd been at first.

She still thought about Ben sometimes, but less and less often. She'd pretty much gotten over her disappointment in him and in the Friends. All she felt now was regret that she'd allowed herself to be so taken in. And even though she understood that her newfound peace of mind came, at least in part, from the influence of the CloudNet sphere over her bed, it didn't bother her much. After carrying the secret weight of her dual life for so long, it was a relief to let the burden go. It wasn't as if the Friends had turned out to have had anything real to offer. They had abandoned her. That much was obvious by now. So, for a change, why not allow herself to be *happy* that InfiniCorp was taking care of her?

Life wasn't really so bad here.

In fact, it was pretty okay.

By then she rarely left her bed. She knew the facility's whole CloudNet menu practically by heart. For hours at a time, she explored its passageways and lost herself in her favorite dream games. She appreciated the way the sphere kept everything else at bay. As if a switch had been flipped, her worries would disappear, and all that remained would be a light-headed, radiant feeling. She'd never experienced it like this at home. Even the room was starting to glitter.

One day Tabitha awoke from her afternoon nap overflowing with gratitude for this place, which had made her feel so cared for even after everything she'd done. She wanted to do what she knew was right. She yearned to make Representative Shine proud of her. So the next time the angel-faced girl came in to clear away the snack tray, she stopped her.

"What's the matter, Tabitha? Something wrong?"

"Nothing," she said. "I—I just wanted to let you know, I'm ready now."

Representative Shine didn't say anything. She stepped back to the side of the bed, set the tray down, and took Tabitha's hand.

She looked so happy.

* * *

Throughout that night, her last in the white room, Tabitha drifted in and out of sleep, imagining what might lie ahead for her the next day. Whatever it was, it would be very different from her old job at the Department of Intern Relations, that was for sure. She hoped she would live up to company expectations this time.

Early that morning, about an hour before wake-up, a blue-uniformed employee came to disinfect her bathroom. This wasn't unusual. Twice a week since she'd been in the tower, they had come in to sterilize the toilet and run a mop over the tile floor. There were no robots here—at least, none that she'd seen. It was as if nothing in this facility had been modernized in many years. The Cleaners never said a word. They just came in, did their job, and left. Tabitha had learned to ignore them by then.

But that morning the Cleaner was one she'd never seen before. A muscular girl with a wide nose and a mole under one eye, she appeared to linger near the end of the bed, sorting through the sterilizers in her equipment cart longer than seemed necessary. And Tabitha got the weird feeling she was watching her. To be honest, it made her uncomfortable. Had she done something wrong? Was she in some kind of trouble?

She closed her eyes and pretended to fall back asleep. But that was when the girl whispered to her:

"Sister Tabitha . . ."

She opened her eyes. The girl was standing over her now, looking into her face. She spoke again: "A single thread of reality can be hard to distinguish in a complex fabric of illusion."

Tabitha thought it was an odd thing to say. Yet at the same

time it stirred something unexpected in her, like a distant memory. She felt sure she'd heard it before, but when?

"The sour milk smell. Think about that. Concentrate on it."

It was funny, but until that moment she'd almost forgotten about the bad smell. She'd become so used to it, in fact, that she hadn't thought about it in what seemed like ages. But now she realized it was still there.

"It's the stench of the ocean acidifying," the girl continued, "the marine macrofauna collapsing. The ocean is almost dead now, but you can use the smell as a lifeline. Focus on it. Follow it out of the haze and back to reality."

Somewhere in the deep recesses of her consciousness, Tabitha felt a vague rush. Yes, she did remember something about this from the secret meetings and whispered conversations. Something about the end of the world. With the Cleaner's dark eyes on her, Tabitha did what she was told. She concentrated, trying her best to isolate the unpleasant odor from all the other distracting sensations. Soon she could feel it burning at her nose once more, and as it did, her other perceptions seemed to come back into sharper focus. The room stopped shimmering. All at once she experienced clarity like she hadn't felt in days, maybe even weeks.

She sat up. "Get me out of here."

"It wouldn't be easy," the fake Cleaner answered. "This place is a fortress, and we're three hundred miles from land."

"Are you saying it can't be done?"

The girl paused. "There would be risks, but the Friends have the means to make it happen."

"I don't care about the risks! I'll take the chance!" She slipped out of bed and started to reach for her clothes. "So, how is it done? Are you going to sneak me onto a boat or something? Smuggle me out in a box? Tell me what to do and I'll do it."

"Whoa, hold on. Escape isn't what the Friends have in mind for you."

Tabitha stopped. It took a moment for this to sink in. "But . . . but I have to get out of here. I want to go home, back to the domes."

The girl shook her head. "You can't go back to the artificial cities, Tabitha. Not ever. You need to accept that."

Tabitha's stomach sank. She took a deep breath. "All right. Outside, then. I'll live in the desert. Somehow I'll find a way to survive out there."

"You don't understand, and we're running out of time. The Elders have already decided what you'll do. Your ability to fight the spheres is exceptionally strong. There aren't many who could snap out of a CloudNet trance like you just did— not in *this* place, anyway. Do you realize that?" She glanced nervously at the door. "We have a new mission for you. Things happen for a reason, Sister. The Elders never intended for you to be captured, but now that you're here, they believe this is what was meant to be. The best way for you to aid the cause is to remain here as our operative. You'll be a lone conscious agent, an unsuspected Friend among the sleeping Waywards."

Tabitha couldn't believe what she was hearing. "So . . . you're just going to *leave* me here? How could that help any—?"

"I have news about Brother Ben."

That stopped Tabitha midsentence. By then Ben felt like a distant part of her life, an old, shameful mistake that was behind her now. "You don't have to tell me. I already know. Ben was a traitor. He gave up names, including mine. And then he killed himself."

The girl shook her head. "Not true. If that's what they told you, it was a lie."

Tabitha opened her mouth to speak but then closed it. Standing by the side of her bed and blinking into the face of this girl, she felt like the whole world had frozen to a halt.

"Ben wasn't a traitor. He didn't give anybody away. He tried to find you. After you were taken, he disobeyed the Friends and snuck Outside to search for you. He called out your name in the ruins. That was how he ended up getting captured, and then soon afterward he died trying to escape. But it was all for you. He did everything he could to try to get you back."

She felt like the air had been knocked out of her. So she'd been wrong to lose her trust in Ben after all? After weeks of believing that he betrayed her, now she was supposed to switch gears again and accept that he'd been a good friend—and a good *Friend*—all along? As much as she wanted to, it was hard. She'd been twisted back and forth so many times, she wasn't sure whom or what to trust anymore. Why should she doubt the Friends any less than she doubted the company? Hadn't they *both* done enough damage to her already?

"Ben devoted his life to serving the Greater Purpose," continued the whispering Friend. "He would have wanted you to do this for us. Now is not the time to lose faith. You know what's coming. You know that securing any future at all will require personal sacrifice from each of us." She leaned in closer. "We all have our tasks, Sister Tabitha, and this is yours. The Friends are counting on you."

Tabitha's jaw tightened. Where were the Friends when she'd been surrounded by company thugs Outside by the St. Louis dome? Where had they been all this time she'd been in the tower, counting on *them*? The girl with the mole went silent, waiting for an answer, but Tabitha was struggling with the wave of heat rising inside her. She clenched her fists.

"What's wrong with you people?" she said at last. "How could you use me like this? How can you ask me to stay here, rotting my life away for you?"

"Sister, you made a solemn oath. If you really believe, as the Friends do, that el Guía is coming, then why should you doubt the wisdom of the Elders?"

Tabitha blinked at her. She realized that this was the problem. She *didn't* believe. After all she'd given up for the Friends, she wasn't willing to give any more for a savior who wasn't coming. It was just another illusion. She spoke through her teeth now: "You're as bad as they are."

Suddenly she reached back and slammed her fist into the girl's face. The fake Cleaner's hand flew to her nose. She staggered backward, sinking against the wall.

Tabitha took a step forward and stood over her. "Tell the Friends no thanks. I'm done making sacrifices for them or anyone else."

The girl gaped at her, eyes wide. A thin line of blood trickled down her wrist. After a moment she pulled herself to her feet. With Tabitha still glaring, she wiped herself with a napkin and then wheeled her cart back to the door. She turned to Tabitha one last time.

"The Elders won't take this lightly."

When it was clear she would get no answer, the fake

Cleaner wheeled her cart into the corridor and closed the door quietly behind her. Tabitha's fists were still clenched. She almost wished the Friends hadn't woken her. At the end of all things that mattered, would it really have been so wrong to leave her feeling okay? Maybe it would have been better that way.

She didn't know.

All she knew was that she was alone. Nobody was looking out for her. Not the Friends. Not the company. Nobody. She'd almost let herself forget that nothing was black and white, just shades of gray everywhere you turned. But she was done trying to figure out what was right and wrong. So little was in her control, anyway. She couldn't save the world any more than she could have saved Ben. The only future she had any chance of rescuing was her own.

If she was ever going to find her way out of here, then she couldn't count on help from anybody else. Which was fine by her. Because from now on the only person she was going to look out for was herself.

12

through the looking glass
and what eli found there

The reflecting door swung shut behind him. Eli and Marilyn found themselves in a long, cramped room with a low ceiling and a musty odor. In here the coolers were so strong, there was a chill in the air. From somewhere up ahead they heard a soft mechanical hiss, followed by silence, followed by another hiss, at regular intervals. Eli squinted into the gloom. Across the long walls were shelves piled high with what looked like salvaged parts from electronic equipment: burned microchips, light generators, wire scraps, lengths of pixel tubing, and countless other gadgets and electronic parts Eli couldn't even identify.

"It looks like a high-tech junkyard," Eli whispered.

What now? Marilyn asked, hiding under his cloak.

"I don't know."

He took a tentative step into the clutter, then another, squeezing his way between wooden crates that were scattered all over the floor. The room seemed to go on so far that he couldn't even see the opposite end. The intermittent hiss grew louder as he moved deeper in. Long shadows flickered across the ceiling like ghosts.

Suddenly Marilyn squirmed. *Wait! Don't move!*

Eli froze. "What's the matter?"

We are not alone.

Eli peered across the mess and tried to scan the room, but he didn't see anything that caught his attention. What he heard, though, was the hissing machine, close now, cycling through its repetitive process. *Hisss.* Stop. *Hisss.* Stop. *Hisss.* What was it, anyway?

Out of the corner of his eye, he saw something move.

Eli!

He spun around. A figure was crouched on the floor. Eli's breath caught. It wasn't just that somebody was there, watching him from the shadows; it was that this stranger was one of the most frightening visions Eli had ever come across. His face was covered with so many leathery scars, it was painful to look at. He had long gray hair and a dirty white beard. He was obviously an Outsider. He wore a hooded environment suit, threadbare, and a menacing black glove that went all the way up his left arm. His other hand was exposed, and the skin was wrinkled and lined with veins. He looked ancient, at least as old as Grandfather. Then Eli noticed something hanging over his shoulder, a metallic cylinder that swelled and shrank with each breath the savage took. It appeared to be some kind of respirator, and Eli realized it was making the hissing sound.

Eli felt his courage return. Whoever this poor creature was, he was too old and frail to be dangerous. "What are you doing here, Outsider?"

"Waiting for *you*," he said, his voice as raspy and dry as the desert, "the errant Papadopoulos, the grandchild who called out for the truth. I wanted to meet for myself the boy who would risk climbing the sky just to find out what nobody else would tell him."

Eli stared. He had only just finished climbing the sky. How could this old man have known what Eli would do before it even happened?

"No," he said. "I meant, how did you make it past the perimeter Guardians?"

"There are ways. Hidden paths. If you know where to look."

Eli couldn't help shivering. He'd been in here only a short while and already he was cold. He glanced around at the jumble of boxes and equipment again. "What is this place?"

"This is a sky chamber, one of several hidden in the inner crust of the dome." His respirator hissed. "Some are for sky control, some for storing test equipment. This one holds refurbished dome parts." He gestured at the space on the floor beside him. "Sit."

Eli took a step forward.

Don't, Eli! I don't trust him.

Marilyn had kept so still under his cloak that he'd almost forgotten she was there. But Eli didn't need the warning. This was only the second Outsider he'd ever spoken with, and he was already wary. He squatted to get a better look at the decrepit old man, but he wasn't about to sit next to him.

"So," he said, "do you believe the same crazy stuff the kid on the Bubble does? About how the world is about to come to an end and all that?"

The Outsider smiled, revealing two uneven rows of jagged yellow teeth. "Tell me, in your InfiniCorp training, have you learned much about the rapid rise of carbon levels in the planet's atmosphere? Have they shown you charts or graphs or anything that demonstrates its alarming rate of increase over the past few decades?"

Eli considered but shook his head.

"Then let me be the one to enlighten you." The old man paused while his respirator expanded again. "The point of no return for Earth is about four hundred and fifty carbon-equivalent units per million. Do you have any idea what that number is at the present time, Eli Papadopoulos, as you and I sit here in air-conditioned comfort?" He bent forward so that his nose was uncomfortably close to Eli's. "Nine hundred and eighty."

Eli rose and took a step back. This Outsider was giving him the creeps.

"There's something very wrong out there," he continued. "Long after the passing of the Great Sickness, it's still gathering strength. For now, the machine that runs your life keeps your attention elsewhere, but just beyond your vision lies an ever-expanding wasteland of desert and death. Eli, the end of the world as we've known it has already happened, you just haven't realized it yet. You're like an oyster in a steaming pot, blissfully unaware that you're being cooked alive."

Eli studied him. "If it's already over, then why are you

here? What do you and the other Foggers hope to gain by coming into the domes?"

The old man's lip curled. He pointed a gnarled finger at Eli. "If your house was on fire and your family were asleep inside," he shouted, "would you do *nothing*?"

Eli took another step backward. Coming here had been a mistake. He spun around and dashed to the door. It wouldn't budge.

"It's locked!" When he turned to look back again, the bent figure was standing. His nose stuck out from between the two curtains of dirty gray hair that framed his face. Eli felt his blood rush. "You did this!" he shouted. "You can't keep me here—my family will never let you get away with it! Unlock the door!"

The Outsider's voice was calm. "I didn't lock it. If it won't open, it means the sky must be rebooting."

"Rebooting? What does that have to do with anything?" Eli grabbed the knob again and started yanking with all his might, but it wouldn't move. "Let me out! Let me out!"

"Listen to me, Eli. When the system resets, the dome is at its most vulnerable. It's standard procedure for the company to secure all the sky chambers during any reboot. In a few minutes they should be released automatically, but in the meantime both of us are locked in here."

Eli slammed his fist against the door. "Why should I believe you? How would you know how the domes work?"

"Because," he answered, "I designed them."

Eli felt Marilyn scrambling under his cloak. *Enough lies! I'll make him open the door!* She burst into the air, baring her teeth.

In an instant she bounded across the tops of the crates and flew at the old man. He held up his gloved hand, so she sank her teeth into his forearm. But the Outsider didn't even flinch. While Marilyn dangled from his arm, hissing and scratching, he calmly reached with his free hand and dislodged her as if he didn't feel a thing.

Marilyn's whole body went rigid. Eli watched the grizzled figure lift her by the scruff of the neck, dangle her, helpless, in the air, and then gaze into her face with what looked like a strange mixture of amusement and reverence.

"There you are, little altered creature, cheated queen of the wild. I was wondering when you'd come out of your hiding place and say hello."

Panicked, Eli charged across the room. "Don't you dare hurt her! Leave her alone, filthy desert snake!"

Before he was even halfway to Marilyn, though, the Outsider had already lowered her gently to the floor and let her go. The instant she was free, she dashed at Eli and leapt into his arms. He pulled her close. *Are you all right?*

Her orange eyes were wide with surprise and fear. *I think so . . . There's something wrong with his arm. It's—it's not alive!*

Eli looked her over. She appeared dazed but okay. He glared across the room again. "What just happened? She tells me your arm isn't alive."

"*Does* she, now?" He raised his glove and gazed at it. "Well, she's right. I lost my original years ago. This one is a prosthesis, a mere substitute." He flexed the fingers and tapped his forearm. Where Marilyn's teeth had torn through the leather, Eli could now see shiny blue plastic. It looked like the same material sometimes used for droid casings.

190

The Outsider's left arm was robotic.

"I assure you I mean Marilyn no harm," he said, his respirator still expanding and contracting on his back. "After all, I believe that before this is all over, she'll have an important role to play."

"How do you know her name?" Eli demanded. "And what do you mean, she has a role to play? How could you possibly know what's going to happen?"

"Know?" He shook his head. "I don't *know* anything. What's yet to come isn't fixed like the scenes of a play, waiting only to be acted out onstage. The future is misty and forever shifting with the changing tides of the present. What little I have foreseen came to me only as a possibility in a vision—as fixed as the wind, as substantial as a cloud."

"You saw Marilyn in a *dream*?"

Marilyn climbed onto Eli's shoulder. *Can there be any doubt his brain is fevered?*

For a moment the old man didn't respond. He seemed to recognize the incredulous tone in Eli's voice, because finally he said, "I've lived in the wasteland a long time. The desert has a way of enhancing one's perceptions. It expands the senses and sharpens the mind."

Eli grunted. "Some would say it *twists* the mind."

The Outsider smiled almost imperceptibly. "As you wish."

Eli noticed something on the floor near the old man's feet. It was the *Alice* book. In all the confusion it must have slipped out of his pocket. The Outsider saw it too. He reached down and picked it up.

"What have we here?"

"Give that back!" Eli demanded. "It's mine!"

"Is it, indeed? Then you might want to be more careful with it. They aren't making any more of these, you know." He examined the cover. "So, tell me, what do you think of Lewis Carroll?"

Eli only glared.

"Since I was a boy, I've been captivated by Alice's story. The genius is in the author's inventiveness with logic and facility with the absurd. You can read it again and again and each time find something new and intriguing." He ran his finger tenderly along the binding, and as he did so a realization dawned on Eli.

"The Outsider I saw under the streets," he said. "It was you, wasn't it?"

He nodded.

Eli studied him with renewed curiosity. How could such a decrepit old desert rat make his way so easily in and out of the dome's support systems? The ragged figure took a step toward him. He narrowed his eyes at Eli and recited:

> "'The time has come,' the Walrus said,
> 'To talk of many things:
> Of shoes—and ships—and sealing-wax—
> Of cabbages—and kings—
> And why the sea is boiling hot—
> And whether pigs have wings.'"

As he spoke, he inched forward. Now he was so close that Eli could make out the individual wrinkles on his scarred face. If there was ever any question whether he was crazy, this speech should have been Eli's proof. Yet there was something in his eyes that kept him from backing away.

"The world is overheated," the old man said, handing the book back to him. "The polar ice caps have long since melted away. The oceans have risen and acidified. All over the planet, entire ecosystems have already collapsed: animals, plants, fish, birds—countless species, gone forever. Many others are greatly reduced in number and barely surviving, whether through adaptation or migration in search of cooler temperatures. And people are no exception. Pestilence and dwindling resources have already reduced our numbers too and continue to cut the average human life span shorter. There used to be a lot more old people, but sickness and hardship take most of us earlier than they once did. It's evolution on steroids, survival of the fittest. In or outside the domes, those without youth, strength, and cunning rarely last long in this harsh new landscape. Those few of us old-timers who survive do so only with the aid of exceptional resourcefulness and extraordinary luck—not to mention special technology." He gestured toward his respirator. "I don't say this to frighten you, Eli. It's just the new reality. Human life as we've known it is drawing to a rapid close. And, despite what you've been told, it's still heating up out there. The old world is gone, and only the insects rejoice. Bugs are the only winners in the Great Warming."

Eli hesitated to speak. He didn't really believe what he was hearing, but he wasn't sure either. "Even if what you say is true, we must be able to reverse it somehow. There has to be something we can do."

The Outsider shook his head. "It's too late for that. We're

at the end of a process many years in the making, triggered back when the massive overuse of oil, coal, and natural gas for energy first began to trap the sun's heat in the atmosphere. Mankind has been preparing the groundwork for its own undoing for a long time."

"And nobody knew?"

"Oh, many knew. Scientists across the globe were long ago in agreement about what was happening and spent years raising the alarm. Unfortunately those with the ability to do something about it on a large scale simply chose not to."

"That doesn't make sense," Eli said. "Why would anyone choose not to?"

The old man shrugged. "All the power in too few hands. Few incentives for those at the top to act against their own short-term interests. It was easier to deny the evidence in favor of assuming it was mere science fiction, a case of Henny Penny calling out that the sky was falling. Believing meant making changes. Why risk ruining a good thing when there was wealth and power to cling to? And make no mistake, Eli, those at the top wielded mighty power indeed. They held even the ability to convince massive numbers of people that the science itself was simply wrong. And it's no surprise they were able to persuade the general public of this. Everyday people *wanted* the science to be wrong. Who could blame them? Who wants to believe that worldwide calamity is just around the corner?"

He took another drag through his respirator. Eli could sense that even Marilyn was waiting anxiously for him to continue.

"But soon the impact of accelerating climate change grew too obvious to explain away. Rapid disintegration of glaciers, diminishing shorelines, parched farmland. Increasingly violent weather brought frequent tornadoes and record flooding to major cities all over the world. Island nations started to disappear under water. Diseases like malaria were spreading. Even the timing of the seasons had changed. Soon the evidence of a heating planet became so undeniable that the company had to find another way to conceal the truth. So they came up with a new strategy: the domes."

"Wait," said Eli. "So you're saying the company leadership—my *family*—knows all this stuff but is *hiding* it? That's outrageous! If it weren't for Grandfather, we'd all be dead!"

The old man nodded. "That's true."

"So how can you accuse my family of wanting to deceive everyone? It's ridiculous!"

"Is it?" The Outsider's eyebrow was raised, but then his voice went softer. "For what it's worth, your family elders weren't the only ones who inadvertently helped along the warming process—the same process that triggered the Great Sickness in the first place, before your Grandfather's leadership and luck prevented it from wiping us out of existence. In some ways the Papadopouloses were no worse than anyone else in earlier days who stood by and didn't act. But the fact is, from its first years running the country, InfiniCorp fanned the flames of an irresponsible and unsustainable lifestyle. Eventually the damage to the earth's ability to cool itself became irreversible. Mother Nature's vengeance was like an oncoming steamroller nobody could stop. In time the senior leadership of InfiniCorp came to recognize the world's fate. I'm sorry to be the one to tell you, Eli, but they understood long ago that the end is coming."

"No, that's a lie!"

"In some ways, building the domes was an act of mercy. It provided a way to fend off despair, to prolong the old, comforting ways and delay facing reality for a few decades. And why not? Management had the power to pull it off, and they saw no better alternative. By isolating the employees in cocoons of illusion, they can at least keep their consumer base for a while, the powerful can stay in control, and the money and good times can keep rolling—until the resources at last run dry or the storms knock the domes out of commission. Either way, they've always known it's only a matter of time before the party comes to its inevitable, blistering end."

"You're wrong!" Eli shouted. "Your brain is fried! My family cares about the employees!"

"Eli," he said, his voice steady and calm, "Grandfather is scared. Your aunts and uncles and parents too. They know what's coming. The company is already losing control. In your heart you know what I'm saying is true."

"How would you know any of this? You don't have any idea what my family was thinking. Why would a Fogger like you know anything about the inner workings of the company?"

"Because," he said, "I was there. Long ago I was part of it, a senior leader at the very elbow of your grandfather. Oh yes, we were quite close. Childhood friends, in fact. Almost like brothers. You find this hard to believe? Well, I can't say I blame you. These days you'd be hard-pressed to find evidence. Any record of me or my service has long since been wiped from the archives."

Eli's head was spinning. On his shoulder Marilyn was getting even more agitated. He felt her claws digging into him.

Try the door again, Eli. If he was right about the reboot, maybe it's over by now and we can get out of here.

Eli started backing away again. What he was hearing couldn't be true, and yet he remembered what Grandfather had hinted at, that there really might be cases in which the company felt that hiding the truth was in the best interest of the people. But surely not with something so gigantic as *this*— the end of the world! Besides, he'd also said the earth was cooling, not warming, and Grandfather would never lie to him. Eli made a decision. He was going to find out the truth, no matter what it was. The moment he got back home, he would ping Grandfather. He wasn't supposed to interrupt him at work but he felt sure Grandfather would take his transmit. And then Eli would tell him everything, no matter the consequences. Grandfather would clear it all up. In the meantime Eli wasn't about to accept what some brain-addled Outsider said about his family.

He refused to believe it.

"I made a mistake coming here," he said, still backing off. "Now I want you to keep away from me. I don't want to hear from you people ever again."

"You can deny us, but not forever. It won't be long before you'll be with us once and for all."

At the door now, Eli grabbed the handle and pulled. This time it opened without undue effort. A sudden gust of warm air blew into the room, bringing some relief from the frigid air.

Eli and Marilyn gazed out at the dome ceiling. The bright, swirling light they'd climbed through only minutes earlier was gone. Now there was only the glow of the digital moon and a sky full of beautiful stars. The dome was in nighttime mode. Whatever the issues were, InfiniCorp had finally taken care of them.

Marilyn chirped with relief as Eli ducked through the door and onto the ledge. Just when he started toward the ladder, though, something seized his wrist. It was cold and hard, and it held tight. He spun around.

"Join us!" the old man hissed. "Help us defy the authority whose negligence helped send all humanity down the path to extinction!"

Eli tried to struggle but the robotic grip was too strong. "If you're asking me to work against my own family, to be your mole inside the organization, I won't do it! Never! If you really could see the future, you would already know that! I'm a Papadopoulos!"

"Yes, but you're a special case. You always have been, Eli, and you've always known it. It's why you've never been able to follow the road your family laid out for you."

Eli's pulse was racing. He remembered the day of the blast and the damage the bomb had done to the air filter. He could still picture the dead girl in the mud. He would never be a part of that. This man, if you could even call him that anymore, was out of his mind. Eli flailed his legs and his free arm, trying his best to punch or kick the Outsider so he'd let go. He was concentrating so much on escaping, though, that he lost track of where he was on the ledge.

Just as Marilyn was getting ready to pounce again, Eli lost his balance and slipped.

Marilyn shrieked. *Eli, look out!*

But it was too late. He tumbled over the edge. The next thing he knew, he was dangling in the air hundreds of feet over the city of Providence. The *Alice* book slipped from his pocket, and he saw it tumble down, down, toward the rooftops until it was too small to see. The Outsider still had him by the wrist, but he was gritting his teeth with the effort of holding on. There was no telling how long he would last. Eli's legs kicked uselessly among the pixels.

Help me! Marilyn!

Marilyn peered down at him in horror. Beside her the old man grunted and cursed, all his concentration focused on keeping hold of Eli. But Marilyn could only watch. She screeched, jerking her head back and forth as she tried to think of what to do.

I can't, Eli! I'm too small! Don't let go!

Eli had no intention of letting go if he could help it, but even as adrenaline flooded through him, he couldn't stop himself from thinking how pathetic his life was. After everything he'd been worrying about—wasting his life away in a low-level job assignment, being kidnapped and dragged away by Foggers, even facing down the end of the world—how ironic that he would end up falling to his death after slipping on a ledge. He couldn't even scream, because there was still a part of him that cared if people on the ground looked up and noticed him dangling in the night sky.

But soon the Outsider's efforts paid off. With surprising

strength he managed to lift Eli back toward him, close enough that Eli was able to grab the iron grating himself. Seconds later he landed in a heap on the ledge. Even then the robotic hand still didn't let up. It grabbed Eli by the collar and yanked him to his feet.

"I know what you feel when you close your eyes," he said, breathing into Eli's face now. "I know the emptiness, the awareness of change coming. But you should know that all hope is not yet lost. Your broken animal friend wasn't the only one I saw in the dream prophecy. There was another, an indistinct shadow of a child, a powerful desert thief whose disciples would follow him anywhere."

Over his shoulder Eli could see Marilyn creeping up behind him. *I can jump him again, Eli! I can scratch his eyes out! What do you want me to do?*

No! Eli said silently. *Wait!*

"This shadowy figure I saw," the old man continued, "held the final fate of humanity in his hands. Save or destroy. His choice would determine our destiny. For years I've been watching for him, el Guía, the great leader who will launch the final revolution. And now at last I've found him." His face came even closer. "It's *you*, Eli. Guiding the battle march at the end of the world is your special destiny."

"You're crazy! I'm no leader! I'm just a kid!"

"Is it such a crazy idea? You're the grandchild of the CEO of all InfiniCorp. It's not a stretch to imagine that his cunning might have been passed on to you. What's more, you've already shown abilities that few possess, including the strength to resist the pull of the CloudNet. No, it *is* you. I can feel it. You're the one Fate has chosen to fulfill the prophecy. Whatever hope is left for the ragtag remains of humanity, you hold it in your hands. The day of reckoning is almost here. Come. Lead us. Guide us through the approaching upheaval to the place we all must go."

Eli couldn't believe what the Outsider was saying. Even as the respirator hissed and the robotic grip tightened, he could only stare into the cold, intelligent eyes that were searching his own.

"Where do you mean?" he asked, his voice barely a whisper. "Are you talking about the Wild Orange Yonder?"

The old man didn't respond, but in his gaze the answer was clear.

"Who are you?"

"In the wasteland I have many aliases: Samuel the Trickster, Old Gus the Fool, el Viejo del Desierto, just to name a few. To keep my anonymity I've even feigned my own death. Seldom do I reveal my true identity, even to my allies, because those who know it face great danger. But *you,* Eli, need to know if you're ever going to understand." A lock of gray hair fell into his eyes, and he brushed it back with his natural hand. Eli noticed something on his palm. A tattoo. It was that image again: the blazing sun with the jagged, twisting rays. "Long ago the official company records showed my name as Dr. S. G. Friedmann, but always my middle name was the one used by those who knew me best. My real name," he said into Eli's ear, "is Gustavo."

At last he let go. Eli's feet hit the metal grate again, and for a moment he stayed frozen, still gaping at the ancient creature. Marilyn tugged at his trouser leg.

Eli, let's go home!

He took a step back. This time the Outsider didn't try to stop him. At the far side of the ledge, and with Marilyn clinging to his cloak, he swung himself onto the ladder. Then he scrambled down through the night sky. After a few rungs, when he felt the immediate danger was over, he craned his neck upward again.

The grizzled old face was still peering over the ledge, still watching.

13

the way of the future

Safe on the ground again, Eli and Marilyn made their way home through darkened streets. Eli kept checking over his shoulder in case anybody was following. Now that he'd firmly and finally refused to join the Foggers, who could guess how they might try to take their fanatical vengeance on him?

It just doesn't add up, he observed silently to Marilyn. *How could an old desert rat have designed the domes? And why would anyone say such unforgivable things about my family? That Outsider must have been so brain fevered, he didn't know what he was saying. When the masked boy told me Gustavo was taken by the desert, I thought he meant he was dead.* Eli kept his head low and ducked down Angell Street. *How is anybody supposed to figure out what's real and what isn't?*

I don't know, my love.

Within minutes they were home again. They shot inside and Eli locked the front door behind them. His dinner was still waiting for him on the kitchen table, but he rushed past it.

He found Claudia dozing on the sofa with the CloudNet still on and a flashing party hat tilted on her head. She'd been out celebrating on the street with all the others, Eli guessed, and now she was spent. Nobody appeared in the sphere to tell him there were any messages, which was a relief. It meant he had at least until morning before he would have to face Mother and Father.

He charged up the stairs and into his room. "Heather, please put me through to Grandfather."

Marilyn trailed behind him. *Do you think it's such a good idea to admit you climbed the sky and met this Outsider? It's only going to make things worse for you.*

What am I supposed to do? Grandfather knows the truth, and he's the only one I can trust to tell me. Besides, if Grandfather really did know this guy once, then maybe if I help the company track him down, it might lead them to forgive me someday.

Marilyn looked skeptical.

Heather appeared in the sphere. "Oh hi, sweetie," she said, looking adorable in a short-sleeved blouse with swirling colors and the words *I Survived the Providence Sky Freak-out, and All I Got Was This Lousy T-shirt* written across the chest. Behind her a mariachi band played peppy music while a crowd of digital people danced. "I'm heading out to join my friend Betty at the afterparty at Club Babyhead! Want to come?"

Eli ignored her. The Heather program was constantly coming up with new ways to maintain the illusion that she was real. Everybody knew she wasn't, of course, but the company had done extensive market research and found that consumers enjoyed the fantasy that CloudNet assistants had lives of their own. Last month Heather had gone through an emotional breakup with a fictional boyfriend.

"Didn't you hear me? I have to speak with my grandfather."

"Oh, don't get all in a huff. I heard. God, you can be a ping-kill sometimes, you know that?" The music wound down and the dancers walked dejectedly away. After that, Heather was all business. "Okay, so what's this about? Grandfather's a busy guy, and you know you're not supposed to disturb him at work."

"But he's *always* at work. Listen, I'm his grandson and I need to ask him something. Just ping him, please. I think he'll answer when he hears it's me, especially if you say it's important."

She rolled her eyes. "All right, all right, Mr. Man on a Mission. I'll put you through, and you can tell him yourself." She faded, and a moment later the sphere filled with the smiling face of Grandfather's personal assistant, Doug. Doug was synthetic too, an earnest-looking guy with a tweed jacket and just a touch of gray around the ears. Eli had spoken with him before, but not often.

"Good evening, Eli. I hear you're looking for Grandfather. Unfortunately he's in a meeting at the moment."

"This late?" He looked at his watch. "It's almost ten at night."

"I'm afraid so. Is everything okay?"

Eli bit his lip. Even though he should have expected this, he couldn't help feeling disappointed. "No, actually, it's not."

"What's the matter? I can take a message if you'd like."

Eli was surprised he didn't seem to know about his job

assignment yet, but then again maybe it wouldn't be coded into the CloudNet until it was official. At Eli's feet Marilyn's whiskers twitched, her eyes still on him.

"I don't know. . . ." He curled and uncurled his fingers in his pockets. "It's kind of . . . private."

"I assure you, any message left with me will be kept in the strictest of confidence."

Eli considered. How could he leave just enough information to ensure that Grandfather would ping him back but not enough to get him in trouble before they had a chance to talk? He had to choose his words carefully. "All right," he said. "Tell him I met somebody today, someone who says he used to be friends with him years ago. He told me a bunch of crazy stuff, stuff I don't believe. Anyway, please ask Grandfather to ping me as soon as he can. I have some questions."

"I'll make sure he gets this as soon as his meeting is over. Is there anything else I can help you with?"

"No, that's it."

"Very good, sir."

Eli sat hunched on his bed with his back to the wall and his knees pulled tight to his chin. It'd been several long minutes since he'd left the message. Claudia had already called up the stairs to him, saying good night before dragging herself to bed. Now, as he sat staring at his bedroom door, he jumped at every noise, trembling at the thought of what the Outsider had said:

It won't be long before you'll be with us once and for all . . .

What if the Foggers were coming for him? As crazy as the old Outsider had been, he knew how to sneak his way into the

206

crust of the dome. If the Foggers could manage that, who knew what else they could do?

He told himself he was being ridiculous. Silently he begged Grandfather to hurry up and finish his stupid meeting and ping him back. All this waiting was driving him nuts.

Eli, I found something interesting. It was the first time Marilyn had spoken in quite a while. All this time she'd been balled up in a corner with her eyes closed. Now she chirped excitedly and hopped onto the bed.

"What? Tell me."

Ever since we saw the Outsider, I've been searching the Cloud-Net. I started by looking for text on Dr. S. G. Friedmann, or Samuel G. Friedmann, or S. Gustavo Friedmann—any combination I thought might work. In the end, though, I found nothing that matched anybody who was ever involved in building the domes.

"What does that prove? He told us he'd been erased from the archives."

Wait, darling, I'm not finished. When I didn't find any text files, I started scanning the image files. I sifted through a few billion of them, starting with the oldest I could find. She was staring into his eyes now, excited. *You wouldn't believe how many archived databases there are in the far recesses of the CloudNet. It's like wandering through a gigantic museum full of secret doors and hidden passages to rooms people seem to have forgotten about. There are storage systems that have sat unnoticed for decades. And in one of them I came across something that caught my attention. Oh, if only I could take you there!*

Still gazing into her eyes, Eli suddenly felt something new, a fizzing sensation inside his head. He sat up and pressed his

207

palm against his temple. It was as if Marilyn had mentally grabbed his hand and was pulling him along behind her through a digital tunnel. He was on some strange electronic thrill ride across a series of interconnecting highways, bridges, and footpaths that went on and on in every direction, twisting and turning around him while he held on for his life. Soon the rush was over, and he gasped. He was back in his room, but now his scalp tingled, and he realized there was an image forming inside his brain. A bunch of executives standing around a table. He was sure he'd never seen or imagined this picture before in his life. So why could he see it now?

But he already knew the answer. It was just too weird to believe.

"Marilyn, did you feel that?"

She looked as surprised as he was. *Yes. Somehow I carried you with me through the CloudNet.*

"I can see the file even without a sphere. Somehow you downloaded it into my brain. How?"

I don't know! I just . . . did it.

Eli could hardly believe it. It must have been a feature of the chip they'd never come across before. It wasn't just weird— it was scary.

Look at the image, Eli.

He closed his eyes and concentrated. The file was almost like a memory except much clearer and more detailed, as if there were a physical screen right in front of him. The shot, of a bunch of smiling men and women in old-fashioned business suits, had obviously been taken long ago. From the pose and the location—there was no mistaking Grandfather's board-room—Eli realized this was a room full of senior executives

208

from decades past, an early picture of the Leadership Council. Grandfather was in the center, shaking hands with somebody and grinning into the camera. It was weird to see him with hair and looking so much younger than he did today. He didn't recognize any of the other people. On the table in front of them was a model of a city not unlike Grandfather's music box, complete with tall buildings, stadiums, houses, and roads, all in miniature—and a wire dome shell that completely enclosed the model. Beside the mini city was a sign with thick purple letters:

THE INFINICORP DEPARTMENT
OF EMPLOYEE PROTECTION ANNOUNCES
INFINI-DOMES: THE WAY OF THE FUTURE!
A TRIUMPH OF SECURITY, SHELTER,
AND LUXURY LIVING!

"Okay, this is an old shot from when they first created the domes. So what?"

Do you see the man your grandfather is shaking hands with? Look at his name tag.

Eli did. He was a skinny, mustached guy with a sloping nose and cropped black hair. At first the letters on the tag seemed too small to read, but then Eli found he could zoom in closer.

Dr. S. G. Friedmann.

"All right. So now we know there really was a man called S. G. Friedmann, and whoever he was, he used to be important enough to be on the Leadership Council. But that doesn't mean we're looking at Gustavo from the Friends of Gustavo or that the Outsider we met is the same person as the one in this picture. Who knows? That nut job could've somehow heard of this Dr. Friedmann and could be only pretending to be him."

Why would he do that?

"I don't know. He's crazy. He's a Fogger. Why would somebody on the Leadership Council end up as an Outsider?"

Marilyn couldn't answer.

Eli studied the picture again. The man with the mustache didn't look anything like the ancient Outsider he'd seen, but then again the picture was very old, and the Outsider's face had been badly scarred. There was no way to tell for sure. He checked Dr. Friedmann's hand, the one held casually at his side. The skin of his fingers looked natural. But there was something else.

"Hey, Marilyn, look," he said. "There's something in his hand."

Whatever it was, Dr. Friedmann was holding it at an angle, so it wasn't easy to see, but it looked like a manila binder, one of those old-fashioned things they used for keeping papers together back in the Old Days, when people still recorded things on paper. Eli zoomed in and bent the image to adjust for the angle. Now he found he could make out the words on the front cover:

CONFIDENTIAL UPDATE
GREENHOUSE RECOVERY PROJECT

Marilyn must have seen it too, because Eli heard her reading it just as he saw it. Then she asked, *What do you think it means?*

210

"I have no idea."

Grandfather was the only one who would be able to shed any light on all this. Eli checked his watch. Ten-fifty-two p.m. The meeting must have ended by now. He wondered if he should try pinging Doug again. In the end he decided against it. If he kept bugging the office, it would only end up annoying Grandfather, and that was something Eli definitely wanted to avoid. He would just have to keep waiting until Grandfather got back to him.

Eleven-twenty-four p.m. Still nothing.

Eli remained slumped on his bed, his eyelids growing heavy. It had been a long, emotional day, and he was exhausted. In the past few minutes, he'd caught himself dozing off twice. Marilyn was no longer in sight. She'd told him the effort of downloading the file into his brain had given her a bad headache—she'd been getting a lot of them lately—and it had left her weak. She'd crawled under the bed and was now either asleep or comatose in a dream game.

Part of him was still marveling at the chip in her head.

Being able to tap into household appliances and link to the CloudNet without a sphere was impressive enough, but she'd managed to send a file into Eli's brain, which was entirely flesh and blood, not some system of digital processors. What else could the chip do? What startling abilities still lay dormant inside Marilyn's little cranium, waiting to be discovered?

And yet, at the same time, Eli worried about Marilyn. Ever since she'd started linking into the dream games, she'd been getting headaches that seemed to be growing worse and worse.

The more she used the advanced features of the chip, the more it seemed to leave her lethargic.

What was it doing to her?

He made a mental note to press her about this later. Right now he couldn't afford to be distracted. He focused his thoughts on the Outsider and on planning what he would say to Grandfather once he finally got in touch with him.

Where *was* Grandfather, anyway? This was getting ridiculous.

Eli checked the time again. Twelve-thirteen a.m.

One thing was obvious: Grandfather wasn't going to ping him back tonight. He'd probably gone to bed by now. As frustrated as Eli felt, he decided to do the same. He would ping again first thing in the morning. For now, Eli would at least get some rest.

He slumped onto his bed and closed his eyes.

Within moments he was asleep.

Eli woke with a start, his heart pounding. He thought he'd heard something out in the hallway. It sounded like the faint *squeak, squeak, squeak* of floorboards, as if someone were creeping up the stairs to his room.

He checked the time. One-twenty-one a.m.

Marilyn? Was that you?

She didn't answer. He could hear her breathing under the bed. She was deep asleep.

He raised himself onto his elbow. He held his breath and strained to hear any break in the quiet. In his mind he could picture Foggers coming to get him, crouching on the other side of the door, waiting. The silence continued for a long time, and finally he let himself relax. He'd only dreamed the sound, he decided. It was understandable. He was still jittery from everything that had happened. But now he breathed a sigh of relief and let his head drop back to his pillow.

Suddenly his door swung open and they were on him.

There were two of them: dark, hulking figures with cloaks and sunglasses. Eli didn't get a long look, but in the dim glow of a streetlight through his window, he caught a quick flash of mottled, leathery skin. He tried to scream, but they were so fast he didn't have time. As soon as his mouth was open, he felt a sharp jolt that began at his shoulder and rapidly spread across his entire body. He couldn't make a sound. Terrified, he tried to struggle but found he was unable to move. He called out to Marilyn, but she didn't answer.

Everything happened quickly after that.

The Outsiders didn't say a word. They grabbed his arms and dragged him from bed. Within seconds, and more quietly than Eli would have thought possible, they lugged him down the stairs. As they carried him through the front door, he noticed that the security system was disabled. Inside his useless body he kept struggling, desperate to move his limbs or to scream, but it was no use. What was happening? Where were they taking him?

In the dimly lit street in front of the house, a transport pod was waiting for them. The Outsiders carried him toward it. Long, low, and menacing, it had enormous road tires, red illuminators, and jagged tail fins shaped to look like angel wings. Eli knew this style of pod. Everyone did. It was a Department of Loyalty transport. But obviously this one wasn't real because these weren't Department of Loyalty agents, they were Outsiders. It was a good trick, he realized, a disguise that would enable the Outsiders to travel Inside unchallenged and undetected. He tried again to struggle, but his body was dead to him. If only he could call out for help! If only he could demand that they tell him what was going on!

But somewhere in his heart, he already knew. This was the end. He was being taken away and no one would ever hear from him again.

One last time he wondered how he could have been so foolish. Marilyn had warned him not to get involved with the Foggers, and yet he'd kept on ignoring her. Why had he let his childish curiosity get in the way of his better judgment? Was it that all along he'd believed something like this could never happen to him? Or was it that he'd secretly *wanted* it to happen?

He felt himself lifted into the air, and then, with a gasp, he landed hard on his elbows. Just as he realized he'd been stuffed headfirst into the back of the pod, a cloth bag was shoved over his head. Now he couldn't even see.

Marilyn! Wake up! Help me! Help me!

But it was too late. The pod was already carrying him away.

PART II

the tower at the end of the world

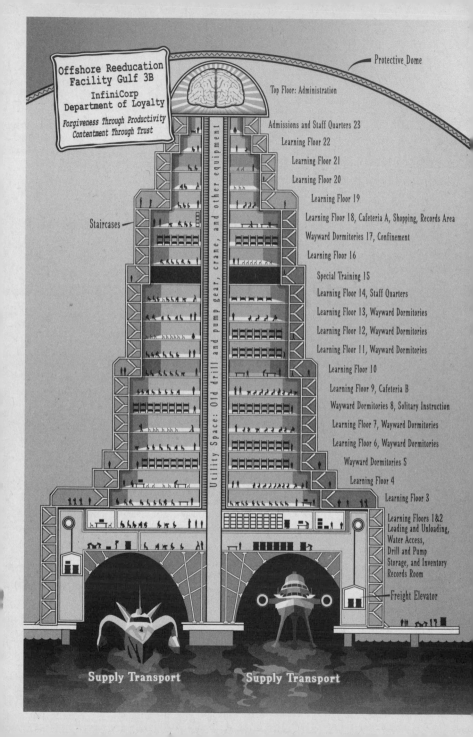

Offshore Reeducation
Facility Gulf 3B
InfiniCorp
Department of Loyalty
Forgiveness Through Productivity
Contentment Through Trust

Protective Dome

Top Floor: Administration

Admissions and Staff Quarters 23

Learning Floor 22

Learning Floor 21

Learning Floor 20

Learning Floor 19

Learning Floor 18, Cafeteria A, Shopping, Records Area

Wayward Dormitories 17, Confinement

Learning Floor 16

Special Training 15

Learning Floor 14, Staff Quarters

Learning Floor 13, Wayward Dormitories

Learning Floor 12, Wayward Dormitories

Learning Floor 11, Wayward Dormitories

Learning Floor 10

Learning Floor 9, Cafeteria B

Wayward Dormitories 8, Solitary Instruction

Learning Floor 7, Wayward Dormitories

Learning Floor 6, Wayward Dormitories

Wayward Dormitories 5

Learning Floor 4

Learning Floor 3

Learning Floors 1&2
Loading and Unloading,
Water Access,
Drill and Pump
Storage, and Inventory
Records Room

Freight Elevator

Staircases

Utility Space: Old drill and pump gear, crane, and other equipment

Supply Transport

Supply Transport

14

control and disposal

While the black-robed Outsiders dragged Eli from his room and out of the house, Marilyn lay under his bed, unaware. It seemed that in recent weeks every time she did anything more mentally demanding than a simple CloudNet search, it left her feeling as though there were a hot spike in her skull. She had long suspected the brain chip was damaging her each time she used it. At first it hadn't felt like much, just a sensation like a tiny spark going off. She'd barely noticed it. But the more time that went by, the more intense the feeling had become, as if the chip were frying her brain cells one tiny burst at a time.

It was a real concern, of course, but what could she do?

She'd never mentioned it to Eli. There was no point in worrying him.

Tonight, though, after piggybacking him across the CloudNet to show him the image of Dr. Friedmann, she'd ended up so weak, her whole body trembled. After a while her

thoughts had clouded over and she'd blacked out. Still comatose under the bed, she imagined she could hear Eli's silent
voice calling out to her from somewhere far, far away. It was
unsettling, but some part of her realized she was asleep, so this
seemed like just another piece of her troubled dream.

But then she heard it again, this time even more desperate:
Marilyn! Can't you hear me? Help! Help! Please!

Something in the urgency of the voice stirred her to attention this time. At the far edge of her consciousness, she sensed
something was wrong and she needed to wake up. She tried to
swim to the surface of her dream but it was as if there were a
weight dragging her down, and the pain in her head was growing. She ignored it and kept fighting. After a great effort, she
became aware again of the cool floor under her belly and the
smell of clean sheets over her head. She opened her eyes.

It was dark. The room was quiet. She was curled in a tight
ball. The door was open. And there it was once more, Eli's
voice:

Marilyn! Wake up! Help me! Help me!

She pulled herself up. As she did, the throbbing in her
skull was so intense that for a moment the walls spun around
her. But she could sense Eli wasn't in the room anymore. So
where was he? Following the direction of his signal, she crept
into the hallway and down the stairs. The front door was ajar,
so she headed that way. There was already a sinking feeling in
her stomach.

Eli? Are you there . . . ?

She reached the darkened street just in time to see cloaked
figures hop into a black transport pod like the ones used by the
Department of Loyalty. She knew in an instant something was

terribly wrong. Eli's signal was faint and unresponsive, and it was coming from inside that pod. Even more disturbing, before the pod skidded away from the curb, she caught a brief glimpse of a mottled red face.

Outsiders! They were taking Eli away from her!

She tore after the pod, hissing and screaming. She was ready to face down the desert rats, rip them apart and scratch their eyes out. *Darling, I'm here! I'm coming for you!*

But the pod was moving fast. When the long black shadow rounded the corner of Angell Street, she lost sight of it. By the time she charged around the corner herself, the red illuminators looked like dots in the distance. She hurtled after it. Soon, though, it disappeared from view. Marilyn dashed ahead to where she thought the pod had turned, but it wasn't there. She spun the other way. Nothing.

It was gone!

Eli! she called, desperate now. *Where are you? Tell me so I can follow!*

There was no response.

She stretched herself up on her haunches and cast her gaze to the top of the dome. Still panting, she wondered if it had taken flight and she'd missed it. At this time of the cycle, in the wee hours of the morning, the sky was programmed to give off only a dim light and the stars were brilliant and beautiful. The red illuminators could be lost among all the drifting multi-colored dots, some of which were probably other pods. But maybe Eli was up there. The black pod could even have flown Outside already, if that was where they were going. There had been enough time, and Marilyn had been concentrating on the street too much to even think about looking up at the sky.

219

Helpless to know what else to do, she sprinted down Angell and glanced into every cross street. All she saw were shadows and darkened houses and InfiniCorp shops that were closed for the night. She cursed herself and the burning fire in her head. Even now she felt like she'd been hit with a sledgehammer. Something dreadful was happening to Eli, and tonight of all nights she had been too slow-witted to stop it.

Eli, hold on! she cried. *Don't give up—I'll find you!*

She spent half the night prowling the streets of Providence for any sign of the black, angel-winged transport pod. As much as she realized deep down that Eli and his captors were long gone, she couldn't bear to give up the search in case she was wrong. Miserable, and with little energy left, she at last succumbed to her exhaustion and collapsed in a little alley by a power-storage box near the perimeter of the city.

The pixels at the far edge of the morning sky were just starting to glimmer an electronic silver when Marilyn awoke to the sound of footsteps.

Something was creeping up behind her.

Something that was trying not to be heard.

She leapt to her feet and spun around. Only a few yards away, two boys in purple uniforms were slinking in her direction. Their eyes were fixed on her, and in their hands they carried long wooden clubs. At first Marilyn didn't understand, but then she noticed an InfiniCorp truck parked in the street behind them, lit up on the side by glowing purple words: *Department of Pest Control and Disposal.*

With sudden dismay she realized that to these boys in this

dim light, she must have looked like a rat or a raccoon or some other stray creature, maybe something that'd wandered in from Outside. They paused when they saw she was awake and aware of them, but then they raised their clubs even higher.

They rushed at her.

In a frantic split second, Marilyn tried to assess her options. She couldn't communicate with them to let them know they were making a mistake. Behind her and on both sides were concrete walls several stories tall. To escape this narrow alley, she realized, she would have to fight her way past these boys.

She sprang at the closer of the two, a square-jawed kid about fifteen, with close-set eyes. In midair, just as her claws were about to lash at the boy's collar, she felt a stunning blow that took her square in the shoulder. It was his bat, and it sent her flying against the left wall. She slammed against the concrete and dropped to the ground.

"You devil!" the boy shouted. "Coming at me, are you? Maybe this'll settle you down!"

He swung his bat again, except this time Marilyn saw it coming. With a squeal she rolled aside just in time, and the bat cracked against the concrete where her head had just been. The pain in her shoulder was excruciating, but as the boy reared his arm back for another swing, she had the presence of mind to change direction.

"The net! The net!" he shouted to the other boy as she scurried between his legs. "Don't let it get away!"

The other boy, dark-haired and taller than the first, was already in her path, and he showed just as little fear as the first boy did. He let her rush at him and waited until she'd leapt

221

into the air before striking a blow of his own. This time the bat connected just below her ribs and knocked the wind out of her. She landed in a heap on the ground. Something coarse and light dropped onto her. It was a mesh of sticky rope, and it wrapped itself tight around her body. Dazed and gasping for breath, she tried to twist herself free, but she found she couldn't move.

She was defenseless as she watched the second boy rear back his bat for a final blow.

But that was when the square-jawed boy called out again. "No, don't kill it! I want to take a look!"

With a dubious glance over his shoulder, the second boy stopped his arm in midswing and then lowered his bat. When the first boy came back into Marilyn's view, he was holding what looked like a long wooden rod, at least ten feet in length, with a circular metal band at one end. He shoved it through the net, and then Marilyn felt cold metal wrap tight around her neck.

"Slippery little devil, isn't it?"

"A lot of fight in this one. I whacked it good, and it's still going."

The next thing Marilyn knew, she was being lifted into the air, her whole body dangling from the end of the rod. With a vicious animal snarl that came from somewhere deep inside, some ancient, fearsome place she hadn't even known was there, she began slashing and biting and flailing her claws, trying somehow to rip through the choking metal. But it was no use. She realized she was beaten, and she went still. She had never known such misery.

For a moment the boys only watched her, wide-eyed, as they held on to the other end of the rod.

"What the heck *is* it?"

The taller boy leaned in close—but not *too* close—and squinted into Marilyn's frightened eyes. "Don't know. Some kind of deformed weasel, maybe. Or a squirrel mutation?"

"That's no squirrel," said the square-jawed boy. "We see plenty of mutants, but I never saw anything that looked like *that*."

After a pause the taller boy reached into his pocket and pulled out an InfiniPencil. Still keeping his distance, he prodded her exposed belly with it, perhaps to see what reaction it might bring. For Marilyn this indignity was too much, and she hissed at him again with such sudden fury that it startled him. He jumped back.

"All right, then," he said, chuckling as he slipped the pencil back into his pocket. "Let's load it into the truck with the others—but we better give this one its own cell."

Still dangling Marilyn from the end of the rod, the boys opened the back of the truck, and she found herself being forced into one of dozens of small wire cages that lined the inside walls. In the confusion of the moment, she didn't get a good look, but she could tell there were other animals because she heard a chorus of growls and hisses. It sounded like some of the caged things were throwing themselves against the metal bars at her appearance. The air smelled of fear and fury. At last the metal collar released its choking grip on her neck, but an instant later the cage door slammed shut. Then the boys closed the back of the truck. Marilyn was trapped.

Shaking and in pain, she could feel the eyes of the animals watching her from every direction. Despite the darkness, she could make out some of them. A couple of sick-looking dogs. A tank of snakes. Something that looked like a hairless cat with a malformed paw. Mostly, though, what glared out at her from behind the bars of the cages were the same pointed faces, pink-eyed and hateful, over and over again: rats.

Large, evil-looking rats.

The cage next to hers was stuffed full of them. They growled and spat at her, pressing their long teeth between the metal bars as if trying to force their way through. When Marilyn looked closer she noticed there was something horribly wrong with every one of them.

Some had multiple tails.

Many had extra legs.

And the biggest one of all had three eyes.

Marilyn shrank back. As the engine started and the truck began to move, she trembled not only because of these terrifying creatures but also at the thought of where the boys might be taking them. She remembered again the words she'd seen on the side of the truck: *Department of Pest Control and Disposal.*

It was the *disposal* part that bristled her fur.

15

savages and kings

Eli woke up with his face against a cold tile floor. He had no idea where he was or how long he'd been there. He was covered in sweat and his left shoulder ached. He thought he could hear the wind howling. With a great effort he used his elbows to lift his body to a kneeling position.

Then he raised his head and looked around.

He was in the center of a small, dark room, empty except for him and an oversized CloudNet sphere that floated overhead, dormant but still providing the little light there was. In waves he remembered climbing up the sky.

And the strange old man with the respirator.

And the Outsiders bursting into his room.

And Marilyn! Oh god, where was she? *Are you there?* he called silently. *Marilyn, are you all right?*

There was no answer. Maybe the Outsiders had grabbed her too. After all, the man who called himself Gustavo seemed to know all about her and her chip. If he was taking his revenge on Eli for refusing to join the Foggers, why stop there? Hadn't Marilyn been just as clear about where she stood?

Eli pulled himself to his feet. In the center of one of the four walls was a black door. He tried it, but it was locked. What was this place? Some kind of criminal den where twisted Fog conspirators brought victims to be tortured—or worse? He'd read InfiniBook stories about secret Fog dungeons, but never did he imagine he would find himself a prisoner in one. How long before somebody came for him? Had they brought him here to rot forever?

Whatever they were planning to do, whatever horror lay ahead, he wanted it to hurry up already and happen. Waiting and not knowing was more than he could stand.

"Hello?" he called toward the closed door. "Anybody here?"

Somebody must have heard him, because he heard something move on the opposite side of the door. First a distant sound like animals grunting, then a *clomp, clomp, clomp* like boots approaching. He backed against the opposite wall and eyed the door. Whoever it was, they were on the other side now, working the latch.

And then the door swung open.

Two savages—large, muscular boys with scarred, sun-damaged complexions—stepped through the door. One had a prominent lower jaw and sharp yellow teeth; the other had a gaping hole on the side of his head where an ear had once been. Both wore the black InfiniCorp uniforms of the Department of Loyalty. Neither said a word. In an instant they were on both sides of Eli, each taking an arm. They yanked him from the wall and dragged him forward, closer to the CloudNet sphere.

Eli was too scared to speak.

Then from overhead a voice, thin and lethargic, whispered, "Finally back among the living? How considerate of you." The sphere was already glowing brighter and seemed to swell in size. From the haze inside it materialized the Infini-Corp logo—smiling employees cupped in the palm of a giant, protective hand—and then, in front of it, a much larger face, pale and narrow, with white hair and cold gray eyes. The sight gave Eli chills.

"Spider . . . ? Spider, you have to help me!"

His cousin glowered down at him. "What a difference a day can make. Only yesterday you seemed repulsed by my presence. Not so contemptuous anymore, *are* we?"

Eli felt fingernails digging into his arms. "Wh-what's going on?" he asked, his voice shaking. He took a quick, nervous glance at the Outsiders.

"Ah, I see you've met my special assistants . . ."

"Special assistants?" Eli repeated, confused.

"That's right. I have an understanding with these two gentlemen. They do whatever I ask, and in exchange I provide them shelter from Outside. It's an equitable arrangement. Their barbarian nature makes them far fiercer than other Department of Loyalty agents and less prone to . . . *taking pity* at inconvenient moments. These are valuable qualities that make them ideal for certain . . . *tasks*. Covert assignments that require a special sensitivity, not to mention stealth." He snickered. "But you've already experienced how soundless they can be. After all, it was they who visited your home last night."

Outsiders working for the company? Eli had never heard

227

of such a thing before, and the idea terrified him. He struggled, but the two barbarians held tight.

"Let me go!" he cried. "You're hurting me!"

"Oh, don't try to converse with them," Spider said, his voice still eerily dispassionate. "They're trained to respond only to me, aren't you, boys? Besides, I had their tongues removed, so they don't speak. It makes things much easier."

Eli could hardly believe he'd heard right. When the Outsiders responded with low grunting noises, it made Eli's heart pound even harder. He'd cut off their tongues? His own cousin was a monster!

He noticed something peculiar about the sphere too. It wasn't just its size. He tried to look away from the image of Spider's head, but he found it wasn't easy. The very thought of taking his eyes off the glowing ball brought on a panicky feeling. What if the masked boy in the Bubble had been right that CloudNet spheres had influence over people? This sphere did seem to have a compelling power. Not only that, but the more Eli stared into the haze, the more he felt his thoughts drifting from him. He had to look away or soon he wouldn't be able to think at all. Sweat dripped into his eyes. He gritted his teeth and forced himself to ignore the panic. Only after a tremendous effort was he able to squeeze his eyes shut and turn his head away.

"Impressive," Spider said. "Your will is strong. But that, unfortunately, is the real tragedy, little cousin. Because it was this same willfulness that led to your undoing." Feigning a pained expression, he sighed. "But you can't fight the sphere's influence forever. Trying to do so would be both foolish and pointless, so I suggest you don't bother. Keep your eyes on the sphere and I think you'll find that things will be a lot easier for you."

Eli felt a rough hand under his chin. The Outsider with the missing ear twisted his head back toward the image of Spider. Eli tried to shut his eyes, but the other Outsider, baring his yellow fangs, held his eyelids open with two of his filthy fingers. Eli screamed. He had no choice except to look at the sphere.

"I don't understand any of this!" he called out. "Why are you doing this to me, Spider? Why did you bring me here?"

Spider's expression hardened. "Don't try to play innocent with me. The Department of Loyalty knows all about the Fogger-hacked funbot you followed yesterday. And you were spotted climbing the sky. Tell me, what happened up there? Who did you meet? What did you discuss?"

Eli opened his mouth but nothing came out. The company *knew*. But of course they knew, he realized. What else had he expected? He'd been so upset yesterday that he hadn't cared what would happen to him. But that was yesterday, and now he knew he'd screwed up worse than ever.

Spider's eyes were still boring into him from the sphere. Eli was still so frightened that he couldn't bring himself to speak.

Then something bizarre happened. The two Outsiders seemed to fade away. Eli lost even the feeling of their grip on his arms. The room colors began to swirl, and the walls, floor, and ceiling melted away. When the movement stopped, Eli found himself on a gigantic field of black and red squares. He was standing on an enormous checkerboard that went on for a great distance in every direction. Placed all over the board were huge black checkers the size of boardroom tables. Stranger still, Eli realized that he *himself* was a checker, the only red piece on the whole playing field. His breath caught in his throat. If he hadn't been seeing it with his own eyes, he wouldn't have believed it.

This was just a trick, he told himself. It was an illusion created by the CloudNet sphere. He was still in the gray room with the Outsiders.

A face appeared high above him. Spider was a giant now, several stories tall. "What's the matter, Eli? Isn't this the game you and our dear grandfather enjoy so much? Well, now it's *my* turn to play. And what do you know? It's my move."

Spider reached out one of his long, skinny fingers and slid the nearest of the huge black pieces toward Eli, almost knocking him over. Eli had to leap out of the way to avoid getting crushed.

Spider grinned. "Go ahead. Your move."

"Stop it!" Eli cried. "Whatever this is, turn it off! What do you want from me?"

A giant fist slammed down onto the table. The impact sent a few of the game pieces flying into the air and then crashing back down to the ground. Spider's voice was low and even. "I don't believe you heard me. I said it's *your move*."

Eli leapt forward to another square, any square. It didn't matter which, he knew. There were black pieces everywhere he looked, and in any case it was clear that Spider wasn't going to let him win. He wasn't interested in a fair game. This wasn't a game at all.

As if studying the board, Spider lowered his chin thoughtfully into his hands and gazed down at Eli. "Now then," he said, "why don't you tell me what happened in the sky?"

So Eli did as he was asked. Voice shaking, he told him how he'd found the mirrored door during the dome malfunction. He described the sky chamber, and the strange old Outsider who called himself Dr. S. G. Friedmann, and how he'd talked about the end of the world. He even mentioned how the old Outsider had the crazy idea he'd seen Eli in a vision. What would be the point in lying? It was obvious Spider already knew plenty. It was even possible he knew the whole story and was only testing to see if Eli would hide the truth.

Spider's face was expressionless at first. By the time Eli's story was over, though, his lips showed the slightest hint of a smile.

"Oh, Eli, Eli . . . ," he said, shaking his head. "How it pains me to hear of such treachery, especially from a member of my own family. As I'm sure you're aware, Dr. Friedmann was an agitator from the past, the original Fog turncoat and a deceiver of the lowest order. That old traitor has been a thorn in our heel for long enough, but we'll get him now, rest assured. There will be no tears shed for him when we do. No, the real heartbreak here is *you,* Eli, because now it's tragically obvious what you've let yourself become."

"What do you mean?" Eli's voice was suddenly weak. "It wasn't the real Dr. Friedmann. So what are you saying? What am I that's so tragically obvious?"

Spider's finger appeared again, and, almost casually, he slid three black checkers up close to Eli. One. Then another. Then another. Eli felt them pressing around him. He couldn't escape. He was like an ant in a trap.

"A Fog agent, of course," Spider said with a grin. "That's what you are. A conspirator of the most treacherous nature."

"But . . . it's not true!"

Spider shook his head again. "You can deny it all you like, but the Department of Loyalty already has sufficient evidence to put you away for a long, long time. You've been plotting the overthrow of the company, foolish boy. Admit it. You've been involved in anti-InfiniCorp activity for much of your short life."

"No! That's wrong! You have to believe me!" Eli's mind whirled. "Ask Sebastian! I know he told you I've been anxious, but he also knows I would never be disloyal to the family! Let me ping Grandfather! Please, I have to talk to somebody!"

"Sebastian can't help you, I'm afraid. And I wouldn't count on Grandfather coming to your defense anymore."

Something in Spider's voice made Eli pause. "What—why?"

"Perhaps you haven't heard?" He grinned again. "Oh, it's been quite a momentous evening for our family. You'll be interested to learn that the old warhorse has fallen ill. At this moment he's breathing through a tube and is close to death. It's all so very tragic."

Eli's insides went tight. It was too awful to imagine. But it was true that the last time he'd seen Grandfather, he didn't seem well. All Eli wanted now was to be with him. He would have given anything to be at his bedside, to hold his hand and maybe even talk with him for the last time. But he could tell that Spider had no intention of letting that happen. In fact, he seemed to take cruel pleasure in watching Eli's face pale at the news.

Spider was enjoying every minute of this.

All of a sudden the checkerboard rose under Eli's feet.

Spider had upended his side of the game board, and all the checkers began sliding downward to the opposite end. Several of the table-sized game pieces were bearing down on Eli, and in a flash he understood that unless he did something quick, he was in danger of being crushed. He leapt aside and felt the first one brush against his hand. Then he jumped on top of the next one and rode it as it slid down the board. A moment later he was on his back, on top of a jumble of checkers. One of them had knocked painfully against his arm, but otherwise he was unhurt.

Spider snickered again. "It seems there will soon need to be a few . . . *changes* in company leadership." He brought his giant face down close to Eli. "King me!"

Eli was so scared, he couldn't breathe. Spider had lost his mind.

"All right," he said, glancing somewhere behind Eli, as if he were talking to someone Eli couldn't see. "That's enough, I think."

Eli felt as if somebody were dialing down a knob in his brain. A moment later he found himself in the gray room again, the two Outsiders' fingers still digging into his arms. Spider's sneering face was still hovering overhead, although now his cousin was back to being just an image inside the CloudNet sphere. Eli was trembling. He was covered in sweat and too weak to do anything but blink into the glowing orb.

"Such a disappointment you turned out to be," Spider said, his voice soft once more. "The family will be devastated. I confess I'm surprised you managed to keep up the conspiracy for so long. And right under our noses!" Eli was about to protest, but Spider waved his hand. "Enough pretending!"

233

Then to the Outsiders he said, "Take this pathetic excuse for a Papadopoulos away from my sight!"

As the Outsiders dragged Eli toward the door, Eli summoned his last remaining strength to call out, *"Wait! I'm still part of the family! You can't do this to me! Where are you taking me? Let me go!"*

But there was no answer.

The whole world seemed to rock and sway as the two Outsiders pulled him into a narrow gray hallway. Eli's head slumped. He was all alone and nothing made sense and nothing would ever be right again. Somewhere in the distance he thought he could hear waves crashing. And there was a smell burning at his nose, a faint odor like sour milk.

16

animal instinct

Still trapped in the cage, Marilyn kept her body in a tight, defensive ball and did her best to block out the horrifying growls of the mutant rats, only inches away. Her entire left side throbbed from the impact of the wooden bat, but she was pretty sure nothing was broken. Even as the truck carried her through the city she continued to call out silently to Eli, but she got no response. Still, she could sense his signal, faint but somewhere out there.

At least she knew he was alive.

Soon the truck squealed to a halt and the engine went quiet. The animals quieted too, perhaps sensing, as Marilyn did, that death was near, that they had reached the Department of Pest Control and Disposal's final destination. But Marilyn's eyes were shut tight in concentration. She'd noticed a steadily glowing blue light above the wire doors of each of the cages. The locks were electronic. If she could somehow find a way to mentally tap into the lock on her cage, then perhaps she could pick it open. The trouble was, her head was still fried from last night. Plus, she didn't know if the lock mechanism used a logic chip she could access. And even if it did, figuring out how to hack her way in and then release it would take time.

And time was something she lacked.

The back doors of the truck swung open, and the two purple-uniformed boys appeared again. Grim-faced and wearing bulky gloves, they climbed inside and each grabbed a couple of the cages by the handles. One by one they began unloading them behind the truck. Many of the animals whimpered or snarled in protest. Marilyn's cage was one of the first. She was dropped roughly onto a hard surface, and now she found herself at what looked like the back entrance to a small brick building where two other purple-uniformed employees, both of them teenage girls with ashen faces and dull-witted expressions, stood watching the boys unload.

"A pretty good crop for one night's work," the square-jawed boy called out to them.

Behind the girls was a garage door opening into a dark space, with a couple of tired-looking cleaning robots, just visible, slumping against the wall. Marilyn couldn't see far inside, but what she saw looked cheerless and uninviting, with a low ceiling and walls painted a dismal gray. There were flickering shadows too, and heat, waves of it, as if somewhere in that dark space, a furnace burned hot, waiting for them. There was also something foul in the air, something unspeakable.

The smell of smoke and flesh. Of fire and terror.

Marilyn noticed the sign above the entrance: Organic Waste Incinerator.

In a frenzy, she tried again to hack her way into the lock. She couldn't feel any pathway in, though, perhaps because the lock was impenetrable to her chip, or maybe just because she was too desperate to think clearly.

It wasn't long before all the animals were out of the truck.

"That's the whole load," the taller boy announced, removing his gloves and closing up the doors. "They're all yours now. See you tomorrow."

While the truck pulled away, the girls stood a moment, scowling at the field of caged animals as if deciding where to begin a big task. "All right," one of them said, "let's get this over with."

Seconds later Marilyn saw two boots appear in front of her. To her dismay she felt her cage being lifted into the air, and then two flat gray eyes peered at her through the wire mesh.

"You first, little rat. Or cat. Or . . . whatever the heck you are."

Marilyn shook with fear. If only she had a little more time! But the girl was carrying her into the dark room now, and Marilyn could feel the air getting warmer, the temperature rising on her fur and skin, as they moved closer to the furnace. She closed her eyes and forced herself to concentrate as hard as she could. It took all her focus, and it felt like a tiny hot coal was burning somewhere behind her eyeballs. With only seconds to work with, she abandoned her attempt to pick the lock and turned all her attention to the building itself, searching for something, *anything,* that might help buy her a minute or two.

At last she found something.

When the overhead sprinkler system kicked on, it sprayed water in every direction.

"Aw, crap! What's this?" The girl stopped in her tracks and spun toward the other girl. "What's going on? Nothing's on fire!" Almost at once the girl's hair and clothes started to soak, and so did Marilyn's fur. Water dripped through the bars of her cage.

The other girl, still dry on the other side of the entrance, looked just as confused. "No idea," she called back, eyeing her now-soggy friend. "A malfunction, I guess. Try shutting off the main water supply. The valve is under the sink."

"Crap!" the first girl said again. "Crap, crap, *crap!*" She dropped Marilyn's cage to the floor and stormed over to the other side of the room.

Marilyn saw her chance. Heart pounding, she concentrated her thoughts on manipulating the closer of the two robots, an ancient-looking lowrider with a cracked blue chassis, a few feet away and unnoticed in the confusion. She instructed it to step over to her cage. Marilyn had no idea how the lock worked, but it didn't matter anymore. She directed the robot to stick its rubber fingers between two of the cage's metal bars and then pry them apart. A moment later there was a space wide enough for Marilyn to climb through.

And then she ran.

* * *

238

Limping and exhausted, Marilyn darted into an artificial hedge on a side street just off Branch Avenue. Her shoulder stung, and her entire left side below her ribs was stiffening up. Eli was out there somewhere—she could still sense him—but she was beside herself that she didn't know where he was and couldn't communicate with him. And if that weren't upsetting enough, she'd seen two disturbing Info Updates flash across the CloudNet as she was scurrying past the glowing street spheres.

The first had been news about Grandfather. He'd collapsed the night before and had been in and out of consciousness ever since. Which was distressing news for everyone but would be especially upsetting for poor Eli. At least it explained why Grandfather hadn't returned Eli's ping.

The second Info Update, though, was of even more immediate concern to Marilyn. It was an All-City Security Alert: *Have you seen this creature?*

To Marilyn's surprise, her own image had filled the sphere.

"As part of an ongoing investigation into the criminal activities of the Fog," said a voice, "the Department of Loyalty asks for your assistance in locating this dangerous mutant. At this moment it is believed to be loose in the city of Providence and is considered a threat to health and security. Anyone seeing a creature that looks like this must report the sighting to the nearest Guardian at once."

She stared at the image of herself. Surely the escape of one small animal from the Department of Pest Control and Disposal didn't justify an All-City Security Alert. Did this mean they knew about the sky climb? Is that what they meant by "criminal activities of the Fog"? It was ridiculous to suspect her or Eli of Fog activity, of course, but it would at least explain why Eli had been taken away in a Department of Loyalty vehicle. Was it possible they'd been looking for her all along and had only just discovered where she was?

And if that was it, if Eli had been taken by the Department of Loyalty, why then had she seen Outsiders climbing into the pod with him?

So many questions. So many unknowns. It was all too confusing and distressing! In any case, she would have to think about it later. She had no time to lose.

She had to get out of sight.

At that very moment a street-sweeper droid had rounded the corner, and Marilyn had charged away down a side road. Now it was minutes later, and she was still concealed in the artificial hedge, peering through the plastic brambles. The city was awakening. Employees were already beginning to fill the sidewalks. Where was she supposed to go?

She closed her eyes and mentally scanned the CloudNet in the hope that somebody had seen Eli since last night. But no. Instead, what she found left her even more puzzled. There was a new report about how Eli's parents had been selected by the company to go to Arizona as permanent Papadopoulos family representatives in the Retirement Dome. Their son Eli, the report said, had chosen to accompany them. There were images of the three of them golfing, attending parties, and visiting smiling patients in luxurious hospitals. Marilyn knew it had to be fake. Not only would Eli never have left without taking her with him, but it didn't match what she'd seen with her own eyes.

On a whim she decided to tap into the cache of Eli's In-finiTalk system. It turned out he had an unread urgent ping from Mother.

"Eli, where *are* you? Oh, I hope I'm not too late. If you get this, listen to me very closely. I know it sounds strange, but I want you to leave the house *right away.* Go this very minute to Wickenden Station and ride the Bubble tram. Someone will meet you there and explain everything, but for now don't waste a moment. *Just go. Right now.* Oh, Eli . . . I hope you get this. Something awful is about to happen, I can feel it—"

That's where it cut off.

The message made the fur on Marilyn's neck stand up. Frantic, she closed her eyes once more and, ignoring the low sizzle in her brain, hacked her way into Sebastian's InfiniTalk system. Then she left him an encrypted electronic message of her own:

Sebastian, your brother is in danger. Last night he was taken by Outsiders in a Department of Loyalty transport pod. I don't know where he is anymore. I'm not sure where else to turn. Please, please, help me find him.

She left it unsigned. It was all she could do for now.

Behind a transport-maintenance station off Charles Street, Marilyn cowered in a jumble of broken pod parts. All over the city the CloudNet systems were looking for her. The surveillance cameras, the taxi-pod robots, even the credit machines. She couldn't see how she could go on much longer without somebody or something finding her.

And then what? She didn't want to think about that.

241

By now she could tell from the distance of his signal that Eli wasn't Inside anymore, at least not in Providence. She was convinced that the reason she couldn't communicate with him was that there was at least one dome wall separating them. The same thing happened whenever Eli traveled to New Washington. Their signals had trouble penetrating the domes' magnetic fields. Which meant that her only real chance of avoiding capture and finding Eli would be to leave the dome herself.

The idea terrified her.

In recent weeks the thought of leaving even the *yard* had made her anxious. Some mongoose she'd turned out to be, she couldn't help thinking. Mongooses were supposed to be adaptable. They lived to explore. She remembered again the mutant animals in the truck. As horrifying as they'd been, weren't they her kin, in a way? Due to no fault of their own, they'd become something they were never intended to be. Yet even they seemed to sense there was something particularly wrong about Marilyn.

And it was true. There was no denying it.

She decided to make her way south, toward the dome's exit on Hartford Avenue. She was careful to stay off the roads as much as possible. She crept behind buildings, scrambled over walls, and took the time she needed to be sure nobody saw her. And always her eyes were open for CloudNet devices that might be watching for her.

Finally she could see the gate, no more than fifty yards away. She peered around a low stone wall and saw a blond girl with triangular ear plates, an employee of the Department of Dome Maintenance, by the look of her uniform. The girl was talking with the gate monitor and seemed to be getting ready to pass through the arch to Outside.

At last, Marilyn thought, *a little luck.*

But then she noticed that not far away, just a few paces from the archway, two Guardians stood chatting. There was no going back, though. She'd made up her mind about what she was going to do, and if she didn't follow through now she might never get another chance. It wouldn't be easy to get past the Guardians, she knew, but she was small and fast, and this gave her an advantage. If she could surprise them after the gate opened for the girl, then she might just make it through the archway before it closed.

It wasn't much of a plan, but it was all she had.

And then the gate opened.

With no time to overthink her strategy, she shot from behind the stone wall and dashed headlong into the open. Just when she was halfway across the pavement toward the archway, though, she heard an alarm go off. Ahead and to her left, a stubby green street-sweeper droid was zipping into her view, rolling as fast as it could to block her path. Marilyn had been so focused on the gate that she hadn't even noticed it.

The Guardians looked up.

Adrenaline pumping, Marilyn bared her teeth and kept running. She knew she couldn't slow down or turn around anymore. It was too late for that. Up ahead the blond girl had already stepped through, and the gate was starting to close.

The droid was blocking her path now and reaching out its little tentacles, dozens of them, to grab her. Just before Marilyn reached the droid, she leapt into the air and over it, surprising even herself that she could jump so high. She landed on the other side without losing momentum. But the Guardians were still ahead, standing in front of the gate as it continued to shut.

So Marilyn did the only thing she could think to do. She flung herself at one of them, hissing and clawing and hurtling her weight into his chest. He screamed and cussed and flailed his arms, but not for long, because in an instant the other Guardian had Marilyn by the tail and neck, and he ripped her off him with one wrenching yank.

"Got ya, mutant!"

Just behind him, barely three feet away, the gate was almost closed. Marilyn had no time to think. What she did next came from pure instinct: she bit the base of his thumb with such force that she felt the bone. The Guardian howled. When he let go, she unclenched her jaws and dropped to the ground. Just before the gate slammed shut, she slipped through.

Right away the heat enveloped her, and the bugs swarmed around her eyes and ears.

She was Outside.

17

learning floor 9–b

Eli woke up with a terrible headache in a strange white bedroom, under yet another glowing sphere. Still bleary, he tried to ping home, but for some reason the sphere wouldn't let him through. Then a white-uniformed InfiniCorp Guardian named Representative Tinker, a pretty girl with wispy blue hair and a friendly smile, brought him a meal and told him he was in the admissions ward of an InfiniCorp tower surrounded by water. It was a special offshore program for the reeducation of Wayward Employees, she said, and Eli was going to join other Wayward Employees on one of the facility's many production floors. Everything was going to be all right, she told him. There was nothing to worry about.

At once Eli jumped into his story.

"I need to speak with somebody right away," Eli told her, glad to have found someone who seemed to care. He almost asked to ping Grandfather but then he remembered what Spider had said. The thought of Grandfather near death made

Eli's insides tight. "Let me talk to Father," he said at last. "Or Mother. She might be easier to reach. But if neither of them is available, we can try Sebastian or even one of my uncles or aunts."

"All in good time, Representative Papadopoulos," she said, patting his hand. "First we need to get you back on your feet. You've had quite a shock."

"But there's been a mistake," he insisted. "Don't you get it? My cousin Spider put me here because he thinks I did something I didn't do. My family must be worried, and when they find out what happened, they'll be furious!"

"Oh, I believe you, and I'll see what I can do, I promise. But for now you need to get some rest."

Eli blinked at her. How could anyone act so calm about this? Didn't she understand this was a nightmare? What he needed wasn't rest. He needed to get out of here! He yanked back the sheets and started to climb out of the bed. "No, I won't wait. I need you to take me to somebody who'll help. I have to get back home!"

Representative Tinker looked startled. "Goodness! What are you doing, Representative Papadopoulos? You're not ready to be discharged from the ward yet!"

"I don't care! I demand to speak with whoever's in charge!"

Before he could even swing his legs to the floor, though, he felt the pinch of a hypodermic needle in his arm. Right away his strength left him and he dropped back into the sheets.

Representative Tinker's face was red and upset. "I'm sorry that was necessary, but you must understand that you're not thinking right yet. You're distraught." Quickly she tucked him in again and headed to the door. Before switching the lights out, she looked back. "You shouldn't worry, Eli. You're going to like it here. Everybody does."

As he peered over the edge of the sheets at the closed door, he already felt the drug lulling him to sleep. Soon he had to shut his eyes.

He woke up feeling as though his head were filled with mush. Still bleary-eyed, he tried contacting Marilyn again, but it was no use. He wondered again if something had happened to her too, but he pushed those worries aside, reminding himself that she was alive. He could feel her signal somewhere in the distance. That was something, at least.

For the next few hours, a series of other Guardians visited him in the room, all of them cheerful and attentive, all of them apparently concerned about his well-being but also curious to meet the grandson of Grandfather Papadopoulos.

"It's an honor to have a celebrity here," they would say. "We all hope you have a pleasant visit."

"Why can't I speak with my family?" he would ask them, his voice still weak from the drug. "When will you let me?"

"Don't worry about a thing," they would answer, or, "Wait a little while and I think you'll feel a whole lot better." Whatever assurances they tried to give Eli, he couldn't help noticing that as they left his room, they always locked the door behind them.

Hours later—or was it minutes?—he felt strong enough to leave the bed. He slipped across the room and banged on the wall, demanding to speak with someone about going home. This worked about as well as it had the first time. Within seconds the Guardians were back with another hypodermic needle and Eli found himself on the bed again, drifting out of consciousness.

After a while the days started to blend together. Representative Tinker seemed always in good spirits, always sympathetic to his concerns. But now Eli knew better than to demand to speak with anyone. He would have to go along with whatever was happening here until he found some other opportunity to send out a message. In the meantime all he could do was try to avoid gazing into the sphere, which was always there, glowing over his head. This one didn't seem to hold quite the grip on his mind that the powerful one in the gray room had, but he could feel that its pull was still stronger than what he was used to. He didn't want to look at it, but despite himself he sometimes did. There wasn't much else to do. That, and sleep. He slept a lot.

Every day he woke up feeling a little less troubled, a little more resigned to reality.

One morning Representative Tinker came into Eli's room with an orange uniform in her hands.

"It's time," she said. "I believe you're ready for the next step. Why don't you put this on, and I'll take you to your new classroom?"

Eli took the uniform. Lately he'd found that everything was easier when he just did what he was told. And besides, he didn't have the energy to argue anymore. He felt light-headed, as if his thoughts were so weightless they floated away as soon as he thought them. He slipped on the uniform like he was drifting through a dream.

"This tower used to be a giant oil rig," Representative Tinker explained as she led him down a series of narrow stairways. "We still pump oil here, of course—at least for now—but there isn't much left under the seabed anymore. The pump team takes up only half a floor now, which is good news for us, because the company converted all the extra space just for the Waywards."

There were windows in the stairwell. Eli could at last see the sea. It looked reddish, but maybe that was a trick of the light. Perhaps two hundred yards away, his view was blocked by a curved wall of glowing blue that started above the edge of his vision and fell at a sharp angle. The tower had its own little dome. Unlike the sturdy domes over the cities, though, this one seemed less substantial, with an arc that ended before it reached the water and a sky so thin that Eli could make out the metal grid that formed the dome's outer shell.

"Where are we going?" he asked, still trudging behind her.

"You'll see!" When she smiled back at him, Eli felt his face flush. He couldn't help it. She was like an angel.

At last they came to a door with a sign that read Learning Floor 9-B. Representative Tinker opened it and led him into a long, dismal room with exposed steel girders and ancient blowers. Along the length of the floor ran wooden tables where rows and rows of kids, maybe as many as a hundred of them, sat working, some sitting at antique sewing machines, others digging through what looked like piles of cloth.

"What is this place?"

"A textile-assembly team!" Representative Tinker said with a sweep of her hand. "This is where you'll learn to be a productive member of the company, Eli. You're going to help in our garment-manufacturing process!"

Eli peered into the gloom, trying to take it all in. Except for a handful of CloudNet spheres floating overhead, the room seemed to have few modern devices. There were no robots in sight—Eli hadn't seen any since he'd been in this strange place—and despite the blowers the air felt stale and muggy and smelled of sweat. The only breeze seemed to come from a few metal fans that squeaked as they pivoted back and forth. On the walls hung a few sad arrangements of plastic flowers, thick with dust, and from the girders flaked grayish paint that might once have been purple. It was as if somebody long ago had tried to cheer the place up a little but had failed miserably.

It occurred to Eli that maybe he should run. He couldn't, though, he realized. If he tried, he would only end up getting another hypodermic needle stuck in his arm.

Besides, where could he go?

He felt Representative Tinker's hand on his shoulder. "Don't be nervous. It's going to be fine. It's normal to have a little case of the jitters on your first day, but you'll get in the swing of things in no time—you'll see."

A square-jawed employee in a drab green uniform approached them. She wore a sweatband around her head, and her blond hair swooped up and over like a water fountain. "Welcome to Learning Floor Nine B, Representative Papadopoulos. I'm Representative Dowd, one of the Productivity Facilitators here. Come. I'll show you to your Contribution Team."

Representative Tinker whispered into Eli's ear, "I'm so

250

proud of you!" She gave his arm a reassuring squeeze. "Have a productive day!"

Representative Dowd led him deeper into the room. Eli scanned the long tables, where the kids worked diligently at their tasks. He guessed they ranged in age from perhaps twelve to eighteen years old. He couldn't help noticing how quiet the place was. Other than the squeak of the fans and the soft echo of their footsteps, the room was silent.

"Unnecessary discussion is discouraged," Representative Dowd explained, her voice low. "It distracts from efficiency. All the workers are Waywards, just like you, so everyone learns that meeting the daily production quota is the best way of making amends for the indiscretions they've committed against the company."

On a sign on the far wall was the same message Eli had seen posted everywhere he went: Forgiveness through Productivity, Contentment through Trust.

Wandering between the tables were several other kids in drab green uniforms like the one Representative Dowd wore. Eli watched them look over the laborers' shoulders, apparently checking their work. The Productivity Facilitators seemed to be the supervisors here. More intimidating, though, were the white-uniformed Guardians standing sentry along the walls like prison security. Unlike Representative Tinker, these were all large, flat-headed kids with impassive expressions. Eli didn't like the look of them.

Representative Dowd walked him to the only empty seat, at the end of one of the tables. "This is Representative Papadopoulos," she announced.

The nearby workers, all of them kids about his own age,

looked up from the piles of shirt parts they were working on. Everybody smiled, glassy-eyed. No one seemed overly moved at hearing his famous last name.

"Hello, Representative Papadopoulos," they responded in chorus.

Representative Dowd gave a quick demonstration of what Eli was supposed to do. His job title would be Matcher. The work was simple enough: he would sort through piles of shirt parts—sleeves, collars, fronts, and backs—and match sizes together. Completed sets were then passed down the table to the Rippers, who removed numbered tags from the material. Next the sets were passed to the Operators, who sat at antique sewing machines and stitched the different parts together, and finally to the Packers, who packed them in crates.

Representative Dowd left, and soon Eli was struggling to keep up with the others. He sifted through his mound of shirt parts, making occasional surreptitious glances at the other kids at the table. They were all working fast. Nobody ever seemed to look up. The boy to Eli's left was pencil thin, with short black hair, freckles, and eyes so big that he looked a little like a bug. He seemed about the same age as Eli. The beefy girl to Eli's right was ghostly pale, with mousey brown hair and drooping eyelids. She looked older, maybe seventeen or eighteen. Even though she appeared half-asleep, her hands seemed to have energy of their own as they sifted through her pile. Eli worked up the courage to speak to them both.

"Hi," he whispered, "I'm Eli. What are your names?"

Instead of answering, the girl glanced over, curled her lip, and growled at him. Then she turned back to her pile. Her hands never stopped moving. Eli wanted to sink into his chair.

The boy seemed a little friendlier. He looked nervously around, perhaps to see if any of the Productivity Facilitators were nearby, and then, with his eyes on his work again, he whispered, "I'm Clarence. She's Geraldine."

Eli decided to ignore the strange tension. "It's nice to meet you, Clarence. Why are you here? What did you do wrong?" After a moment Clarence looked over as if he were going to answer, but then his face went red and he dropped his gaze once more.

Eli felt a hand on his shoulder.

"Maybe you didn't understand when I told you about the no-unnecessary-talking rule?" He turned. Representative Dowd didn't seem angry. Her expression and tone of voice were like those of a patient parent reasoning with a disruptive toddler. "It's not surprising. You're new. But we have a quota to meet, three hundred seventy crates by the end of the day, which means each Matcher will need to process over nine hundred shirts. Reaching our goal will take everybody's full attention. Please concentrate on your task, Representative Papadopoulos. You of all people should understand that everybody's work is vital to the well-being of the organization."

Eli wanted to argue with what seemed like an unreasonable rule, but he decided against it, for now. Geraldine was giving him the evil eye and Eli could feel his face burning. Soon everyone went back to work. For a long time Eli didn't look up at all. He kept his mouth shut.

Lunch was served in shifts in a spacious cafeteria with tables and an area where Waywards could stand and stretch their legs if they wanted to. The moment the hungry workers stepped into the room and lined up for their meals, the place filled with loud conversation. Talking, it seemed, was okay here.

Eli found an empty table near the back and set his tray down. He was starving. He examined his lunch: lumpy meat loaf, green mush, and some kind of yellow desserty thing that looked like it had sat out in the sun for a while. Just as he was working up the courage to test the meat loaf, somebody spoke just behind him.

"I stopped working."

Eli turned. The freckled boy from the worktable was standing there with his tray.

"You asked what I did wrong to end up here, and that's the answer. One day I told my boss at the tanning salon that I wasn't showing up to work anymore, and that was that. I meant it too. For days and days I didn't go back. People kept coming up to my room and knocking on my door to tell me I had to report to my job, but I just stayed in bed."

"Why did you do that?"

He shrugged. "I don't know. I just felt . . . sad. I had this terrible, empty feeling all the time. So I stayed in my room. I didn't go to parties, I didn't do *anything*. Eventually they sent me here." He set his tray next to Eli's and sat down. "I know. It was a stupid thing to do. I guess I was so wrapped up in my self-absorbed wrong thinking that I didn't consider the consequences. No worries, though. I'm better now." He held out his hand. "Sorry we couldn't talk earlier. Let's start again. I'm Clarence."

"Eli." He shook his hand. "Nice to meet you."

Clarence picked up the grayish pizza from his tray and took a bite. He covered his mouth as he spoke. "Listen, I know

254

what you're going through. The first day is always the hardest. I see it all the time. Everybody here remembers what it was like to be a newbie."

"Thanks. What's up with that no-talking rule, anyway?"

"Yeah, they can be kind of a pain about it," he said with a half smile. "But you can get away with talking if you learn how not to get caught. Like I said, don't sweat it. You'll get with the program soon enough. I bet it'll only take a few days before you learn to like it here."

"That's hard to imagine," he admitted, glancing at the line of Guardians watching from along the far wall. Eli couldn't help feeling grateful to this kid, who was obviously going out of his way to be nice. Now that he saw him away from the frantic pace of the work line, he seemed normal, like any regular boy Eli might have passed on the street at home. Not somebody he would have pictured working in some faraway dungeon on the sea. "How long have you been here?"

"Eight months. More than some kids, not as long as others." He nodded in the direction of a table where the big, pale girl from the work line sat alone, her expression vacant and her mouth moving as if she were talking to herself. Everybody else seemed to steer clear of her. "Geraldine was here long before I started."

"What's her problem? The way she looked at me, I thought she was going to bite my head off."

"Oh, she's harmless. Just stay out of her way and you'll be fine."

"No, really. There's something wrong with her. What is it?"

Clarence was quiet a moment. "Well," he said, "most kids

get with the program pretty quickly, but the ones who *don't . . .*" He shrugged. "They sometimes end up like her. Kind of freaky and quiet." He leaned in close and dropped his voice. "Geraldine was a *Resister.*"

Eli could only blink at him.

"A holdout," he explained. "An unrepentant Wayward who clings to wrong thinking and refuses to get it that we're all on the same company team. It's a shame. After a while just about everybody comes around on their own, but every now and then we get somebody who doesn't. When I first got here, Geraldine was kind of scary and violent. People got hurt. She went to Solitary Instruction a few times, but even that didn't work. Finally they brought her up to the fifteenth floor. That's what fixed her."

"The fifteenth floor?"

Clarence nodded. "The Special Training area. When Geraldine came back, she forgot all about resisting. Now she's one of our most productive teammates."

"What the heck is Special Training? What did they do to her?"

"Nobody knows, but whatever it was, it sure fixed her head up quick."

Eli recalled the powerful sphere he'd faced for a short time in the gray room and how it had played with his mind. He shuddered at the memory. "I think I may have already seen the Special Training area," he said. "As soon as I get the chance, I'm going to stop my cousin Spider from doing this to people. When my grandfather finds out about this place, he's going to shut it down." When Clarence didn't react he added, "My grandfather is *the* Grandfather. The man who saved humanity? I'm Eli *Papadopoulos.*"

Clarence only smiled amiably. If Eli didn't know better, he could almost have believed the kid had never even heard the name.

Eli glanced over at Geraldine again. Her eyes were closed, and she appeared to be in some kind of trance. "Why was she brought here in the first place? What did she do to end up in an InfiniCorp reeducation facility?"

"Oh, I hear she snuck out of her dome without telling anyone. They found her wandering around Outside in the desert." Clarence took another bite of his pizza. "So anyway, that's why my advice to you is, don't try to fight it. Do the right thing and admit you were wrong. You'll feel better once you let yourself go with the flow. Really, it's pretty cool here. You'll see."

Back at the worktable again, Eli's hands shook. He was still mulling over what Clarence had said about Geraldine, how after her visit to the fifteenth floor, she'd just *forgotten* about resisting. And yet nobody appeared troubled by this, or by anything else in this cheerless place.

In fact, everyone seemed *happy.* It was weird.

How could this be?

The answer seemed a little clearer a moment later, when the overhead spheres suddenly glowed bright. All at once everyone set their work down and looked up, gazing contentedly at the glimmering orbs. Eli felt the pull of the CloudNet drawing his own eyes upward. He tried, but he couldn't stop himself from looking.

The stream in the sphere was short, a series of brief statements from famous celebrities about the high quality of company T-shirts and their importance to the InfiniCorp community. When it was over, Eli went back to his work feeling refreshed and invigorated. He was suddenly eager to meet the challenge of making his daily quota—even *excited* about it.

Then he caught himself.

This sudden feeling of euphoria wasn't real. He would have to keep reminding himself of that. He had to stay alert to reality if he was ever going to find a way to contact anyone beyond the tower.

It was past eight in the evening when the three hundred seventieth crate was packed. Eli was exhausted. At the sound of a whistle, he followed the other Waywards to the cafeteria where, still caked in sweat, he shoveled down cold spaghetti as though he hadn't eaten in weeks. After that, everyone split into groups—boys on one side, girls on the other. Eli was told to stick with a group from his table. He followed Clarence down one flight of stairs to a cramped dormitory area with twelve bunk beds along the walls, several broken-down sofas, and yet another CloudNet sphere, floating in the center. Eli was shown to the only empty bunk, the one just below Clarence's, where a clean uniform was waiting for him.

After an unsatisfying shower where the water came out in a feeble stream, he discovered all the other boys lazing on the sofas, watching the CloudNet.

"Come join us," Clarence called, his eyes only briefly looking away from the sphere. "This is our Rewards Time. We earned it."

"Uh . . . no, thanks." Inside, Eli was desperate to find a way to avoid watching any more of the CloudNet than he already had, but there didn't seem to be anything else to do. In the end he climbed onto his bed and faced the wall. None of the other kids seemed to mind that he was being antisocial.

In fact, nobody said a word, not even to each other.

Much later, after lights-out, he lay awake, listening. Apart from the gentle snoring of the other boys, he thought he could hear the sound of heavy machinery grinding somewhere far below. The clang of metal on metal. A distant *shoosh, shoosh, shoosh* of pistons. He thought about the old man in the sky and the boy on the Bubble tram, and he wondered if what he was hearing was an oil pump, the sound of the last petroleum on earth being sucked from deep under the seabed.

If only his family would contact him. Surely Mother and Father wouldn't abandon him here. Not Sebastian either. They would come for him eventually. But by now a new set of worries was creeping into his thoughts:

What if they didn't know where he was?

What if Spider was hiding him from everyone and was planning to keep him here forever?

As his first week on Learning Floor 9-B came to a close, Eli's hope began to fade. The Guardians watched everything, and nobody seemed willing to help, not even the other Waywards.

Every day was pretty much the same. Work started at

seven a.m. and ended when the quota was completed. Way-wards were kept busy all the time, and every few hours the CloudNet spheres would blaze bright. Whenever Eli felt the pleasant numbing effect taking hold of him, he would make an effort to pull his eyes away, but it was hard to block it completely. Each morning he dragged himself to the work line less convinced he would ever get out of this place. He'd spend the rest of his days here, long hours filled with nothing but T-shirts and glowing spheres—a dismal, empty existence, despite the promise of contentment on the signs that were posted everywhere.

But after a few more days, he started to feel a little different.

For one thing, he began to appreciate his job. It was less stressful than his old life of tedious management studies. Compared with that, the mindless busywork of matching shirt parts was a welcome relief. Plus, there was something to be said for the fact that everyone really did seem happy. Eli was getting faster on the production line too. Several times a day Representative Dowd or one of the other Productivity Facilitators would look over his shoulder and comment. "Good work, Representative Papadopoulos," they would say. "We're so glad to have you on the team."

It was nice to finally feel valued.

He still missed Marilyn and worried about what had happened to her, but even those thoughts started to seem distant somehow, as if he were standing outside himself and looking in. More and more, what he felt was regret that he'd let the company down. It seemed that Representative Tinker had been right when she'd promised that productivity would be the best thing for him.

He spent his days working on the Learning Floor, and at night he joined Clarence and the other boys from his group as they trudged down to the glowing sphere in their dormitory bunk room. After just a few days he realized it simply wasn't possible to block out the spheres completely. In spite of himself, he even began to look forward to CloudNet breaks from the production line. They were always brief. A short infomercial, an inspirational clip about some new InfiniCorp product, perhaps a sneak peek at an upcoming docudrama about how great it was to work for the company.

Whatever it was, as he watched he felt his worries disappear like magic.

"Believe in yourself," a smiling boy might whisper as he stood at the edge of a high cliff. Then, closing his eyes and taking a deep breath, he would let himself fall backward off the edge, and the camera would follow him as he plummeted down, down, down, until finally he would land in the protective arms of a company executive. Then the boy would open his eyes again and whisper the words that appeared in the air above him:

"Trust yourself. Trust InfiniCorp."

An attractive girl would show off her artificial ears, over-sized and blue, which shimmered with light. "DESPERATELY SEEKING GLOW LOBES?" Every Wayward on the production floor would nod. Eli even caught himself doing it. After all, it really *would* be cool to have ears like that. "THEN BE THE FASTEST PRODUCER OF THE WEEK AND WIN A TRIP TO THE EIGHTEENTH FLOOR TO VISIT . . . THE GLAMOURAMA!"

"Ohhhh!" the Waywards would murmur with excitement

as the spheres dimmed. Everyone including Eli would throw themselves back into their work with renewed energy.

At the back of his mind he realized his enthusiasm for these things came, at least in part, from the influence of the CloudNet, but that thought no longer bothered him as much. After all, what did it matter, really? It wasn't like life was so horrible here. Everyone was nice, the work made him feel useful, and at night he slept on a comfortable, soft bed. The production area no longer seemed as dreary as it had at first. The air wasn't as stale and the heat didn't bother him. Even the fake flower arrangements on the wall seemed less depressing now. In fact, he kind of liked them. Leafy green vines had grown up the walls, along with little white and yellow flowers—many more than he'd noticed at first—and it totally brightened the place up.

How could he have missed that before?

It wasn't that he no longer thought about contacting his family, it was just that it didn't seem quite as urgent as it used to. Every morning he woke up more or less resigned to the idea of putting in another full day's work for the team. And at night when he sank, exhausted, into his bunk, he slept peacefully.

After two weeks of making T-shirts, Eli's life had taken on an otherworldly quality, as if he were living in a beautiful dream game where smiling, friendly people helped each other by helping the company. The production area practically glowed. It was lush and green, alive with zillions of flowers of countless varieties and colors. They grew on all the walls, up the purple girders, and even across the ceiling. It was like working in a beautiful jungle. It was amazing. It made him happy.

Deep down he knew this feeling wasn't real, that it was just the CloudNet messing with his head. He would still remind himself of this, but less often now, and with less conviction. After all, what did it matter if this happy glow wasn't exactly genuine? Considering everything he'd done—turning his back on his family, betraying the company by meeting with members of a criminal organization with nutty ideas about the end of the world—living this way was better than he deserved.

And the fact was, he was too tired to care anymore.

Eventually he stopped worrying about it at all. He worked through his pile of T-shirt parts, feeling content for the first time in what seemed like forever. He didn't need to feel inadequate anymore. He was productive, life was okay, and each day that passed seemed better and better.

One morning on the production floor, he was vaguely aware of one of the other Waywards, a Packer, watching him from the other end of the room. A tall, broad-shouldered girl, she had a tangle of frizzy hair that was so long and out of control that she looked deranged, like a wild beast.

This wasn't the only time Eli had caught her watching him. A recent transfer to his Learning Floor, Eli had first noticed her about a week earlier. From that initial day, she'd seemed to take a special interest in him. Several times he'd looked up and caught her eyeing him, and she'd looked away, her expression returning to that empty, glassy-eyed stare that all the Waywards had. For this reason Eli had been avoiding her all week. Whenever she moved nearer to him in the cafeteria line, he would pretend to wander in another direction. Before he sat to eat, he would always wait until she'd set her tray down somewhere so he could choose a different table.

There was something about her expression, and how she seemed to track his every move. It made him nervous.

He didn't want any trouble.

Later that afternoon he had to pee. He raised his hand to alert one of the Productivity Facilitators, who nodded that he had permission to leave the table and go to the bathroom. This was the standard procedure. As he made his way down a short hallway and then around a corner to the bathrooms, his thoughts were on his work, not the frizzy-haired girl.

Which was why, after he finished with the bathroom, he nearly jumped when he found her in the hallway, standing in his path. Her glassy-eyed expression was gone. It was as if she'd been waiting for him.

Eli froze.

"I've been watching you," she whispered. "You're not like the others. The CloudNet doesn't have the same hold on you as it has on them. Don't deny it. You're like me. You're stronger."

A sudden sick feeling gripped Eli's insides. Whatever this was, he wanted no part of it. But when he tried to step around the girl, she blocked his path.

"What are you doing?" he demanded, keeping his voice low. "Are you crazy? Do you want the Productivity Facilitators on us for slacking off? Let me go! I need to get back to my work!"

But she didn't budge. Her eyes stayed locked on his. "Listen to me," she said. "You have the ability to fight the influence of the spheres. I know you already figured out how because I've seen you do it." She stepped even closer, and Eli found himself backed against the wall. "Ignore the dream things," she whispered. "Look past them. Concentrate on my eyes. Follow my voice. Resist. You can do it. *Wake. Up.*"

Eli was sweating, and it wasn't the heat. He glanced over her shoulder. If he craned his neck he could just see around the corner to the hallway. As far as he could tell, it was clear. For now.

"Go away," he said, barely able to get the words out. "Leave me alone or I'll call the Guardians."

The girl narrowed her eyes. "I'm sorry," she said, "but you leave me no choice but to do this the hard way. Remember, this is for your own good."

And with that Eli felt her fist slam hard into his stomach. The pain was sharp and sudden. If he could have screamed, he would have, but nothing would come out. He buckled over. He wasn't hurt, but the wind had been knocked out of him for a moment. When he straightened up, he looked back at the girl, clenched his fists, and got ready to rush at her.

But then he stopped himself.

Because at that instant he realized something had changed. The hallway had lost its glow and had returned to being dreary and gray. For the first time in a long time, his head didn't feel muddled, and his thoughts and feelings felt like they were really his own.

Except it didn't feel like such a great thing, because all at once terror gripped him. In a flash, everything he'd all but forgotten came rushing back: The Friends of Gustavo. The end of the world. Eli was a captive somewhere far, far away from home, a prisoner trapped by Spider in some secret tower for brain-dead InfiniCorp slaves. It all seemed too crazy to be true, and yet here he was. He was having trouble breathing. What was he going to do? He was all alone! He'd lost contact with Marilyn, and Grandfather was sick—or worse. For all Eli knew, he could be dead by now!

And then he remembered his parents. Somehow he had to contact them! He had to tell them everything! He wanted to run, but this strange, wild-haired girl had him by the shoulders now. He tried to shake her off but she was stronger than he was.

"Hold on, Eli. Don't you panic on me. Get a grip on yourself. In just a few seconds the Guardians are going to come looking for us, so if you know what's good for you you'll listen to me very carefully." He stopped struggling, and she went on. "You need to do what I do. Keep focusing on the things that are *real*. Never stop fighting the spheres. You can do it. But no matter what happens, you also have to keep acting like the others, the drones. Never let your guard down. Never let the Guardians suspect for one second that you're not under their complete control."

Terrified, Eli stared into her gray eyes. "Who are you?"

"My name is Tabitha. You and I are going to break out of here."

18

another resister

Tabitha estimated she'd been at the reeducation facility for four or five months by then, and she knew how to stay under the radar. No matter what happened, she worked hard and kept to herself. The trick was to hold her expression blank all the time, with only the slightest hint of fear and submission. She realized early on that if she was ever going to escape, her abnormally high resistance to the spheres had to stay a secret.

After her stay in the admissions ward, she'd been sent to Learning Floor 1-C, on the tower's lowest level, where Waywards loaded and unloaded supply transports. It was tough, sweaty work. The heat on the dock was dizzying, and the sour milk stench of the acidified ocean, red from all the algae, made her retch. But as difficult as the conditions were, she'd also grown strong here, stronger than she'd ever been. For the first time in her life she was aware of the muscles in her back and arms, the power in her legs and shoulders. There didn't seem to be any mirrors in the tower, but she once caught a flash of her own reflection on the surface of a CloudNet sphere and barely recognized herself. Gone was the foolish intern from St. Louis, the failed dissident who'd spent her every moment living in constant fear while trying to appear respectable. Staring back at her was a steely-eyed girl with hair that hadn't seen a comb in ages, a wild kid who looked like she could handle herself in a fight.

She looked like a survivor.

Tabitha fought a smile. A survivor was exactly what she was. As far as she knew, she was the only Wayward still in command of her own thoughts, the only one in control of her own destiny. None of the Guardians or Productivity Facilitators seemed to suspect she was just biding her time, waiting for her chance to break out.

For weeks she'd kept alert for information, any weakness in the system she could exploit. One thing that struck her was how low-tech the place was. Not only were there no robots and few other modern devices beyond the CloudNet spheres and the electronic locks on the doors, but often she noticed the Guardians walking around with paper documents, like in the Old Days. The records on each of the Waywards were stored in hard copy in a room on the first floor not far from her own work area. Whenever a newbie arrived, Tabitha would see Guardians going in there with paper files labeled with the newbie's name. She didn't know why they used this quaint storage system, but perhaps it was to be sure the records were well hidden and off-line. If need be, they could shred them out of existence.

Tabitha had toyed with the idea of stowing herself in one of the larger supply transports, but it was hard to see how she could pull off such a stunt without getting caught. Too many Guardians kept watch over the docking area. All the ships and pods were searched at every departure and arrival. Every crate that entered or left was inspected.

One night, while the other Waywards on her team were sleeping, she'd climbed through an air vent in her fifth-floor dormitory room. It was a risky move, but she'd gotten away with it. In the cramped darkness and heat she'd crawled through a series of ventilation ducts—at one point forcing herself to squeeze down a narrow vertical section despite her fear of heights. Eventually she'd found herself peering into the room where they kept the files on the Waywards. The walls were lined with metal cabinets, many rusting and dented. There was nobody in there, but she didn't dare climb down. She kept crawling. Soon she was over the docking area of Learning Floor 1-C, the same place where she worked all day, every day.

Even at night the place was crawling with Guardians.

Back in her bunk she lay awake, thinking. What she needed was a diversion. If she could distract the Guardians' attention, she could sneak into one of the smaller pods and fly it away herself. This seemed more realistic than stowing herself in one of the large, water-bound transport ships and hoping not to be discovered. The trouble was, how could she distract the Guardians without drawing attention to herself? If they grabbed her and realized she wasn't under the spell of the spheres, any chance of escaping would be gone forever.

She knew she would only ever get one opportunity to do this right.

In the days that followed, Tabitha felt her optimism slipping away. Despite her decision to go it alone, there was no avoiding the conclusion that she needed help. But where was she going to find anybody willing to sacrifice themselves for her? In this tower full of InfiniCorp drones and Wayward zombies, it wasn't going to happen. So every night she curled up in bed with her face in her hands, sure she was doomed to work in the reeducation facility for whatever was left of her short life.

But then one day they transferred her to Learning Floor 9-B.

And that's where everything changed.

On her very first morning packing T-shirts into crates, she noticed something strange about one of the other Waywards, a stocky, black-haired boy sorting fabric at one of the tables. There was something different about the way he behaved, something subtle but important, and it drew her attention to him right away. His eyelids drooped a little less than the others. He was just a little slower to look up at the spheres when they glowed bright. Some part of his brain appeared to be struggling to remain alert. Few people would have noticed, but Tabitha recognized the signs right away.

This boy was demonstrating an impressive resistance to the spheres.

True, he seemed to be *losing* his battle against them, but he was the only other Wayward she'd ever come across with the strength to even try. The realization that she wasn't alone, that she'd found another Resister like herself, gave her hope.

She kept watching. The kid obviously hadn't been trained to hide his efforts, because he seemed to make no attempt to conceal the subtle struggle in his expression. If he wasn't more careful, Tabitha worried somebody else would eventually notice too.

And there was something else that struck her about him. Something familiar about his face. At first she couldn't figure it out, but then she realized what it was: he looked a lot like someone she remembered seeing in a photograph. It was in a company zine she'd read before she was taken from St. Louis. The article was about Sebastian Papadopoulos, one of Grandfather's most ubiquitous and tiresome grandspawns, and how he was about to start his career at InfiniCorp, but for some reason Tabitha's eye had been drawn to the sullen-faced boy reading in the background. According to the image notes, it was Sebastian's little brother—Ari or Leo or some short name like that. She couldn't remember.

Anyway, if she didn't know better, she would have sworn this was the same kid.

But of course it couldn't be. Why would a member of the ruling family end up here, doing grunt work with a bunch of Waywards? It didn't make sense.

And yet the more she studied him, the more she wondered. The resemblance was so striking, and the Productivity Facilitators even seemed to talk to the boy with unusual deference.

On her second day she saw the kid do something stupid. In the middle of the shift he stood up from his work, glanced around the room, droopy-eyed and confused, like a sleepwalker on the point of waking from a dream, and then started shouting.

"Help!" he called, to nobody in particular, it seemed. "There's been a mistake! Let me—let me talk with someone! Let me ping home! Please!"

Right away one of the Productivity Facilitators was on him. "Settle down, Representative Papadopoulos," she said, her voice calm but commanding. "You need to take your seat or you'll fall behind on your work."

For a few seconds he just stood there squinting at her, as if he were having trouble processing her words. Then he said, "But . . . I don't belong here."

"I said *sit down,* Eli!" All at once her expression softened, and she put her hand on his shoulder. "The spheres will be coming on again in a moment. You don't want to miss that, do you?"

He hesitated, but then he slumped into his seat again. A moment later he was back to sorting fabric.

None of the other Waywards seemed to notice any of this. Everybody kept smiling their empty smiles and working as fast as ever, as if nothing had happened. Tabitha pretended not to have noticed either, but her thoughts were swirling. So he *was* a Papadopoulos! How was this possible? How on earth did he end up here?

She didn't have long to wonder. Just after the boy settled back into his work, the Productivity Facilitator stepped over to Tabitha's end of the room and spoke in low tones with one of the nearby Guardians. Tabitha strained to listen. She didn't catch it all, but she heard them discussing the boy's case. He'd been caught leading a group of anti-InfiniCorp criminals. There was no mistaking the name of the group either. She heard the words distinctly.

It was the Friends of Gustavo.

When Tabitha heard that, she nearly dropped the box she was carrying. It was almost too much to take in. The idea of a Papadopoulos enslaved in an InfiniCorp labor facility was bizarre enough, but that he'd been accused of being one of the leaders of the *Friends*? No, it was too incredible. She glanced over at him again and saw only a sweaty, confused kid tangled in a dream, like all the other Waywards. She couldn't picture him with a secret life as a Fog agent. Even if the company believed it, Tabitha didn't. In fact, he looked so pitiful that she couldn't help feeling sorry for him.

But she reminded herself that he was a Papadopoulos, which meant he didn't deserve her sympathy. The Papadopouloses were a family of tyrants. This was one point she believed the Friends had right. Grandfather and his oppressive clan of thugs were at the very center of the problem she'd risked so much to struggle against. They were the whole reason she and the rest of the Waywards were stuck in this tower. So why should she feel bad for this boy? If the Guardians decided to drag him away because of the shouting incident, why should she lose any sleep over it?

The Guardians didn't drag him away, though. For the rest of the day they let him stay working at his table. Maybe it was because he was a Papadopoulos, or maybe it was because the Guardians decided that he wasn't a real threat, that he would fall fully under the spell of the spheres soon enough anyway. Tabitha didn't know. Whatever the reason they'd let it go this time, Tabitha doubted he'd ever get away with causing a second scene like that, which meant he needed help learning to fight the spheres while appearing not to. So over the next few days she kept her eyes on him and struggled with what to do. She'd been thinking about her escape plan again. An idea had come to her, but she wasn't sure she could bring herself to carry it out.

In the end she made her decision.

Which was why she confronted him in the little hallway outside the bathrooms. It wasn't easy, but she managed to pull him out of his half trance just before the Guardians came looking for them. Now she was waiting for her next opportunity to get close to him.

She wondered if she would regret her decision. If there had been an option that didn't require the assistance of a Papadopoulos, of all people, she would have gone for it in a second. But she couldn't think of any other way.

That evening there was another storm, the worst since Tabitha had been in the tower. All night she lay in her bunk, listening to the howling wind and the thunder that shook the walls. The whole room rocked and swayed. Tabitha tried not to think about the waves out there, but it was hard not to picture them growing higher and stronger as night wore on. She couldn't help imagining every crash as the beginning of the end, as if the sea itself were reaching out to grab the tower by the neck and drag it into the depths.

It would happen eventually, she knew.

She wasn't sure if there was a God, but maybe if she prayed hard enough she could hold off the inevitable for a while. She closed her eyes and mouthed the words over and over again.

Not now. Not yet.

274

* * *

By early the next morning, the rumbles of thunder sounded farther away. The worst of it had passed, for now. The air was hotter and heavier, though, and Tabitha's shirt was caked in sweat. As she filled crates with T-shirts and stacked them in the loading area, she kept glancing over at the Papadopoulos boy. He sat at his table, looking pale and cheerless as he did his work.

This was worrying. If he wasn't more careful, the Guardians were going to notice.

At lunchtime she found him sitting alone in the cafeteria, so she sidled over to him. For once he didn't wander off the moment she got close.

"You again," he said without looking up. Even his sandwich looked sad. Crumbly bread, dried-up lettuce, and some kind of meat.

"Welcome back to earth," she whispered. "Consider me your tour guide."

He didn't even crack a smile. Once again Tabitha almost felt sorry for him.

In the distance there was another murmur of thunder. "Look," she said, "you can't mope or they'll catch on to you. You have to keep acting like everything's beautiful and you feel terrific. Try not to look anyone in the eye too long. If you do, smile. And don't trust anyone."

"Why should I trust you, then?"

Good question, she thought. In spite of everything, she found herself liking the kid. "Because I'm all you've got now." She examined her own lunch. A dry roll with some kind of dirty, watered-down soup. "A few days ago I saw you arguing with the Guardians. Don't do that again unless you want to take a trip to Special Training and come back a walking basket case. Never let your emotions control you. Most of all, whenever the spheres kick in, you need to pick something genuine to focus on. Sensations are good. Pinch yourself if you have to. Force your eyes to look to one side of the image."

"How am I supposed to do that? The spheres are so strong."

"Don't worry. You can pull it off, I can tell. And it gets easier with practice."

For the first time he looked at her. "What do you want from me?"

"I told you yesterday. In this crowd of sleepwalkers, a kid who can think for himself is a rare commodity. We can help each other." She filled him in about Learning Floor 1-C, about the shipping boats and transport pods. She was careful how much detail she went into, though, especially about all the Guardians who kept watch down there. The kid already looked terrified enough, and she couldn't afford to scare him away. Like it or not, she needed him.

"I don't see how you expect to get away with stealing a pod," he said when she was finished. "Even if you somehow make it out of here without getting shot out of the sky, then what? Where do you go?"

"Where else? We can't go back to the domes, so our only choice is to hide in the wasteland." His eyes fell back to his tray. Tabitha could tell he thought she was nuts. This wasn't going to be easy. "There are safe places out there," she said. "Sanctuaries where people know their way around the desert."

"What people? Outsiders, you mean? Cutthroats and lunatics and cannibals? You expect them to lend a hand?"

"No, people like you and me. Friends who can show us how they survive. They're out there, Eli—we just have to find them."

"How can you know that for sure? Have you been out there? Do you know anyone who has?"

Tabitha hesitated. This wasn't going as well as she'd hoped. And the truth was that she knew nothing for sure. She was making a leap of faith, hoping the Friends were right about this. Because what other option did she have?

"No," she admitted, "it's just what I've been told. But no matter what, don't you think even the *chance* of surviving Outside beats the certainty of living like a zombie in here? We sure can't go back to InfiniCorp."

Eli played with his napkin. "Listen, I know you're trying to help me, and I appreciate it, but I think you and I are in different situations. Maybe you can't go back to InfiniCorp, but I'm only here because of a mistake. I won't be here much longer."

Tabitha stared. Was he serious or was he playing with her? Could he really be that naive? "Let me get this straight," she said, careful not to raise her voice. "You're waiting for dear old heroic Granddaddy to burst through those doors and save your precious Papadopoulos butt? Well, forget it. I hate to be the one to break it to you, Prince Eli, but if you're here it means somebody *wants* you here. This tower is the end of the line, and there's no going home. Not for any of us, not even you."

His face went pink. "That proves how little you know."

"Oh really? So what's this I hear about you and the Friends of Gustavo?"

That seemed to catch him off guard. His mouth opened and closed, and then he dropped his gaze again. "That was my own fault," he said, "my own stupidity. Yeah, I spoke with a Fogger. Two, actually, and now my cousin Spider has it in his head that I'm part of some conspiracy. What I did was dumb, I know, and I won't do it again. But just because I screwed up, it doesn't mean I was working against the company. I wasn't." He looked up. "Why, what do you know about the Friends of Gustavo?"

"I know a little," she said. "It's hard even for me to believe it now, but I used to be one of them."

As soon as she said it, she realized she'd made a mistake. Eli's expression hardened. It was a few seconds before he spoke again. "Oh, I get it now. I should have known. So that's what you meant about finding help Outside. You people are still trying to rope me in. Or maybe you're just setting me up for some kind of trap."

"No, that's not—"

"What's the matter with you people? I already told the old man I'm not interested in joining. I'm not like you! And now because of you Foggers I'm stuck here. Haven't you done enough to me already? Why can't you *leave me alone*?"

"Keep your voice down," Tabitha said through her teeth. All around them kids were eating and talking, and the last thing she wanted was to draw anybody's attention. She leaned in closer. "First of all, the Friends—the Foggers, as you call them—didn't arrange for you to be here. It's not how they work. Second, I believe you that you're not Friend material. That's obvious. And anyway, didn't you hear what I said? I'm not one of them anymore."

"Oh, I see. You *were* a traitor, but now you're all reformed."

Tabitha's blood rushed. Of all the people she might have ended up with, why did it have to be *this* kid? Here he was, imprisoned in a slave tower, and even now he was so confused that he wasn't ready to admit the truth. He obviously wasn't going to understand.

She should have expected this.

"You're not the only mistake the Friends ever made," she said at last, trying to stay calm. "They ruined my life and then abandoned me. And, no, I don't believe most of the stuff they believe in anymore. Gustavo. The Wild Orange Yonder. I tried to for a while, but I don't think I ever really did."

"Then why go running Outside, looking for them?"

"You have any better ideas? Or are you okay with the prospect of rotting your life away?" Tabitha's fists were clenched. She had plenty more to say, but that was when, over Eli's shoulder, she noticed one of the Guardians wandering between the tables not far away. She swallowed her anger and forced a vacant smile. She'd had plenty of practice hiding her emotions, but she worried about Eli. He was a newbie. But when she started sipping at her lumpy soup and making happy sounds like it was the most delicious soup she'd ever tasted, he

279

seemed to get it that something was up. He smiled too and started murmuring about glow lobes.

She was glad to see that at least he wasn't a complete fool.

Even after the Guardian moved on, it was a while before either of them spoke again. The storm Outside wasn't quite finished yet. The wind picked up, and Tabitha could feel the tower sway just a little.

"What about the end of the world?" Eli asked, calmer now. "If you don't believe in most of what the Friends say anymore, does that mean you don't believe these are the Final Days?"

Sweat trickled down Tabitha's neck. Glancing around at the room, all she saw were zombie slave children sitting empty-eyed in the heat and stink of the cafeteria while Guardians stood watching. Even away from the spheres of the productivity area, many of the kids still gazed at a glowing screen on the wall, an ad for yet another dream game. Just at that moment there was another distant peal of thunder. To Tabitha it all seemed so pathetic and sad that it was almost funny.

If the Guardians hadn't been watching, she might have laughed.

"I can't deny that one," she said. "If this isn't the end of the world, then I don't know what is."

Eli stayed quiet awhile. "I'm not saying I believe, and I'm not saying I don't," he said at last. "All I know is, as soon as I have the chance, I'm going to tell my family about this place. I'm going to have a lot to say." And then he mumbled something as if only to himself. " 'The time has come,' the Walrus said, 'to talk of many things . . .' "

"What was that?" Tabitha wondered if she'd overestimated him. Was he falling back into the Wayward trance again?

But then he gave her a half smile. "Oh, it was just something the old man said."

"What old man?"

"One of the Foggers I met. A crazy old guy who told me he was Gustavo."

Tabitha raised an eyebrow. "Well, you're right about one thing. He must have been crazy if he thought he was Gustavo. He couldn't have been. Not *the* Gustavo, anyway. If that guy really existed at all, he must have died years ago."

Eli nodded. "I know. And I admit he had me wondering at first, but now I realize it had to be his brain fever talking. He told me he used to work for the company and that he knew my grandfather. I even saw an old image and started to convince myself it might have been him. The craziest part was that he said he saw me in a dream and that I had a special destiny to fulfill some prophecy about saving or destroying the world. Which is ridiculous. He called me a weird name too—el Guía."

"He called you *that*?" Tabitha wasn't sure what to say. What he was telling her was completely whacked. No wonder the kid was such a mess. "Trust me, Eli, it had to be his brain fever talking. Whoever the Outsider was, he was playing with your head."

The bell rang, warning that only four minutes remained before they had to head back to the Learning Floor. All around them Waywards began to get up from their tables and shuffle over to the tray conveyor belt.

"Listen," Tabitha whispered, "like I said, we don't have

much time. I'm offering you a chance to break out and *live* for the rest of your life, however long that might be. Are you in, or do you still have so much faith in your virtuous relatives that you're willing to risk wasting away in this place?"

Eli narrowed his eyes at her. "Don't act like you know anything about my family. You don't. When I tell my parents the whole truth about how my cousin is running this tower, they'll shut it down." He turned away. "Risking my life with some crazy Fogger escape plan isn't the answer."

"Your family's going to shut down the work tower?" Tabitha repeated, unsure if he was kidding. "Eli, how do you think the domes have stayed running so long? All those people living their little bubble lives. How do you think they make it all function? What, you think this tower is the only one? Don't try to pretend you never knew. Your whole clan runs this organization, not just some bad-egg cousin of yours. You people *built* this system."

Eli's face reddened. "I don't believe it. My family isn't perfect, but we're not monsters. Grandfather is a good man. Whether you want to admit it or not, he saved us from extinction and made the cities work even when the rest of the world was dead. We Papadopouloses kept everyone safe and alive." His jaw tight, he pushed his chair back and stood up.

"You're making a mistake."

"Maybe. But I already listened to you people once, and look where it got me."

"Eli, you can't be serious—"

"Leave me alone."

Tabitha watched as he picked up his tray and joined the

others. She wanted to run after him, take him by the shoulders and shake him. Instead, though, she grabbed her own tray and headed as calmly as she could to the back of the line. This wasn't over. She hadn't made it this far only to lose her one chance of escape because of somebody else's misguided loyalty.

She wasn't finished with Eli Papadopoulos.

19

the nature of nature

Soaking wet and covered in mud, Marilyn limped down the median strip between two lanes of broken asphalt.

It had been raining for four days. She'd spent the previous night shivering under one of the thousands of abandoned cars she'd passed along the highway. Near exhaustion, she'd tucked herself up among rusted pipes and decayed rubber tubing in hopes it would at least partially shelter her from the downpour. Instead of sleeping, though, she'd spent most of the night listening to the wind and rain. In her brief moments of slumber, she found herself besieged with the same torments she'd faced every day since she'd been Outside.

Wind and sodden earth. Lightning and hunger and wild dogs.

Even in her dreams, she couldn't escape these things now.

She'd been following Eli's distant signal for five days, ever since she'd left the Providence dome. Always moving, she'd kept to the same road as much as possible because she didn't trust her own ability to navigate through the unfamiliar. Once, back in the Long Ago, it had been a highway known as Interstate 95. Marilyn knew this because there were rusted green and white signs that said so. Every now and then she passed under them—ancient signposts for travelers who no longer existed.

It had been days since she'd seen a human being. As far as she could tell, she was the only traveler out here now.

According to the signs, she was somewhere in Connecticut, just beyond the ruins of a city called Bridgeport. Every mile she covered looked more or less the same. Disintegrating pavement. Barren fields of mud and rubble. Dead trees like corpses. Now and then she came across the ruins of a former city or town, some deserted business center with crumbling bridges and empty, dilapidated buildings. And since the rain began, everything.was flooded.

Worst of all was the hunger. In all her life she'd never known it like this. On the first day, before the rain began, there had at least been the insects that swarmed in thick clouds through the air. But the rain had made bugs difficult to find, and now she was ravenous. Every once in a while she came across the remains of dead things, mostly animals her own size or smaller, their bones picked dry. But even if she'd had the stomach for such things, there was never any meat left on them.

After four days of running, hunger burned inside her like a fever. The ache in her belly consumed her thoughts and never left her alone. She was feeling weaker by the hour.

Toward the end of that afternoon she stopped to catch her breath. Resting behind a large rock at the crest of a hill, she could see for miles across the desolate landscape, even through the rain. A sea of empty land vehicles. An overturned bus, its rusting hulk half-submerged in water. The highway ran like a river, and, as warm as the air was, above her the looming sky was gray and cold. She closed her eyes.

I know you're still out there, my darling. Hold on. I'm coming for you.

She could still feel Eli's signal, but he made no response.

Marilyn had already had one close call with wild dogs. It had been before the rain, on her very first evening out of the dome. Any genuine animal of the wild would have sensed something approaching, Marilyn was sure, but her attention was elsewhere. She was standing in the middle of a clearing in the woods and was looking straight up at the gathering clouds, which were lined in pink and red as the hazy daylight faded. The colors were softer out here and yet at the same time more intense. She was mesmerized by the idea that these were real clouds, actual formations of crystallized water droplets that had collected up in the atmosphere and reflected natural light from the sun. There was no programming involved. Nobody had encoded them with drift logic or advertising.

These clouds simply *were*.

Watching the real sky, so vast and uncorrupted, made her feel for the first time a part of Nature, an unspoiled creation of an immense system of randomness. Yet the colors were so beautiful, they made her wonder if this system could be so random after all. Maybe there really was a Leonardo up there somewhere, overseeing things. In the unknowable scheme of the universe, wasn't it possible that someone or something might have planned all this? The clouds, the sky, even Marilyn herself? Could it be that even a brain-chipped mongoose was here for a purpose?

Looking back, she could almost feel her animal ancestors chirping at her in alarm. There she'd been, exposed in an open field and lost in pointless ruminations—hardly the thoughts of a feral mongoose fit to survive in the wilderness—and the distraction had almost killed her.

Wild dogs sprang from every direction, five of them, scraggly things with rib cages clearly visible on their emaciated bodies. They lunged across the field with their teeth bared, their yellow eyes burning with a look she understood better now. It was hunger. They'd been lured by her scent, the smell of food. They were nearly upon her.

The only reason she survived was luck.

Just as she felt the biggest and fiercest of the dogs snapping at her heels, she happened upon a narrow hole in the ground. She'd passed several of them as she'd walked into the field, and now she darted down into one. In that instant all five dogs reached the top of the hole, growling and tearing at the dirt above her. They barked and howled in frustration, but they couldn't get to her. Marilyn scratched and flailed her legs through the dirt to move herself forward. She was deep in a tunnel, and now she had time to wonder what creature had dug it and whether it might still be down there, somewhere in the gloom, ready to attack any intruder. But she wasn't going back. She took her time crawling through the darkness, uncomfortable in such a tight space. The hole smelled musty and old. Whatever animal used to live in this place, not even its scent remained. Eventually she found another way up and out of the tunnel and ended up in a thicket perhaps forty or fifty yards from where she'd leapt into the hole. By then it was pouring rain. But the dogs were gone.

From then on she'd been more careful. As she traveled, she kept her eye out for escape routes, anything she could climb or dig under or hide inside at a moment's notice. A concrete wall. A car with a half-open window. Even the water itself could be used as cover.

At night she dreamed of the wild dogs—fearsome, starving creatures with tongues that lolled out of their mouths as they ran at her. She knew they were still out there, packs of skeletons hunting the wasteland.

Every now and then she heard barking in the distance.

Late in the morning she came to a stretch of road so flooded, she was forced to leave the highway. She climbed through a grove of overturned trees and eventually stumbled onto a passable road, this one narrow and winding. She followed it awhile, moving slower and slower as her energy waned.

At a curve in the road she stopped to rest again, wondering how long she could last without finding something to eat. A small, desolate village lay ahead and, just in front of her, a sign that tilted to one side. Most of the paint had been chipped away, but she could see it had once been blue with carved gold letters:

Welcome to Hartsburg
Population 1,061
"Home Is Where the Hart Is!"

Minutes later she was slinking through the town's sodden, muddy streets. Collapsed wooden houses, windowless and dripping. More deserted vehicles. A simple white church with a steeple that, incredibly, still stood upright even as the wind whipped garbage across the road. Marilyn moved with caution, alert for anything that might jump out at her. Wild dogs weren't the only danger. She wondered when she would run into more barbarians like the old man in the sky or the hag that had nearly killed Eli. But she saw nobody. This place was empty, a ghost town.

Up ahead a small clapboard building caught her eye. It had a sign that said HARTSBURG GROCERY. Its exterior was weatherworn and many of the clapboards were missing, but the building itself was still upright, and it still had a door. Her heart beat faster. With energy she didn't realize she still had, she ran toward it. Maybe her luck had turned. The perishable food would be long gone, of course, but maybe she would find *something* inside. Canned goods, perhaps? Opening a can would present a problem, but, given the chance, she was sure she could figure a way to get to the food. After all, she was desperate.

At the side of the little building she stopped to consider how she was going to get inside. All the windows were broken, but they were too high to reach. After a moment she went back to the street and found a long, dead tree branch. She dragged it to the side of the store, propped it against the wall, and then climbed to the window. Her pulse was racing. Food, at last! She could almost taste it. She hopped inside and dropped to the floor.

There was nothing. Just bits of twisted metal that might once have been shelving, all broken into pieces and strewn about the room. Somebody had been here first and had already ransacked the place. From the thick layer of dust, it must have been a while ago. The room stank of mildew, and even the wood flooring felt spongy under her paws.

When she turned her head she noticed a faded message spray painted across the entire back wall. The spelling was poor and the letters were misshapen and crude, as if a child had written them:

SALGAN O MUERAN! GET OUT OR diE!!
THiS STuF FOWNd BY Big diEGO
AND HiS dETH RADERS
WE EET inTRudRS

The skin on her neck prickled, but not because she thought whoever had written it might burst into the room. It was obvious nobody had been here for a long, long time. But still the message itself left her breathless, especially the last part. She wondered if it was true or just a threat. And what had happened to these people, whoever they were? After the food was all used up, where had they gone? And if they and everybody else were dead or dying somewhere, what was the purpose of anything? Why would the great architect of all natural things allow this?

But she couldn't let herself get distracted with pointless questions. All that mattered now was that she was still weak with hunger and there was nothing here to eat. She was on her own in the middle of the Outside wilderness during a storm, and if she didn't find food soon, she was going to starve. And Eli still needed her help.

Marilyn dragged herself down the road again, away from the town. The thunder seemed louder and more frequent, and the wind and rain blew hard in her face. After a while she stopped under a low bridge to take a drink and caught a glimpse of her reflection in the water. She didn't recognize herself. She was skinny and haggard, and her fur was matted with mud. She looked like a drowning rat on the brink of death. Suddenly all she wanted to do was collapse. She didn't want to give up, but she felt so famished and weak. After all, she'd been running for almost five days.

Just beyond the bridge she noticed a long four-story building with open concrete walls, and floors that slanted in alternate directions. She'd seen pictures of buildings like this, old-style parking garages for the road vehicles of years long past. Surely she could find a dry place in there, a safe corner at the top of an incline where she could rest awhile, just until the storm ended. She staggered to it and climbed the first staircase to avoid the rising flood. In the center of the second level she found an elevator car that had long since stopped working. The sliding door was open, though, and despite the darkness, it was dry and comfortable and smelled relatively clean.

This would do nicely, she decided. She could lie here and get some sleep while she dried off. A few hours, that's all she needed. After that, maybe she would feel better.

She tumbled into a corner of the floor, glad to take the weight off her aching legs. Almost immediately her eyes grew heavy and she felt sleep start to take hold of her.

But that's when there was a sudden rattling sound.

She opened her eyes.

On the opposite corner of the elevator floor was a rattlesnake. Its body was coiled and its head was upright. It was staring at her, threatening to strike. Like her, it must have stumbled into this dry, comfortable place after it came into the garage seeking shelter from the storm.

She kept still, sure she was about to die.

But then, as she stared into the snake's murderous eyes, she felt something stir deep in her soul. As terrified as she was, she was overcome by a powerful wave of hate, inexplicable and primal. She realized she *despised* this slithering thing.

She wanted it dead.

After all she'd been through, why should she let it take her life?

All at once she knew what to do. Instead of making an immediate dash for the doorway, she took a half step *toward* the snake, just within striking range, tempting it to come for her. It did. Its head moved like a whip, but she was ready for it. The instant it made to spring at her, Marilyn leapt back through the doorway and out of its range. Despite her hunger she was still agile, and just fast enough to get away with it.

The snake was angry. It slid across the elevator floor, its fangs glistening with venom. But this was what Marilyn wanted. She let it come. She led it into the open space of the garage and saw it clearly for the first time. It was perhaps four feet long, with a thick, muscular body and a repeating diamond pattern on its brownish scales.

The snake hissed as she danced around it in a wide circle. In spite of her desperation—maybe because of it—she'd found strength she wasn't aware of. She taunted the confused reptile, stepping just within its reach and backing away the moment it attacked. It shook its rattle in fury, but Marilyn kept doing it over and over again. She was wearing it down, letting it use up its limited energy as she kept moving around it, always circling, circling. Hungry as Marilyn was, she was determined to outlast it.

Finally, after what seemed like hours, the rattlesnake was moving noticeably slower. Its head wobbled as it tried to follow Marilyn's erratic movements, and it took longer to respond when she teased it. Marilyn decided now was the time to make her own attack. She lunged at it with her claws outstretched. Just as she did so, the snake made one last dive at her, and she felt its fangs whip across her shoulder. But her fur was thick, and the venom didn't penetrate to her skin. Before the viper got a second chance, Marilyn had her jaws clamped around the narrow section of its neck, just under the head. She shook it with all her strength. The snake's body went suddenly limp.

It was dead! She'd actually killed it!

She dragged the carcass back to the elevator and started ripping hungrily into its flesh. With every delicious mouthful she felt her heart beating faster and her strength returning. She was experiencing the ecstasy of her first blood kill. It was different than she'd imagined it would be. It wasn't awful or disgusting. It wasn't even sad. It was noble and logical, the true nature of the world. She could feel a change coming over her, the dawning realization that she would never be the same again.

For the first time in her life, she felt as if the eyes of all her ancestors were watching with approval.

The next morning the rain stopped. The sky cleared and the sun blazed again. Marilyn was amazed at how quickly the bugs reemerged. By afternoon many of the puddles had all but evaporated.

She was growing stronger now, and making better time than ever.

For miles there had been an evil smell in the air, sharp and foul and unidentifiable. Faint at first, it grew stronger as she made her way south, until it burned in her throat and lungs. Something about it made her afraid.

Just before sunset she crossed the New York state line. Whatever the stench was, the air was thick with it here. It made her wary. Since she didn't know what she was afraid of, she wasn't sure how to avoid it. She climbed one of the dead trees to the highest branch that would support her and looked ahead.

There it was. She could tell right away she'd found the source of the odor. Just a quarter mile or so ahead, she could see a vast lake unlike any other she'd yet come across. Even from here she could see there was something very wrong with it. The water was an odd purplish color, and clouds of smoke billowed off its surface. Parts of the lake were on fire.

Near the edge of the ooze she could make out what looked

like the remains of dead things, hundreds of them, perhaps. Most were skeletons, stripped clean of flesh. Without moving closer she couldn't tell exactly what they were. And she wasn't going to go any closer.

One thing was sure: she couldn't stay anywhere near here tonight, even to sleep. She would have to find a path around this terrible place, even if it meant traveling in darkness many miles out of her way.

She climbed down the tree and soon she was moving west, keeping what she hoped was a safe distance between herself and the edge of the foul-smelling sludge. Minutes later, as she emerged from a patch of dead brush, she came across something crouched at the edge of a steaming pool, lapping at the ooze. She was almost on top of it before she noticed. The sky was beginning to darken, but there was still enough light to see. Whatever it was, it was skinny and hairless and long, perhaps twice the length of an adult human. It was obviously some kind of mutant. Marilyn could see right away there was something horrible about its body, something peculiar and startling. She blinked and looked again, unsure if she could trust her eyes.

Its hide was so thin, it was barely there.

She could not only make out the ridges of its backbone, but she could see the backbone itself, right through the skin. Its muscles were visible too. And what looked like internal organs.

All of a sudden it raised its gourd-shaped head as if it sensed it was being watched. Standing erect on its hind legs, it pulled itself to its full height and turned in Marilyn's direction. She wanted to run, but for a moment she couldn't. She was too terrified at what she was seeing. Its face was almost featureless. Its nose was sunken into its skull, and where its eyes should have been were only two thin circles of skin. She could see into the empty sockets behind them.

It lowered its head as if trying to take in her scent. Then it lumbered toward her.

Marilyn took a step back into the thicket. And then another. Soon she was running. Behind her she heard the thing make a low, plaintive wail that seemed to hang over the wilderness. It sent shivers through her bones and filled her heart with dread. But she didn't stop. She would run all night if she had to. And after that she would keep moving, continuing south as fast and hard as she could, for as long as it took. She had a great distance yet to go, she knew, but even now she could sense she was getting closer to Eli. She could still feel him.

As long as she could follow his signal, she wasn't going to give up.

Not ever.

20

faith and doubt

Eli tried to keep up a brave face. No matter what Spider thought of him, he was still a Papadopoulos.

How long had he been in this place? A few days? A month? He wasn't sure anymore. The powerful spheres seemed to warp time, and every day felt more or less the same. The manual labor never ended, and most of his waking hours were spent fighting the CloudNet. As Tabitha had suggested, he'd been finding real things to focus his mind on, but keeping alert here was a lot harder than living in the dream haze.

In a way, he almost wished she had left him there.

Every now and then the spheres gave updates about Grandfather. He was getting weaker by the day and wasn't expected to live much longer. Huge crowds were gathered in domes all across the country. The biggest crowd of all held a vigil in front of Papadopoulos Mansion, in New Washington. Watching all this, Clarence and the other Waywards would get teary-eyed. But for Eli it was different. It wasn't simply some sad, historic moment to him. This was *Grandfather.*

He kept trying to imagine why Mother, Father, and Sebastian hadn't come for him. There were two possibilities: First, maybe Spider had dragged them off to secret work prisons too. It was hard to imagine that he could get away with it. Father and Mother, especially, were high-ranking family members within the company. Still, it was a possibility he couldn't ignore. The second possibility was that Mother and Father were *okay* with Spider taking him away. After the Fogger incidents maybe they were furious with him, thinking he'd betrayed the company. Eli worried about both of these possibilities and what it would mean if either was true. For now, all he could do was cling to the dimming hope that someone would eventually come for him. And when that happened, he would make sure Spider paid for what he'd done, and maybe someday Eli would be forgiven.

In the meantime he did his best to keep Tabitha at a distance. He wasn't going to give her away as a Resister—he owed her that much—but it didn't mean he wanted to risk exposing himself to more trouble. She had once been a Fogger, after all, and anything he did to cause suspicion would only give Spider more ammunition to use against him later.

Unfortunately Tabitha seemed to have no understanding of what he was going through.

She had her own ideas.

Even though he'd told her to keep away from him, the next day she approached him again in the cafeteria. He tried moving to another table, but she wouldn't take the hint. She followed him. She'd gotten so good at drifting, blank-faced, among the Waywards that she could do it without drawing attention to herself. There was nothing Eli could do to stop her without causing a scene. So he gave up.

"I've been thinking about what you said," she began, as if she hadn't even noticed he'd been avoiding her. She didn't seem to care. "Here's why the old man you saw couldn't have been the real Gustavo."

"Leave me alone," he whispered. "Don't you get it? I'm not interested."

"Well, listen anyway. Maybe you will be. Keep in mind, I'm not telling you what I believe, only what I heard. How much do you already know about Dr. Friedmann?"

Eli didn't know much of anything, but he didn't answer. He pretended she wasn't even there.

Again this didn't seem to faze her. "Gustavo Friedmann was a radical figure from the early years of InfiniCorp. He was a petrogeologist and a design engineer who came up with designs for experimental city-shelters with sophisticated people-management systems—what eventually became the CloudNet and the domes. After that, his continuing research into the changing climate got him kicked out of the company's inner circle." She stopped to sample her lunch. Today it was soggy rice and some sort of meat pudding. As appetizing as ever. He waited for her to go on, but she didn't. She took another spoonful and chewed it slowly.

"So?" he said. "What happened to him?"

"I thought you weren't interested."

He glared at her.

She gave him the slightest of smiles. "It depends on who you ask. For a while the official company word was that he was one of the earliest victims of brain fever and that his condition led him to commit suicide. But the Friends say he went into hiding and lived Outside for years, until the desert finally took him. Either way, he's dead now. Which proves that whoever your sky-dwelling friend was, he couldn't have been Dr. Friedmann. He probably wasn't even as old as you thought. The desert takes a heavy toll on the people who try to survive out there. Everyone knows that."

"All right, so what was the Greenhouse Recovery Project?"

"So you *do* know something about Gustavo. You've been hiding it. If not, how would you know about the Greenhouse Recovery Project?"

"I told you yesterday, I saw a picture that seemed to be this Dr. Friedmann guy. The project name was on a folder he was carrying."

Even through her jungle of hair he could sense her eyes studying him. "Boy, either you're a good liar or they couldn't have picked a more clueless Papadopoulos to accuse of being with the Fog. But dumb as it sounds, I believe you. You really don't know anything about this, do you?"

Eli's face warmed. "Are you going to tell me or not?"

So Tabitha went through the story as she'd heard it from the Friends. She described how after Dr. Friedmann had spent years working with the company, his research led him to recognize how dire the climate situation had become. He put together a plan for what they had to do: the Greenhouse Recovery Project, he called it. It was a detailed list of immediate, sweeping changes to the way the company did business and the way people lived their lives. He said InfiniCorp and its employees needed to break their addiction to fossil fuels like coal and oil by switching to cleaner, renewable energies. They needed smarter power-delivery grids to get energy more efficiently from where it was generated to where the people actually lived. In the meantime everyone had to make more efficient use of the energy they already produced. All this was going to be expensive and difficult, he warned, but the consequences of *not* making such dramatic changes were unthinkable. If the company didn't act right away, the end was certain to come. But the good news, he said, was that the solutions to the climate crisis already existed. The technologies were currently available. And, while moving forward with them was absolutely necessary to ensure human survival, they also presented a huge revenue opportunity for the company. Best of all, InfiniCorp was big and powerful enough to make it all happen. This was the moment for the company to exercise its wisdom and leadership to save the world.

But when Dr. Friedmann took his work to the other InfiniCorp leaders, they weren't willing to accept his conclusions. They felt the measures he recommended were unnecessary and extreme. They didn't believe the situation was as urgent as he was warning.

"And that was when, according to the company, Dr. Friedmann lost his mind and killed himself." Tabitha was keeping her voice steady and low. "But if you believe the Friends, that's not what really happened. They say that before Dr. Friedmann was out of the picture, he went to the other leaders again and again, trying to get them to listen to him. They were making a terrible mistake, he said. It was an error that could end up in the destruction of everything that mattered, including humanity itself. What's more, he told them that if they didn't agree to address the problem right away, he would bring his findings directly to the people so they could decide for themselves." Tabitha paused, giving Eli a chance to let the words sink in. "After that, according to the Friends, some of the company leaders decided he was dangerous. They sent a secret order to have him arrested. Some even say they were going to kill him. But Dr. Friedmann supposedly found out they were coming for him, and he disappeared. That was less than a year before the Great Sickness."

"Do you think any of it could be true?" Eli asked.

She shrugged. "What do I know?"

He tried to keep his face blank. A Guardian against the far wall was looking in their direction. "Let's say your people were right, and Gustavo really did end up living in the desert. If so, then how can you be sure the Outsider I saw *wasn't* him?"

She gave him a sideways glance. "God, you're stubborn. I told you, I'm not a Friend anymore, okay? They're not *my* people. And in any case, it doesn't matter which story is right. My point is that it was a long time ago, and whichever way you look at it, Gustavo is dead."

Eli wondered who she was trying to convince—him or herself? It was almost as if she were more troubled by his story about the old man than he was. "Well, okay. . . . But whoever the Outsider in the sky was, he told me there might still be hope. He was crazy, but at least *that* part I want to believe. Don't you?"

"This was the same guy who said he thinks you're el Guía,

302

right? You. A Papadopoulos. So what does that tell you?" Her lip curled. "No, Eli, I don't believe in fantasies. No one can stop what's unavoidable. Not some crazy old man. Not some fictitious desert warrior. Nobody. However long we have before we're all dead—whether it's days, weeks, or years—the only thing left to hope for is one last gasp at self-preservation in the desert before the time runs out. So to hell with your old Outsider. To hell with your grandfather, and everyone else. I've learned the hard way that nobody's looking out for anyone but themselves, no matter what they tell you. I'm a survivor. Right now that means figuring a way out of here, not putting my faith in some dead man's hallucination of a hopeful future. I don't have time for pipe dreams."

"So, if you don't believe in InfiniCorp or the Friends, then what side are you on? What about the other kids trapped in this tower? Don't you care what happens to them?"

"It's not that I don't care, Eli. It's that I'm just one person and there's only so much I can do. If I don't put myself ahead of everything else, then no one will. I'm on nobody's side but my own."

Eli wondered if it was true. It couldn't have been long ago that she'd given up an awful lot to join the Foggers. As misguided as that decision may have been, it meant that back then she'd at least believed in something, an idea she felt was greater than herself. Eli looked down at his tray. He'd hardly touched his food and the lunch break was almost over. He would be starving by the end of the workday and he didn't care.

"My cousin Spider seems to think he could still be alive."

"Who?"

303

"Gustavo. When I told him the old man called himself Dr. Friedmann, he said the Department of Loyalty would go after him. He said something about that old traitor being a thorn in the company's heel for long enough, and how he was finally going to get him now."

She stared at him. "That's not true. You're making it up."

"Now who's being stubborn? But it doesn't matter. You still have no idea who he really was, and neither do I. In any case, whatever happened to the real Gustavo makes no difference to me, because nothing justifies what the Foggers do. After the attack on the Providence dome, I saw the wreckage. Dead bodies on the ground. Blood and debris everywhere. I don't understand you people at all. And, yeah, maybe you're no longer with them, but you *were*. How could you defend what you did? How did you sleep at night, knowing you were part of a group that works with Outsiders and tries to blow up innocent people?"

Tabitha's fists were clenched, but her voice stayed low. "Don't blame the Friends for the damage to the domes. Whatever else they are, the Friends are against using violence as the way forward. *That* I can promise you. Defiance, yes. But carnage and destruction? It isn't their way. All they want is to identify those willing to see the truth so they can recruit them to join the great quest. Apart from anything else, setting off bombs to attack the company would only turn the employees further against them. The Friends are smarter than that."

Eli blinked at her. "So . . . if the Foggers aren't the ones messing up the domes, then who is?"

She shook her head in amazement. "You've flown over the wasteland, right? You must have looked out at some of the ruins down there? Destroyed cities? Entire towns, washed away? Did you think the domes were immune to the hurricanes, the floods? Lightning strikes are doing real damage. There have been fires, explosions. People have been getting killed. Wake up, Eli. You're not in a trance like the others." She leveled her gaze at him. "Don't you get it? Every time there's obvious damage to a dome, the company puts out word that the Foggers are up to their old tricks again. The name of the game is *denial*. Keep everyone from worrying about the worsening climate and how long the domes can last. Because as soon as they open their eyes, the illusion starts to unravel."

"I—I don't believe you."

"Yeah, I guess I'm not surprised anymore. I thought you were different, but I see they have you all wrapped up in their little fantasy just like everybody else." She grabbed her tray and stood. "Keep dreaming, Eli. Maybe Mommy and Daddy will show up tonight to take you home."

Tabitha lay in the darkness, listening to the gentle snoring of the other Wayward girls, asleep in their bunks. She'd been wide-awake for hours, stewing about Eli.

Over the past few days she'd watched him struggle with the spheres and with his own peculiar position in this strange place. He could have given her away, but he hadn't. Instead he'd worked hard and kept his head. His will was strong, even stronger than she'd guessed at first. She respected him for that. And as misguided as his belief in Grandfather was, she admired that too, in a way. She wished she could still feel that kind of faith in someone.

Sooner or later, though, he would have to face the reality that his entire family had abandoned him. After that, he would have to trust her, and she would probably end up disappointing him too. Because the way she saw it, somebody had to make a sacrifice. Escape from the tower was impossible without a diversion, but whoever created the diversion was unlikely to escape before falling back into the hands of the Guardians. Even if he made it out of the tower alive, she wasn't sure how long she could stick with him in the desert. In a fight-or-die world, she couldn't be expected to babysit a pampered Papadopoulos. She would do what she could, but as soon as he became a burden, she would have to think of her own survival.

One way or another, there was a good chance she would have to abandon Eli, like everyone else had. The thought made her uneasy. But she *needed* him now. It frustrated her that she was second-guessing herself. Why should she feel bad for him? Didn't the Papadopouloses use her and all the other employees for their own purposes all the time?

Still, no matter how she looked at it, there was something peculiar going on. That any member of the ruling family would be accused of conspiring with the Fog was curious enough, but *this* kid especially. . . . He seemed to know so little about the true nature of the company and the world around him. What made the Papadopouloses so sure he was part of the resistance? Was talking with Foggers really so bad that it justified sentencing a member of their own family to slavery in a work tower?

Maybe.

And yet something about it didn't feel right. Tabitha

wondered if there was something else, some other part of the story Eli wasn't telling or, more likely, didn't know. For a long time she'd been wondering whether it was time she took another trip to the room with the file cabinets. If anything could shed light on this mystery, Tabitha guessed it would be in there.

She made up her mind. Careful to move without making a sound, she twisted her body to the other end of her bed and dug her fingers around the vent cover.

Ever so gently she pried it open.

Seconds later she was crawling through the darkness on her hands and knees. It was cramped inside the vent, and so hot she felt like she would melt. Keeping her balance was hard too, because the tower was rocking back and forth with another approaching storm. She couldn't let herself slip. Any sound she made could give her away.

Soon she came to the narrow, vertical section. This was the part she was dreading most. Just peering down at the long drop made her dizzy. She took a deep breath and climbed in, feetfirst. Trying not to think about the distance she had to descend, she inched downward little by little, applying outward pressure to the shaft wall with her palms and feet so she wouldn't slide too fast. Sweat dribbled into her eyes. After what felt like forever, her feet at last touched the bottom.

But she couldn't afford to relax.

The vent split off in several horizontal directions, and she struggled to remember which one led to the Records Room. She chose one, and a moment later she was crawling on her hands and knees again. After a couple of turns, she saw the grate she was looking for. A dim light shone up through the metal grid, and just as her face inched close enough to look down at the filing cabinets, she heard a sound that froze her in her tracks.

Whistling.

There was somebody in there.

She held her breath and tried not to make a sound. Through the mesh she saw it was a Cleaner, a boy with droopy eyes and hair that fell like a wet rag around his head. He was shuffling between the metal cabinets, pulling his cart behind him as he wiped the floor with a mop. It was lucky she hadn't attracted his attention already. All he had to do was look up and he would see her peering down at him. But if she tried to back up now, it was possible her shifting weight might cause the vent to creak. She kept as still as she could, hoping her sweat wouldn't drip through the mesh and down to the floor.

She watched the Cleaner work. His movements were slow and methodical, and his eyes held a glassy expression. Another Wayward sleepwalker. At one point his gaze turned toward a high shelf not far from where Tabitha waited, and for a moment she felt sure he saw her. She choked back a gasp but held still. After a few seconds he went back to pushing his mop.

It seemed like ages before he packed up and left the room, shutting the door behind him. Tabitha continued to hold still in case he was nearby. There was even a chance he might return. She counted out the seconds, letting about ten minutes pass. Then she waited a little more.

At last she decided it was time to make her move. As quietly as she could, she unclipped the grate and dropped herself to the floor. While the boy was working, she'd noticed that each cabinet was marked with a letter of the alphabet, and along the far wall was one with the letter *P.* She rifled through its drawers, starting at the top. In the second drawer from the bottom she found what she was searching for, a manila folder labeled with evenly spaced block letters: *ELI PAPADOPOULOS.*

She pulled it from the cabinet and looked inside.

21

one small victory

Eli was in a foul mood as he drifted with the rest of the sleepy-eyed Matchers down to the production area. He didn't like to admit it, even to himself, but he was secretly beginning to wonder if Tabitha was right.

Just as he was making his way to the matching table, somebody bumped into him, almost knocking him over. He turned. Tabitha was staggering past, along with the other Packers. Part of him wanted to shout back at her, to demand to know what her problem was. But he let it go. What would be the point of attracting the attention of the Guardians?

He dropped into his seat and everyone got right to work. The day had only just begun and already the heat was stifling. The blowers were useless. The ancient metal fans seemed to do little except push the hot air around. Even the Productivity Facilitators were moving slower than usual. Overhead, a growing patter of rain echoed against the tower's small dome, and every now and then the wind rose in pitch and the whole room rocked to one side. Eli could tell another big storm was on the way. By the sound of the rising wind, it could be the roughest one yet. None of the other Waywards appeared to notice.

His mind wandered while his hands sifted through the fabric. He'd been doing it long enough that his fingers seemed to know what to do on their own. After a while he shifted in his chair, and as he did so he felt something in his pocket, something he was sure hadn't been there earlier. Curious, he pulled it out. It was a piece of paper folded into a small triangle. How strange. He looked closer and noticed that somebody had penciled three short words in two lines:

ELi
READ ME

He dropped the paper triangle onto his lap and went right back to the T-shirts. He glanced around the table to see if anyone had noticed, but the other Matchers looked as zonked as ever, too caught up in their work and their dream thoughts to pay much attention to anything else. He knew at once who had slipped him the message. He shot a quick glance at the Packers and wasn't surprised to catch Tabitha looking right back at him. She must have been waiting for him to discover the piece of paper, whatever it was.

He looked away. Why couldn't she just leave him alone? Why did she have to put him at risk yet again for what was sure to be another of her crazy ideas? Whatever message this paper contained, he didn't want to know.

Except that he did. He couldn't help feeling intrigued. And as the minutes wore on, it only got worse.

Eventually he raised his hand to go to the bathroom and the fountain-haired Productivity Facilitator, Representative Dowd, gave him the okay. Head down, he stepped between the long tables and then out to the bathroom. Once he'd closed himself inside a stall, he unfolded the paper.

Right away it puzzled him.

It appeared to be some kind of official document from the Department of Loyalty. There was the InfiniCorp logo, along with Spider's name and signature. At the top, in thick red letters, was the word *CONFIDENTIAL,* and below that somebody had scribbled, *File with Rep. Eli Papadopoulos's records.* This page seemed to be from some secret file the company was keeping on him. But how was that possible? How could Tabitha have gotten her hands on anything like that?

And yet here it was.

Eli read the subject line: *Daedalus and Paloma Papadopoulos: Fogger Traitors.*

That took a moment to sink in.

Father and Mother? Foggers? It was a crazy idea.

He jumped down to the main body of the memo, which was several paragraphs long. At first he only skimmed it, unable to take it all in fast enough. Certain phrases popped out at him: . . . *caught working in secret with the enemy . . . a foiled plot against InfiniCorp's most senior leadership . . . documented evidence . . .*

He reached the end and started at the top again, only this time he went through it more slowly. The sound of the wind and rain rose once more. The tower tilted a little to one side, so Eli shifted his balance, leaning against the stall wall. But his eyes never left the page. He couldn't believe what he was reading. According to this memo, the same night Eli was taken from his bedroom in the Providence dome, his parents had been arrested. They'd been trying to stage an executive takeover within the Leadership Council, but at the last moment their plan had been discovered. After years of conspiring against the company, it said, Grandfather's own son and daughter-in-law had been identified as Fogger agents and enemies of InfiniCorp.

The words echoed in his mind. *Enemies of InfiniCorp.*

His own parents!

It wasn't true, of course. How could it be? But now at least he knew what Spider meant when he'd accused Eli of being part of a conspiracy. If his cousin had somehow got it in his head that Mother and Father were agitators, that explained why he might think that Eli, their son, could be one too. And Eli hadn't exactly helped to dissuade him of this idea when he'd climbed the sky. But then again, Spider hadn't just made a mistake, had he? He'd known all along that Mother and Father weren't Foggers—he'd made it all up. He deliberately framed them, and Eli too.

At last he understood why Mother and Father had never come for him. Not Sebastian either. If Spider had been willing to lock Eli up just for being the son of Daedalus and Paloma Papadopoulos, then why should it have been any different for Sebastian?

God only knew what Spider had done with them.

This was even worse than Eli had imagined. What was he supposed to do now? He couldn't just go back to the matching

313

table and start working again as if nothing were different. Tabitha was right. Nobody was ever going to come for him. In his mind he could almost see his cousin's cruel eyes gazing down from the sphere, laughing. Spider had not only ruined Eli's life, but Mother's, Father's, and Sebastian's also. He'd done it intentionally, and out of pure spite.

Eli's hands were shaking. He gripped the paper so tight that his knuckles went pale.

The moment he stepped back into the production area he almost slammed into Representative Dowd, who seemed to have been heading in his direction. Her face was pallid.

"Representative Papadopoulos, empty your pockets!"

Eli was so surprised, he could only sputter. "Wh-what? Why?"

A hulking figure slouched up beside her. Greasy hair over drooping eyelids, beefy arms swinging loose from slumped shoulders. Geraldine. She smirked at Eli.

"It has been brought to my attention," Representative Dowd said, "that there may have been something hidden in the palm of your hand when you walked to the bathroom. I see it's not there now, so I want to find out if it's still with you. Or perhaps you already flushed it away?"

"I—I don't know what you're talking about."

Eli tried to walk on, but the Productivity Facilitator blocked his path. Her hands moved to her hips. "Empty your pockets!"

He wasn't sure what to do. He was caught! With no other choice, he pulled out the folded note.

Representative Dowd stared. "Where did you get that?"

"I . . . found it on the floor." As soon as he said it, he realized how feeble it was.

Geraldine shook her head. Her voice was quiet and scratchy. "No, it was hidden in his pile. I saw him drop it into his lap."

Representative Dowd grabbed it from his hand. Eli stopped even trying to pretend anymore. He backed deeper into the room. "This is why I'm here, isn't it?" he asked, his voice rising and starting to shake. "Because of some ridiculous story that Mother and Father are Foggers?"

"You're here only because you're a Wayward employee," Representative Dowd said, unfolding the note. "Your self-absorbed wrong thinking led you off the path of teamwork and company values."

Eli was suddenly so filled with emotion that he couldn't stop himself from letting it show. "That's a *lie!*" he shouted. "It's *all* a lie! *Everything happening here, this whole place—it's one big deception!*"

His words cut through the silence. A few of the Waywards looked up from their work. Eyes glazed, they peered around as if unsure of where the sound was coming from.

As it happened, on the production floor that day were Representative Shine and Representative Tinker, the two pretty Guardians from the admissions ward. It wasn't unusual for one or the other of them to visit Learning Floor 9-B. Sometimes they came with new Waywards, but not always. Like all the other Guardians and Productivity Facilitators, they turned at the sudden commotion.

The blue-haired one, Representative Tinker, was the first to reach him. "My goodness!" she said, her forehead wrinkled with concern. "How can we help you? What on earth is all the fuss about?"

But Eli wasn't fooled by her gentle manner. What was the point of pretending to go along with them anymore? "I'll tell you what it's all about! I'm stuck in this tower because of a pack of lies!" He pointed at the document. "It's all in there!"

Representative Dowd thrust the page at her. "He was sneaking around with this."

With a frown Representative Tinker took the document. By then the other Guardian girl, green-haired Representative Shine, had also reached them, and the two stood together like twin angels. This was the first time Eli had ever seen them standing so close, and for a moment it startled him. He'd known, of course, that they looked alike, but until then he hadn't realized just how *much* alike. Apart from their hair color, they were like clones.

"Why didn't you tell me?" Eli demanded. "You must have known about this from the very beginning—don't try to deny it! Why didn't anyone ask for my side of the story?"

The identical Guardians didn't study the page for long. By the sudden way their expressions darkened, it was obvious to Eli that he was right—they'd seen it before and already knew exactly what it was and what it meant. They glanced at each other. When Representative Tinker spoke again, her voice was cold.

"How did you get this document, Representative Papadopoulos? Did you break into the Records Room yourself, or were you working with someone?"

He stopped breathing. Tabitha wasn't far. As a matter of

fact, at that very moment he could see her over the shoulders of the Guardians' white uniforms. Like the other Waywards, she had returned to work as if drawn back into her dream, unaware of anything else. But Eli knew better.

"It doesn't matter who gave it to me," he said after a pause. "The point is, I was never involved in any crazy anti-InfiniCorp plot. My cousin Spider made the whole thing up! It's not true! Now, if you would let me contact my family, I can explain myself to them and we can work this whole thing out."

He could see right away he wasn't getting through. Their expressions grew darker, and their normally friendly eyes narrowed to icy stares. "You're disappointing us." Representative Shine sounded deadly calm. "We asked you a question, and we expect an answer. Who gave you this document?"

Representative Dowd stayed quiet, deferring to the higher authority of the twin Guardians. Other Guardians, the ones who had been standing all along the walls, started to close in around him. There were seven or eight of them, moving in from every direction. All at once Eli realized how serious a mistake he'd made. He should have been more careful. He'd let his emotions compromise his judgment, and now it was too late to go back.

"No more delaying, Eli. Give us the *name*!"

He took a step backward. "I—I don't know it."

Representative Tinker's face contorted with rage. She stamped her foot. *"Wrong answer!"* To Eli's astonishment, she leapt at him, kicking his chest and knocking him clear across the floor. She was surprisingly strong. He started to scramble back to his feet, but now Representative Shine was coming at him, her lip curled in a snarl as her shoes click-clacked across the floor. Before he could stop her, she grabbed him by the hair and slammed him to the ground. Like her double, she was much stronger than she looked. Eli tried to pull himself upright, but he felt an electric jolt at the base of his neck. The pain was excruciating. He buckled forward and dropped back to his knees. What he found most incredible was that none of the nearby Waywards even looked up.

For the next few seconds, two of the Guardian boys held him while the two girls huddled nearby with the Productivity Facilitators. He didn't catch much of what they said, just a few whispered phrases here and there:

"*. . . Resister . . .*"

"*. . . special case . . .*"

"*. . . danger to the company . . .*"

Eli could barely move. When he tried to struggle, another jolt shot across his shoulders. "Stop!" he gasped. "Listen to me! My parents aren't traitors and neither am I! You—you have to believe me!"

Finally one of the girls said, "Let him go." Eli couldn't see which one it was, but her voice was calm. The boys released their grip and stepped away, and Eli was able to lift his head.

Representative Shine and Representative Tinker stood a few feet away from him now, their faces serene and pretty once more. "This doesn't have to be so hard," Representative Tinker said, casually brushing a few strands of wispy blue hair from her eyes. "We're reasonable people, and hey, it's totally understandable that you're confused. This whole adjustment thing must be especially difficult for you. Just tell us what we need to know and everything will be so much easier. That's a promise. But if you refuse . . ." She shrugged.

"If you refuse," Representative Shine continued for her, "then you force us to take drastic action that we don't want to have to take. Don't make us do that, not to you, of all people."

Eli's whole body ached. Once again he saw Tabitha watching from where she was lifting crates. Her face was pink and her jaw was tight. He could see in her eyes that she was flustered.

"Maybe you don't understand." Representative Tinker stepped toward him again. "Maybe you think you've already experienced the full force of the Special Training room. Believe me, you haven't. When the sphere is set to maximum strength, the nightmares are . . . well, let's just say they're *intense*."

"Dreams have power, Eli. If they're strong enough, when they tap into the darkest, most terrifying recesses of the unconscious mind, they can leave people haunted and empty. When it's all over, people don't care to resist anymore. They don't care about anything at all."

"They're like empty shells, walking zombies staggering around in a nightmare that never ends. Sometimes it's necessary. But such a high price to pay."

Eli looked over again at Geraldine, who had drifted back to the matching table and gone back to her work as if nothing else mattered.

The two Guardians were very close now, and Eli found himself staring up at two copies of the same face. Representative Shine crouched beside him. She took his hand. "But we don't want that for you, Eli. No matter what you've done, you're still Grandfather's grandson. All we care about is the productivity and contentment of the Waywards in this tower. They're everything to us."

"If somebody accessed a classified document without authorization," Representative Tinker said over her shoulder, "then it's a serious breach of tower security, which is a big problem. As a Papadopoulos, you should appreciate that better than anyone."

"Whoever you're trying to protect, it's pointless. Now that we know there's another Resister, we *will* discover him or her before long. So we're going to ask you one last time, and we hope you choose the easier path, the way of *right* thinking."

"If you do, then your dreams will be good dreams. You'll have no reason to be afraid."

They smiled. They weren't angry anymore. They were being reasonable. Representative Shine gave his hand a gentle squeeze. "So, what's it going to be, Eli? In or out? Are you with us or against us?"

A bead of sweat trickled down his forehead. Even though he couldn't see her anymore, he knew Tabitha was still there, nearby, watching. It would be so easy to give her away. But, Fogger or not, she'd tried to help him, which was more than he could say for anybody else here. In an odd sort of way, she was his friend.

He leveled his eyes at them. "I already told you. I don't know who gave me the document. I have no idea."

Their smiles faded. Rage flashed across their eyes once more, but it didn't last. Representative Shine let go of his hand. "Disappointing."

Behind her Representative Tinker scowled. "Such a shame,

Eli. We expected so much more of you." And then to the other Guardians she called, *"Take him upstairs!"*

Seconds later two Guardian boys dragged Eli across the Learning Floor. As he passed between the long tables, he couldn't help wondering at how, even now, none of the Waywards seemed aware of any of this. They kept working and smiling, lost in their own worlds. The only ones who even looked in his direction were Clarence and Geraldine, and that was only briefly, and only because Eli managed to knock their seats with his foot as he went past. They glanced up and seemed to take in a little of what was going on, at least that Eli seemed to be in some kind of trouble. Instead of appearing concerned, though, Clarence caught Eli's eye and shook his head in disapproval. Geraldine curled her lip and growled.

After that they both went right back to their work.

The rain was pelting harder against the dome, and the door to the stairway was just ahead. The Guardians' expressions were grim, and their fingers dug painfully into his shoulders and under his armpits. But this was good, Eli decided. It was something real to concentrate on, a way to keep from sinking back into the CloudNet dream for what could be the final conscious moments of his pathetic life. Spider had won. Everything that could ever have been good about Eli's future was gone now, and who knew where Mother, Father, and Sebastian were? The only thing he had left to cling to was his one small victory: at least he hadn't given in to Spider's people.

Even as they dragged him through the doorway, he was careful not to look in Tabitha's direction.

22

special training

The Guardians lugged him, kicking and screaming, up many flights of stairs until they reached the fifteenth floor. There was a narrow hallway there, and Eli recognized it as the same corridor the two Outsider savages had carried him through after his terrifying checkers game with Spider. The rain was louder up here, nearer the top of the dome. The Guardians led him through a black door, and all at once the memory of that awful night came flooding back.

The Special Training room was almost the same as he remembered it: small, gray, and nearly empty. The oversized sphere was still floating near the ceiling, but now there was a metal chair on the floor just below it. That's where the Guardians dragged him. One of them held him down while the other one strapped him in, forcing his arms and legs into metal clasps. A bracket was clamped around his forehead.

"Stop!" he screamed. "Where's Spider? Tell him he can't do this!"

He tried to struggle, but they were too strong. The chair tipped back. All at once the sphere hummed to life, and the room swirled with light. Eli felt the power right away, an irresistible force drawing him in as gravity draws a falling body toward the earth. There was nothing he could do about it. He couldn't turn his head. He couldn't bring himself to close his eyes. His thoughts became muddled, and soon he no longer felt the chair underneath him. He was floating. The room was gone, and he was drifting up, up, into the ball of pulsing color.

The next thing he knew, he was in a clearing in the woods. He was running through a field of grass as tall as himself. Only it wasn't normal, synthetic grass. It was the real thing. It scratched his arms and face as he scrambled through, desperate to make his way forward. The trees ahead were real too, their branches thick with natural green leaves, like the trees of long ago. If he weren't so terrified, he would have thought it was beautiful here. Except the air was too dry and the sky overhead was darkening with smoke. Behind him, the grass was on fire, and so were the trees. If he didn't find a way out, he was going to die.

He tried to remind himself it was just a dream, but it didn't feel like it. It felt real.

"Eli!" somebody called. "Eli, over here!"

Up ahead two shadowy figures stood at the edge of the woods. They weren't far. Eli made it to the end of the grass, and now he could see their silhouettes waving him over. They called out again:

"Run, Eli! Don't stop!"

He could feel the heat at his back. He pressed on. The figures ran ahead, though, and he was having trouble keeping up.

The flames felt closer and closer behind him. With every breath his lungs filled with ash. Already he was exhausted. "Wait!" he called, wheezing and stumbling. "Wait for me!" Then he made a mistake: he turned around. He saw a wall of fire as wide as the woods and taller than the tallest tree. It charged at him, moving faster than he ever would have imagined. He gasped. As he took a step back, his foot caught on something, and he fell. Too late to save himself now, he realized. Not even enough time to get up and run. As the heat intensified around him, as his scream caught in his throat, he tried to sense the chair underneath him. He forced himself to focus on the clamps at his wrists and ankles.

"It's working," said a whispered voice.

"No," said another. "He's still fighting. He's stronger than we thought. Turn it up higher."

Seconds or hours later, Eli opened his eyes. The flames were gone, and the woods were gone, and he was on his back, staring up at a cloudless sky. The air smelled faintly of salt—and something else. What was it? Not far away he could hear a sound like gentle waves. He lifted his head.

He was on a beautiful beach lined with palm trees. And here was the ocean—not the foul-smelling sea he could sense from the tower, but a clean expanse of blue that went on and on to a distant, perfect horizon. He sat up. This was how it once was. He knew it without question. He rolled up his trousers and stepped to the edge of the surf. The sand felt cool and rough between his toes. He waded in. The water was so clear, he could see the bottom. When he was up to his knees, a school of tropical fish—curious yellow and blue things—shot between his feet, making him jump. Then he laughed. He'd never experienced anything like this before. Whatever this dream was, it didn't feel like much of a nightmare.

And yet . . . And yet . . . something was wrong. Other than the sound of the wind and the waves, it was perfectly quiet. The beach seemed to go on forever in both directions, and there was nobody else in sight. Not a soul. There was something spooky about it.

"Hello?" he called. "Anybody here?"

Nothing. Only the echo of his voice.

He realized he was all alone, *totally* alone, for the first time in his life. He'd lived all his years in domes crammed with activity, and now the isolation felt unnatural. *Where were all the people?*

The sun blazed at his back. While he'd been standing in the water, the heat had grown almost unbearable. He looked down. In the water's reflection, dark clouds were filling the sky behind him. The water itself went hazy too, as if the rising temperature had allowed something foul and sickly red to grow and thrive in there. Within seconds he could no longer see the bottom. And then, just a few feet away, something bubbled under the water. There was a faint *pop* at the surface, and when Eli looked, he saw a dead fish floating on its side. For a moment he only stared. Another one appeared just a few yards ahead. *Pop.* And then two more. *Pop. Pop.* His stomach rose into his throat. It continued to happen faster and faster all around him. In a panic he began to fight his way back to shore, but the water was much heavier now. Soon Eli was knee-deep in a vast, unbroken field of dead fish and bloodred water as far as he could see. Desperate, he thrashed his arms and pushed his weight through the filth until at last he made it back to the beach. The moment he reached dry sand he fell to his knees and threw up.

By then the odor of the ocean was unmistakable. Sour milk. He gasped for breath. When he looked up, he was surprised to see two figures standing over him, the same shadowy people he'd seen before, by the woods, except he recognized them now. He couldn't believe his eyes.

"Mother? Father?" He was overjoyed to see them. "What's happening? Do you know? Can you help me?"

They smiled. "Don't worry, son," Father said. "It's going to be all right."

"Come with us," Mother said. "We'll show you what we can do for you."

They held out their hands for him to take. Behind them the sky was growing even darker, and Eli could see what looked like a giant tornado moving across the water. But everything was going to be okay now. His parents were here. He reached up, took their hands in his, and pulled himself to his feet.

But something wasn't right. They wouldn't let go, and their grips—both of them—were unexpectedly powerful. He struggled. They were hurting him. Mother and Father curled their lips and laughed. Their faces were changing. Terrified, Eli found himself in the crushing grasp of two red-faced demons with mottled skin, long, pointed chins, and horns on both sides of their foreheads. With sudden horror he realized it was all true what the secret document had said. Mother and Father really *were* working against the company. His parents were Foggers.

He screamed.

The demons laughed harder. While Eli kicked and writhed, they dragged him back into the filthy, stinking water. He was among the dead fish again, and the sea was rising all around him. His parents were going to drown him. *"No! Let me go! Let me go! Please!"*

The ruined ocean was almost up to his mouth. He started to cough and sputter, but then he got hold of himself. He craned his neck toward the clouds. Two pairs of eyes gazed down at him from the sky. He stopped struggling. He concentrated on the eyes, only on the eyes.

The clouds morphed. Soon he could make out the shapes of two identical faces. They were studying him. Eli pointed his finger and shouted, "It's you! Don't think I don't see you up there! I know none of this is real! I'm still strapped to the chair!"

The cloud face on the left frowned. "He's still fighting," it whispered. Eli couldn't tell if it was Representative Shine or Representative Tinker. But he supposed it didn't matter.

"It doesn't go much higher," the other one said. "Careful. If we push too far, we could totally fry him."

"Take the chance," the first one said. "Do it."

* * *

327

The demons disappeared, and so did the water. Now Eli was hovering in space, floating through a weird purple mist. The cloud faces solidified until the massive heads and bodies of the two Guardian girls were perfectly clear, drifting in circles around him. Only it wasn't them, exactly. Their stomachs swelled, and their mouths grew bloated and ugly. Their white uniforms morphed into identical striped shirts with caps, and white trousers that stretched over their bulging bellies. Eli recognized them. Somehow they'd transformed into Tweedledum and Tweedledee, the demented, fighting twins from the *Alice* stories. He wondered if the Guardians had chosen this nightmare for him, or if it was just his unconscious mind spilling into his dream.

They were everywhere. Every way Eli turned, he saw their ugly, round faces. It wouldn't take much for either of them to reach out and crush him. From somewhere deep in the mist he heard music, some insane melody played in the familiar tink-tonk of the funbots. Arm in arm the two Guardians began to dance, and while they danced, they chanted:

> *"Tweedledum and Tweedledee*
> *Agreed to have a battle;*
> *For Tweedledum said Tweedledee*
> *Had spoiled his nice new rattle!"*

They repeated it over and over, the music and voices echoing so loud in Eli's head, he covered his ears.

After that, everything went even crazier.

In a blaze of fire, the twins disappeared and colors burst and flashed all around him. The music continued while images darted past and melted away—strange, upsetting visions that made him cower. Many of them spoke to him. "What a disappointment you turned out to be . . . ," said a voice coming from a swarm of squirming, fat slugs with the faces of his uncles and aunts. A giant caterpillar smoking an enormous cigar floated past. "You're a disgrace, boy," it said in Uncle Hector's voice. "We expected so much more of you." The mist billowed and swirled. In the distance Eli heard a peal of thunder. He wasn't sure if it was real or part of the nightmare. A boy in an Outsider mask drifted close and leered into his face, making him squirm. It was the kid from the Bubble tram, except now he had a respirator and a fake arm. Beneath his demonic mask there was something terrible and frightening about his eyes. Eli tried to look away but he wasn't able. *"Leave me alone,"* he pleaded. *"Go away!"* But the boy's gaze stayed fixed on him. Without a word he reached up and pulled back the mask. When Eli saw the twisted, sun-scarred face underneath, his heart nearly stopped. He was looking at himself.

Eli's breaths came in rapid gasps. "No! No!"

The whole world was shaking, and so was he. Surely he was losing his mind. All he wanted was to let go, to somehow shut himself down so it would all go away. In the end he curled himself into a ball and wrapped his arms around his head as the nightmare images continued to swirl and flash around him. In the distance somebody was screaming. It was a long time before he realized it was his own voice.

He woke up, not for the first time. Only he didn't trust it. Maybe he was awake, but maybe it was just another part of the dream. It had been going on for what felt like days. He seemed

329

still to be in the Special Training room, except now he was alone. It seemed odd at first that the Guardians would leave him unattended, but then he realized it wasn't so strange. After all, he was strapped to a chair, and the sphere surely could make the nightmares on its own. Everything was dark around him except for the light from the orb, which glowed dimly now. His clothes were soaked in sweat, and it felt like all his energy was gone.

He wondered how long he'd been there.

He wondered if he was dead.

Suddenly the sphere brightened and the room started to rumble. The walls were closing in around him. Now he knew this really *was* just another part of the long nightmare. Ghost images flew at him, whispering and shrieking as they whipped around his head. "InfiniCorp is taking care of everything! InfiniCorp is taking care of everything!" He reached out to grab them, but his fingers passed right through them cold, leaving him weak. The walls were very close now. They were almost on him. In seconds they were going to crush him to death.

But that was okay. He didn't care anymore. In a way, he hoped they *would* crush him.

He was too weak to fight.

He closed his eyes and passed out again.

In Eli's dream he was deep, deep asleep and had been for quite some time. But now he tossed and turned. He sensed something. It felt like a mosquito buzzing around his ears. Something prickling at the back of his mind.

And every now and then he thought he heard a voice.

Eli . . . Eli, wake up. . . .

He tried to shut it out. This was just the newest phase of the endless nightmare, another whispering ghost to terrify him into submission. But he was beyond that now, *way* beyond. Already he felt trapped in a shadow world, and his thoughts—the few he could still muster—were foggy with dark visions. Didn't they realize they'd already worn him down into submission? Even if he wanted to fight, he had so little energy left. They had won. So why did they bother to torment him further?

Come back. . . . Follow my voice. . . .

He heard himself groan. He wondered if they would ever stop, or if this was how it would continue on, forever. When the voice spoke again, the words were louder and clearer. *Don't give up, Eli. . . . You can do this. . . . I'm right here. . . . Come back, darling. . . . Come to me. . . .*

This time something about the voice itself, low and gravelly in his mind, made him pause in his dream. He wondered. Was it possible?

No, it couldn't be.

He felt movement on his chest, as if something small had shifted its weight. But that didn't mean anything. It could still be part of the dream. Probably was, in fact. And yet his pulse sped up. Gathering his remaining strength, he managed to fight his way just a little closer to the surface of consciousness. He opened his eyes. The sphere was dormant now, and there seemed to be a shape, a dark blur, not far from his face. He blinked a few times and soon he could make out a vague outline of something smallish and gray perched on his uniform. It did *look* like her. The creature, whatever it was, was leaning over him, its whiskers twitching not far from his face.

Marilyn? Is that you?

Yes, my love. You had me worried. I thought I'd lost you.

But Eli still wasn't convinced. She pulled back, and when the light caught her, he could see her a little more clearly. She looked awful. Filthy. Emaciated. Her fur was tattered and patchy, and some of it appeared to have turned from gray to white, especially around her snout and around her eyes. There was also a nasty gash across the left side of her body, and one of her ears was ripped open.

His suspicions returned. This might still be a nightmare after all, a dream that something horrible had happened to Marilyn. Why not? If the sphere was dredging his psyche for one last way to send him into despair, there were few things left that could do it like this could. At the same time, though, this moment felt somehow different from the rest of the nightmare. For one thing, there was the buzz in his ears that he hadn't experienced in any other part of the dream.

How do I know it's really you?

She stood over him and leaned close. His scalp started to tingle, and he felt a sensation like a gentle caress in his brain. All at once the two of them were lying in his backyard again, and he could feel the cool, smooth plastic of the artificial grass at his neck and under the heels of his bare feet. From a distance came the sounds of activity: the hum of transport pods, the murmur of the crowds on Thayer Street. The Providence dome glimmered a radiant bluish green. As Marilyn chirped beside him, a flock of pelicans swooped across the sky. But it lasted only a moment. In a blink the scene faded, and he was back in the chair again. He was looking deep into her eyes.

"It *is* you," he whispered, his voice trembling. "You're real. You're here. . . ."

Foolish, exasperating child. Of course I'm here. Don't you remember my promise? She nuzzled her snout against his cheek. *I said I'd never leave you.*

23

revelations

The room shook with thunder. From Outside Eli could hear the wind shrieking and waves crashing against the dome. While he'd been lost in his dreams, the storm had grown much worse.

You have no idea how happy I am to see you, he said silently, still amazed. *I'm so, so sorry, Marilyn. I should have listened.*

It's all right, my love. I'm here now.

But how? His eyes fell on a small gap in the wall he hadn't noticed before, and on freshly crumbled plaster on the floor near the far corner of the room. He realized this was how Marilyn must have gotten in. She must have squeezed through the space between the walls. *What on earth happened to you?*

It's a long story, my love. There isn't time.

He considered again her skinny, ragged body. The open gash across her side was puffy and caked in blood. It looked infected. "Tell me," he said aloud. "I have to know."

She eyed him. *Very well. But it's quicker to show you.* Once

334

again Eli's scalp tingled, and he realized she was downloading something to him. And suddenly there it was. As if it were right in front of him, he could see the black-winged Department of Loyalty pod and Marilyn chasing after it. He was there with her as she hid in the streets of Providence and barely escaped the dome. For weeks she'd trudged, exhausted, through the endless wilderness Outside, all the time following his signal. He felt her terror and hunger as she endured storms and fought in countless death struggles with other starving creatures of the wild, many of them mutants. She'd had to learn to fight and kill to survive. Finally she'd stumbled onto an InfiniCorp transport hub just west of New Washington and had managed to stow herself in the ovenlike baggage compartment of a southbound product-delivery transport and, after that, in the sewage piping of an ocean-bound supply vessel heading across the Gulf of Mexico to the tower. It was there, in a fight with a mutant rat, that her ear had been slashed open and she'd received the gash across her side.

All this she had endured for him.

He gazed at her now, with no idea what to say. He'd never felt more love for her than he did at that moment. But now that the download was finished, his brain felt like mush. Somehow it had sapped his energy even further—and, worse, he could feel how the effort of sending it had drained Marilyn's strength even more than his own. Her head slumped and one of her eyelids hung lower than the other.

Marilyn? Are you okay?

I'm fine. Don't worry about me. What's important now is getting you out of here. The transports are on the lowest levels.

Yes, I know, but there's no way to get there. The place is locked up like a fortress and crawling with Guardians. *And besides, look at me. I'm stuck in this chair.*

Marilyn lifted her head. *I think there may be a few things I can do to help.* She fixed her gaze on the clamps around his wrists. Within seconds they started to heat up, until finally they clicked open. Then she did the same with the clamps around his legs and the bracket around his head.

"Thank you," he whispered, impressed. It was a great relief not to feel the metal digging into his wrists anymore.

Come on! Let's get going!

At that moment the wind rose in pitch and the tower creaked to one side. Here on a higher floor, the shift seemed even more noticeable to Eli than it had below, or perhaps it was just that the wind and waves were so much more powerful now. For an instant the sphere blinked brighter, but then the tower rocked upright again.

Let's go! Marilyn insisted. *We're running out of time!*

Eli was about to slide himself off the chair and stumble after her, but he hesitated. The growing storm was making him think once again of what Tabitha had said about Gustavo and the Greenhouse Recovery Project. For so long there had been so many questions burning inside him. He knew of only one person who would have all the answers, and Marilyn was right—time was indeed running out. If Eli was ever going to find out the truth, it had to be now.

"Wait," he said. "Before we go any further, I need you to do something for me first."

She stared at him. *What are you talking about?*

"Remember back at home when you pulled me through the CloudNet? Do you think you can do that again? The

336

spheres here won't allow me to communicate beyond the tower, but I bet *you* can find a way. I need to talk to Grandfather."

Eli, you don't seem to appreciate the urgency of the situation. The system says the Guardians check on you every hour, and I don't know when the last time was. They could be back any minute.

"I'm safer here than if I'm caught wandering the hallways. And anyway, you don't understand. This can't wait. Grandfather is the only one who can really help."

She appeared to study him as the rain rumbled overhead. When at last her voice echoed in his mind again, it was softer than before. *Grandfather isn't well. You know that, don't you?*

He nodded. "All the more reason to reach him now. Wherever he is, I have to find him."

She seemed to consider. *All right, my love. I'll do my best.* She stepped toward him once more, hopped back onto his lap, and closed her eyes. After a few seconds she opened them again. A long moment passed. Staring into her face, Eli began to wonder if it was going to work. Maybe she couldn't do it more than once. But soon he felt a tingling on his scalp. And then came the feeling he remembered from the first time, the faint fizzing sensation deep in his brain.

The sounds of the storm started to fade. He closed his eyes.

Eli was in the digital tunnel again. In his mind he and Marilyn were flying across a field of multicolored lights. She carried him down a long chain of interconnecting highways as countless electronic intersections whipped past. Every now and then they would duck through doorways he hadn't noticed, or they would turn onto side roads like steep, winding staircases. Eventually the lights faded and the feeling of motion slowed.

Now he found himself floating in a CloudNet sphere over a narrow hospital bed. The room had uneven, pinkish walls that glistened with moisture and seemed to expand and contract at regular intervals like enormous living air sacs. Eli realized he was inside some kind of medical apparatus, a giant artificial lung. In the bed below him, twisted amid the sheets, somebody was struggling to breathe. He'd been expecting to come to Grandfather, but this wasn't him. The patient in the bed was too small and frail to be anyone but a child. Hairless and rail thin, his skin was yellow and withered and he had black circles around his eyes. He looked more like a corpse than a living being. Two robot nurses attended him. At that moment one of them was fussing with the plastic tubes that connected his arms and chest with the medical equipment behind his head. The noise of the storm had dropped away by then, and everything was quiet except for the hum of machinery and the rasp of strained breathing.

Marilyn, who is this? Why are we here?

She didn't answer. Although Eli could sense her presence somewhere in the CloudNet, he could feel she wasn't in the sphere with him but instead was lingering somewhere behind. It occurred to him that she was even more worn out than he'd realized and that in her weakened state, she must have carried him as far as she could until at last she'd had to send him ahead without her. He was on his own.

He gazed down again at the child in the bed, only this time

there was something about the face that caught his attention. It was something familiar about the shape of the ears and the way the nose slanted at the top. Eli realized he'd been wrong. The shriveled, ghoulish creature barely clinging to life below him wasn't a child after all.

"Grandfather?" he whispered. "Is that you?"

The old man stirred. When he spoke, his voice was weak and raspy. "Eli? My fat lamb . . ." Then his body convulsed in a series of sharp, rumbly coughs. With each one the walls shuddered.

"I'm here," he said. Even across the CloudNet, Eli felt a lump in his throat.

The robots looked up, but only for a moment. They seemed far more interested in Grandfather's coughing fit than in Eli's presence. After a quick glance at the sphere, their blue faces swiveled back to the patient. One of them adjusted a knob on a nearby machine and the coughing subsided.

"How on earth have you come to me here, child?" he murmured, his eyes still closed. Before Eli could respond, though, a faint smile seemed to form on his lips, and he answered his own question. "Oh . . . the mongoose, of course. They didn't think to look for her until it was too late, did they? And they never found her." His eyes opened just a crack. "Oh, he's a brilliant man, my friend. A genius if ever there was one."

For an instant Eli thought he saw a mischievous look flash across his face. Grandfather must be delirious, he thought. He was also smaller and frailer than Eli ever would have imagined. "What happened to you, Grandfather? Are you going to be all right?"

Almost undetectably he shook his head. "I'm afraid not. Medical technology can do only so much. It seems the particulates have finally gotten the better of my lungs. Still, I've been lucky to fend off the inevitable as long as I have. Raise me."

These last words he directed to the nearer of the two robots. The back of the bed lifted until he was in a sitting position and looking into the sphere. It broke Eli's heart to see him so withered and feeble.

"I'm glad you're here, child. Now that I see you, I realize I've been holding on because I was waiting for this moment. I somehow knew you'd find a way to me."

It was an odd thing to say, but Eli supposed his mind could have been failing him along with his body. He remembered that Grandfather had been sick the entire time since he was kidnapped from home. He wondered if he'd even known that Eli was gone. But it didn't matter. Eli had come here for assistance and he was determined to ask for it.

"Oh, Grandfather," he began, his voice already shaking, "I'm in terrible trouble and I need your help." At last the whole story came tumbling out: how he was trapped in a reeducation tower run by Spider and the Department of Loyalty, how Spider was secretly using company employees as slave labor, how Mother and Father had been accused of working with the Foggers against the company, and how Eli himself had also been accused. The next part was especially difficult for him.

"The thing is, I really did have contact with Foggers. I know I shouldn't have, and I'm sorry, except it wasn't my fault, at least not at first. But then they told me things, things I didn't want to believe but couldn't help thinking about. Stuff

340

about the Outsiders, and the temperature of the planet, and the end of civilization. They told me that the weird stuff happening with the domes—all the explosions, the system problems, the sky glitches—isn't because of Fogger sabotage, like InfiniCorp says. They said it's because the domes were never designed to withstand weather as extreme as we're getting now, so they're starting to fail." Eli was taking it slowly now, trying to gauge Grandfather's reaction. "They said it's only going to get worse and that our family knows it, and that's why the company is blaming the Foggers—as a way to hide the truth."

He waited for a response, but the old man didn't say anything for a long time. He gave a wheezy sigh. "I always knew this day would come."

Eli's stomach tightened. Until that moment he'd been holding out hope. "So, it's true," he said. "About InfiniCorp and the Final Days. *All* of it. You've known what was happening all along."

Grandfather stayed quiet, but the truth was plain in his eyes.

All the pent-up frustration of the past few months rose in Eli's chest. As small and helpless as Grandfather looked, and as much as Eli still loved him (he couldn't help it, even now), he was so furious at him, he could barely speak. When he tried, the words caught in his throat. "How could you let this happen?"

"None of us realized," Grandfather answered, his voice heavy with regret. "And by the time we did, it was already too late."

"Why didn't you let anyone know?"

"What good would that have done? Beyond a certain

341

point, there was no way to change the direction of things. Besides, it's been years since I had any real authority in the company. I've been a mere figurehead for your uncle Hector and, more recently, your cousin Spider. The change in position wasn't my choice. Hector and Spider have kept me around this long only because it suits their needs."

It took a moment for this to sink in. Grandfather wasn't in charge?

"Understand," continued the old man, "I'm not trying to absolve myself of responsibility. I *was* in charge for decades. But all this history is like sand swept behind us long ago in the desert wind. It's all in the past now and can't be changed. Life as we've known it is all but over. There's nothing anybody can do about it. The only remaining question is, what do we choose to do with the limited time we have left? Take desperate action in the face of unimaginable dread and discomfort just to cling to the slim, irrational hope of surviving? Or admit defeat and live out the rest of our days in relative ease? This is what the company's leaders have always believed InfiniCorp offers: Contentment. Peace of mind. A way to keep living a simulation of our old, carefree lives as long as possible without regret for the past or trepidation about the future."

"So we shouldn't care that we're using some of our own people as slaves so others can live well? Or that the CloudNet is turning everyone into mindless zombies with no idea what's happening around them?"

Grandfather's expression didn't change. "As the company sees it, the CloudNet serves a vital purpose. Imagine, for example, if the spheres in a single reeducation facility were to shut down and the Waywards were all to awaken from their dreams. A setback like that could put the whole operation at risk. With the Outside world falling apart, InfiniCorp sees enforced ignorance as a form of compassion. It believes it's providing a service of mercy."

"Is that what *you* believe?"

There was a long pause as the living walls of the lung room expanded and contracted. "I did," Grandfather answered at last. "For a long time I did. Eli, I'm not a perfect man. I've always carried secrets. I've had to. After nearly losing everything to the Great Sickness, my reaction was to safeguard what I thought was the only real asset humanity still had—and that was the company. It wasn't purely selfish, and I never meant to leave people helpless. I simply felt InfiniCorp had the means to protect the employees from despair, at least for a while. I tried to do the best I could for everyone."

Even as Eli gazed down at his grandfather—suddenly so disappointing and pathetic to him—back in the Special Training room, his fists were clenched. "Why didn't you tell me any of this before?"

"For obvious reasons, InfiniCorp's top leaders share these secrets with very few. Even among our family, only a handful know the true purpose of the company. But I always planned to tell you, Eli. I was waiting until after you started in the Program. Perhaps this was another mistake, one of many I've made over my long career."

Eli wasn't buying any of it. The more he listened to what Grandfather said, the more betrayed he felt. "What about the Wild Orange Yonder? Is there any truth to *that*?"

"Believe me, we've looked everywhere. We searched the wasteland but came up with nothing. You have to understand, the company was grasping at straws for any chance for survival. In the end I'm afraid InfiniCorp came to the conclusion there's no such place."

"And Dr. Friedmann? What's the truth about him?"

"Ah, Gustavo . . ." For the first time a smile truly formed on his shriveled lips. "One of the most remarkable people I ever knew. A great engineer, a voracious reader. He was a man of many varied interests. Literature, history, genetics, neuroscience . . . He was fascinated by dreams and the study of the unconscious mind. He was the one who invented the brain systems that eventually became the control centers of the Cloud-Net. We were inseparable as children, you know. The very closest of friends for many years. He was always something of a troublemaker. Not so unlike you, Eli, in your way." Grandfather eyed him with obvious affection. "Even as very young men we were both ambitious. We shared a philosophy that people who follow the rules rarely make the history books."

He looked tired now and took a long, wheezing breath. "But as is sometimes the unfortunate way of things, in later years he and I had a falling-out. As his criticism of the company and its business grew louder, he became more of a problem. When he brought us that Greenhouse Recovery Project of his, I thought he'd lost his mind, that he'd let himself get carried away with his own outlandish ideas. Later I came to recognize that he wasn't as mad as I'd believed, but by then it was too late. Few know, outside of the company leadership, but for a long time I've had to watch, powerless, as my eldest son secretly made all the key decisions."

"So is that what my parents were doing? Getting ready to expose the truth about Uncle Hector and Spider to everyone who didn't know?"

Grandfather nodded, the strain of talking so much starting to show in his drooping eyelids. "Apparently so."

It was like a slam to Eli's gut. Memories came rushing back to him, little things Mother and Father said or did in his presence that should have been clues: How they always warned him to stay on Uncle Hector's good side. The way they often left family gatherings early and seemed to keep themselves apart from the rest of the Papadopouloses. Every once in a while, they'd let slip disparaging comments about InfiniCorp's senior leadership, and even about the company itself. He'd noticed these things in the past but never considered that they might mean anything. Eli had always felt his parents didn't pay enough attention to him, but now he realized he had paid too little attention to *them*.

"What did the Department of Loyalty do with them? Are Mother and Father in another slave facility like the one I'm in?"

Grandfather's eyes grew watery. He nodded. "As far as I know, yes. I'm so sorry, Eli. I let so much happen that shouldn't have. I was wrong about so many things. . . ."

Eli barely heard him anymore. He felt as if he were falling, as if his whole world were sinking into darkness. The old man started to cough again, and the pink, fleshy walls went into spasms. While one of the robots adjusted his pillow, the other tweaked the dials on the equipment beside the bed. Even so, it was a while before Grandfather's spasms were under control once more.

"Now, I'm very tired, child," he said at last, his voice even

345

weaker. "You'll have to let me sleep. But please understand that I accept full responsibility for what I've done. I made my choices, just like you will. I only hope your decisions will prove wiser than mine. Of all my grandchildren, I've always considered you special, and for good reason." He half smiled. "Perhaps I shouldn't have said that. After all, our conversation is sure to be recorded and analyzed later. I'm afraid Hector and Spider don't trust me. They seem to suspect that my allegiance to the company I built may not be as strong as it once was. They have me under constant watch now, so I must always be careful what I say and do." He was looking directly at Eli now. "Before long they're sure to find out about your visit here and how you made it happen. You should be aware of that."

It was at this moment that Eli realized the robots' optical sensors were fixed on him once again. But he was too upset to care anymore. If everything Grandfather said was true, what could anyone possibly do to him to make matters worse?

"But what's going to happen to me, Grandfather? Can't you get me out of the tower?"

"Believe me, I would help if I could, but I'm powerless. In any case, my time is drawing to a close." Grandfather looked as if something had just occurred to him. "Oh, but perhaps there's one small consolation I may be able to offer. Remember the soothing melodies you used to unlock from my music box? Well, music isn't the only key to quieting a troubled mind. And in that spirit I'll leave you with one final riddle."

Eli stared. A *riddle*? *Now*?

The old man must have seen the incredulity on Eli's face, because he added, "Don't worry, this is an especially good one.

It happens to have been a favorite of my friend's, the one who designed the domes. Here it is: When backward is forward, Alice looks through a mirror. What does she see?"

Eli's confusion only deepened. *Everything* appears backward in mirrors. When Alice steps through the looking glass, she finds an entire *world* in reverse. It was part of the whole point of the second *Alice* story! But before he could say so or ask Grandfather to explain further, Eli found himself slipping back into the tunnel of color.

"Goodbye, my dear. Goodbye . . . ," rasped Grandfather, and then he started to cough again, violent hacks that sounded like they were ripping open his insides. But the lung room was getting smaller and smaller. Eli tried to reach out for the old man, realizing it was probably the last time he'd ever see him, but already he felt himself falling backward across the Cloud-Net. Soon the colors were rushing past once more, swooping and twisting around him in a breathtaking canopy of light.

In an instant he jolted awake again. His eyes opened. He was back in the Special Training room.

The walls and floor trembled and rolled with each crash of the waves. The wind had grown louder. It sounded like a shrieking chorus now, as if it might have the power to rip the protective dome away from the tower at any moment.

Eli buried his face in his hands. Grandfather had lost his mind. He'd saved the world only to end up leaving the last of humankind in a defenseless daydream, and when Eli had asked for his help in a crisis, all he'd given him was a stupid riddle. Somehow what stung most was that members of his own family had known the truth all along. Eli almost wished he'd never found out. If only he could go back and warn the others, tell them that the Foggers were right, that InfiniCorp was nothing but a lie.

But there was no chance of that anymore.

Even now he still had the option of living in a dream and ending the growing anguish he felt in his heart. He could give himself up to the Guardians and go willingly into a bottomless reverie. It was definitely the easier option. It would shield him from the terror of the End Times and might even stop him from feeling the shame of what his family had done.

And yet, he remembered, not everybody in his family had been content keeping so many terrible secrets. His parents had *tried* to change things for the better. He was glad, at least, for that. But Eli didn't want to dwell on what had happened to them just then. If he did, he was going to start crying like a little kid. Right now he couldn't afford to do that.

He looked down at Marilyn, lying collapsed on his uniform. Her head had sunk to his chest and her eyelids hung half-closed. She looked even more fragile than before, if that was possible, as if taking him through the CloudNet had depleted her strength so badly she could barely move. He hated to ask any more of her, but he had little choice. He remembered what Grandfather said about the only remaining question, and he had already chosen his answer.

It was time for desperate action.

Marilyn, are you strong enough to unbolt the door? We have to get out of here.

Her echoing voice was faint but clear. *I think so, my love. I'll do everything I can.*

He picked her up and cradled her in his arm. She closed her eyes. It pained him to watch how hard she seemed to struggle as her chest rose and fell. Moments later, though, he heard the electronic latch click open. He gave a silent word of thanks and put her gently into his pocket so she could rest. Then he slid out of the chair and opened the door just a crack.

When he felt sure it was empty, he crept out into the hallway.

24

a cog in the grand design

Tabitha couldn't sleep.

It was the middle of the night, less than a day after she'd slipped Eli the note about his parents. She regretted showing him the document now, but she'd never expected to set off such a firestorm. The strangest part, the part that still amazed her even now as she lay in the darkness of her bunk, was that he hadn't given her away to the Guardians, even when doing so would have made things easier on him. It was an act of self-lessness that had astonished her. And now it was too late for anyone to help him.

It left her thinking again about the old man in the sky.

Deep down she wanted to believe the story and everything it implied—that maybe Eli really *could* be el Guía, that he might actually be the one who could lead the way to safety in the great unknown. But no, she couldn't let herself slip back into that old foolishness. The kid wasn't el Guía because no such person existed. There was no lost sanctuary either, no hidden paradise waiting to be found just so that people could ride out the apocalypse.

There would be no happy ending for humanity.

Only wind and rain and sand and death.

Okay, so maybe the kid did something selfless, but that didn't change anything. Eli Papadopoulos was still just a boy who was in way over his head. Right or wrong, he was as good as dead now, and she was still here. This was all that mattered anymore.

She turned toward the wall and tried to ignore the growing tempest Outside—the frequent crack and boom of thunder, the ever-increasing pitch of the wind. The way the reeducation facility was rolling and tossing in the waves was enough to make her nauseous. And yet none of the other girls in the bunks seemed bothered. They lay motionless through it all, under the spell of the spheres even during sleep. Tabitha took a deep breath and tried to quiet her thoughts.

It was just as she closed her eyes that she heard the electronic bolt on the door click open.

She froze. She didn't dare turn her head to see who it was. It was rare for the Guardians to check the bunk rooms this late at night. By this time most of them were asleep themselves, and besides, the spheres kept everyone in line for them. She pretended to be out cold like everybody else.

Then she heard somebody whisper, "Tabitha? Tabitha, are you in here?"

Her eyes opened. It couldn't be. She turned and saw the shadowy figure standing in the doorway just as there was another crash of thunder. She nearly jumped.

"Eli?" she whispered back, sitting up. "Oh my god!"

But he held a finger to his mouth. "Shh. Careful, or you'll alert the Guardians."

As if she needed reminding.

Her muscles tensing, she glanced around at the other Waywards, but they remained still in their bunks. "But how . . . ? You were in Special Training. . . ."

"No time to explain. You were right. Nobody's coming for me. So now I'm ready to break out of here with you. Right now."

"You're going down to the pods?"

He nodded.

Her thoughts reeled as she tried to take in this sudden turn of events. Somehow the Papadopoulos boy had escaped the nightmares. She didn't think it was possible, and yet here he was, in front of her. The low nighttime shimmer of the sphere gave a ghostly blue sheen to his face.

"And you came back," she said, still trying to make sense of it. "For *me*. Why?"

"What do you mean? I couldn't leave without you. We're in this together. Come on, let's go."

She hesitated. Part of her couldn't help thinking he was a fool. Coming for her had been one more risk he shouldn't have taken. Somehow he'd made it all the way down to the fifth floor without getting caught, which meant he had to be far more resourceful than she'd realized and probably didn't need her help to get to the pods. Surely he knew that. And worse, he didn't realize that he was setting himself up to be used as a distraction for her benefit, a means by which she could be more confident of getting away, even if it meant leaving him behind. As true as it was, she felt guilty for even thinking it.

"What's the problem?" he asked. "You doing this with me or not?"

She looked back at him, and for a split second she thought she saw something curious, something she hadn't noticed before. In the darkness it was hard to be sure, but it looked like he had a small animal's head poking out of his pocket. Her eyes had to be playing tricks on her. Even so, she couldn't help recalling that Gustavo's prophecy spoke of an animal that traveled with el Guía, a deformed creature with strange powers. For a moment she felt uncertain. A surge of emotion was twisting her insides. Misgiving, perhaps. Maybe fear.

This was all too weird.

But everything was happening fast, and she forced herself to stay focused. Here was her one chance of escape, and she wasn't going to blow it because of some crazy superstition. She was a survivor. Everything was on the line. Every second counted.

"All right," she answered, her voice steady. "Let's do this. I know where the pods are. Just give me a moment to pry open the vent cover and I'll lead you through."

Seconds later she was on her hands and knees inside the air duct. It was about as hot as she could take, and already her neck and arms ran with sweat. She had just enough room to look back and beckon Eli to follow.

"You sure this is the best way?" he asked, frowning into the open vent.

"Definitely. It leads to the docking area and there's no chance of running into any Guardians. Come on! Let's go!"

He hesitated, but he climbed in after her and soon they were crawling through the darkness, one after the other. The storm was worse than any she could remember. Inside the cramped space she was even more aware of how the tower swayed in the gale. With each roll of thunder, her hands felt the vibrations in the metal. She realized this must have been part of the reason Eli had been able to make it this far. The hurricane helped hide any noises. On the other hand, she wondered how an escaping transport pod would fare in the storm. She decided not to worry about that yet, though. For better or worse, this was her one shot at escape. First she had to steal a pod; then she'd worry about flying it.

Finally they reached the part of the duct where they could peer down at the loading area. Even here, within the protective hemisphere of the tower's dome, the water rolled and pitched with the storm. There were at least a dozen pods waiting on the deck, and bobbing in the water were several medium-sized InfiniCorp transport boats, a supply tanker, and even what looked like a submarine.

And as always, Guardians stood watch over it all.

"The water really *is* red," Eli whispered.

"It's the algae. When there isn't much oxygen left in the ocean, it takes over."

Eli stared. "How are we going to get past the Guardians?"

A drop of sweat dripped from Tabitha's forehead to her hand. This was her moment, she knew. All she had to do was instruct Eli to swing down first and wait for her behind the crates on the left side of the deck, where there were a handful of pods to choose from. He would hesitate, but he would do it. She could see it in his eyes. He trusted her. But the fact was, there was a good chance that somewhere along the way to the crates, somebody would notice him. If so, when the Guardians called out, they would rush toward him, clearing a path to the pods on the right—which, in a way, would be the best-case scenario for Tabitha. In the chaos she could leap from the vent. She wouldn't need long—only a few seconds—to reach the nearest pod, climb inside, and instruct it to fly. Escape had never seemed closer.

And yet she found herself wavering. She'd convinced herself that she wasn't going to look out for anyone else, but now that it was time to act, the idea of making Eli take the bigger risk felt the same as betraying him. He was looking at her, waiting for her to tell him what to do. She had never felt so unsure.

Just at that moment the wind surged. Below them the water level rose, and there was a powerful *whoosh!*—so loud it was almost deafening—as an enormous wave smashed against the tower. The duct shuddered. The whole facility seemed to groan, and the building tilted steeply to one side. Tabitha and Eli were both sent sprawling. Tabitha felt her head smack into the metal. Unlike during the previous times the tower had swayed, this time it was several seconds before the floor started to right itself. When it did, the whole place lurched in the opposite direction, making everything on the loading dock—the pods, the crates, the Guardians, *everything*—shift. Several of the Guardians slipped and fell, while others called out to each other.

Tabitha turned back to Eli. There was no time to lose. "This is our chance!" she said. "While everything's still chaotic down there I'll pop open the vent and we'll both make a run for the pods. We'll do it together. Get ready." She reached for the grate and started to dig her fingernails around the edge.

But Eli tugged her backward. "No, wait!" he said. "We can't do this! We have to go back!"

She craned her neck toward him again. "What! What do you mean?"

"The storm is too strong! The tower isn't going to hold! We can't just leave everybody here to die! We have to wake the other Waywards so they stand a chance!"

Tabitha gaped at him. Here they were, at the pods. The storm had provided a perfect distraction, and the Guardians were barely paying attention. This was the best chance they could ever hope for, and he wanted to go *back*? The kid was nuts!

"If the storm is bad enough," she answered, trying to sound reasonable, "then it'll knock out the power, and with the CloudNet gone they'll wake up anyway."

"Maybe, but by then the whole facility could be destroyed. We can't take that risk. We need to rouse everybody before it's too late. At least then they'll have a hope of saving themselves."

She was going to argue again, but there was a look in his eyes she'd never seen before. He wasn't going to change his mind. Without waiting for her answer, he twisted around and started crawling back up the duct. Furious, she closed her eyes and took a deep breath. She knew she should forget him. Why should she care about the other Waywards when she had herself to think about? She should just rip open the grate and rush out there while she still could.

Something held her back, though. Something inside her she couldn't explain.

She twisted herself around. Even as she scrambled after him, she was sure she was making a terrible mistake.

By the time Tabitha got back to the dorm room, Eli was dashing from bunk to bunk, taking each Wayward by the shoulders and shaking her. "Wake up! Wake up!" he was calling over the rumble of rain and wind. It wasn't working. They were all too deeply under the spell of the spheres.

"Not so loud!" Tabitha warned. "You're going to alert the Guardians! You'll get us killed!"

"If we don't do something, they could *all* be killed! Help me!"

Her thoughts were going a hundred miles an hour and she wasn't sure what to do. Trying to save the Waywards was noble and everything, but it seemed futile, even suicidal. It occurred to her that it was a miracle the Guardians weren't already on them, but then again, the storm was so loud now that it must have been drowning out the noise Eli was making—and besides, with the tower bobbing in the waves, the Guardians had other problems to attend to just then.

Still, whatever had kept them safe so far, their luck couldn't last.

"Eli, this is pointless!" she said, trying to keep her voice low. "Even if you somehow figure a way to rouse all the kids in this room, there must be hundreds of Waywards in the facility! What are you planning to do, sneak onto every dormitory floor? Unless you know a way to kill the CloudNet all at once, there will always be more Waywards we'll have to leave behind. Face it—it's time to give up on them and take care of ourselves!"

He looked up. "If your house was on fire and your family were asleep inside, would you do nothing?"

It took her by surprise. This was something Ben and the other Friends used to say. She stared at him. And then she saw the animal again. When Eli turned, the dim light of the sphere floating beside her was just bright enough for her to make out a slumped creature in his pocket, its claws clinging tight to his uniform. Her breath caught. Before, when she'd first thought she'd seen it, she'd convinced herself it was just her imagination. But no, here it was again. Grizzled and cut, it looked like a rat that had been in a fight. Its eyes were only half-open, but even so, it seemed to gaze at her with suspicion.

"Eli . . . ? What on earth is th—?"

She didn't get a chance to finish. With another howl, the wind seemed to lift and drop the floor under her feet, and she lost her balance. Her arms flailed to break her fall, and her hand passed through the CloudNet sphere. The moment she felt the cool tingle on her fingers, she knew it meant disaster. All at once the sphere came to life. The room filled with light.

Suddenly an alarm blasted through the air.

Tabitha hit the floor. She was unhurt, but for a second or two, she and Eli both froze. There was no going back now. The alarm was loud and seemed to come from every direction, yet none of the Waywards stirred.

"Oh my god." The full horror of the situation swept through her. "I—I'm so sorry, Eli. That's it. They're coming for us. We're dead!"

When she turned to him, though, the look of determination in his eyes startled her. It was as if a switch had gone off inside him. In a flash he was standing over her. He held out his hand and helped her to her feet.

"We have to hurry!" he said. "Follow me!"

Behind him a loose wooden rail hung off the end of one of the bunks, and in one motion he snapped it off in his hand and headed for the door. After he'd first arrived, she'd heard the automatic lock reset itself when the door had swung shut behind him, but now, just as he reached for the handle, Tabitha thought she heard the electronic bolt click again. He swung the door open without much effort.

"How——?" she began, but then she stopped. She must have only imagined that the door had closed all the way.

She stumbled after him down the hallway. Eli was swinging his makeshift baton like a madman, whacking every sphere he passed as he headed down the long corridor. There were seven or eight of them, floating in regular intervals along the narrow ceiling. Some he struck several times. Sparks flew, but instead of breaking, they seemed to glow brighter.

"Disturbance on level five," came a voice from the spheres. "Resisters in Wayward Dormitory corridor B."

"Wake up! Wake up!" Eli shouted over the blaring alarm. He slammed his fist against each bunk-room door he passed.

Tabitha ran after him. "Eli, stop!" She had a desperate idea. Maybe if they hurried back to the air duct, they could still slip away. With luck they might reach the pods before the Guardians figured out what had happened to them. It wasn't likely, but it was the best she could think of. They had to at least try. "What are you doing, Eli! We need to go back!"

"We can't go back! We're the only chance the Waywards have! Come on, hurry!"

"There's nothing you can do for them! Eli, please!"

Eli stopped at an arched door near the end of the hallway. She caught up with him, but it was already too late. She could hear footsteps rushing up the stairway. In seconds the Guardians would swarm the corridor, and their passage back to her bunk room would be cut off. Frantic to find another way out, she tried the door but of course it was locked, just like all the others. They were trapped.

Another crash of thunder shook the walls. Adrenaline pulsed through her veins and she wondered how on earth she'd allowed this to happen. Back at the pods she could have just let Eli go. Even up until moments earlier she could have dashed back to the open air duct while she still had a slim hope of making it to the pods without him. But she hadn't, and now that option was gone. Why had she done this to herself? With one bad decision she'd let everything crumble to nothing.

The footsteps were closer. The first of the Guardians was about to appear from the stairwell.

And then something strange happened: the door in front of them slid open, even though Tabitha had been positive it was locked. "Follow me!" Eli said. Astonished, and with no idea where she was going, she shot behind him into what looked like another dark, narrow passageway. Just as three Guardians came into view in the corridor, the door slid shut again. There was shouting, followed by the sounds of the frustrated Guardians pounding at the door.

Eli waved for her to keep moving. "Don't worry. They won't be able to get it open right away. The unlock mechanism is blocked from them for now. It should hold at least a minute or two."

Tabitha was still shocked. After a few steps she stopped. "H-how did you do that?"

"It's Marilyn," he said, gesturing at the rat in his pocket. "She's a friend. She's going to help us find our way." When Tabitha only gaped at him, he stepped back to her and grabbed her hand. "Come on, there's no time to explain. Trust me. Let's go!"

She staggered after him. Wherever they were, it was hot and damp and smelled vaguely of sewage. Thick metal pipes ran along the length of the passageway, and in and out of the walls and ceiling—so many, there was little room to move. As they scrambled through the tight space, the tower continued to rock and the echo of rain and wind against the nearby dome was so loud it hurt Tabitha's ears. She couldn't help wondering if this was the end—if, despite their inexplicable escape, the tower was about to crumble into the sea, making everything meaningless. But no. She couldn't think about that possibility. She couldn't allow herself to.

Soon they came to a low opening near the floor, and they squeezed through. It was even darker on the other side. Just as Tabitha was about to take a step into the gloom, Eli grabbed her by the arm and pulled her back. An instant later she saw why. When her eyes adjusted, she realized they were on a short ledge over a steep drop. It went down perhaps fifty feet, all the way to the water. If it weren't for the storm crashing all around them, she would have heard the waves.

She screamed. She had to hold tight to the wall as the tower dipped and swayed.

"What are we doing here?" she said, forcing herself not to look down. Straight ahead she noticed something else. Perhaps six feet across the gap stood an ancient structure of metal girders that began somewhere below and got narrower as it rose high into the darkness above.

Eli had to shout to be heard over the noise. "Marilyn says this is part of a utility crane they used to use back when this tower was only for drilling oil! It's inactive now, but it looks like we can climb it!"

"But what about the Guardians?" she called back.

"This whole section is blocked off for now! With luck, it'll be a few more seconds before they can unjam the locks, and then they'll have to figure out what level we're on! Let's go!"

Only then did it fully sink in what Eli had in mind. He wanted her to jump across the gap and then scale the metal structure, use it like a ladder. Just the idea sent her stomach into her throat. Despite herself, she looked down again at the drop, and her knees went weak.

"What's the matter?"

"I—I'm scared . . . ," she admitted, taking deep breaths. "I'm no good with heights."

His eyes were on her now, and for a moment she was ashamed. But his expression was calm, and when he finally spoke, his voice was gentle, even over the noise. He put his hand on her shoulder. "Tabitha, you can do this. Think of all the months you spent here in the tower, fully aware of what was going on. You are one of the bravest people I've ever met. You'll be okay. I'm right here with you."

His words calmed her a little. Besides, she didn't have

much choice except to do this. She bit her lower lip and took another deep breath.

"Don't think about it," he said. "Just jump."

She summoned all her courage and leapt into the air, stretching her arms toward the nearest girder. When she felt metal she held tight, let her body slam into it, and then wrapped her legs around it for dear life. She'd made it! She was on the crane!

An instant later Eli was hanging on to the girder beside her, the strange animal still partly visible, clinging inside his jacket. Somehow Tabitha knew what was coming next. She could see it in the direction of his gaze. He was looking up, not down.

"You're not going back to the pods, are you?" she said. It wasn't really a question.

He shook his head. "You were right about shutting down the CloudNet," he answered as the tower groaned again. "That's what I have to do. But it doesn't mean you have to come. You can climb down and try to find a path back to the pods. I wouldn't blame you, and you might even make it. But I can't do that. I'm a Papadopoulos. My family is responsible for so many mistakes, and I feel like I have to at least try to do something right. I know it must sound crazy, but I've made my decision. Now you have to make yours."

He started climbing up the crane. Tabitha could hardly believe what was happening. From the moment she'd first found out the kid was a Papadopoulos, she thought she understood everything about him that mattered. She thought he would be arrogant. She was sure he'd be self-centered and tyrannical. But she'd misjudged him. Here he was, ready to sacrifice himself for the Waywards. He was making her question everything she thought she knew. Now she felt awful for the selfish way she'd behaved toward him, and for all the secret thoughts she'd held from him. Suddenly she wanted to tell him everything, to let him know she realized now how wrong she'd been.

By then he'd reached the girder just above her. She pulled herself a little higher, toward him. "Eli, I don't think you'd want me along with you," she said, "not if you realized the truth. Because you're a Papadopoulos, I was ready to abandon you down at the pods while I got away. Even if we'd made it to the desert, I was thinking of leaving you alone there too." She paused. "I wouldn't do any of those things now. And I'm sorry."

This seemed to take a moment to sink in. He stopped and looked back. His eyebrows pulled together. "It's okay," he said. "It doesn't matter anymore."

When his eyes met hers, she felt a rush of something she didn't understand, a dizzy feeling as though she were part of something much bigger than herself. The boy, the animal protector, the storm—was it possible it could all be a coincidence? Maybe the Friends were right after all. Maybe she, like everyone else, had always been a single, tiny cog in a complex system far larger than she'd ever imagined. All at once, with the tower rocking and the sound of waves crashing and wind howling, she had the idea that perhaps there really was a plan, a grand design with a special role she was meant to play.

She made her decision.

"Wait!" she called. "I'm coming with you!"

Trying not to look down, she followed Eli up the crane. It went for quite a distance. Every now and then they could hear the alarm blaring through the walls. Occasionally they even heard shouting.

"How far do we go?" she asked. "Where are we headed?"

"Every dome has a CloudNet brain—that's what we're looking for," he called back. "Marilyn says there's an orange door on the top floor. We have to find it!"

Tabitha was in a daze now, concentrating on keeping a steady footing on each girder and holding on tight as she moved upward. The top of the crane leaned against a metal rail that wrapped around a steel enclosure. Climbing off was easier than jumping on, as long as she didn't look down. She followed Eli across a short passage that led to another vent. There were Guardians on the other side of the wall. She could hear them. And yet somehow she wasn't as worried as she might have been. Eli had already led her this far, with doors that locked and unlocked for them, through dark passageways in hidden recesses of the facility. It was as if his animal companion knew exactly where to go, as if it somehow had the blueprints of the tower and access to the hidden cameras.

They crawled on their stomachs through the vent. This was the twenty-fourth level, the top floor of the facility. The sound of driving rain filled the air, and the cramped space shook with thunder. Soon the three of them were looking out at a small alcove with a tiled floor. With the animal's assurance that the passage was clear, they climbed out. Tabitha's heart was pounding. Just ahead, somebody was shouting orders as waves continued to crash against the dome and rock the tower. The floor listed to one side. Clinging to the wall so they wouldn't lose footing, she and Eli crept to the end of the alcove. They peered around the corner.

There it was, just as Eli had said.

A corridor with a stairwell and a single orange door.

It was guarded by three beefy kids in white uniforms. From the hint of unease in their expressions, Tabitha guessed the Guardians were as concerned by the storm as she was, but she also knew that, like the Waywards, they were under the spell of the spheres. In the meantime, finding a way past them was the only way to get to the door. It wasn't going to be easy.

"What do we do now?"

Eli was still trying to catch his breath from the climb. "I don't know. I'm out of ideas."

But an idea was beginning to occur to *her*, and it hit her once again that the Friends had turned out to be right. Everything happened for a reason. All of a sudden she knew what she had to do, though the thought terrified her.

"Tell me something about the man in the sky," she whispered in Eli's ear, although she already knew what he was going to say. "He had a tattoo, didn't he?"

He looked surprised at the question, but he seemed to consider. "He did. An orange sun—it was on the palm of his hand. How did you know?"

Before she realized she was going to say it, she heard herself whisper, "A single thread of reality can be hard to distinguish in a complex fabric of illusion."

He must have seen the transformation on her face. "It doesn't mean anything, Tabitha. Anybody could have a tattoo."

But she no longer doubted. In a rush she understood why she was here in the tower, why she'd had to endure all those

366

months on the Learning Floors. This was it. This was her moment. As she started to move toward the Guardians, Eli grabbed her arm.

"What are you doing? You'll get caught! Don't be stupid!"

"There's no time to discuss it. You have to shut down the CloudNet." She turned to gaze into his face, probably for the last time. "I do this for you, el Guía. Everything depends on you. Wait ten seconds and then go."

With that she shook off his hand and stepped into the corridor.

25

the brain room

Eli watched Tabitha race toward the Guardians, calling out to them. The moment they saw her, they left their posts. She disappeared down the stairwell and they dashed after her. Eli struggled to stay where he was. There was little chance she could make it far before they caught her. If only there was something he could do!

Let her go, Eli. It's too late.

Marilyn's voice was so weak, it was barely there anymore. The mental exertion of accessing the tower's systems had left her gasping for breath, and now Eli worried about losing her too. Why was everything he cared about slipping from him? He put his hand in his pocket and stroked her fur. She was safe—for now, at least. Tabitha had cleared the path to the orange door, and that was all he could allow himself to think about.

I'm sorry I can't take down the CloudNet for you, my darling. I would if I could.

I know, he answered, even though he realized instinctively that it never would have been possible. Even if she were at her strongest, her chip was no match against the power of an entire CloudNet, and the effort of trying to shut it down might even have killed her. *Don't worry, Marilyn. You've done plenty.*

He'd waited long enough. The corridor was clear, so he leapt from the alcove and ran to the door. It unlocked just as he reached for it, and after he stepped through, it slammed shut behind him.

It was the steep drop in temperature that startled him most.

Right away the sweat on his scalp and back started to grow clammy, and he could see his breath in puffy clouds. In his entire time in the tower, he'd never felt air this cool. He was in a long room cluttered with shiny equipment and flashing lights. There was a musty smell and a deep electronic hum he could hear even over the howl of the wind. Shadows flitted across the low ceiling as the tower creaked again. The place reminded him of where he had met the old Outsider, and he realized this was another sky chamber. He was inside the shell of the tower's little dome.

He glanced around at the equipment. Most of it was large and unfamiliar to him. He wondered why nothing appeared damaged or upended from the storm, but then he noticed that everything was bolted to the floor. He stepped deeper inside, following the sound of the electronic hum. Soon he found what he was looking for: near the center of the room stood a gigantic enclosed tank filled with translucent pink liquid, and floating inside was a mass of grayish goo with lights and glowing fibers that jutted in all directions.

The CloudNet brain.

He hurried to the tank and began searching for a control panel—any buttons, keypads, or whatever looked like it might help him shut it down. There wasn't much, just a small, shimmering plate at one side of the base. It had a knob and a couple of switches, so he flipped the switches. Nothing seemed to happen. He spun the knob, and the light in the tank grew a little brighter, but otherwise the brain continued to hum and throb just the same as before.

How do I do this?

Marilyn didn't answer. Eli realized she was unconscious. He was on his own.

But there had to be a way! The wind rose, and the floor pitched to the side again. Eli gripped the edge of the tank until his knuckles went white. He was so close and yet he was going to fail! He wanted to scream—at Representative Shine and Representative Tinker, at Spider, at every one of his uncles and aunts. Even Grandfather had been so warped with age and disease that he hadn't helped him. He slammed his fist against the glass.

And it was then, with his eyes fixed on the throbbing mass of electronics in the tank, that a curious new thought occurred to him. What was it Grandfather had said when he gave him the riddle? Something about how music wasn't the only key to quieting a troubled mind? At the time, Eli had assumed he meant that the riddle was a diversion to make him feel better, but now, as he watched a cloud of pink bubbles rise around the artificial brain, a different possibility dawned on him: What if it wasn't *Eli's* mind Grandfather had been talking about? What if, like with Grandfather's music box, the original designers of the domes had built in a Master Key, a secret phrase that could control a dome's entire CloudNet system? What if, despite the fact that their conversation had been monitored, Grandfather had been trying to help him after all?

He leaned closer to the glass and said, "Good night, folks. Time to go back to sleep."

Nothing happened.

But of course not, he thought. The Master Key to the CloudNet, if there really *was* such a thing, wouldn't be the same as the shutdown words for the music box. It would have something to do with the riddle, or else why would Grandfather have given it to him? Perhaps the question itself was the key. He tried it, careful to speak in a loud, clear voice: "When backward is forward, Alice looks through a mirror. What does she see?"

Again, nothing. It was no use.

His thoughts were interrupted. Two figures appeared out of the shadows, one on each side. He spun to look. To his left a hulking boy with an oversized jaw and long yellow teeth was moving toward him. On his right, another large kid, this one missing an ear. Eli's stomach sank. They were Outsiders, the same two savages who'd first brought him to the facility.

"It's all right. Keep your distance, gentlemen," whispered a listless voice. Eli wasn't sure where it had come from, but then he noticed something happening inside the tank. A holographic image seemed to be forming in the pink liquid all around the brain. At first he could make out only a giant mouth—two rows of teeth and thin lips forming a wide smirk. But then above it two gray eyes appeared, followed by white hair and the rest of a pale, familiar face.

Spider.

"Curiouser and curiouser," said the enormous, grinning head. "It seems I was alerted to your escape attempt just in time." On his order the savages had halted in their tracks, but Eli could still hear their raspy breathing and impatient movements, as if they were itching to pounce on him the moment Spider gave permission.

"Spider, please don't do this! You don't understand!"

"Oh, but I do. I'm told our dear, unfortunate grandfather regained consciousness for a while and that you and he had a little chat. Naughty, naughty, little cousin." Pockets of gas bubbled up through the goo, and his grin widened. "But I think you'll find I'm going to be surprisingly reasonable with you. You see, after reviewing your illicit conversation with the old fossil, my father has the outlandish idea that—now that you better understand our state of affairs, not to mention your own hopeless situation at the moment—you might be more open to reason. With the right incentive, of course. My father was never comfortable with my decision to cleanse you from the organization in the first place, I'm afraid. It turns out your uncle Hector is a sentimental man. *Foolishly* sentimental, if you ask me. Still, there it is. Against my better judgment, I've been instructed to offer you a deal."

Eli's muscles went tight. A deal? What was this?

"Cooperate with the company," Spider continued. "Agree to come back without causing any more trouble, and my father has agreed to overlook your indiscretions. He'll ask the Leadership Council to assign you to a position you don't deserve, something respectable in middle management where you can't do much damage but you'll live a comfortable life befitting a Papadopoulos."

"What are you talking about? What life? Don't you hear the storm Outside? The tower could collapse any second! The whole world is falling apart!"

Spider seemed to shrug. "I suppose there's no denying that the clock is ticking on the planet. But don't let this passing Gulf drizzle fool you. The company's scientists believe we still have time before the curtain closes, time enough for some of us to enjoy the many pleasures InfiniCorp can still provide. And while it's unfortunate that we can't shield *everyone* from the discomfort of the days ahead, the company can arrange it for *you*, at least for a while, and starting sooner than you think. As we speak, a pod is on its way to fly you from harm. You'll be safe from the hurricane, I assure you." Even as Spider made this offer, his expression made it clear that he didn't approve of it. Still, his tone was rational. Reasonable. "Now, what do you say? Are you ready to return to the family fold?"

Eli stood there, frozen. Was he serious? After all his time in the tower, InfiniCorp was going to take him back? They were offering him everything he'd always wanted: a life in the city domes, a good position in the company, the respect of his family. And yet even as he tried to take it all in, he couldn't help thinking of Tabitha, and of his parents. The floor rocked and the walls trembled. There was another crashing wave, and as the tower groaned he pictured all the Waywards, asleep in their bunk rooms. He thought of Clarence and even Geraldine, so lost in their dreams that they would remain unconscious even while the tower sank into the sea.

It didn't take him long to make up his mind.

"You monster! How do you sleep at night?"

Spider's expression darkened. "I can't say I'm surprised by

373

your attitude. I told my father that trying to reason with you was a waste of effort. I think his judgment was thrown by the impressive way you managed to contact the old geezer on his deathbed despite the CloudNet restraints. But not me. I always suspected that you and Grandfather were up to something, plotting ways to overthrow my father and me from authority." At this he raised an eyebrow. "Which leads me to one last piece of business. Tell me, where is that little furry abomination of yours? Marilyn is her name, right?"

Eli's face flushed. "Don't you dare! You'll never get your hands on her!"

The holographic head seemed amused. "Oh, but of course we will. Surely you realize that. Now that InfiniCorp understands what she is, we can't allow her to remain a threat to our systems. Yes, we'll find her. Even now she must be somewhere nearby, perhaps hiding in this very room, listening to everything we're saying."

The savages took another step closer.

Eli felt the hairs on his neck stand on end. "What are you going to do?"

"I've put up with you for long enough, troublesome cousin. Now I'm arranging for you to have an accident. Quite unfortunate. Everyone will be so, so sad. But take heart. The Great Savior will be joining you soon, and once you and Grandfather are both dead, you'll have an eternity of quality time together. In the meantime, don't worry, InfiniCorp is taking care of everything." His gigantic, near-transparent face formed a sneer. "All right, boys. He's all yours."

The Outsiders leered at him now, their eyes yellow and cruel. They started creeping in his direction. Eli took a step backward and almost fell. And yet his mind was still scrambling for any way he might be able to shut down the Cloud-Net. All he had was the vague hope that Grandfather's riddle meant something. He was desperate to reason it through, to find some hidden meaning he might have missed. After all, the Master Key could be anything, any series of syllables.

When backward is forward, Alice looks through a mirror. What does she see?

By then the savages were closing in on him, so he made a dash toward the far wall, squeezing through a passage in the jungle of bulky equipment in hopes it would buy him some time. His thoughts raced. The first part of the riddle surely referred to when Alice was in the looking-glass world, but he'd already guessed that, so now he ran through the things he remembered her seeing there. In the very first room, he recalled, there were pictures that moved, a clock with a human face, chess pieces that talked, and a book of nonsense poetry. After that she came to a staircase, a winding path that didn't lead anywhere, and—oh, it was no use! The list was too long, and the savages were almost on him. Plus, Eli realized, Alice wasn't looking *through* a mirror to see any of these things, because she herself was *inside* the mirror!

But then he caught himself.

No, that was wrong. In a flash he remembered there *was* one thing she'd seen through a mirror, even in the looking-glass world.

He reached the far wall, where the curved metal girders that shaped the dome's exterior met with the shimmering electromagnetic field that was the dome's outermost layer of protection. In the gloom it looked like a grid of glowing rectangles, a concave wall of high, tinted windows that curved inward as they went up. He could almost feel the rain pounding and the wind blasting on the other side. But there was nowhere left to run. Heart in his throat, he spun around and saw the two freakish boys rushing at him, squeezing their large frames through the narrow rows of blinking generators and vibrating neurofiber systems. Seeing Eli trapped, the savage with the missing ear slowed just a little. He licked his lips. In the tank behind them, Spider's giant head grinned.

And that's when the answer came to Eli at last.

It was the book of poetry. Since everything in the looking-glass world was reversed, all the words Alice saw in the book were printed backward, which meant she had to hold it up to a *second* mirror to read it. What she saw was a poem—a backward image of a backward image. The riddle wasn't a riddle at all. It was simply directions to a particular passage in the story. As it happened, the poem Alice found was one of Eli's favorite parts of the whole book. He knew it by heart. But was it the Master Key?

There was only one way to find out.

"Wait!" he called, holding up his hand just as taloned fingers reached out at him. For the briefest of moments, the Outsiders stopped. Perhaps the tone of Eli's voice startled them. Perhaps they were just curious. In any case, Eli began calling out the first verse of the poem:

> " 'Twas brillig, and the slithy toves!
> Did gyre and gimble in the wabe!
> All mimsy were the borogoves!
> And the mome raths outgrabe!"

The lights started to blink. The head in the tank began to dim. Even the Outsiders took notice. They turned to watch.

Spider's eyes grew furious. "What's happening? *Stop him!*"

But Eli didn't miss a beat. He called out the next verse as fast and loud as he could:

> *"Beware the Jabberwock, my son!*
> *The jaws that bite, the claws that catch!*
> *Beware the Jubjub bird, and shun!*
> *The frumious Bandersnatch!"*

There was a thunderous groan like the sound of a giant engine winding down. The lights flickered, and Eli heard a series of sharp, echoing bursts—*crack! crack! crack!*—that seemed to grow closer as the tower powered down one floor at a time. Even in the dim light, he could feel the energy of the spheres diminish. The Outsiders must have felt the change too. Their eyes went wide, and they looked around in terror. One of them had a hold on Eli's uniform, but now he loosened his grip.

With one final *crack!* everything went dark.

Spider howled with rage, but after a few seconds his voice faded to nothing. In the relative quiet that followed, Eli felt a rush of wind and water on his back.

He turned. The electromagnetic outer shell of the dome wall had disappeared, and only the structural girders of the tower's dome stood between him and a twenty-four-story drop into the sea. The view was terrifying. It was night, but he could make out the raging water below, a vast field of enormous, angry waves as far as he could see.

377

He grabbed on to the nearest girder and held tight.

There was a roar so loud, it felt like the whole world shook. With an earsplitting creak the tower lurched backward. If Eli hadn't been clinging to the girder, he would have slipped. The Outsiders tumbled down the floor, but they caught themselves, grabbing on to nearby equipment. This time the tower didn't right itself. It settled at an angle, like a low table that had lost two of its legs, and it stayed that way. But the savages still weren't finished. Within seconds they were climbing up the floor.

They were still coming for him.

With nowhere else to run, Eli swung himself around the girder and started climbing. The sour milk smell was almost overpowering. He was Outside, hundreds of feet high, clinging to the outer skeleton of what remained of the tower's dome. The wind whipped through his hair, and the storm roared all around him. Within seconds he was soaked through. Rain dripped from every part of him and weighed down his uniform. But he couldn't stop. He didn't see the Outsiders anymore, but they must have been back there somewhere, still following. He silently called out to Marilyn, still in his pocket. She didn't answer. His only consolation was that he could sense her signal. It was weak, but she was still alive.

By the time he reached the top, the gust had slowed a little. Through the pounding rain ahead of him, he saw what looked like a small, empty transport pod. But could it be? Yes, that's what it was. He felt a rush of adrenaline. But whose was it, and why was it here? It might belong to the Guardians, he decided, or whoever ran the Brain Room. Perhaps moments ago there had been more pods besides this one, pods that had fallen into the sea as the tower shifted. There was no way to know, and in any case it didn't matter. Here it was, one last chance of escape! Still clinging to the girder, he scrambled for it.

Just as he got close, though, a bright light appeared in the sky overhead. He craned his neck. A black transport pod was descending from the clouds. Within seconds it landed across the girders beside him. It was long and low, with red illumina-tors and dark tail fins like the wings of a demon.

It was from the Department of Loyalty.

The doors lifted open. Eli tried to climb away, but before he knew what was happening, he felt a stabbing pain down his spine. He could barely move. Faceless employees dressed in black took him by the arms, dragged him to the transport, and stuffed him into the rear compartment. It all happened so fast that Eli hardly had time to think. Then the pod started to rise, slow and steady, despite the wind. Exhausted, Eli could only peer through the window as the tower began to drop away. How had everything gone so wrong, so fast? Tabitha had let herself get captured, Marilyn was limp in his pocket and des-perately hurt, and now he was back in the hands of the De-partment of Loyalty! After everything the three of them had gone through, nothing good had come of it.

He felt like throwing up.

But as the pod continued to glide, he had a view of what was going on at the base of the tower, and what he saw sur-prised him: other pods, dozens of them, were rising into the air. In fact, the whole area around the giant oil rig was begin-ning to swarm with escaping transports. As the waves crashed and fell, he even caught brief glimpses of the chaos on the slanted deck. Under the bright lights of the docking area, people were running—Waywards, by their orange uniforms, and even some white-clad Guardians, mixed in with them. Free from the influence of the CloudNet, crowds were pouring onto the lowest level and into the tankers and pods. Eli was stunned. Now he could only hope that the awakened Waywards would all find their way to safety.

And that Tabitha would be among them.

His shoulder slumped against the wall, Eli rested his head on the cool glass. He was so tired. His whole body hurt. Below him the tower continued to shrink, finally disappearing behind a curtain of mist.

The black Department of Loyalty pod ascended through the clouds and above the storm. For a long time it traveled. Eli's compartment was dark, and the heat grew oppressive. He wondered where they were going and what the black-uniformed employees were planning to do with him. After a while he noticed, at the front of the cabin, a digital face beginning to form on an overhead screen. He was breathing quickly again, sure he was about to confront his cousin one last time. He readied himself for the stare, the listless gray eyes and pale, sickly gape of the one person who had caused him so much trouble. There was nothing Eli could do to save himself now. Spider had him under his control.

But the head that materialized wasn't Spider's. It had dark features, long black hair, and a sloping nose—a face not so unlike his own. Eli's heart leapt.

"Sebastian!" he cried.

"I hope you realize how much I just stuck my neck out to save your sorry butt," his brother said, his voice strangely cool. "I'll catch a world of crap for this."

Eli wasn't sure what to say. He didn't understand his brother's chilly tone, but at the same time he couldn't help feeling elated—and shocked to see him. Until this moment he'd assumed that on the same night the Outsiders had kidnapped him from Providence, the company had also taken Sebastian. He'd worried for so long. "I'm glad it's you!" he said. "You have no idea how relieved I am!"

Sebastian narrowed his eyes. "You didn't think you were going to make it out of the tower alive on your own, did you? You wouldn't have. Even if you'd reached the pod on the roof and managed to get it into the air, Spider had already sent out orders to track you down. You're lucky my people got to you first."

Eli's chest swelled. In a gush of emotion, all the terrible things he'd learned, the appalling secrets about the company and the warming climate, came pouring out: The true nature of the reeducation facilities, and how he'd been held prisoner, like so many other misused employees. How Grandfather wasn't in charge anymore, and how Spider and Uncle Hector had been secretly running things for years. How the Cooldown was a big lie, and how the overheating atmosphere was making the storms grow so destructive, they would eventually destroy the domes. "The company knew all along," he told him, "and Mother and Father were trying to expose the truth when they got caught. Now you and I need to alert everybody so they can make their own choices while there's still time!

381

Maybe it's not too late to reverse the damage to the planet! There has to be a way!"

For a long moment Sebastian eyed him. Finally he shook his head and said, "Eli, I've known about the climate since my first days in the Program. Don't look so surprised. What, did you think that my mentor, Spider, wasn't going to tell me? Sure, it was a shock at first, but what's the point of kicking and screaming when there's nothing anybody can do? As far as Uncle Hector and Spider, I already know about that too. But it's the best way, the *only* way, because Grandfather has been feebleminded for years. His time is over."

Eli couldn't believe what he was hearing. "But . . . what about Mother and Father? Don't tell me you're okay with what happened to them."

Sebastian's face reddened. "Mother and Father were trying to ruin all the good that Uncle Hector and Spider have been doing. Don't you get it? It's not just our family that benefits. It's all the employees. Instead of suffering and dying in the desert, they get to live without worrying about the future. But I guess you've been too blinded by Foggers to understand that."

"And Spider? He *kidnapped* me. He held me prisoner!"

"I'm not surprised you see yourself as the victim. You always have. And yet the night you forced Spider to cleanse you from the Providence dome, he was only doing what he had to, for the sake of the company. He could've had you killed right then and there, but he didn't. That's loyalty, Eli. But you wouldn't know anything about that, would you?" He curled his lip. "I'm so disappointed in you. I never thought you'd turn out to be a traitor—just like Mother and Father."

Eli felt like all the air had been sucked from his chest. He tried to protest, but no sound would come. It was clear his brother wasn't going to hear him anyway. When he managed to talk, his voice was weak and shaking.

"What are you going to do to me, Sebastian?"

He didn't reply, but even as Eli asked the question, he could feel the pressure growing in his ears. The pod was descending. Within seconds the cabin shook, and there was the familiar *whoosh* of landing. Then the rear door lifted open. From the front cabin, one of the black-uniformed Department of Loyalty agents appeared and grabbed him by the shoulders, and the next thing he knew, he felt himself being dragged through the door and landing face-first in warm mud.

He lifted his head.

Before the heat hit him, he felt the bugs. They swarmed his ears and flew into his nose. He coughed and sputtered them out as he raised himself to his knees. He looked around. It was still nighttime. They had flown out of the storm, but he could see another one raging in the distance—or perhaps it was the same one. The horizon flashed with lightning and crackled with distant thunder. The heat washed through him in waves. As hot as it had been inside the pod, out here it felt like he was being cooked alive. The pod had landed in the middle of a vast field of nothing but mud.

He knew right away where he was. He didn't have to ask.

This was Deep Outside.

The middle of nowhere.

Next to the pod Eli noticed a growing cloud of glimmering light—another holographic image. Soon Sebastian's angry face was glowering down at him again. "Only because you're my brother, I'm taking this risk for you," he said, his voice flat. "But this is the last time. Don't expect me to stick my neck out for you ever again."

"Don't leave me here, Sebastian! I'll die!"

Sebastian bared his teeth. "Go away and don't ever come back. These guys in the pod are on my team, and we're loyal to each other, but this is the absolute limit of what they'll do for me. They agreed to give you five minutes before they report that you escaped on your own, and then they're going to look for you as hard as anybody else. And understand, they'll shoot to kill. So run, hide, and don't ever be seen again, brother. This is goodbye."

The pod rose into the air. In the dark distance another jagged flash of lightning split the sky. The edge of the storm was moving swiftly, heading his way. Eli checked his pocket and felt Marilyn, still unconscious. He was sweaty and thirsty, and his heart felt like it might pound through his chest. He had five minutes.

He started to run.

26

wasteland

Eli scrambled across the mud. He soon realized he'd been wrong about the terrain. In addition to bare earth, he found himself moving over stretches of rock and low brambles. In the darkness he'd missed them, but now he had to watch his step. The storm was closing in fast. Even as he searched the sky for any sign of the black pod, he was aware of how fast the wind was rising around him, blowing up dust from the few dry patches. His sides hurt, and he gasped for breath. But he couldn't stop.

When the rain reached him, it was as if somebody had thrown a switch. The sky shook, and then—with sudden, violent force—the full strength of the gale let loose all around him. Almost instantly he had to slog his way through widening pools of water. The earth grew soft, so soft his feet sank with each step. Twice he slipped, and as he fell he had to twist his body to avoid crushing Marilyn when he smacked into the mud.

It wasn't long before he realized he couldn't go much farther. Struggling to the top of a rise, he found a patch of brambles tucked in a low space between two large rocks. It wouldn't provide much shelter, but it was better than nothing. And it was a place to hide. He crawled inside and curled around Marilyn to shield her as best he could. Then he lay shivering. He closed his eyes, bracing himself against the downpour and the howling wind.

It was a long time before exhaustion finally claimed him.

When Eli regained consciousness he was still shivering. He remembered waking several times during the night, but now, as he opened his eyes, the sun shone bright, even through the patchy clouds. The rain had stopped. Tiny insects buzzed near his ears again.

The storm had passed, it seemed. At least for now.

He pulled himself from the brambles. He was covered in dried mud. His whole body ached. Before stepping away from the rocks, he checked the sky for the black pod. He saw nothing. In the distance there was another flash of lightning.

Marilyn? Are you still with me?

There was a long pause. Then her signal, fragile and unsteady. *Still here, my love.*

The muscles in his neck relaxed just a little. They were alive, both of them. They had made it together to another day. He was grateful, at least, for that.

He squinted into the hazy distance. Miles and miles of nothing, as far as he could see. All right, he thought. Now what? They needed food and shelter. If he didn't find help for

Marilyn soon, he wasn't sure she was going to make it. And yet he had no idea where they were or how far it was to civilization. He was famished, his throat was dry, and already he felt like he was melting under the hot sun. With no environment suit to protect him, how long could he expect to last?

But there weren't many options. He knew what he had to do.

He found a nearby puddle and knelt beside it. Hoping it was clean, he cupped his hand and spooned it to his mouth. It tasted okay. He took Marilyn gently from his pocket, lowered her to the water, and let her drink. Only when she was finished did he take more for himself, swallowing in thirsty gulps until he was satisfied. Then he stood again. After another glance around, he chose a direction at random.

He started walking.

Hours later Eli was still walking. Now it was sometime in the afternoon. He knew this because his shadow had grown small and was now stretching longer again behind him. There was no way to gauge how far he'd gone. Mile after mile the landscape stayed more or less the same: Rocks. Patchy brush. Red earth, hardening under the sun. The ground didn't even slope much anymore. It seemed to have settled into an endless, level plain of nothing. Every now and then he caught a faint whiff in the air, a burned smell.

One of the things that unnerved him most out here was the silence. Throughout his entire life in the domes—even in the tower—there had always been background noise. The hum of machinery. The drone of blowers. Funbots. Crowds.

Street sounds. But here there was barely anything. Just the wind and the soft crunch of his own footsteps.

The sky too was unsettling. The sheer immensity of it. No adverts. No digital birds. Just blue and puffy gray, forever, in all directions. Never in his life had he felt so small.

He was heading west, more or less, following the course of the sun—the *actual* sun, which blazed so impossibly bright and hot that it felt artificial to him. He'd been exposed to it so long, his skin hurt. Dust blew into his eyes and coated his throat. He tried not to think about water. There were no more puddles to drink from. They'd dried up quickly in the heat. For a while his mind had been playing tricks on him, making him see lakes in the distance, but always they disappeared as he got closer. For the past mile or so, he'd started to feel dizzy, and now he was aware that he was a little slower. It worried him. He was dehydrated and hungry, and his strength was beginning to fade.

He slapped another bug biting at his neck, although he wasn't sure why he bothered anymore. He wiped the sweat from his eyes.

Eli . . . ? Want to know what I was just dreaming about?
All right. Tell me.

Marilyn had spent much of the day unconscious. For long stretches she lay straining to breathe, cradled in his arm. Occasionally, though, she would awaken and do her best to keep him company. He was glad for the distraction. Now, in a signal that was barely a whisper, she recited:

> *I sent a message to the fish:*
> *I told them "This is what I wish."*

388

He smiled. It was from another *Alice* poem, yet another work of beautiful nonsense. He continued for her, this time speaking aloud as he stumbled through the dusty earth:

> *"The little fishes of the sea,*
> *They sent an answer back to me.*

> *"The little fishes' answer was*
> *'We cannot do it, Sir, because—'"*

She picked it up again, but already her signal was even weaker:

> *I sent to them again to say*
> *"It will be better to obey."*

> *The fishes answered, with a grin,*
> *"Why, what a temper you are in!"*

> *I told them once, I told them twice. . . .*

He waited, but then he realized she'd fallen unconscious again. So he finished the line aloud for her:

> *"I told them once, I told them twice:*
> *They would not listen to advice. . . ."*

He couldn't recall what came after that, and for a long time he tried to remember. It gave him something to do. A tumbleweed drifted past. Far away a tornado moved across the horizon.

After several minutes her voice came to him again.

There's a good chance I'm going to die, my darling. You know that, don't you?

Eli stared hard into the distance. Other than the bugs and the brambles, they had seen nothing all day that was alive. No other plants. No animals. They hadn't even come across a road.

He didn't answer. He kept walking.

The shadows stretched long across the hard earth of the desert. Eli was moving much slower now, stumbling in a near delirium. His face and neck stung with the effect of sun exposure, and his lips were swollen. They felt as if they might crack open. His eyelids were growing heavier by the second, and he had to fight the urge to drop to the ground.

His thoughts were muddling together. They darted from one random place to another until they ended up tangled in a disjointed swirl in his mind. One moment he would feel overcome with regret, and in the next a strange wave of euphoria would wash through him. It occurred to him that all his life he'd been under the influence of the CloudNet at some level, but out here, for the first time ever, he was finally free of it. The subtle tug on his thoughts, the constant temptation to think about something unimportant—it was gone. He'd always felt ashamed of wasting so much time with his imaginary adventures, but at least they had been his own dreams, not those of the CloudNet. Maybe shutting himself off with his storybooks had been his unconscious way of freeing himself all along. Now his imagination, unshackled and entirely his own, was all he had left. What had once seemed childish now felt beautiful and noble, the final resource nobody could take away.

On the other hand, what good had it done him? The world was so much bigger, far more dangerous and unforgiving, than he'd ever realized. If only he'd paid more attention and recognized the dangers sooner, perhaps he could have done things differently. Maybe he wouldn't have ended up like it appeared he was going to—dead of exhaustion out in the wasteland.

There was no point in denying it anymore. There was nothing out here.

Nothing except dust and emptiness. Thirst and death.

Eventually his knees gave out. He collapsed on the ground. Still curled and gasping in his arm, Marilyn lay in the dirt by his head. He pulled her closer.

I'm sorry. It wasn't enough, he knew. It was all he could think to say.

Her eyes were open. Her ragged little body strained for each breath. *It's all right, my love. It's not your fault.*

With their heads pressed to the warm, hard earth, they watched the sun drop slowly into the horizon. The lower it sank, the wider it seemed to grow, its edges shimmering like the giant ball of fire Eli knew it really was. Little by little the entire sky took on new, brilliant shades that changed by the moment and reflected off the edges of the clouds—amber and pink, purple and silver—a breathtaking panorama of color. All along he'd thought the dome sky was the most beautiful sight in the world, but now he realized he was wrong. And all at once he began to have a feeling about the place the Foggers were searching for. Grandfather said InfiniCorp looked everywhere and didn't find it, but now Eli was desperate to believe it was still out there. Maybe the company just hadn't looked in the right place. Or maybe it wasn't a place, exactly. Perhaps it was only a dream to aspire to, the possibility of a better world beyond the apocalypse. Maybe the Wild Orange Yonder was simply another word for hope.

Next to him Marilyn wheezed.

They lay watching the colors progress. After a while, something appeared out of the sky. It was a pale-feathered bird with black spots on its wings, and it landed on the ground just ahead of them. Taken aback, Eli stared. He held his breath as it picked at something beside a low clump of brush. He wondered where it had come from and how it had managed to survive out here in the emptiness. If there was one bird, perhaps there were others like it somewhere out there. Perhaps there was something to hope for after all.

A few seconds later it flew away again. Barely able to lift his head, Eli followed its path into the sunset at the end of the world, one of the last, he supposed, to be witnessed by human eyes. Up ahead new storm clouds were already gathering. And yet he felt grateful to be alive. Grateful that he'd been here for this one brief, thrilling moment. With his cheek still in the dirt, his gaze stayed fixed on the dimming sky, so vast and orange and wild. It was beautiful—so beautiful it made his sides ache. His eyelids grew heavy again. He started to dream. He imagined a place where clean water was plentiful and storms didn't kill. He imagined he could see shadows moving closer, the outlines of desert people in tattered environment suits, ambling toward him in the growing darkness.

Already he was asleep.

epilogue

The nights grow ever darker and the days less welcoming. This year the season of rain seems to have no end. The six of us that remain have taken to hunting in pairs. We gather earlier each morning and we take turns keeping watch. We have had to wander deeper into the desert to escape the mutants and the highwaymen, but some of us are saying these terrors were no worse than what we face now. Better to take our chances with slave traders than to die of starvation in the wasteland.

I was among those who said no to this, but now I am beginning to agree.

Four days ago Rosalia and I found a boy collapsed in the desert. In his arm was a strange animal I have not seen before, although Rosalia claims it is not a mutant. We brought them back to the shelter. After some discussion it was decided that we would take them in, but only until they are strong enough to go out on their own. We no longer have resources enough to share outside our clan, as we once did. To be honest, I agreed to allow them among us only because Rosalia insisted, and because I believed they were going to die anyway. But it appears they are doing better now. Rosalia spends much of her time with them, whispering to them in their sleep and nursing them back to health. Even the animal. I tell her she is a fool but she does not listen.

Some among us worry that finding a fallen stranger so far out in the nothing is a bad omen. But Rosalia is not one of them. Each day as the boy and the animal grow stronger, I have noticed her scanning the horizon more and more often. This morning I asked her what she was searching for and she told me there is a great storm brewing. It will not be long now, she said, but the old man of the desert knows that the ones we have been waiting for are with us at last.

He will be here soon, she said. He's coming for them.

AUTHOR'S NOTE

Global warming remains a controversial issue. While most scientists agree that the world is warming at a faster-than-normal pace, and that humans are at least partially responsible for this warming, they disagree about the possible consequences for our environment. After reading Eli's story, you may be wondering just how I came up with some of the crazy scenarios (Dome cities? Creepy mutants?) described in the book. Well, I'll be honest with you: some of them might not be so crazy, if the world continues to heat up at its current pace. Others, however, are completely made up (this is a work of fiction, after all), and perhaps the majority are a murky mixture of fact and fiction. These ideas were inspired by real science pushed to an extreme and unlikely degree.

When I first began to think about a fictional future in which the Earth is overheating, I called my scientist friend Dr. Julio Friedmann. I went to school with Julio—we met in kindergarten—and now he does climate and energy research for Lawrence Livermore National Laboratory in California, so he knows a lot about what's real and what's just hype in the climate change debate. Julio was generous with his time. He started by walking me through some of what scientists do and don't know, and patiently brainstormed with me as we speculated on some extreme scenarios. What if the world really did get super warm, and very quickly? How might it all play out? What might it mean for the future of the planet? For humanity? I also did some reading on my own. A few of the ideas from this initial research ended up in *A Crack in the Sky*, but, as I said, I often exaggerated things.

Here are some examples of where I did this:

CO_2 IN THE ATMOSPHERE

The truth: Burning carbon-based fuels like oil, gasoline, and coal releases carbon dioxide—or CO_2—into the atmosphere. Our planet can use this gas; rain forests, for instance, play an important role in absorbing CO_2 and converting it back into oxygen. The oceans, too, absorb much of it. A certain amount of CO_2 in the atmosphere is normal. Carbon dioxide helps regulate surface temperatures on the planet by trapping some of the sun's heat as it reflects off the Earth and tries to get back out of the atmosphere—this is what we call the greenhouse effect. Currently, though, humans are changing the equilibrium of this process by creating so much CO_2 (35 billion tons in 2008, and increasing every year) that the land and the ocean can't absorb it all. Deforestation adds to the problem: extra CO_2 builds up in the atmosphere because of the sudden absence of huge numbers of trees that would have naturally converted CO_2 into oxygen and kept carbon in the soil. Scientists can tell what atmospheric CO_2 concentration levels have been in the distant past by studying Antarctic ice samples. Not only has the global concentration of CO_2 in the atmosphere been rising since preindustrial times, but today it is significantly higher than its natural range over the past 650,000 years.

The fiction: In Eli's fictional future the situation is so dire that the amount of excess carbon in the atmosphere measures a whopping 980 CO_2-equivalent units per million (let's call that parts per million, or ppm). By way of comparison, today, as I write this, it's at about 385 ppm. It appears that at 450 ppm, major habitat loss may be inevitable, but questions of exactly what might happen to our environment at specific CO_2 concentrations are hotly debated. In any case, saturating our atmosphere to the level described in Eli's story would require about three hundred years of today's emissions, or one hundred years if our emissions continue to grow at the current rate.

WARMING CLIMATE

The truth: The Earth is billions of years old, and climate change—including periods of warming and cooling—is a natural part of its history. The concern of many scientists today isn't that climate change is happening, it's the rate at which it seems to be happening now. Global temperature records show that the Earth has warmed, on average, by more than half a degree centigrade over the past century. That might not seem like much, but even a small change in average temperature can have a big impact on things like biodiversity, agriculture, and the oceans. According to the National Oceanic and Atmospheric Administration (NOAA), the rate of warming since the 1970s has been about three times greater than the rate over the last hundred years. Seven of the eight warmest years on record (since 1850) have happened since 2001. Many of the world's leading climatologists think this rise in temperature has been caused in large part by man-made greenhouse gases, like CO_2, in the atmosphere.

The fiction: In the future imagined in this story, the Earth has warmed to a drastic degree. The polar ice caps have melted, entire ecosystems have collapsed, previously fertile land has turned to desert, and the remaining resources are dwindling away. While it would be difficult to predict the real distribution of warm and cool geographical zones, Eli's world has clearly undergone a sweeping transformation, an overall warming well beyond what is currently predicted for the near future.

RISING SEA LEVELS

The truth: Sea levels rise because of two things—water warming, which causes the oceans to swell and expand onto land, and melting of ice from landmasses. Using current information to estimate future CO_2 emissions, many scientists—including the Intergovernmental Panel on Climate Change—are predicting that the oceans could rise by three to six feet by 2100, which would potentially displace tens of millions of people and cost trillions of U.S. dollars in damage. There is evidence to suggest that sea levels could rise faster, perhaps ten or fifteen feet by 2100, because more land-based glaciers seem to be melting than we once realized.

The fiction: In *A Crack in the Sky*, ocean levels have risen by about sixty meters, an increase that could theoretically result from a melt that included all of the mountain glaciers worldwide, all of Greenland, all of the West Antarctic Ice Sheet, and about half of the East Antarctic Ice Sheet. That rise would completely submerge Florida, much of the Mississippi River Valley, the central valley in California, and many coastal cities. This is an extreme scenario, highly unlikely in the next hundred years, and has not happened, as far as we can tell, in the last thirty million years of Earth's history.

ACIDIFICATION OF THE OCEAN

The truth: CO_2 that enters the atmosphere and is absorbed by the ocean becomes carbonic acid, which in turn lowers the pH, meaning that the ocean becomes more acidic. Over the last century, the average pH of the surface of the ocean has dropped measurably. There is evidence that acidification may already be negatively affecting the way some animals make their shells, including microscopic animals (zooplankton like foraminifera) at the base of the food chain, coral (which are both food and habitat), and others (like cuttlefish) that are the staple diet of many large marine animals. If acidification continues, by 2050 key components of the marine food chain may be permanently lost.

The fiction: For my novel I took this idea and amped it way up. The Gulf of Mexico over which Eli and Tabitha find themselves is an ocean that smells bad and is tinged with red due to the proliferation of algae. This would indicate a sea destroyed, a far-flung, grim depiction of acidification and deoxygenation combined.

SICKNESS AND MASS EXTINCTIONS

The truth: Climate change threatens the existence of thousands of species when environments change too swiftly for them to adapt. Polar bears are often cited as examples of animals struggling to survive as the Arctic ice melts, but there are many other species all around the world that could potentially die off with the loss of their habitats, food, or water. Others could perish as higher temperatures give rise to destructive parasites such as the mountain pine beetle. Pine beetle infestations have been increasing dramatically in recent years and have already resulted in the destruction of millions of acres of forest in western parts of the United States and Canada. Warming temperatures may also increase the ranges of infectious diseases such as yellow fever, malaria, West Nile virus, and Lyme disease.

The fiction: My novel describes an imaginary future in which this destructive potential is played out to the max. Most of the human population has been killed off by a fast-moving, deadly illness—the Great Sickness. The remaining Outsiders live in a desolate wilderness that has suffered mass extinctions of much of its plant and animal life. Add this to the violent hurricanes, heat, floods, and droughts, and you end up with a harsh landscape indeed, a wasteland where only the strong and resourceful survive.

So here's the thing: while some elements of *A Crack in the Sky* were inspired by actual science and current theories, in the end it's a work of fiction, and many of the details of Eli's world came wholly from my imagination. The lumbering mutant that Marilyn stumbles across near a lake of toxic ooze, for example, is based on no climate change science I'm aware of. I just thought it would be creepy. As far as I know, there exist no imminent plans to build protective domes that enclose entire cities. I just like domes. And finally, as far as I know, animal neurobiologists are not, at this moment, secretly working on ways to boost the brains of small carnivorous mammals.

But then, you never know.

Here are some of the sources I used to learn about the climate change topics discussed here. For a more complete list of sources, check out my Web site at www.markpeterhughes.com.

BOOKS

Berne, Emma Carlson. *Global Warming and Climate Change* (Compact Research Series). San Diego: Referencepoint Press, 2007.

Henson, Robert. *The Rough Guide to Climate Change, 2nd Edition*. London: Rough Guides, 2008.

Lynas, Mark. *High Tide: The Truth About Our Climate Crisis*. New York: Picador, 2004.

Speth, James Gustave. *Red Sky at Morning: America and the Crisis of the Global Environment, Second Edition*. New Haven: Yale Nota Bene, 2005.

INTERNET RESEARCH

"Climate Change—Science, State of Knowledge: What's Known, What's Very Likely, What's Not Certain." United States Environmental Protection Agency.
http://epa.gov/climatechange/science/stateofknowledge.html

"Global Warming: Frequently Asked Questions." National Oceanic and Atmospheric Administration.
http://lwf.ncdc.noaa.gov/oa/climate/globalwarming.html

"IPCC Fourth Assessment Report: Climate Change 2007." Intergovernmental Panel on Climate Change.
http://www.ipcc.ch/publications_and_data/ar4/wg1/en/contents.html

"Ocean Acidification: The *Other* CO_2 Problem." Henderson, Caspar. August 5, 2006. NewScientist.
http://environment.newscientist.com/article/mg19125631.200

INTERVIEW

Dr. Julio Friedmann, PhD, Carbon Management Program Leader, Energy & Environmental Directorate, Lawrence Livermore National Laboratory, Livermore, CA.

SUGGESTIONS FOR FURTHER READING

Cherry, Lynne, and Braasch, Gary. *How We Know What We Know About Our Changing Climate: Scientists and Kids Explore Global Warming*. Nevada City, CA: Dawn Publications, 2008.

David, Laurie, and Gordon, Cambria. *Down-to-Earth Guide to Global Warming*. New York: Orchard Books, 2007.

Evans, Kate. *Weird Weather: Everything You Didn't Want to Know About Climate Change but Probably Should Find Out*. Toronto: Groundwood Books, 2007.

Flannery, Tim, adapted by Sally M. Walker. *We Are the Weather Makers: The History of Climate Change*. Cambridge, MA: Candlewick Press, 2009.

Gore, Al. *An Inconvenient Truth: The Crisis of Global Warming*. New York: Viking Children's Books, 2007.

Haugen, David; Musser, Sandra; Lovelace, Kacy, eds. *Global Warming (Opposing Viewpoints)*. Farmington Hills, MI: Greenhaven Press, 2010.

Nardo, Don. *Climate Crisis: The Science of Global Warming (Headline Science)*. Mankato, MN: Compass Point Books, 2008.

Sommers, Michael, A. *Antarctic Melting: The Disappearing Antarctic Ice Cap*. New York: Rosen Publishing Group, 2007.

For even more information about the science of climate change, check out these Web sites:

epa.gov/climatechange/kids/index.html
Climate change information from the U.S. Environmental Protection Agency (EPA).

climate.nasa.gov/ClimateReel/
Videos and visualizations of climate change from the National Aeronautics and Space Administration (NASA).

pewclimate.org/global-warming-basics/kidspage.cfm
Information from the Pew Center on Global Climate Change.

ACKNOWLEDGMENTS

A sincere thank-you goes to my amazing editor, Stephanie Lane Elliott, and to all the people at Random House who helped put this book together, especially Beverly Horowitz, Chip Gibson, Krista Vitola, Trish Parcell, Tamar Schwartz, Natalia Dextre, Colleen Fellingham and Barbara Perris, Katharine Gehron, Emily Pourciau, Annette Szlachta, Per Haagensen, Joe LeMonnier, and all the wonderful people on the sales and marketing team whose early feedback was so helpful. I'm indebted also to the following for their assistance and support: Andy McNicol, the Commando Writers (Michael A. Di Battista, Peter DiIanni, Scott Fitts, Geoffrey H. Goodwin, Dalia Rabinovich, John Smith and Abby Walsh), J. L. Bell, Dr. Jean Brown, Greg R. Fishbone, Susan Green, Michael Healey, Carolyn Hughes, Jennifer Hughes, Shauna Leggat, Kevin McGurn, Tucker Moody, Alison Morris, Claudia Sorsby, John Winnell, Ana Wons, and Janet Zade. My son, Evan, deserves a special thank-you for providing his thoughtful insights. For some of the climate change information used in this book, I am grateful for the assistance of Dr. Julio Friedmann, whose expertise in climate change science helped lay a factual foundation on which I took many liberties to create this work of fiction. For all those liberties, the blame is entirely mine.

Most of all, I want to acknowledge Evan, Lucy, and Zoe, and especially Karen, my first reader and best friend. *Les quiero con todo mi corazón.*

ABOUT THE AUTHOR

Mark Peter Hughes was born in Liverpool, England, and grew up in Barrington, Rhode Island.

Mark Peter Hughes's first novel, *I Am the Wallpaper*, was a Children's Book Sense 76 Summer Pick and a New York Public Library Book for the Teen Age. His second, *Lemonade Mouth*, was a Book Sense Children's Spring Pick, a Richie's Pick, a Bank Street College of Education Best Children's Book of the Year (Outstanding Merit), an ASTAL Rhode Island Book of the Year Award winner, and a Boston Authors Club Award finalist.